“Hey look! There’s Lucas!”

Gracie beelined down the hall, and Naomi had no choice but to follow her daughter right to the man she’d spent so much time avoiding.

Her heart took a dive. Just one look at him and she was going down in flames. Her hand instantly rose to smooth her hair into place, like it always had when she’d seen him around the halls in high school. When she finally caught up, the roar of her heart stole her breath.

Lucas knelt in front of Gracie and handed her a single yellow rose.

“Thank you!” Gracie squealed, smooshing the rose against her nose and inhaling deeply. “No one’s ever given me a flower before! Look, Mom!”

Naomi smiled down at her daughter, though her heartbeat came in painful hard thumps.

“She’s incredible,” Lucas said, watching Gracie run off. “I can’t believe how much she reminds me of you.”

And Naomi couldn’t believe how the simple act of standing close to him brought her body to life. Blood surged, flooding her with a tingling heat she hadn’t experienced in so long…

ACCLAIM FOR SARA RICHARDSON'S PREVIOUS NOVELS

HOMETOWN COWBOY

"Filled with humor, heart, and love, this page-turner is one wild ride."

—Jennifer Ryan,
***New York Times* bestselling author**

"An emotional ride with characters that come alive on every single page. Sara brings real feelings to every scene she writes."

—Carolyn Brown,
***New York Times* bestselling author**

"[The] story is sensitive, charmingly funny, satisfyingly spicy, and dedicated to ensuring both protagonists grow to earn their lasting love. This will satisfy Richardson's fans while welcoming new readers to a sweeping land of mountains, cowboys, and romance."

—Publishers Weekly

"In the debut of her Rocky Mountain Riders series, Richardson creates an engaging small-town setting, filled with a richly detailed population, including two hurt and lonely protagonists, whose funny and moving journey together is sure to earn plenty of new fans...there is plenty to enjoy in this spirited, heartwarming story."

—RT Book Reviews

NO BETTER MAN

"Charming, witty, and fun. There's no better read. I enjoyed every word!"

—Debbie Macomber,
#1 *New York Times* bestselling author

"Fresh, fun, well-written, a dazzling debut."

—Lori Wilde,
***New York Times* bestselling author**

"Richardson's debut packs a powerful emotional punch. [Her] deft characterization creates a hero and heroine who will elicit laughs in some places and tears in others."

—Publishers Weekly

"4 stars! Hot! [Richardson's] brisk storytelling and the charming, endearing characters set within a solid, engaging plot make this sweet romance shine. A strong and vulnerable Bryce, coupled with a determined, lighthearted Avery, will appeal to readers, especially with their sizzling chemistry. This is a truly delightful read."

—RT Book Reviews

SOMETHING LIKE LOVE

"The author's compassion shines through her beautifully flawed and earnest characters and takes readers on an emotionally wrenching journey to the elusive goal of love."

—Publishers Weekly

"4½ stars! Second in Richardson's Heart of the Rockies series is a delight. 'Resist the drawl,' [Paige] she tells herself at one point, but in the end, she can't resist him—and neither will readers. A wide cast of sharp, well-drawn secondary characters adds depth to the story, as does the beautiful landscape."

—***RT Book Reviews***

"A quick read with vivid characters and a few great twists... sizzles with sexual tension on every page. The ending was a perfect, lovely, and sigh-worthy happy-ever-after... and still kinda romantically hot, as befits the rest of the novel."

—*USA Today*'s "Happily Ever After" blog

MORE THAN A FEELING

"Fans of Robyn Carr will undoubtedly enjoy the Heart of the Rockies series."

—***RT Book Reviews***

Comeback Cowboy

Also by Sara Richardson

Hometown Cowboy
No Better Man
Something Like Love
One Christmas Wish (ebook)
More Than a Feeling
Rocky Mountain Wedding (ebook)

Comeback Cowboy

A ROCKY MOUNTAIN RIDERS NOVEL

SARA RICHARDSON

FOREVER

NEW YORK BOSTON

This book is a work of fiction. Names, characters, places, and incidents are the product of the author's imagination or are used fictitiously. Any resemblance to actual events, locales, or persons, living or dead, is coincidental.

Forever
Hachette Book Group
1290 Avenue of the Americas
New York, NY 10104
forever-romance.com
twitter.com/foreverromance

Printed in the United States of America

First Edition: June 2017
10 9 8 7 6 5 4 3 2 1

OPM

Forever is an imprint of Grand Central Publishing.
The Forever name and logo are trademarks of Hachette Book Group, Inc.

ISBN 978-1-4555-4077-8 (mass market edition)
ISBN 978-1-4555-4078-5 (ebook edition)

To Melissa Lee,
one of the best mamas I know.

Comeback Cowboy

Chapter One

The best thing about grand vintage houses was not the ornate crown molding, or the heavy wooden five-panel doors, or even the charming antique accents.

Nope. Those details were nice and all, but the best thing about old houses were the secrets protected within their walls.

Naomi Sullivan could relate to secrets. She'd carefully guarded a few whoppers of her own. While her own secrets tended to stalk her, she found other people's secrets fascinating.

Admiring the large bow window that welcomed in the early morning sunrays, Naomi breathed in the scent of old wood and dust. Truly, the place was a mess. No one had lived here since old Mrs. Porter had passed away four years ago. The original parquet floors were scuffed and dirty, the thick cherry trim discolored with grime. But somehow the Porter House still charmed her the same way it had when she was a young girl and she'd ride her bike past it every morning on her way to school.

It had always reminded her of something out of a storybook—whimsical and romantic. The structure itself was a Queen Anne Victorian with a steeply pitched roof, a dominant front-facing gable, and overhanging eaves. The siding had been well kept and was painted a lovely cloud blue, with the trim accented in an elegant cream. Classic columns held up a wraparound porch complete with intricate spindle work.

Naomi wandered to the window and peered out at the front lawn. The gardens had gone to ruin, but the grass still grew green and thick. She supposed that was something. Turning back to Colton, her real estate agent, lawyer, and oldest childhood friend, she felt that telltale flicker of passion spark in her chest. "It's perfect. I'll take it."

Colton simply *tsk*ed at her and shuffled his four-hundred-dollar loafers over to where she stood. "No so fast. It's not even officially on the market yet." His head tilted with a healthy dose of sass. "And how's that business loan coming, hmmm? Are the papers signed? Is the money in your account?"

"It will be," she fired back, though she wasn't nearly as gifted in the sass department as he was. "It's all in process." And everything *would* go through. She *would* get that business loan. She *would* move off the Cortez Ranch, and she *would* open her own bed and breakfast by next winter.

Damn it.

"'In process' won't cut it," Colton informed her. "If you want me to make a deal with the Porter family before they list it, I'll need the cash, honey."

"I should have it by the end of the week." At least, she'd better.

She passed underneath an archway and carefully ran her hand over the solid banister that swirled up the staircase in the foyer. She'd done everything required to submit the loan application and the banker had all but told her she was a shoo-in. Working at the Cortez Ranch and living there rent-free for the last ten years had allowed her to save plenty of money, so she only had to borrow enough to purchase the house, do some renovations, and buy the furniture. Besides that, she had outstanding credit and always paid her bills on time.

There was no way the bank would turn her down.

She peered over her shoulder and flashed Colton her most persuasive smile. "Tell the Porters not to bother putting the house on the market. I'll take it. As my lawyer, you can do all the paperwork and cut your rate in half."

He laughed. "You know I'm not that generous."

"Come on now," she scolded. "I've done you plenty of favors over the years. I *always* covered for you whenever you got home late." Seeing as how they'd grown up next door to each other, she'd been around to bail him out when he needed it. "And then there was that time sophomore year when I pretended to be your homecoming date so your parents wouldn't know you were really going with Thomas." Which meant she hadn't had a real date to her own homecoming. She stabbed a pointer finger into his chest. "You owe me big for that."

"True enough," he conceded, heaving out a martyr's sigh. "All right. Fine. I'll have a talk with the Porters and get the ball—"

Her cell phone broke out into song and cut him off.

He eyed her with disdain. "Still haven't changed that awesome Bieber ringtone, huh?"

"I don't know how," she snapped, digging it out of her purse. Her friend Darla had changed it as a joke. "If it annoys you so much, why don't you change it?" she asked, glancing at the screen.

"Who is it? Tell them you'll call them back so I can change that appalling ringtone."

Her heart sped up. "It's Lance." Her boss at the Cortez Family Ranch, who'd actually become more like her big brother. The man who'd given her and Gracie a place to live after her ex had walked out on them. The man who was marrying her best friend, Jessa, soon.

"You haven't told them you're quitting yet?" Colton asked when she clicked off the phone and stuffed it back into her purse.

"Not yet." She looked around the room again, fear swirling in with her excitement. "It doesn't seem wise to say anything until I'm sure it'll work out." There was no reason to get anyone riled up. And all Jessa had talked about recently was the fun they'd have living as neighbors on the ranch.

"You have quite the connection with the Cortez family," Colton reminded her. "Once you move here things will change."

"Things need to change." Lance and Jessa deserved to have their own space. He'd just retired from bull riding and would be reorganizing things at the ranch anyway. In the last several months, he'd started a stock contracting operation to supply bulls on the circuit, which meant he was heavily involved in the day-to-day operations now. He wouldn't need her to keep the books anymore. "Besides, this has always been my dream."

"You sure you're not just running away from Lucas?" Colton always liked to hit people between the eyes with the truth. He knew exactly how she'd once felt about Lance's brother. But she refused to flinch.

"This has nothing to do with Lucas." As the lie tumbled from her lips, she fell back through the years, forced to relive the memories she'd tried so hard to block out.

The day Lucas Cortez, the love of her young life, had been arrested for arson. When they'd taken him away in handcuffs, she'd run after him, sobbing, begging the officer to let him go, insisting he wouldn't have done it. He wouldn't have burned down the rodeo grounds intentionally.

Lucas had turned to her, this seventeen-year-old man she'd known most of her life. The man she'd loved for two years. The man she'd dreamed about building a future with. His face had been cold when he'd told her to go back home. "It's over, Naomi. I'm going to prison. You need to move on."

For years, she hadn't known how. Lucas had taken a chunk of her heart that day, leaving it paralyzed. After a shocking pregnancy and a failed marriage, she'd done what she'd had to do to raise her daughter by herself. Then, last fall, Lucas had come home when his father was diagnosed with Parkinson's.

"How long is he planning to stay in Topaz Falls anyway?" Colton asked innocently.

Yeah right. He knew good and well this topic was off limits. "I don't know." Over the last months, Lucas had split time between his family's ranch and his full-time employer, the McGowen Ranch, but eventually he'd go back to Pueblo for good. And it was just as well. She'd shut the door on the what-ifs of her past long ago. She'd carefully locked up her own secrets, and she didn't need them breaking out now. "I haven't talked to Lucas much," she reminded Colton.

The truth was, she hadn't been able to face him. She'd made sure to keep extra busy, volunteering at school and at Jessa's animal rescue. She'd even taken Gracie to visit her parents for a month over winter break.

When she'd seen him for the first time in ten years, her heart had buckled, filling her with a pained joy. But so much time had passed. They were both different people. Now everything in her life came down to her daughter.

The moment Gracie was born—that moment she'd held her in her arms and cuddled her against her breast—every fear went away, and Naomi realized she'd never be alone again. She was a mother and she would forever be connected with another soul. That bond had changed everything for her. It had made her brave.

"So this is what you want," Colton asked, dipping his chin to give her eyes a good cross-examination. "You're sure?"

"Yes." *Be brave.* It was time for her to show her daughter she could do anything she wanted.

It was time to prove she could make all of her own dreams come true.

* * *

The decision shouldn't be this hard.

Lucas brought his arm back over his head and launched the fishing line, arcing it in a perfectly timed dance, striking the fly against the water to entice the cutthroat trout he knew to be hiding in one of those deep holes on the edge of the riverbed. Ripples circled the small fuzzy hook at the end of his line, mimicking a real fly's movements on the water's sleek surface.

He did his best thinking out here—standing waist-deep in his thermal waders, still feeling the chill of the snow runoff that barreled down the mountain streams and into the Topaz Falls River. It was high for this time of year—the weather had been unseasonably warm for weeks, melting the mounds of snow that had built up on the peaks.

The sun had only just started its descent to the west,

hovering stubbornly over the rocky horizon, casting enough light and warmth that he didn't need a coat. In some ways, he loved it here. After being away from Topaz Falls for ten years, coming back had been nostalgic. He couldn't go anywhere in town without memories flooding him—good memories of him and his brothers riding their bikes to the general store for candy, of building forts in the woods, of riding their horses up the mountain trails.

But his best memories had taken place right on that riverbank over there. Long evening picnics with Naomi, his high school sweetheart. The woman he'd left behind so long ago.

They'd stuff a saddlebag full of food from the pantry and ride out here. He'd spread the blanket on the ground and they'd eat in the surreal glow of a setting sun. When dusk had settled, they'd wrap themselves up in that blanket, kissing and touching each other, and eventually making love in the tall grass.

Memories of Naomi constantly seemed to churn through him, dredging up the past, giving him glimpses of their two years together. Those images were etched into his soul...her head tipped back while she laughed, that long, wavy red hair spilling down over her shoulders and catching the sun's light.

That—*she*—was what made his impending decision so hard.

With no strikes at his line, Lucas wound the fly rod's reel. He had to get back to the ranch, anyhow. His younger brother was throwing yet another shindig in honor of Lance's wedding. Or should Lucas say Levi was throwing it for himself? No one loved a good party as much as Levi.

As he worked the reel, the fly slowly skidded across the water's surface, closer and closer, tying up his scattered thoughts along with it.

A relationship with Naomi now wouldn't be practical. Hell, she didn't even seem to want him. Ever since he'd been back, she'd avoided him. And why wouldn't she? Why would any woman want to be with a convicted felon who'd done time? The rest of the town surely didn't want him to stick around. They'd made that abundantly clear.

Small towns like Topaz Falls, Colorado, had long memories and no one wanted to welcome back the man who had supposedly burned down a stable, killed two bulls, and forever ruined the town's chances of hosting another rodeo on the circuit. Regret rebounded against the walls he'd put in place to hold it off.

All these years, he'd never let himself question if he'd done the right thing covering for Levi. Out of the three of them, his younger brother had taken it the hardest when their mom left, and got into all kinds of trouble. He'd set the fire after finding out their father was having an affair with the rodeo commissioner's wife. Trying to protect his brother, Lucas had stepped up to take the blame, sure he'd get off easy. Instead, he'd gotten the maximum sentence—three years in prison. But sometimes it felt like he'd pay for that fire his whole life.

Didn't matter that he hadn't done it. Didn't matter that he'd gotten out of prison early on good behavior. Didn't matter that he'd built a fucking empire for the McGowen Ranch outside of Pueblo in the years since.

Didn't matter who he was now.

That's why he figured he should head back down south. Bill McGowen had called him up last week and told him he was sorry Lucas's father had been diagnosed with Parkinson's but they were gearing up for the competition season and he needed him back. Which meant he needed Lucas to make a decision. Return to manage his stock, or he'd have to find someone else.

Lucas trudged to the riverbank, his legs fighting the current. He should've told the man then that he'd come back, but his mind had conjured up this image of Naomi in his arms and, before he knew what he was saying, he'd told Bill McGowen—one of the most powerful men in the rodeo world—that he'd need to think about it and he'd let him know after Lance's wedding.

Damn the power of hope.

Sighing, he kicked off his rubber boots and stepped onto the soft bank, where he peeled off his waders. Then he took apart the fishing pole and stored it in the cylinder carrying case.

After shoving the gear into his backpack and slipping into his leather boots, he hoisted the pack onto his shoulders and tramped down the narrow trail that led back to the highway where he'd parked his truck. Even before he reached it, he knew something was wrong.

All four tires were flat—slashed, the shredded rubber lying limply on the asphalt. And there was a glaring orange word spray-painted across the tailgate.

Felon.

That label. That damn label. It'd be slapped on him forever. He jogged down to the road to assess the damage. At least they hadn't shattered the windows. Shaking his head, he dug out his phone, but of course there was no service out here in the river valley.

If he needed confirmation that he didn't belong in Topaz Falls, there it was.

Looking over the damage again, his hands fisted. But anger wouldn't do him much good out here. Hiking his backpack higher on his shoulders, he sucked it up and set off on foot, following the curve of the highway, boots pounding the packed gravel on the shoulder.

He'd have to walk the eight miles back to the ranch.

This was the whole reason he hadn't come home after he'd been released from prison. He'd wanted freedom—a life where no one knew about his past. McGowen didn't care that he'd served time. Hell, he thought it made Lucas more of a badass. When he'd shown up at Bill McGowen's front door after he'd been released from prison, the man had laughed at him. But Lucas begged him to give him one week to prove what he could do, and the man seemed to appreciate that.

He'd never worked as hard as he did that week, doing anything that needed to be done. From cleaning up shit to wrangling the bulls, he'd proven that nothing was above him or beneath him. At the end of the week, an impressed McGowen hired him as a ranch hand, and over the years he'd worked his way up to be the man's right hand. He couldn't give that up now…

The hum of an engine broke into his thoughts. He stepped off to the side to give the car room and glanced over his shoulder.

A yellow Volkswagen Beetle blitzed toward him, picking up speed. Yep, he'd know that car anywhere. Naomi. No one else around here drove a bright yellow bug complete with flower-shaped taillights. Completely impractical for life in the mountains, but that was one thing he loved about her. She didn't care much for horse sense. If something made her happy, she did it.

He watched her car draw closer and closer, and just like it always did when Naomi got near, his heart picked up. Would she stop and give him a lift to the ranch? They hadn't exactly been alone since he'd come back to Topaz Falls. She'd made sure of that.

As the yellow anomaly sped around the curve, he lifted a hand to flag her down, but the car didn't slow.

Maybe she hadn't seen him. Waving his arms, he stepped onto the shoulder…

Shit! The car was coming right for him! Adrenaline fired through him and sent him rolling into the ditch just as the car's brakes screeched. The thing skidded and fishtailed, likely taking out half of the tires' tread.

Breathing in the scent of burnt rubber, Lucas stared up at the sky. Well, that'd been one hell of a close shave.

The car door opened and out Naomi flew, stumbling down the embankment in her polished red heels, to where he lay on the ground.

"Oh my God! Oh my God! Lucas!" Her hands visibly shook. "What are you doing standing in the middle of the road?" she demanded, her voice about twenty octaves higher than normal.

"I wasn't in the middle of the road," he said calmly, though the *swoosh* of blood still roared in his ears. He couldn't tell if adrenaline surged from almost being mowed down, or from finally being able to stare at her the way he'd wanted to ever since he'd walked back into her life all those months ago. Whenever they bumped into each other, she'd always turn away, but now she stood over him, staring down into his eyes.

And God, she was perfection. Wavy red hair finer than silk, and those bright eyes, green as the swaying grass in a meadow. She wore a flowered dress, and her legs were made for wearing a dress. Long and toned, tensed from the way she stood in those heels.

He didn't want to move. Nothing hurt, but if he moved she'd look away from him.

"Mom!" Gracie squealed from the backseat. Her ten-year-old daughter stuck her head out through the open window. "Is he alive?"

"I'm alive," he confirmed, waving. "And I was standing on the *side* of the road," he said, admiring the view of the woman's tanned legs. Yeah, he could pretty much admire that view all damn day.

As usual, Naomi turned away from him. Her breaths came in gasping puffs. "God, Lucas. *God.* I was so distracted I didn't even see you." Her delicate hands covered her face. "I almost hit you. My God, I almost *hit* you." She staggered a few steps.

That got him off the ground. Didn't need her collapsing on the side of the highway.

"Hey." He hurried over to her, brushing the gravel off his ass. "I'm fine." He'd been through a hell of a lot worse than a tumble down into a ditch.

"He looks fine to me!" Gracie offered, still leaning out the window. "He's not even bleeding."

"Exactly." He ducked his head closer to Naomi's, catching her gaze. "See. No blood. I'm good."

She nodded, but seemed to be on the verge of hyperventilating. Which meant she was in no condition to get behind the wheel of that car.

"Why don't I drive you back to the ranch?" Risking her hasty retreat, he slipped an arm around her waist to support her, and he couldn't resist drawing her close to him, closer than she'd been in ten long years. She still smelled like carefree summer afternoons—a subtle hint of lemon along with the coconut oil she used to use to soften her hands.

That scent, the feel of her leaning into his body, roused a sudden overpowering greed. He'd never hungered as desperately for something as he hungered for her. To turn her fully to himself. To feel those breasts he used to kiss so intimately against his own chest again. He knew that body, remembered every curve and bend, every fine detail...

"I'm okay," Naomi whispered, shaking him off. "I can walk."

Of course she could. If she had a choice between keeling over and letting him touch her, she'd gladly opt for hitting the ground. But she did hand him the keys before hurrying to climb into the passenger's seat without his assistance.

Lucas folded himself into the driver's seat. Even with the seat moved all the way back he hardly fit. But he'd take it if it meant he got to sit beside Naomi for ten minutes. Even if she wouldn't look at him. Even if she wouldn't talk to him.

He'd take it. Especially knowing he was likely going back to Pueblo in a few short weeks.

Lucas glanced in the rearview mirror. "You buckled?" he asked Gracie.

The girl nodded with a shy smile.

"All right, then. We're off." He started the engine and backed up, then turned carefully out onto the highway.

Naomi directed her gaze out the passenger's window, but Gracie eyed him dubiously from the backseat.

She looked so much like her mother with those red curls and inquisitive green eyes.

"How come you were walking on the road?" she asked.

"My truck broke down. Back where I was fishing." Not worth mentioning that it'd had some help. "So I was planning to walk back to the ranch. Until you two lovely ladies swooped in to rescue me."

The girl grinned, dimples poking into each cheek. "You bet you were lucky," she laughed. "Especially since Mom almost hit you!"

He stole a glance at Naomi. She stared straight ahead, her face a mask of worry.

God, he wanted to reach over and rest his hand on her thigh, tease out a smile...

"Did you catch anything?" Gracie asked, leaning between the seats.

"Nah. Not tonight. Sometimes I just go out there to think." And whenever he started to think, those thoughts inevitably led to the silent woman sitting next to him.

"I've always wanted to learn how to fish," Gracie babbled. "But I don't want to touch a worm or anything. And I wouldn't keep the fish. That would be mean."

"I never keep them either," he admitted. He'd never developed a taste for trout. "And I'd be happy to teach you how to fish sometime. If it's okay with your mom."

"Can I, Mom? Can I go fishing with Lucas?"

"We'll see," Naomi said stiffly. Parental code for *hell no*.

"What about you guys? What have you been up to tonight?" he asked, trying to soften the woman.

"I had drama practice at school," Gracie said proudly. "I'm the fairy godmother in *Cinderella*."

"Wow." He drew out the word in a theatrical compliment. "Congratulations. That's a starring role."

Her smile was addictive. "I know! I had to memorize all these lines." The girl paused and cleared her throat dramatically. "Bibbity! Bobbity! Boo!"

Lucas widened his eyes with exaggerated awe. "You're a natural."

"Really?" Gracie gasped. "You think?"

"That was better than the movie," he insisted.

"You've seen *Cinderella*?" Naomi asked, finally acknowledging him. The skeptical curve to her sexy lips made him ache.

"Of course I've seen *Cinderella*," he said, looking at her longer than was safe. "It's a classic."

Gracie leaned forward again, straining her seat belt. "If you like *Cinderella*, you should come to my show! It's tomorrow night!"

"Oh honey..." Naomi broke in before he had the chance to answer. "I'm sure Lucas is too busy."

She likely *hoped* he was too busy, but he pretended not to notice her obvious discomfort. "Actually I'm free tomorrow night."

"Yay!" Gracie squealed.

But Naomi's worried glare returned. "You don't have to come."

"I *want* to come," he said, eyeing her. He wanted to spend time with her. To see if he had any reason to stick it out in Topaz Falls. He glanced in the rearview mirror. "One line and the Fairy Godmother has me hooked."

Gracie beamed. "Wait 'til you hear the rest of them!"

"I can't wait," Lucas said, directing a pleading gaze at her mother.

Naomi relented with a sigh. "It starts at seven." Her soft lips twitched as she studied him. It wasn't her full bright beautiful smile.

But it was a start.

Chapter Two

On a normal summer evening, Naomi loved the drive out to the ranch. She'd roll down her window and drape out her hand, letting the crisp air cool her palm and run between her fingers. She'd swear it was more calming than a full glass of good merlot, the way the retreating sun softened the mountains with hazy shadows, the way the trees swayed and the grasses swished as the car rolled by.

But tonight, even though she had her eyes fixed on the world outside the passenger's window, everything seemed dull and gray. Instead of making her feel that all was right with the world, the curves and dips of the lonely mountain road stirred up her stomach, bringing a swell of nausea.

She snuck another peek at the man sitting next to her, still trying to wrap her heart around the fact that Lucas Cortez was driving her car. Sitting not even a foot away from her. Easily chatting with her ten-year-old daughter about "the bestest fairy tales" in the entire world.

She cranked her head back toward the passenger's window. *God, if you can hear me, please let me come out of this fifteen-minute drive with my heart intact. I'll do anything.* It wasn't as if she'd have to give up much. She'd practically been a nun for the last ten years anyway.

But the truth was, not even God could protect her from this. From the havoc Lucas's presence would wreak in her life. In *their* lives. Nothing could protect her from the havoc that was already starting to infiltrate, in the form of emails from her long-lost ex-husband. She'd never meant to keep a secret like the one she now guarded, but that was the funny thing about secrets. They were never truly safe, no matter how deeply you tucked them away…

"You okay?" Lucas asked her quietly.

"Yes," she said quickly, smoothing her dress.

"Mommy, can Lucas come over and watch *Snow White* with us?" Gracie asked in that cherubic voice she used whenever she worried Naomi would tell her no.

Naomi opted for alternative phrasing. "Not tonight, honey. I'm hosting book club at our house." And she had the feeling she'd be doing a lot of drinking.

She felt his stare as Lucas turned onto the ranch's driveway, easing the car along like he was a ninety-year-old man out for a Sunday drive.

"Maybe another time," he said cheerfully.

"Maybe," she mumbled, gathering her purse.

She couldn't help but notice how he took his time parking the car. When he cut the engine, she forced herself to look at him. Big mistake. Her heart buckled and her joints got all loose and disconnected.

The years had only made him sexier, engraving wise lines of experience into the corners of his hazel eyes. Eyes that somehow still smiled, even with all he'd been through. He wore his bronze hair a bit longer these days, so that the ends of it fringed the tops of his ears. It was still thick and luscious, but it was his smile that had lured her in and stayed with her all these years. His smile spoke.

A familiar tremble tightened her hands into fists—a tremble that made her fear fuse with anticipation at being so close to him, at having felt his arm slide around her waist so easily back on the highway.

The encounter had struck her—an electrical current splitting her into two different people: the woman who wanted to be wrapped up in him again and the girl he'd once left behind. The girl who'd made mistakes but righted them all on her own. The girl who'd grown up overnight. The girl who still feared his power over her.

Because she couldn't do it again. She couldn't let herself feel a connection with him only to have him disappear for another ten years. She couldn't risk revealing everything to him.

No matter what, she would not risk Gracie's heart, too.

Naomi blinked, realizing she'd been staring at him too long.

Not that he seemed to mind. His lips simply quirked as though he enjoyed it.

"So thanks for driving," she said briskly, fumbling with the door handle. Finally, she was able to push it open and release herself. Straightening, she focused on leaning the seat forward so Gracie could climb out.

Lucas came around the car and stood too close. He handed her the keys, his fingers brushing hers.

She quickly stuffed them in her purse. "Sorry about almost hitting you and everything," she muttered, sidestepping him. "Come on, Gracie." Tucking her daughter close, she quickly headed for the porch.

"Bye, Lucas! See you soon!" Gracie called.

"I'll see you both at the play," he said, lifting his hand in a wave.

As if she needed the reminder. Naomi quickly shuffled Gracie into the house.

"Why're we in such a hurry?" her daughter demanded.

Was it that obvious? "I have a lot to get ready for book club," she lied. Her friend Darla was bringing pretty much everything. Darla owned the local wine bar–slash–chocolate shop in town and was so picky no one else even tried to make dessert anymore. "And we have to get you to bed at a reasonable hour," she went on, hanging her daughter's backpack on a hook behind the door.

Bogart, their faithful German shepherd, greeted them with his regal, low bark. Naomi bent to scratch his ears, feeling the fatigue of a roller-coaster day catch up with her. It'd been a long evening with the dress rehearsals for tomorrow night's performance. Normally, she let Gracie stay up past eight on Fridays, but not tonight. Gracie needed rest and Naomi needed her friends.

Over the next hour, Gracie tried every excuse in the Book of Bedtime Stalling—dry throat, sore toe, fear of a ghostly stowaway under her bed—but finally, Naomi had her tucked in so tight and cozy that her daughter's eyes started to close. Bogart had curled up on his special pillow near the foot of Gracie's bed and was already snoring.

A pink glow emanated from the flower-shaped night light her daughter had picked out when she was three and they'd been decorating her big-girl room. Soft music played from the clock radio on the bedside table. Oldies. Gracie's favorite. Holding her breath, Naomi leaned over her. "I love you, Gracie girl," she murmured, kissing her forehead, then her nose. This girl was her life. Her reason. Her everything. Tears stung like sparks in her eyes. The secret still sat in her stomach as solid and heavy as a stone. What would it do to them? What would it do to the safe and happy life she'd built for her daughter?

She didn't have time to reflect on the question before the doorbell rang. Eight o'clock on the nose. Her friends were so punctual when there was a promise of wine and chocolate.

Bogart lifted his head as though unsure he should leave Gracie's side to go check on the door.

"It's just the girls, Bogy," Naomi whispered. But he trotted down the hall behind her anyway. As the man of the house, he always wanted to be sure there was no threat.

Opening the door let in a flood of relief. These women were her safety net, the only place she let herself fall. They always caught her with love and wisdom and humor. They always helped her spring back up, somehow feeling stronger. God knew, she needed strength now.

Darla came through first, her petite shoulders weighted down with bags. Although she was the oldest member of the group at thirty-six, she could also be considered the hippest. Her black hair was cropped in a trendy pixie cut made even cooler with smart red streaks. "Hellloooo," she cried. "I brought truffles! And a local zinfandel!"

"Perfect." Naomi unburdened her of one of the bags, peeking in and instantly catching a whiff of luscious dark chocolate.

"And I brought bridesmaid gifts!" Jessa announced, squeezing past them while she waved miniature gift bags in the air. Although she and Lance had been together for nine months, her friendly brown eyes still shone like a woman caught up in the richness of new love. Tonight, she had her long blond hair pulled back loosely, making her look even more like a young bride.

"I can't believe the wedding is only three weeks away," Cassidy Greer squealed, cramming herself into the entryway along with them. Even her vivid blue eyes seemed to be sparkling more than normal. Usually, the poor woman seemed tired and stressed—working as an EMT while she put herself through nursing school—but tonight the wedding excitement seemed to have given her a second wind.

"I'm so glad you're here," Naomi told them all, leading them down the hall and into her small kitchen. While Gracie had been in the shower, Naomi had taken the time to set out her good china plates and wineglasses, along with festive flowered napkins.

"Me too," Jessa sighed. "I need some girl time. Living with Lance is so wonderful, but there are just some things boys don't get."

"I'll have to take your word for it." Naomi laughed. She hadn't lived with a boy in a very long time. And even then it had lasted less than a year.

"Not that I'm complaining," Jessa said quickly, giving Naomi an empathetic pat on the arm.

"You'd better not complain." Darla unpacked enough wine from her bags to serve a wedding party. "You're the only one who gets sex whenever she wants it."

"Yeah," Cassidy agreed. "That's one perk to living with a man."

"I know, I know." Jessa pulled out the boxes of chocolate truffles and dipped pretzels, spreading them around the table. "But I've been so stressed. You're not going to believe what happened today. The minister ran off with the pianist!" she wailed. "And now I have no music and no one to officiate at the wedding."

"Whadda you mean they ran off?" Naomi asked, popping the cork on the zinfandel.

"They're gone." Jessa slumped at the dining room table, already reaching for a wineglass. "Together. I guess they left notes for their spouses or something. It's all over town."

"Wow." Naomi sat across from her while Darla took the head of the table and Cassidy scooted into the chair next to Jessa.

"So what're you gonna do?" Cass asked, eyes rounded with concern.

"I have no idea." Jessa helped herself to a few of the truffles. "I mean, I've already called every other religious official in town—including that guy who owns the tarot card shop—and *no* one is available."

"Maybe Levi will do it," Darla suggested, topping off her glass. Apparently, Naomi hadn't poured her enough. "God, I wouldn't mind seeing him all dressed up in a starched black suit and white collar." She licked her lips suggestively.

"I'm *not* having Levi do the wedding." Jessa rolled her eyes. "You never know what's going to come out of that man's mouth."

Naomi didn't blame her. The youngest Cortez could be a bit of a wild card.

"What about Lucas?" Cassidy proposed thoughtfully. "He's pretty well spoken." She slid a quick glance to Naomi. Her friends always seemed to do that whenever anyone spoke the man's name. As if they were all afraid of what it did to her.

Not that she'd admit it out loud, but it did quite a lot.

Hopefully, they'd missed the bright red flush that turned her face molten.

"I thought about that..." Jessa seemed to study Naomi longer than the rest of them. "But he's so busy getting everything ready to go back to the McGowen's ranch for good..."

A gasp hitched her breath. "He's going back?" The words harnessed the strange mix of relief and sorrow that gathered in her heart. "When?"

"Right after the wedding, as far as I understand." Jessa eyed her as though trying to gauge her reaction. "Bill McGowen told him he needs him back or he'll have to find someone else." She gave Naomi a pointed look. "He's not here much longer. So there's not much time."

Naomi focused on her wineglass, on the shimmery rose-colored liquid. Jessa had hounded her for months to talk to Lucas about her unresolved feelings for him. But her friend didn't know the real reason those feeling still existed. No one did.

"Not much time for what?" Cassidy demanded, looking back and forth between them suspiciously.

"To screw him, silly," Darla put in. "To see if he's still got it."

"That's not what she meant," Naomi said. That wasn't a concern. Something told her he still had it. "I can't believe he's leaving again." He hadn't said anything in the car. Though she hadn't given him much of a chance. "He's supposed to go to Gracie's play tomorrow night."

"You invited him?" Jessa asked happily.

"Not exactly," she admitted. "Gracie invited him."

Darla munched on a pretzel. "Maybe you two should go out after the play," she proposed with peaked eyebrows.

"I'm not going out with him." They'd all been on her

case since he'd arrived back in town, but didn't they get it? Lucas wasn't going to stick around. She knew he'd leave again. He wasn't happy in Topaz Falls. So what good would going out with him do either one of them? He wanted to leave and she was staying. She was opening a bed and breakfast.

Not that she was ready to share that news yet.

"So Gracie invited him," Cass mused.

Yeah. Her sweet, loving, extroverted daughter had invited him. Which meant she liked him. Which meant she'd get all attached to him and then he'd disappear again. Naomi couldn't tell if the sadness weighting her heart was for Gracie or for herself.

She stamped it out with anger. "He has no business going to that play." Why would he be trying to build a friendship with Gracie when he was planning to leave?

"What're you so upset about?" Darla asked, setting down her wineglass. "You've hardly even acknowledged his presence in Topaz Falls. You've gone out of your way to avoid him for months."

Naomi's face burned. She was upset. She was sad and angry. But not at Lucas. She was upset with herself. The truth was she couldn't look Lucas in the eyes because she had kept things from him. Things she should've told him a long time ago.

"Naomi?" Cassidy reached over to pat her hand. "What is it? What's wrong?"

They all stared at her with concern and sympathy. Her friends. The ones who'd each spilled their own secrets at one time or another. Darla had told them all about the pain of watching her husband slowly slip away from cancer. Jessa had sobbed over her father's death. Cassidy had shared everything about taking care of her mother, whose life was shattered after Cassidy's brother Cash had been killed in a bull-riding accident five years ago.

These were practically her sisters, and though she'd talked about the challenges of being a single mom after Mark left her, she'd never told them all her deepest regret. The secret she'd carried for so many years.

The one she didn't want to carry anymore.

She rested her forearms on the table, ready for this weight to be lifted off her. Ready to be free of it. "Lucas might be Gracie's father." She spoke the words quickly, boldly. That was the only way they could come out. Fast. Direct. Honest. That was it. The truth in all its ugliness.

Darla busted out in gut-splitting laughter.

Cassidy shook her head. "Good one," she said.

"No. I'm serious." Her voice had gotten brittle, the last words falling apart. "I never found out for sure, but I might have been pregnant before he was arrested." In the wake of Lucas's arrest, she'd fallen apart and found herself in a relationship with Mark. Things had happened so fast. When she'd told Mark she was pregnant he'd asked her to marry him right then and there. She'd told him she had to think about it, and that night she went home and wrote Lucas one more letter. Over the previous two months, she'd written him eight letters, one each week, and all of them had been returned unopened. All these years, she'd kept that final letter. In it, she'd told him there was a chance he was her baby's father and begged him to write her back, but he hadn't. He hadn't even opened the letter. After that, she'd realized she couldn't do it anymore. She wasn't angry with him, but she couldn't hold out hope for someone who kept shutting her out. It had hurt too much. So she'd forced herself to move on.

"Shit." Darla gawked at her. "Shit! You're not kidding."

"Oh my God..." Jessa mumbled, mopping her mouth with a napkin.

"I'm not kidding," Naomi confirmed, pushing away her plate. She couldn't even stomach a bite of chocolate right now. "I've never told him. Never told anyone. But Mark emailed me twice last week."

"*Mark?*" they all said in unison.

"He said he wants to talk to me. About Gracie." He'd actually used the word "daughter." His daughter. But she wasn't. He'd been gone for ten years. And Naomi had always wondered whether he was Gracie's biological father, but it hadn't mattered. It hadn't mattered because Mark had left them and Lucas was gone and they didn't need anyone. She'd taken care of everything. She'd raised her all on her own.

"That son of a bitch." Darla slammed her palm on the table, causing a wave of ripples in Naomi's wine. "I'll email him back for you. Tell him exactly what I think of his sorry ass."

"While I'd love to hear that conversation, I don't think it'll help much." Naomi heaved a sigh. "I haven't written him back." She wanted those emails to go away. Wanted him to disappear. "I don't know what he wants, but I'm afraid he'll try to see her." And he couldn't. He couldn't come in now and destroy everything she'd built for her daughter.

"You have to tell Lucas there's a possibility he's Gracie's father," Jessa said, still gawking at her. "You have to. He deserves to know."

"Yes. He does," she uttered in an aching whisper. He deserved to know everything. Finally. After all these years.

She just wasn't sure how to tell him.

Chapter Three

Just like old times. Lucas rambled into his older brother's kitchen, greeted by the greasy smell of bacon and eggs and the sizzle of the fryer. Lance stood at the stove stirring and flipping while Levi and their father sat at the table discussing the latest PBR standings as they waited for their breakfast.

"They've got you trained, huh?" Lucas asked, lightly socking Lance in the side as he moved past him and sat at the other end of the table.

"I don't think Levi even knows how to hold a spatula," his brother said, low enough so that the other two didn't hear. "And have you ever tasted Dad's eggs?"

"No, actually. I can't say I have." That was because Lance had cooked breakfast for all of them ever since their mom left. It likely had something to do with the fact that Lance had watched her leave early one morning before the sun had even crested the peaks. Lucas had walked into the kitchen when Lance was putting the finishing touches on omelets.

Before that, he hadn't known his brother even knew how to crack an egg. But he'd figured it out that day. They'd all spent those years figuring things out.

"Morning, son." Luis folded the sports section of the newspaper into neat quarters and laid it on the table in front of him.

"Morning, Dad." Didn't matter how many times he said it, that never got old. After he went to prison Lucas didn't talk to Luis for ten years. He couldn't stomach the shame he'd seen on the man's face. But then his father had been diagnosed with Parkinson's and Jessa had called him to come home. That was all he'd needed. An invitation. He'd been welcomed by his father, who was hunched and arthritic, suffering from persistent tremors and balance issues, though the most recent medication they had him on seemed to be making a difference.

"What happened to your truck?" his father asked. "Didn't see it outside this morning."

"It broke down." The last thing his father needed to hear was *how* it had broken down. He had enough to worry about.

"I'll take you to pick it up after our meeting this morning," Lance said, lugging the food over to the table.

"What meeting?" Levi wasted no time piling his plate full.

Lance hesitated, and Lucas didn't blame him. They didn't exactly involve their younger brother in much of the ranch's business. He was too busy reveling in his bull rider fame and sponsorship opportunities to concern himself with the logistics of a stock contracting operation.

"I'd forgotten Jones was coming today," Luis said gruffly. He hated forgetting stuff, that much was obvious, but it happened more and more.

"Jones?" Levi repeated skeptically. "As in Brady Jones?"

Everyone connected to the bull-riding world had heard of Brady Jones. The former champion who'd once competed against Luis was now the director of livestock for the largest rodeo circuit in the country.

"Yeah. It's a big day," Lance said, his face grim. Over the last six months Lance had invested in new livestock, mainly bucking bulls, to get his operation up and running. Lucas had consulted on a limited basis, but he'd been down in Pueblo off and on, and Bill McGowen had all but told him he'd fire his ass if he sensed any conflict of interest between the two operations. Lucas wasn't sure he wanted to lose that job.

"If Jones doesn't contract two or three of our bulls, I'm screwed," Lance muttered, still looking doubtful.

Lucas wished he felt better about things than his brother did, but he'd seen the bulls Lance had purchased. While they had promise, they weren't there yet, and Jones was coming today to scout for the next several events. If they didn't get picked, Lance didn't get paid, and Lucas happened to know his brother had invested most of his savings.

"I'm happy to stick around and shoot the breeze with him," Levi offered. He'd already wolfed down most of his breakfast and was casually sipping coffee. Lucas marveled at how young he still looked. It was obvious the three of them were related, but while he and Lance looked more like Luis, Levi reminded him of their mother. His skin was fairer and unmarred by the stress Lance and Lucas had endured over the years.

And yet he didn't resent his brother. He was glad one of them had had it easier. That'd been the idea when he'd taken the punishment for Levi. He was proud of him. Given the way things had gone after their mother left, Levi could've been a complete screwup, but he'd straightened out, left home to train with bull-riding legend Gunner Raines, and become one of the infamous Raines' Renegades, a group of traveling riders who also made quite the haul in sponsorships.

"Actually, I could use your help patching some siding today," Luis said to his youngest son. Lucas had to smile. Their father didn't think Levi should get involved any more than they did. Besides that, someone had to watch Luis when he did projects. They couldn't have him falling off a ladder or something.

"Lance and I have got this." He finished off his own breakfast quickly then shoved his plate toward Levi. "And since Lance cooked, you're on dish duty." Before Levi could argue, Lucas motioned to Lance and the two of them pushed back from the table and walked out of the house grinning. Yep. Just like old times.

Over the next hour, they worked with Tucker, the stable manager, to get the bulls ready. But even hosing them down, feeding them, and getting them riled up didn't put Lucas at ease. He'd been purchasing and training bulls for McGowen for so long, he could spot a potential bovine champion, and these bulls didn't seem to have it.

"You're worried," Lance said, standing next to him on the outside of the corral while Tucker gated Inferno.

Was his worry that obvious? That bull was supposed to be Lance's best bet, but he didn't have the fire, and Brady Jones would recognize that right away. "How much did you pay for him, again?" he asked, dreading the answer.

"A couple hundred grand." Lance seemed to dread saying it, too. Lucas didn't tell him he'd gotten screwed. He likely already knew.

The sound of a truck crawling up behind them made his stomach pull into a tight knot. Brady Jones got out and sauntered over, thumbs hooked into his belt loops, tall cowboy hat casting a shadow over his eyes. He was a good five years younger than their father, but his face was marked by a few scars and the same sun damage. “Gentlemen,” he said, giving each of them a hearty handshake.

“Good to see you, Jones. Thanks for coming,” Lance said.

“Surprised to see you here, Lucas.” The man eyed him suspiciously. “You give up on McGowen? Or just home for a visit?”

“Home for a visit,” he said quickly. Word would travel fast, and Bill McGowen would not appreciate the fact that Lucas was attending a meeting for the competition. He hung back and let Lance walk Jones around the facilities, showing off each of the bulls his brother had purchased.

When they came back to the fence, Lucas could tell Jones had already made a decision. He’d done enough business with the man to recognize that dispassionate expression. “Well, Cortez, I gotta say, I’m not seeing anything I haven’t seen before.” The man was always direct. It was something Lucas used to appreciate about him.

“You’ve got a good start here, but none of these guys are ready for the big stage.”

Lance didn’t seem to know what to say. He simply nodded.

Jones clapped him on the shoulder. “Give me a call in a few years when you’ve got more experience under your belt.”

“Sure. Of course.”

Lucas had to hand it to his brother. He wasn’t letting his disappointment show. But he could feel it, and he couldn’t let Lance lose what he’d worked for.

"Wait," Lucas said, just as Jones started to retreat to his truck. The man stopped, turned, made a show of glancing at his watch. He didn't like people wasting his time, but Lucas knew he'd want to hear him out. "Come back in a few weeks." Preferably after the wedding.

Irritation pulled at the man's mouth. "I shouldn't have come this week. This operation isn't ready."

"He's got another purchase in the works."

"I do?" Lance mumbled.

Lucas shut him up with a look and strode over to Jones, facing him directly. "There's a private auction next week. For one of Day of Reckoning's offspring." Day of Reckoning was the most decorated bovine champion to ever grace the sport. Bill McGowen had enlisted Lucas to go to the auction and outbid everyone else. He'd also told him not to spread the word, but Lance was desperate. Reckoning II had already competed in a few lower level events and he'd thrown every rider within three seconds. "Lance has an in and it's looking like a done deal. So you'll want to come back soon and take a look at him."

"You get Reckoning's offspring and I'll be here," Jones said. Without a goodbye, he climbed into his rig and left them in a cloud of dust.

His brother eyed him. "Let me guess. You're supposed to purchase that bull for McGowen."

He shrugged. "McGowen has plenty of bulls." The man ran a multimillion-dollar operation. It wouldn't kill him to lose out on one.

"I don't know what I was thinking." Lance glanced over at Inferno, still penned up in a stall. "I don't have much more to invest in this." Not a shock, considering all of the stock he'd purchased recently. His brother had won some significant purses and a championship last year, but that didn't go so far when you were talking millions to get an operation up and running. And Lance had never gravitated toward the sponsorships to supplement his income the way Levi had.

"You can't give up yet," Lucas insisted. "We'll sell some off some of your stock. All you need is one champion. I'll help you figure it out."

His brother seemed to assess him. "You gonna lose your job for this?"

"Maybe." He hadn't thought that far ahead when he'd mentioned the auction.

"That okay with you?" Lance asked hopefully. He'd been trying to get Lucas on board to stick around the ranch and help him run the operation. But there was one problem with that. No one else wanted him around. The McGowen Ranch had been his safety net. It'd provided him the chance to start over. And if he came back to Topaz Falls for good, he'd go right back to being the kid convicted of arson. But he couldn't worry about that now. His brother needed him. He shrugged off Lance's concern.

"I'll figure it out. I can handle Bill McGowen."

If only he felt as confident as he sounded.

* * *

The only thing worse than having his truck vandalized was having Officer Dev Jenkins show up to see the mess.

Lucas liked Dev all right, but he hadn't seen much of him in ten years. Back in high school they'd raised all kinds of hell together, which may have been what inspired Dev to become an officer of the law. He'd always been a hell of a guy—honest, hardworking, loyal. If Lucas would've stuck around, they likely would've still been friends. But while Dev worked his way up the ranks and became a town hero, Lucas had become the town's shame, the wayward son who'd gone and stained his family's good name. In everyone else's eyes they'd taken two starkly different paths. And even though Dev never brought it up, it still simmered between them.

"Did you have to call him?" Lucas asked Lance. They were both leaning against the left fender of his damaged truck watching as the patrol car swerved around the long curve from the east. After the meeting with Jones, Lucas told his brother what had happened to his truck. Next thing he knew, Lance was on the phone demanding that Dev come check out the "crime scene." Lucas had planned to go into town and buy some new tires, then hitch a ride out to change them himself. That'd teach him to mention anything to his brother.

"Some punk ass kid vandalized your car," Lance muttered, as ticked as if it'd been his own. "Last I checked that's a misdemeanor."

Lance would know. He'd done plenty of vandalizing back in the day.

"Dev can figure this out. Give the little shit a good scare. Then they'll let you be."

"They're not gonna let me be." Lucas lifted his hand in a wave as Dev pulled up behind the truck. "And what makes you think it was a kid?" It could've been anyone in town. Marshal Dobbins still hated him. His dad had been the rodeo commissioner, and after the fire he'd been out of a job. Then he'd left Topaz Falls and his family behind, headed for greener pastures in California. Even if it wasn't Dobbins, there was a whole list of others who'd made a career out of holding a grudge. Hell, just last week old Mrs. Eckles—who'd earned a reputation for being the sweetest woman in town—crossed the street so she wouldn't have to walk past him. He'd seen her cross back over once she'd cleared the bakery.

"No one but a kid would mess with you," Lance insisted.

"Yeah, well, Dev won't find anything. I've already looked." There was no evidence left behind. No empty spray paint cans, no knife blade. Not even a damn footprint. Whoever had jacked up his truck had done it right. It'd been planned.

"Mornin'." Dev pushed open the door to his patrol car and took his time sauntering over to the truck. He hadn't changed much since he'd played defensive tackle for the Topaz High School Miners back in the day. Still big and brawny. Dark, clipped hair and a broad jaw that put Hercules to shame. Looking at him, most would mistake the man for a big dumb oaf, but before he'd come back to keep the streets of Topaz Falls safe, he'd gone to CU and graduated in the top ten percent of his class.

That's where Lucas was supposed to have gone, too. They'd planned to room together. Instead he'd roomed with a bunch of thugs who found themselves behind bars for assault, grand larceny, and drug-related offenses. Not that he was complaining. It could've been a hell of a lot worse.

"Thanks for coming, Dev." Lance caught the man's beefy hand in a firm shake while Lucas simply gave him a nod. He was pretty sure this was a waste of all of their time.

"So you got any idea who would've come after you?" Dev asked, walking the length of the truck as he sized up the damage.

"Mrs. Eckles?" Lucas joked.

Dev cracked a grin. "Woman sure can hold a grudge." He eyed the sagging tires on the truck. "But I'd doubt she owns a high-quality switchblade."

"What about Shane and Carter?" Lance suggested. "Those two are always doing stupid shit."

"The Werner boys?" Dev shook his head. "Nah. They've straightened up since I let 'em spend a night in jail for trespassing on the Blairs' farm." He aimed a curious gaze at Lucas. "Have you gotten any threats? Had any confrontations?"

"Nope. Plenty of dirty looks and a couple offhand comments at the bar. Nothing serious, though."

"This is pretty damn serious, if you ask me," his brother said.

Dev took a knee and looked underneath the truck. "Whoever did it was careful. Didn't want to get caught." He heaved himself back to his feet. "I'll check into it. Ask around."

"That's it?" Lance demanded, following him to the rear of the truck.

"Thanks, Dev," Lucas cut in before his brother made a complete ass out of himself. Of course that was it. What'd Lance expect him to do? Dust for fingerprints? This wasn't a murder scene.

"No problem." Dev ignored Lance and faced Lucas. "I'm sure this won't be the last of it, so pay attention. Got it? Let me know if anything seems off."

"Will do," he promised, shaking the man's hand. "But I'll only be in town for a few more weeks, so not sure there's anything to worry about."

His old friend tilted his head with a stern look. "Gonna let 'em run you out of here again, huh?"

"That's exactly what he's doing," Lance growled.

Lucas glared back at his brother. "Doesn't count as getting run off if you want to go." At least he'd thought he wanted to go. Then Naomi had gone and nearly taken him out with her car. Now he wasn't so sure.

"You shouldn't let them get to you, Cortez." Dev started to lumber back to his patrol car. "It's been good having you back. And whoever these bastards are...they'll get over it."

"Thanks." It was good to know not everyone in town hated him. Having the law on his side was something, he guessed.

Dev slid into his car. "I'll call out a tow truck for you. Get you all fixed up. Let me know if you need anything else."

How about an idea for how to win over the woman he'd lost ten years ago? Unfortunately, Dev didn't seem any more adept in the relationship department than he was, seeing as how they were both bachelors nearing thirty. "Hopefully I won't need you again, but thanks."

With a wave, Dev turned onto the highway.

"You don't have to go back to McGowen's, you know," Lance said as they walked to his truck.

"Not this again." They'd had the same conversation at least thirty times since he'd been home, but his argument had started to weaken.

"Your family's here. Dad's here." Lance leveled him with a smug look. "Naomi's here."

"I can come back and visit," he said, avoiding the Naomi issue completely. He couldn't let himself go there. If her distance in the car yesterday was any indication, she wanted him to go back to Pueblo. As soon as possible. Maybe she held his past against him, too. Which brought him back to his point. "Would you want to stay someplace you weren't wanted?"

"No," Lance said grudgingly. "I don't know. Maybe. If I had the right motivation."

"Sure. If I had the right motivation, maybe I'd stay." But his brother had no idea what it was like for him here. Lance was the superstar who'd followed in their dad's footsteps. Last year may have been rocky for him, but after he'd won Worlds, everyone had forgotten about his struggles. Now he was getting married to the woman of his dreams. A woman everyone in town seemed to love. And according to their estimations his older brother deserved all of it, while Lucas deserved to suffer the consequences of his mistakes forever.

"What if you could do something to change everyone's mind?" His brother got the same thoughtful look that took over his features whenever he was generating a plan.

He laughed. Lance made it sound so easy. "What'd you have in mind? Hang out on Main Street and help Mrs. Eckles carry her groceries across the street? Become a Boy Scout?" That ship had sailed a long time ago.

"No." Lance straightened, taking on that authoritative older brother stance. The man had never known when to quit. "You could volunteer. Do something to help out the town. I heard they're gonna start some fire mitigation work over on Topaz Mountain. It's been so dry this spring they're worried one bolt of lightning will torch the whole thing."

"And you really think me cutting down some dead trees is gonna win people over?" He was impressed. He'd never thought of his brother as an optimist, but every once in a while Lance surprised him.

"I think it's a start."

"And what if I can't earn my way back into their good graces?" A familiar bitterness slithered through the words. "Why should I even have to earn my way back in?" He'd spent three years in prison. Wasn't that enough?

"You should do it for Naomi."

Those simple words cut through him, bleeding out the excuses, the pride, the desire to run. Lance knew his weakness. Knew he'd do anything for her. "Naomi's not interested," he said, hating the gruff tenor of the words. "She's made it pretty clear."

His brother's humorless laugh mocked him. "You really are as clueless as Jessa says you are."

"I don't need this." Lance might be older, but Lucas didn't have to listen to him. He went to walk around the truck but Lance grabbed his shoulder and turned him around. "If the town wasn't an issue—if people left you alone and didn't treat you like a criminal—would you stay? Would you want a life with Naomi?"

Yes. He couldn't even say it because it was impossible. He didn't have to say it. His brother had always been able to read him the way Lucas read the river when he was fishing.

"Maybe they'll never forgive you. Maybe you'll work your ass off volunteering and subjecting yourself to public humiliation for nothing." Lance leaned in. "But maybe—*maybe*—it would be worth it. Maybe if you stood your ground and went after what you really wanted, something would change."

For the last ten years of his life, Lucas hadn't entertained any maybes. He hadn't had that luxury. He'd had to go with the guarantees. The guarantee for money. For food. For a roof. For the necessities. He hadn't exactly lost hope, but it hadn't been something he'd held onto, either.

"You have nothing to lose," his brother said emphatically, as though offering his closing argument. "If it doesn't work you go back to the McGowen place. But if it does..."

He trailed off, and Lucas filled in the blanks. If it did work, if he won the town over, he could stay. He could work with his brother on the family ranch.

Not only that. He could also make it a hell of a lot harder for Naomi to ignore him.

Chapter Four

How's it going in there?" Naomi stood outside the small closet that acted as a dressing room in Gracie's classroom. Her daughter—excuse her—the fairy godmother star had been holed up in there for a good ten minutes perfecting her look for the big show tonight. Which started in... Naomi checked her watch... fifteen minutes. "The show's going to start soon, honey," she called through the door. Wouldn't do for the fairy godmother to float in late.

After some shuffling, Gracie emerged, dressed in her blue costume, her reddish hair piled on top of her head, complete with a sparkling tiara. "Well, Mom... how do I look?" she asked nervously.

Too grown-up. And *Mom*? Since when had she called her Mom instead of Mommy? Naomi looked her daughter over, taking in the glimmering turquoise eye shadow and the gloss that made her lips shimmer. God, how was she ten already? It was crazy how the years flew by. It seemed like just last week Gracie had been spinning around on stage in her tiny little tutu. Now they only had eight more years together before Gracie would head off to college.

"You look so pretty, honey," she murmured quietly, fearing Gracie might hear the quiver of emotion in her voice. "You're going to be *amazing* tonight."

"I don't know about that, but at least I'll *look* amazing." Gracie threw her arms around Naomi. "Thanks for making me this awesome costume." She leaned in closer. "I think it's even prettier than Cinderella's," she whispered, her eyes twinkling.

Naomi hugged her back. "You're my princess, you know that?"

"Of course I do." Gracie pulled away and looked around quickly, as though worried that some of the other girls might have seen their little display of affection. But most of the girls had already left the room to go backstage.

"Come on, Gracie girl," Naomi said, tugging on her hand. "One more picture, then I'll walk you to the gym."

Her daughter rolled those spry green eyes but a smile broke through. She posed with both hands clasped under her chin, which only proved she loved the spotlight and all of this attention.

"No more pictures until I'm on stage," Gracie instructed, leading her mother out the door. "And don't call me 'Gracie girl' in front of my friends," she whispered. "I *do* have a reputation to think about."

Despite the maternal tug at her heart, Naomi laughed. "Yes, ma'am," she said with a salute.

They paraded down the hall, Gracie a good foot in front of her, nearly skipping in anticipation of her stage debut. Naomi remembered being like that once. Confident. Full of assurances that she could do anything, including standing on a stage reciting lines in front of a whole roomful of people. What had happened to that girl? The fun-loving spontaneous girl who'd once skinny-dipped with Lucas in a high mountain lake?

"Hey look!" Gracie broke into a jog. "There's Lucas!"

Naomi stopped, her eyes searching down the hall where her daughter had pointed. Sure enough, there he stood, just outside the gym doors, dressed in dark jeans and a black button-down shirt, holding his cowboy hat in front of his waist respectfully.

Her heart took a dive. One look at him and she was going down in flames. Her hand instantly rose to smooth her hair into place, like it always had when she'd seen him around the halls in high school. Not that he looked the same as he did back then. He'd always been good-looking, but when they'd dated he'd had that appealing boyish look. Nowadays he went way past appealing to downright arousing. His complexion had darkened from the years of outdoor work, and his eyes had a deeper tint, a hint that he'd become far more experienced in life. To top it off, he carried himself like a man who knew what he wanted.

"Lucas! Hey, Lucas!" Gracie beelined down the hall, and Naomi had no choice but to follow her right to the man she'd spent so much time avoiding.

When she finally caught up, the roar of her heart stole her breath.

Lucas had knelt in front of Gracie and was handing her a single yellow rose. "Good luck tonight," he said. "If that bit in the car was any indication, you're gonna knock 'em dead."

"Thank you!" Gracie squealed, smooshing the rose

against her nose and inhaling deeply. "No one's ever given me a flower before!" She held it up to Naomi. "Look, Mom! Yellow's my favorite color!"

"I know." She smiled down at her daughter, though her heartbeat came in painful hard thumps.

"Oh! I have to go!" Gracie tore away from the two of them, headed for the cafeteria. "Bye, Mom! Bye, Lucas! I'll see you after the show!"

Before she could even give her daughter a good luck kiss, Gracie had disappeared into the sea of horses and mice and pumpkins who were all streaming into the cafeteria.

"She's incredible," Lucas said, gazing after her. "I can't believe how much she reminds me of you."

And she couldn't believe how the simple act of standing close to him brought her body to life. Blood surged, flooding her with a tingling heat she hadn't experienced in so long...

"The rest of the crew's already inside," he went on when she didn't say anything. "They're saving seats. I wanted to make sure I saw her before." He shoved his calloused hands into the pockets of his jeans just like he had back in high school when he was nervous.

She wasn't nervous. She was downright spooked. But she did her best to snap out of it. She couldn't stand here mute, staring at the old love of her life as though trying to erase the years that had put distance between them. She had to say something. Anything...

"Thanks for bringing her a rose," she managed. "That was thoughtful."

His gaze darted sideways in that bashful way. "Jessa said she loved yellow," he admitted. "I'm glad she—"

"Excuse me." Eleanor Bradley, the principal of Topaz Falls Elementary, cut in to the conversation. Though she was short and stocky, she had the power to make a sixth-grade boy cry with just one look. She cast her sternest glare at Lucas. "What are *you* doing here?" she asked in a clipped tone.

His jaw fell open. So did Naomi's, for that matter. Eleanor might be strict, but she'd never seen her act so... *rude*.

Lucas didn't seem to know what to say so she stepped in. "We invited him," Naomi said just as sternly. "He's here to watch Gracie in the play."

"I see." Mrs. Bradley lifted her chin, almost like she wished she could look down at him. "As long as you're here with someone, then," she muttered before quickly retreating down the hall, shaking her head the whole way.

Naomi's face flamed with embarrassment on behalf of the principal. "I have no idea what's gotten into her. She must be stressed out about the play."

"That's not it," Lucas said drily. "Trust me. I get that a few times a week. Pretty much whenever I show up in town."

"Oh God. Really?" She'd never thought about that—about what it must be like for him. Everyone knew what he'd done. She'd heard some people even blamed him for the town losing out on hosting any more competitions. "But it was so long ago." How was it that people still saw him as the same screwed-up kid? She didn't. She recognized pieces of him—his humility, his humor, his kind heart—but there were so many new qualities, too. So much to explore if she would let herself...

"Doesn't seem to matter how long it's been," he said, glancing over his shoulder as if worried Eleanor would come back. "Maybe this wasn't a good idea. I shouldn't have come."

"That's ridiculous." A sudden protective impulse led her

to take his arm. "Of course you should be here." She tucked her arm around his, stunned by the overpowering rush of longing, but she soldiered on down the hall anyway. "Gracie invited you. She wants you here." Gulping a breath of courage, she looked up at his face. "And so do I."

He stopped abruptly and turned so that he faced her. "Really?" he asked, his eyes searching hers. "You want me here?"

That breath of courage got stuck in her throat. Didn't he know? Couldn't he feel her heart drumming? Couldn't he hear it? "Yes," she said, regretting all those months she'd avoided him, looked away, walked away. The way she'd been acting, he probably thought she was no better than the rest of the town, holding some stupid grudge against him.

But it hadn't been out of anger or contempt. It had been out of fear. He couldn't have known that, though. He must've thought she hated him. "Lucas... I—"

"There you are!" Jessa darted over, squeezing herself between them and urging them to the gym. "The play's starting in, like, two minutes," she said impatiently. "And people are giving us dirty looks for saving two seats in the front row."

"Right." Naomi sighed. She snuck a glance at Lucas, who still stared at her as though waiting for her to finish what she'd been about to say. But now was not the time. Later. She would tell him everything later.

* * *

On a typical evening, a woman's hand brushing his thigh didn't do much for him, but tonight every square inch of him seemed to be on heightened alert.

"Sorry," Naomi whispered, and even in the dimly lit gymnasium he noticed the color that flooded her cheeks. He simply grinned at her. Let her read into that whatever she wanted.

He obviously didn't mind her touching him.

Before the performance, they'd definitely had a moment, but Jessa had gone and ruined it. Then, for the last hour, he'd sat next to Naomi in the crowded gymnasium, her delicate shoulder fixed against his, and God help him, he couldn't keep his eyes from wandering over to her. Not because the dress she wore was particularly suggestive. It was one of those wrap thingies, fitted and elegant. Maybe not so striking on any other woman, but the teal color set her red hair on fire. That, combined with her happy, sunshiny scent, kept tempting him to touch her, put his arm around her, hold her hand as if they were here together.

Which they weren't, of course. But she'd said she wanted him here so he figured that was something.

Somehow, in between glimpses of Naomi and trying to keep his body under wraps, he'd managed to take in most of the show. Gracie was a convincing Fairy Godmother, confident and articulate. She didn't fumble one line. Naomi had been the same way back in high school. Captain of the debate team and persuasive as hell. It was those eyes of hers—the deep intense jade of them made people stumble over their words. He sure had when she'd become his science partner sophomore year. The two of them had never really talked before that—they'd tended to run in different crowds growing up, him with the misfits and her with the cheerleaders and jocks. But that first day in science class when they'd sat across from each other wearing their protective eye goggles, Naomi had made him laugh. It had felt like years since he'd laughed, and he was done for. Completely one hundred percent hers. No woman had given him that feeling since.

The show ended with the cast celebrating the wedding of Prince Charming and Cinderella. Gracie twirled around the stage gleefully, her blue tutu flaring. The applause started and swelled into a standing ovation that rang in his ears. He stood with the rest of the crowd, praising the kids for their performance, but mostly Gracie.

"She was the best one up there," he whispered, leaning closer to Naomi. "I could hardly even hear Cinderella." Who should've been the star of the show. With her wit and those dimples, Gracie had definitely stolen that honor.

"Lack of confidence has never been one of her weaknesses," her mother said, face beaming with pride. He felt it, too, though he had no right. He hadn't done anything to make Gracie into who she was. Seeing her up there, it only made Naomi more amazing to him. What did she have to go through in those early years? An eighteen-year-old with a new baby all on her own, on top of dealing with the shame and the rumors her situation had brought. He couldn't imagine.

The music stopped and the stage broke into a flurry of uncoordinated activity.

As though unable to contain their excitement any longer, the kids flooded down the steps and poured into the audience, their parents gathering them into tight hugs.

Gracie ran down the aisle and flung herself into her mother's arms.

"You were amazing," Naomi gushed.

"Star of the show!" Jessa agreed.

"You should've gone for the lead role," Lance said before

Lucas could jump in with a compliment. "Seriously. You would've made a great Cinderella."

"I didn't *want* to be Cinderella," she said with a look of horror. "She doesn't *do* anything."

Lucas laughed. This girl…she was something else.

"I wanted to be the one who *grants* the wishes," Gracie went on, her eyes as bright as her mom's. "The Fairy Godmother is my favorite character in the story."

"Why's that?" he asked.

"Without the Fairy Godmother, Cinderella never would've found her happily ever after. That makes her the most important character in the story."

The wisdom of that statement struck him. What girl cared more about granting the wishes of others than being the beautiful princess?

"Can we get ice cream?" Gracie pleaded, transforming into a typical ten-year-old again. "All of us together?" she looked around at Jessa and Lance, Darla and Cassidy, and then even at him.

Though he wanted to say yes—to grant *her* every wish—he deferred to Naomi.

"Of course we can," she said quickly, gathering her daughter under her arm. "Come on. We'd better hurry or A La Mode will be packed."

They all herded out the gym doors and down the halls in the same elementary school he'd attended, though everything looked so much smaller now. The desks, the drinking fountains—everything seemed miniature.

Once they'd made it outside, Gracie broke away from her mom. "I'm gonna ride with Auntie Cass, okay?" She attached herself to Cassidy's side. According to Jessa and Lance, Cassidy had babysat Gracie since she was two years old.

"That's fine, honey," Naomi said, waving. "We'll meet you there."

The rest of the group paraded into the parking lot, but Lucas hung back and snagged Naomi's arm. For months, he'd been waiting to steal a moment alone with her and while it may not have been the best time, what with the ice cream and all, he also didn't know if he'd get another opportunity.

"Thanks for letting me come," he said, not meaning for his voice to sound so husky and wanting. He couldn't help it. Tonight he'd felt like part of a family. And it'd been a long time since he'd had the luxury of feeling that.

"Of course," she murmured, between what seemed to be quick shallow breaths. "I'm glad you could come. It meant a lot to Gracie."

And what about her? He pressed his gaze into her eyes. There was so much he wanted to say. Years of words that had never been spoken. And God, he was such a coward. He could hot-brand a bull's ass but he couldn't tell this woman how much he'd thought of her. How much he still wanted her after all this time.

What if she didn't want him back?

"Why didn't you answer my letters?" The question was so quiet, he almost didn't hear. "I sent you so many letters," she said, louder. "And you never wrote me back. You never even opened them."

The blend of anger and sorrow in her voice hit him like a shot to the gut. Was that why she'd been avoiding him all these months? Because he hadn't answered her letters?

"I know you might not understand, but I wanted you to move on." It'd killed him not opening those letters. Writing *Return to Sender* and tossing them back in the mail pile. But he couldn't take her down with him. "I thought my life was over, Naomi." The shock of his prison sentence had shut him down completely. "I knew I couldn't come back here after what happened. And I wanted you to have everything you'd ever dreamed of." He'd known he couldn't give that to her. Not then and likely not now, either. Not with everyone in Topaz Falls blacklisting him.

Her humorless laugh dulled the air between them. "Look how well moving on worked for me," she said, staring down at her trembling hands.

He reached for her face and lifted it back up toward his so she could see the truth. What the hell was she talking about? "You're a good mother. You've made a good life for yourself. And for Gracie." Even with that asshole ex-friend of his walking out on them. "You've given her everything. A happy life. A whole community of people who love her. She had more people watching her in that play than any other kid on that stage..."

"Things could've been so different," Naomi whispered, tears shining in her eyes.

That look of pain cut through him. "I know." He focused on her delicate face, the months of subtle yearnings brewing into something fierce.

"I never believed you started that fire." For once, she looked at him directly, as if trying to see the answer to her unspoken question.

He silently pleaded the Fifth. Knowing the truth wouldn't do Naomi a lot of good now. "I'm sorry I let you down." That encompassed pretty much everything he'd wanted to tell her for ten years. The night he'd confessed to starting that fire, he'd lost her. And he didn't exactly deserve to have her back now.

She stared at him, those heart-shaped lips parted. "There

were so many things I never got the chance to tell you. I tried. I wanted to tell you everything..."

"You don't know how much I regret it." Shutting her out. Making the decision to cover for his brother. To save his brother from god knew what. At the time he'd been so sure he'd get off easy. "I didn't want you to give up anything for me."

"You should've let me decide." A tear did fall then, and even though it killed him to see her hurt, it also meant she still felt something for him. Something deep.

"I'm so sorry, Naomi." For whatever reason, her heart had opened to him. Maybe only a crack, but that was all he needed. He stepped closer to her, so that her body was pressed against his. Out in the parking lot, a line of headlights moseyed out to the road, but he didn't care. He didn't know when he'd have this chance again. So he took her into his arms because he couldn't wait. Couldn't analyze. He had to see. He had to feel her. Had to know she was as desperate as he was.

"Lucas..." she whispered, closing her eyes.

He rested his hands on her hips, urging her closer. "I need to know you don't hate me," he said, drowning in the feel of her. His hands slipped down low on her back, until he had her locked in his arms.

"I don't hate you," she squeaked. "God, I don't hate you at all."

That was all he needed. Holding her tightly in his arms, he lowered his mouth to hers, unable to stop himself, unable to hold back anything. Her lips tasted sweet, so warm and wet. He pressed into them, drinking in the scent of her, the feel of her curves that fit so tightly against his throbbing body.

She kissed him back, sighing deeply into his mouth as though letting go of her protests and hesitations.

His tongue sought hers, rekindling that connection they'd always had, electrifying everything else until the sparks of desire flashed through him.

Her soft moan purred into him as her lips clung to his, and those hands of hers, always delicate but strong, climbed their way down his chest. He'd never regretted walking away from her as much as he did now, gripped by this one small taste of how it could've been with her…

Naomi's wandering hands tensed, then pushed him back. "Wait. I can't…we can't…"

"We could," he insisted, not willing to give up yet. That one kiss had stirred up the fight in him. How could he let her go now? How could he leave and go back to the McGowen Ranch? How could anything ever be the same? He didn't have an answer yet, but he would fight for her, he would figure it all out…

"No," she gasped. "I'm sorry. We have to go. Meet Gracie for ice cream. And…" She backed up another step so she was just out of his reach. "There's something I need to talk to you about. Before I can…do any more kissing."

"Sure. Anything." She used to tell him everything. And though he wanted to pull her back to him, to kiss her until she agreed to go home with him, he could be patient. Or at least he could try.

"Not now. Not here," she said, glancing around at the empty parking lot. "I'll find a babysitter and we can go out one night this week."

"Any night." He would make anything work. Two days ago she wouldn't talk to him. He had no idea what had changed in her but he wasn't above accepting small miracles.

"I'll let you know when I find someone to watch Gracie," she said, stumbling down the curb and into the parking lot. "We can meet at Darla's place."

"Name the night and I'll be there." He'd go anywhere as long as it held the promise of kissing her again.

Chapter Five

For the life of her, Naomi could not figure out how long it would take her legs to stop wobbling. She made her way down Main Street as quickly as possible, given the fact that her body was still reeling from Lucas's kiss. It had been nearly two days and the effects still hadn't worn off—which was a problem, seeing as how she had a meeting with the loan officer at the bank. She had to look professional and confident, not all flushed and flighty.

Pausing outside the classy glass doors, she straightened her skirt, smoothed her hair, and tried to think past the mad throb of her heart. All she had to do was recall the way Lucas's mouth had claimed hers and it took her right back to those evenings when they'd made love, when everything was so new and the slightest touches would set her whole body ablaze. Funny how no other man but Lucas could ever have had her aching and panting five seconds into a kiss.

But she had to focus now. With any luck, she'd walk

out of this bank five hundred thousand dollars richer so she could buy the old Porter place and make the necessary renovations to complete the bed and breakfast. Later tonight, she'd see Lucas. And she'd tell him. She'd make sure there were no secrets between them.

But first...

Tilting up her chin with an air of confidence, she marched through the doors and straight into the air-conditioned bank.

Colton was waiting inside the lobby, dressed in his smart James Bond suit. At the sight of her he crossed his arms, tilted his head and smirked. "Well, well, well. If it isn't my own little Scarlett O'Hara." He strode over, his knowing expression igniting a blush in her cheeks. "Kissing an ex-con in the elementary school parking lot. My, my, my. That has 'scandal' written all over it."

Well, shit. She tugged on his elbow until he followed her to a quieter corner where no one would hear. Not that the bank was crowded, but she swore all the walls in Topaz Falls had ears. "How'd you find out?"

"It was gossip of choice this morning at The Farm." Which happened to be the town's breakfast spot. It was a tiny little restaurant attached to an organic farm on the edge of town. They served farm-to-table dishes—eggs and veggie frittatas, sweet potato pancakes. Some of the locals who were too lazy to make their own breakfasts—like Colton—went just about every day.

"Great." It'd been a while since she'd been at the center of the rumor mill, which almost always originated at The Farm. "How bad was it?" she asked, almost afraid to hear the answer. Who knew how many people had witnessed them kissing Saturday night? And who knew how fast the story had evolved into something much more humiliating?

"Let's just say Hank Green is speculating whether you and Lucas had any conjugal visits while he was in prison."

"Oh lord."

"So what the hell happened?" he pressed, seeming hurt that she hadn't shared this with him herself. "Last I knew you couldn't wait for him to leave."

"It's a long story." Dating back to approximately ten years ago. "But we don't have time to go into—"

Her phone blared that annoying song again.

"Seriously?" Colton scoffed, making a grab for the phone. She waved him off and glanced at the screen. A Denver number she didn't recognize.

"Change the ringtone or I'm going to throw that thing in the road and run over it with my Hummer," her friend threatened.

"Hang on," she said, walking to the other side of the foyer where reception was better. She swiped the screen and lifted it to her ear.

"Hello?"

"Naomi?"

That voice. It resounded through her, bringing with it echoes of the past. *Oh my God.* "Mark." She finally understood what people meant when they said their blood ran cold. Because hers was. Cold and thick, icing over her veins.

"Mark?" Colton echoed, racing to her side so fast his fancy shoes squeaked. "As in your ex?"

"Yeah. It's me," he confirmed grimly into her ear. "I've sent some emails but you haven't responded. So I thought I'd call."

Her pulse throbbed in her temples. Emails. The emails she'd deleted, hoping he would go away.

Her lungs folded in on themselves. Air. She needed air.

Clumsily, she stumbled her way outside with Colton on her heels.

"Look, Naomi." The sound of Mark's voice hadn't changed in ten years. It still had that deep rumble, that coarse edge. "I know you hate me. I completely failed when I walked out on you and Gracie. I was a loser."

She didn't argue. That was an accurate description for a guy who had walked out on his wife and infant daughter...

"But I've gotten myself together. I've got my own landscaping business now."

As if that changed anything! In the silent pause, she heard her own breath hiss into the phone.

Colton squeezed her shoulder. "What's he saying?" he mouthed.

She ignored him and concentrated on remaining upright.

"I've changed a lot," Mark said firmly. "And I want to see my daughter. I want to know her. I want that more than anything."

"She's not your daughter," Naomi whispered. "She'll never be your daughter. You left. And she knows nothing about you." She squeezed her eyes shut to alleviate the pounding in her forehead. She should've found out the truth a long time ago. She should've done a paternity test when Gracie was born. All of these years with no word from him and now he wanted to waltz in and change everything...

She sank to an iron bench in front of the brick building. Without missing a step, Colton sat next to her, his arm positioned protectively around her shoulders.

"I know I haven't been her father," Mark said, filling her stunned silence. "I know I don't deserve to be now. But I never terminated my parental rights. I never legally gave her up."

Fear dug its claws into her heart. "You have no rights," she choked out. He'd never cared…

"Yes. I do." He said it almost apologetically. "I've met with a lawyer."

She glanced up at Colton for reassurance, but obvious concern had etched lines into his forehead.

"Look," Mark went on. "I don't want it to be like that. I'd rather you and I could work this out. Together. Everything can be on your terms. I'll do whatever you tell me to do as long as I can have a relationship with her."

She gripped the phone with both hands, afraid she'd drop it. "And what would that look like?" she demanded. "You obviously don't live in Topaz Falls." God, she was not about to let her daughter go off to Denver every weekend to spend time with a man she didn't even know.

"I'm not sure what it's supposed to look like yet," he said quietly. "We can decide that together."

"Together?" A bitter laugh tripped up her throat. "*Together?* I've done everything alone for ten years. *Everything.*" She'd scraped together money to buy diapers and formula. She'd found a place to live, a way to support herself. She'd taught Gracie to walk and talk. She'd taught her to follow the rules, to be a good person. She'd held her while she cried, while she was sick with a fever and the stomach flu. "I figured it all out by myself," she fumed. "And you know what, Mark? She doesn't need you. Not now. Not ever. It's too late." Her thumb moved to the off button.

"Don't be like this." There was a warning in his tone. "Please. Don't make me get the courts involved. It doesn't have to be that way."

The courts. She grabbed Colton's hand and strangled it in her own. He couldn't get the courts involved, could he?

"You can't just come waltzing into her life like this. She doesn't know you. She doesn't even know anything about you." She'd never told Gracie much about Mark. Her daughter hadn't asked much. She didn't need to because she had a whole community of people who loved her—who'd been enough for her. Naomi had built that. She'd given her a safe place in the world.

Her eyes found Colton's, searching for reassurance, but his uneasy gaze wandered away as though he was already thinking through the next steps.

"Listen." Mark sighed. "I'm not going to let this go. I want—"

She stabbed the off button and held the phone tightly in her hand, staring at it. She couldn't listen to him anymore. Couldn't even begin to understand what he was asking of her. "I can't believe he called. I can't believe he wants to see Gracie."

"I always worried he'd pull something like this." Colton stood and hoisted her up to her feet.

She tottered around on stiff legs. "I should've listened to you. I should've made sure he could never claim any rights to her." Years ago, Colton had tried to get her to legally terminate Mark's parental rights, but she hadn't seen the need. She never dreamed he'd come back. In fact, it'd almost been a relief when he left. She never should've married him. She'd never loved him. And she'd always hoped Gracie wasn't his daughter, anyhow.

"The thing is, Naomi..." Colton tipped up her chin until she could look into his dark eyes and read the worry. "He has a case. My guess is he's found a good lawyer. He knows he could fight for visitation rights or shared custody."

"How is that possible?" she breathed. "How could anyone

give him custody after he walked away? He never called. Never sent money. Never even sent her birthday cards…"

Colton slipped an arm around her as though he sensed she needed the extra support. "It's not fair, but unfortunately the courts don't always care about what's fair. The state likes to see kids stay connected to their birth parents. If you work with him, at least you'll still have some control. It sounds like he's willing to grovel and bend over backward to make this happen."

Even though the hot sun beat down on her head, she shivered. "God, Colton. You really don't think the courts would be on my side, do you?"

His grim expression answered for him. Right now, he wasn't her friend. He was a lawyer. A worried lawyer. "I can hire a private detective in Denver to check up on him. See if there's anything we can use against him. But if he's really gotten his shit together, they might let him have a shot at sharing custody."

This couldn't be happening. Not now. They'd been fine for ten years. She sank to the bench again, trying to take in deep, even breaths. "I don't know if he's Gracie's real father," she murmured.

Colton leaned down as though he hadn't heard right. "Pardon?"

"He might not be Gracie's father," she said louder, stronger. "I was with Lucas two nights before he got arrested."

"Whoa." Her friend slowly sank to the bench. "How'd you neglect to mention that all these years?"

For the same reason she hadn't told anyone else. "It was humiliating. And I was so scared. Lucas was gone. For good." At the time, she'd thought that being with someone—

having the baby with someone—would be better than doing it on her own. "All these years, I've had my doubts Gracie is Mark's daughter. Maybe it's wishful thinking, but maybe not."

"Does Lucas know that?" Colton demanded as though still offended she'd left him in the dark.

"No," she admitted. "I...I wrote him a letter and told him, but he never even opened it." Anger battled back the deep sadness that rose inside of her. If he hadn't shut her out, things would be so different. She was sure of it.

"So you married Mark even though you didn't know if Gracie was his?" He didn't speak condescendingly, but his words raised her defenses anyway.

"Yes," she snapped. "Because Lucas was gone. And I wanted Gracie to have a father." But Mark hadn't been ready for it. Naomi had started bonding with the baby the moment she'd found out she was pregnant, but he'd kept his distance.

"Lucas has been back in Topaz Falls for months," Colton reminded her.

"And I haven't found the right time to tell him everything."

"The right time?" Her friend gaped at her, his eyebrows raised nearly to his hairline. "He's been here on and off since last fall. But you haven't found the *right time* to tell him?"

She stared across the street, watching the willow branches in front of the library sway in the wind. "I'm going to. Tonight. We're already planning to meet."

"You should've told him a long time ago," Colton said, pacing while he glared down at her. "If Gracie *is* Lucas's daughter then Mark has no rights to her. He can't fight for custody."

Which meant she could protect Gracie from him. Things could stay the way they were. "What do I have to do?" she asked, rising to her feet, suddenly willing to scale Topaz Mountain if it meant she could keep Mark out of Gracie's life. "How can I find out for sure?"

"You have to submit a DNA sample from one of them. Send it to a lab."

"Okay." That didn't sound so hard. "I'll ask Lucas tonight. After I tell him."

Colton nodded his approval. "In the meantime, I know a private detective in Denver who can check up on Mark. If he does happen to be her biological father, maybe my guy will find something we can use."

"Great. Yes. A private detective." The comfort of a plan evened out her pulse. "What else can I do?"

"You make sure you tell Lucas as soon as possible," Colton said as though he trusted her about as much as he trusted a Russian spy. "Because this is serious. You likely don't have much time before Mark tries to contact you again."

She looked down at her phone, still pressed tightly against her palm. "How long will the genetic testing take?"

"If I call in some favors and rush it, I can probably hear back from the lab within a week. Two at the most. But you've got to do this tonight."

"I will—"

The receptionist stuck her head out the door. "Ms. Sullivan? Mr. Hollingsworth will see you now," she said as though annoyed she'd had to track Naomi down.

"Right." She dug a water bottle out of her purse and took a quick sip in hopes of soothing the terrified squeak that kept breaking through her voice.

"Come on." Colton led her back inside, where they veered down a short hallway. She focused on the breathing techniques she'd learned when she was pregnant and hoped her face wasn't splotched with emotion.

Mr. Hollingsworth greeted them at the door to his office. He was a grandfatherly type, short and stout with the white mustache of a gentleman.

"Naomi, Colton." He shook both of their hands before inviting them in. The office was as small as a closet but held two straight-backed chairs. The walls were decked out with pictures of his family.

"I know you're both busy, so we'll make this as quick and painless as possible." He retrieved a manila folder from a drawer and handed it over. "I'm pleased to tell you that we've decided to grant your business loan. We have all the paperwork ready to go." His twinkling eyes smiled at her. "I hope you brought a pen."

She tried to smile back, tried to claim the happiness that should've been hers in this moment. The start of a dream she'd had for herself a long time ago. But the shock of Mark's call filled her with a cold fear. What if he got visitation? Shared custody? Would she be able to stay in Topaz Falls? Or would she have to move to Denver?

"I brought a pen," Colton finally said, giving her hand a squeeze. He fished it out of his briefcase and handed it to her.

"Do you have any idea when you'll open the inn?" Mr. Hollingsworth asked politely.

"Hopefully before Christmas." She managed a polite smile. Topaz Falls was famous all over Colorado for its festive Christmas celebrations. "But I haven't officially given my notice at the ranch, so I'll see how much longer they'll want me to stay to wrap everything up."

"I'm sure they'll miss you," the loan officer said dutifully. "It sounds like you've done great things for them."

And they'd done great things for her. "I've loved working there, but they're starting a new chapter and so am I." At least she hoped so. She hoped Mark wouldn't screw this up for her.

"Well, let's get you started so we can all get out of here in time for lunch," Mr. Hollingsworth said, sliding the first legal-sized paper across the desk.

She signed paper after paper, doing her best to listen as Mr. Hollingsworth explained the terms of her loan.

"Well, this is it," he eventually announced, sliding one last paper across the desk. "Congratulations, Naomi. I'm sure the bed and breakfast will be a huge success."

"Thanks," she said, rising from the chair. The weight of uncertainty draped her shoulders. Somehow she shook the man's hand, even though hers trembled. One week ago, everything had been so certain: She'd open the bed and breakfast and she and Gracie would start a new life—a new adventure. Now she had no idea what would happen. Whether she'd be forced to spend half of her life away from her daughter…

"Come on." Colton positioned himself at her side, leading her out of the office and down the hallway.

They stepped out in the sunlight and she finally gasped in a panicked breath. "Oh my God, Colton. Oh my God." She gripped his arm so tightly she had to be cutting off his circulation. "What if he gets shared custody? What am I going to do?"

He plucked her fingers off his suit coat and steered her

to face him. “You can’t worry about that,” he said with authority. “Not yet. Talk to Lucas first. We need to get this all sorted out before Mark has time to do anything else.”

“Right.” She took his arm again and started to walk down the sidewalk. “I’ll talk to Lucas.”

She only hoped he didn’t hate her when he found out the truth.

Chapter Six

Lucas couldn't remember the last time he'd been early anywhere, but he found himself standing outside Darla's chocolate and wine bar exactly ten minutes before he was supposed to meet Naomi.

All day, the minutes had crawled by. He and Lance had spent most of the afternoon evaluating each of the bulls and deciding which ones to sell off in order to free up enough cash to make the new purchase. Lucas had even called up a few of his contacts to generate some interest so they could unload them quickly. They'd gotten a lot accomplished, though he wasn't quite sure how, given the way his thoughts kept drifting back to that kiss with Naomi.

Craving another taste of her lips, he pushed through the doors and scanned the restaurant. There were a few patrons at the bar—tourists it seemed—but otherwise it was pretty empty. He hadn't been in here before this—hadn't exactly had a reason to go to a swanky wine bar—

but he had to admit it was a nice place. In contrast to the country clutter most business owners in Topaz Falls stockpiled, Darla seemed to prefer a modern and clean look. The floors were a bronzed concrete and the tall pub tables were made from old wine barrels. Contemporary prints hung on the walls, giving it a much higher-end feel than the Tumble Inn.

"Hey, Lucas," Darla called from behind the bar. "You want to take that table over there by the window?"

He glanced to where she was pointing. The table for two sat in a quiet corner, somewhat secluded, though it had a great view of Main Street and the mountains beyond. The sun was still bright for seven o'clock, illuminating the reddish cliffs of Topaz Peak.

"That'd be great," he said. As one of Naomi's closest friends, Darla obviously knew why he was here. The way Naomi and her friends got together so often, he wasn't surprised.

He'd no sooner made it to the table than Darla stood there with her notepad. "So how you doing?" she asked with a twinkle in her eye.

Yep, she definitely knew about their date. And she seemed happy about it, which meant maybe he could mine her for some information. "I'm good," he said, taking a quick glance at the menu. "How about you? Things going well around here?" He might be out of practice at buttering up a woman, but hopefully it was like riding a bike.

"Things are great."

It was nice to have someone in town smile at him instead of look at him with a scowl.

"It was quiet this spring, but things are starting to pick up," she said hopefully.

Spring was typically a slow season around Topaz Falls, muddy and sloppy with all of the snow melting. But temperatures still tended to be too cold for people to enjoy the summer activities that made the town famous.

"Good. That's great." He set down the menu. "I think we'll take a bottle of your most expensive Shiraz and whatever chocolates you recommend to go with it."

Her dark eyes went wide. "Really? Are you sure? That's a three-hundred-dollar bottle of wine."

What was three hundred dollars when he was finally getting Naomi all to himself? "I know." He handed her the menu. "It'll be worth it. *Right?*" he probed. Naomi was warming up to him. She'd stopped running. Hell, she'd even let him kiss her.

Glancing around, Darla pulled out the chair across from him and sat. "Naomi is worth every penny," she agreed.

"Do you think she'll like the wine?" he asked, easing a deeper question into his tone. Darla knew Naomi better than anyone. Surely they'd discussed this date. Surely she knew exactly how Naomi felt about him.

"Yes. I think she'll like the wine." She leaned in closer. "A word to the wise, though, Lucas. Keep an open mind, okay? Think before you say *anything* tonight."

"Huh?" That wasn't exactly what he'd expected her to say. "What do you mean? Why wouldn't I have an open mind?"

Her lips pursed as though she was considering something. "Just... this moment will define a lot for you two. Okay? Remember that—"

Before he had time to ask what the hell she was talking about, the bells above the door jangled and Naomi walked in.

God, just the sight of her knocked the air out of him, leaving room for nothing but pure astonishment. She was radiant...wearing a long, flowy skirt with a tight shirt underneath a light open sweater. Her cheeks were pinker than usual, and he wondered if it had anything to do with the same passion that was now streaming through him.

She scanned the restaurant and saw him, though her expressionless face made it difficult to interpret how she felt.

As she approached the table, he stood. "Hey." He would've liked to kiss her again, but that would have to wait. She seemed distracted. Was she nervous?

"So I'll go get your order," Darla muttered before quickly rushing away to leave the two of them alone.

Naomi sat on the very edge of the chair across from him. "Hi," she said softly. "Thanks for meeting me."

The formal ring to her words threw him off. On Saturday night, she'd let down her guard and he'd seen the raw emotions that hid behind her walls. But now it seemed that wall was back up. Maybe even stronger than before.

Good thing he wasn't one to hide behind anything. "I'd meet you anytime," he said, nice and direct. Didn't want to risk her missing his meaning. She'd finally stopped walking away, turning away, avoiding him like she was afraid he'd burn her. And he wasn't about to let her go back.

"Naomi...I've been waiting for six months for a chance to just talk to you. To just have you sitting across the table from me." And he didn't want to wait anymore. He didn't want to waste time. "I'm—"

"Hi, you two!" Darla called, approaching the table with a serving tray. "Here's your Armagh Shiraz 2008 Red wine from Australia paired with my signature dark chocolate raspberry, orange, and blackberry truffles."

"The Armagh?" Naomi echoed. She gaped at Lucas. "That's one of the most expensive bottles in the restaurant."

He shrugged. "Yeah. So?" Seemed to him, she deserved to be spoiled. And he was up to the task.

"It's one of the best you'll ever taste," Darla insisted, pouring them each a glass and leaving the open bottle between them. "Enjoy," she murmured, raising her eyebrows at Naomi in some female code he couldn't fathom.

"So you drink the wine, then eat the chocolate?" he asked, lifting his glass.

"Um. Yes." Naomi's hands fisted on the table as though she was trying to stop them from shaking.

He hated seeing that. Hated seeing her nervous and unsure. This was him. And her. They'd spent so much time together. She used to know him better than anyone. "Cheers, then." He waited for her to lift her glass. As they clinked the glasses together, a small smile played with her full lips.

He could still taste those lips. When he finally got to kiss her again he'd savor them. He wouldn't let her push him away.

They both took a long silent sip.

The wine was good—not that he was picky. He wasn't much of a drinker.

He set down his glass. "I'm glad we could do this."

"Me too." Naomi smiled, but then her head turned and she stared out the window.

He definitely wasn't an expert at reading women, but she didn't seem so sure about that. "Listen... I know things have been awkward, but—"

"Oh my God," she gasped. "Oh my *God*!" Her gaze was fixed on something outside.

"You okay?" He turned to the window, trying to figure out what had made her face so pale.

"This is *not* happening." She jumped out of her chair and sprinted for the doors. Lucas scrambled after her, nearly getting nailed by the door as she bolted outside. "Wait," he called, but she didn't seem to hear.

Scanning the street, he saw what seemed to have consumed Naomi's attention. A man. Standing on the opposite side of the road in front of the Blue Jewel Hotel. He squinted—the guy was familiar. Big, stocky build, short clipped hair. It took him longer than it should've to place him.

Mark.

What the fuck was he doing in Topaz Falls?

"Why are you here?" Naomi darted into the street without looking first. A Buick slammed on its brakes and laid on the horn, but she didn't seem to notice.

Lucas sprinted across while the car was stopped. "Hey." He slipped his arm around her waist, but she tore away from him and flew toward Mark.

"What the hell do you think you're doing?" she shouted, stopping the people who'd been walking by on the street.

"Easy, Naomi." Mark's arms went up. "You hung up on me, so I thought I'd come and see you. In person. That's the best way to deal with this."

"The best way?" she practically shrieked.

Lucas laid a hand on her shoulder. He'd never seen her so riled about anything. All around them people gathered, some looking the other way as though pretending they weren't eavesdropping. He recognized Charlie from the General Store and good old town Mayor Hank Green, who was also an old rival of his father's.

Yeah, he was pretty sure whatever was going on here, the whole town didn't need to know about it. "Why don't we go talk somewhere else?" Lucas suggested. This was likely going to consume the front page of tomorrow's gossip column.

"We're not talking!" Naomi yelled. "God damnit, Mark. I told you to leave us alone."

"I've lost ten years of her life," Mark said, and Lucas couldn't believe how calm he sounded. Almost like he was trying to soothe her. "Please. I want to sit down with you. I've changed, Naomi. Everything's changed and I want a place in my daughter's life."

The crowd on the fringes grew. People were whispering, ducking their heads together.

So this asshole was trying to get to Gracie after he'd left them both behind? Lucas fisted his hands. If Naomi gave him the word, he'd tackle him right through the window of that hotel.

"She might not be your daughter," Naomi said.

That seemed to stop everything—the murmuring, the people who were trying, and failing, to walk by without staring…

"What's that supposed to mean?" Mark demanded, the first hint of irritation in his voice. "Who else's would she be?"

Naomi whirled until she faced Lucas. Tears ran down her face. "That's what I wanted to talk to you about."

His stomach clenched. She couldn't mean what he thought she meant. She couldn't mean she'd wanted to talk to him about being Gracie's father…

"We were together right before you got arrested," she reminded him. As if he ever could've forgotten the last time he'd made love to her. He'd taken her up to the lake and put a mattress in the back of the pickup…

But no. Gracie couldn't be his daughter. Surely Naomi would've told him before now. All these years later…

Mark stepped closer to her. "You're just saying that because you don't want me to see her."

And now they really had an audience. People circled them, but Lucas couldn't see any faces. He couldn't see anything. Everything was too hazy to focus.

"No. I'm not," Naomi said quietly. "I always wondered but I never found out for sure. And it never mattered because you left us. God, Mark. You walked out. You didn't look back. You've never sent us a dime!"

Lucas knew he should do something. Stop this spectacle. If only the world would quit spinning around him.

Gracie might be his daughter?

His?

"You have no idea how much I regret all of it," Mark said, approaching Naomi. "I'm so sorry. I'll do whatever I have to do to make it up to you." He laid a hand on her arm, and that tore Lucas out of the fog.

"Don't touch her," Lucas growled. "Get your fucking hands off of her."

Murmurs started up in the crowd again, people on both sides of them debating whether they should call the sheriff.

Naomi turned to him and gripped his forearms tightly. "Go back to Darla's," she said, her tone fully in control.

"What?" She was sending him away? After she'd just dropped that on him? She was telling him to leave her alone with Mark?

"Now. Please." She let go of him. "Go back to Darla's. I'll be there in a minute."

A plea in her eyes begged him not to argue. So he bumped his way through the crowd, blinded by the fast pound of blood in his head. Somehow he found his way to their table and sat, his gaze still directed out the window where he watched the crowd disperse as Naomi pulled Mark aside and the two of them seemed to talk quietly.

"Um, I thought maybe you could use something stronger than the Shiraz," Darla said. He had no idea when she'd come over. She set down a glass of whiskey in front of him. "You remember what I said. This is a defining moment for you and Naomi."

He blinked at her. "Jesus. You knew what she was planning to tell me tonight." Who the hell else knew that he might be a father before he had?

"I only just found out," Darla snapped. "And you have no right to be pissed off. You got that? Naomi's been dealt some shitty hands in her life, and she's always done the best she can. She did right by her daughter." The woman slashed a pointer finger in front of his face. "No matter what happens, you'd best remember that. Don't screw this up, Lucas."

Screw what up? What the hell was happening? He kneaded his forehead, trying to force his brain to think straight. Gracie might be his daughter. He might have a daughter with the only woman he'd ever loved.

Darla marched away as though wanting to make a point.

He turned back to the window in time to see Naomi hustling across the street, head down and arms pumping like she was on a mission. She walked briskly to the table and sat across from him, drawing in a long, measured breath as though steadying herself.

"I know you're probably shocked," she said, searching his face.

Shocked didn't even touch it. He couldn't find the words…

"Mark emailed me a few times. Then he called me this morning." She paused as though wanting him to digest that. "That's why I have to find out if he's really Gracie's father. He might not have a case, but we won't know unless we get a DNA sample from you."

"Hold on," he choked out. That was all he could manage. Once, in prison, he'd made the mistake of trying to break up a fight between two other guys. That's all it had taken for them to both turn on him, shoving him to the ground and kicking him repeatedly in the stomach. This hurt worse. "If Mark hadn't gotten in touch with you…if he'd never come back into the picture, would you have told me? Would you have ever wanted to find out the truth?"

The rigid pull in her jaw answered his question. Answered a lot of questions. He may be the lesser of two evils in this case, but she was only telling him because she had to. Not because she wanted to.

"I tried to tell you a long time ago," she said, her bottom lip quivering. The anger in her eyes bore into him with an accusation. "I wrote you a letter. I wrote you *eight* letters. And you didn't bother to open even one of them."

The weight of pain in her features crushed his shoulders. He closed his eyes to shut out the sight. He couldn't stand to see her in pain. Pain he'd caused. "I'm sorry. I didn't mean to hurt you." It wasn't enough. It would never be enough. He'd done more than hurt her. He'd scarred her. He'd thought he was doing what was best for her. He'd wanted that more than anything. But every decision he'd made back then was now crashing down on him—the decision to cover for Levi, the decision to force Naomi to move on…

God, he could've had a family with her. Ten years of beautiful moments, and he'd missed every single one of them. It was the worst punishment he could imagine. Guilt knifed through him as he stared at her across the table. "I can't change the past." He could regret it forever, but that wouldn't change anything for them now. "Why didn't you tell me right away? Last fall when I came back? Why did you avoid me instead of telling me the truth?" They could've already worked through this. They could've already found out the truth…

"You're planning to leave again," she said evenly, as though she'd detached herself already. She seemed to have regained control over her emotions. But he hadn't. He didn't know if he ever would.

It was too much. All of it. He thought about all the times in the last six months he'd run into her and Gracie at the ranch. Every time she'd seen him, Naomi had known that Gracie might be his daughter. She'd never said anything. God, she'd never said one damn word. Because she was ashamed of him. What mother would want an ex-con to be her daughter's father? The truth hit him hard, forcing tears into his eyes. Even if the test revealed he was Gracie's father, Naomi wouldn't want him to be a part of their lives; she'd made that clear with six months of silence.

Suddenly he couldn't sit there anymore. He couldn't even look at her. "I have to go." He swiped his hat off the table and stood.

"Wait." She grabbed his arm. "You have no right to be angry."

"I'm not. Not at all." But a grief that he'd never experienced—even when his mom left—was swallowing him and he couldn't fight it.

He dug out his wallet and threw money on the table. When he glanced at Naomi, he could tell she was about to cry. He could tell, but he couldn't do anything to stop it.

"I'll do whatever test you need me to do," he told her roughly. "But right now, I have to go."

Chapter Seven

Naomi sprinted after Lucas, dodging tables, knocking her chair over in the process. Once again, she'd drawn the attention of spectators. The few patrons who sat at Darla's bar had all turned around at the loud crash.

She didn't care who saw anymore. She had to catch Lucas. God, that pain in his eyes had torn into her. He'd looked at her like one of Jessa's wounded animals.

She ripped open the door, ready to sprint down the street, but Darla hooked her shoulder.

"Let him go," she said, pulling her back inside.

Naomi wriggled free. "But I have to make him understand why I didn't tell him..."

Darla slipped in front of her. "Do *you* even understand why you didn't tell him?"

Her body stilled. No. She didn't. All these months he'd been right in front of her. Now, after having sat with him through Gracie's play, after having kissed him out in the parking lot, she couldn't for the life of her figure out why she'd been so afraid. "I should've told him last fall. He shouldn't have found out on the street in front of everyone." Naomi sank into the chair nearest to the door.

"Okay, everyone! We're closing." Darla traipsed to the counter and started to shoo people out.

"But I'm not done with my wine," one woman argued.

"And we haven't paid the bill," a man said.

"Don't worry about it. It's on the house." Her friend herded the few customers to the door. "Come back tomorrow and I'll give you a big discount." One by one, she waved them away. "Bye now. Thanks for coming. You can always head over to the Tumble Inn for a nightcap. They've got some killer cocktails. Great drafts on tap," she babbled, not giving anyone a chance to argue. "Out you go now." She all but shoved them out the door. "See you tomorrow," she called cheerfully as she waved. Then she locked the deadbolt and rushed over to the table Naomi had just shared with Lucas. In a haste, Darla snatched the nearly full bottle of expensive Shiraz. She plunked a glass in front of Naomi and filled it, then poured one for herself.

"You didn't have to close early," Naomi said, though the words held no conviction. After the scene she'd made on the street she was relieved to be alone. Maybe she shouldn't have gone after Mark like that. Now the whole town would know. God, they'd have a heyday at The Farm tomorrow morning.

"What'd you tell Mark?" Darla asked, all business. Always pragmatic, the woman was probably already formulating a plan for damage control.

Naomi took a sip of the wine, but it felt so wrong drinking it without Lucas.

Sighing, she set down the wineglass. "I told him he wasn't going to see her until we've sorted this out. And even then I don't know." She'd reminded him how he'd said this could be on her terms, and then told him she'd have the test done to determine paternity as soon as possible.

"How'd he take it?"

"I think he was shocked. As shocked as Lucas was." A heavy weight pressed into her chest. "But he agreed to wait until we have the test results back before contacting me again." Which gave her roughly two weeks to try and find a way to tell Gracie about this mess. Either way, her daughter's father was coming back into the picture and she had no idea how to prepare her. "What am I going to tell Gracie, Darla? How am I supposed to explain this to her?"

Her friend gave her one of her specialty *it's no big deal* looks.

But this was a huge deal. It would change everything.

"You don't have to worry about it now," Darla insisted.

If only that were true. Naomi glanced out to the street. "The whole town will know by tomorrow afternoon." Once news hit The Farm, that was all anyone would be talking about.

"That may be true, but no one'll say anything to Gracie. These people aren't *that* heartless." Darla shoved a plate of truffles across the table. "Besides, this is all a good thing, girl. It's time for you to figure out the truth. Time for Gracie to learn the truth. And time for you to decide what you want."

That sounded so simple. "I have no idea what I want," Naomi admitted. For the last ten years everything had been about what Gracie had wanted or needed. The bed and breakfast had been her first step in trying to plan for their future…

"In case you hadn't noticed, Lucas loves the hell out of you." Darla popped a chocolate into her mouth. "He's *always* loved you. These few months, he's been more patient than any man I've ever met, but that's not gonna last forever, honey. Especially not now."

"He's leaving." Again. "He's going back to Pueblo and I can't. This is my home. As small as this town as, this is the community that embraced Gracie and me, the one that took care of us." After Mark left her, the local quilters club had thrown her a baby shower and made sure she had a year's supply of diapers. And for the longest time after Gracie was born, random baskets of food and formula and little toys would show up on the doorstep of their run-down apartment.

And the Cortez family…They were her support system. Jessa and Lance and Luis…

Even though she was planning to move off their property, she'd still go to their Sunday night family dinners. She'd still spend holidays with them. This town was so much a part of her past and her future. "I'm buying the old Porter place," she blurted. "And I'm opening a bed and breakfast. My business loan went through today."

Darla choked on a sip of wine. "You're *what*?"

"It's always been my dream." Although she'd never voiced it to anyone else. There were times it had seemed unattainable. "And with Jessa moving to the ranch, I figured now was a good time. They don't need me anymore. Tucker can take over the books."

"Why haven't you said anything?" her friend demanded. "This is amazing!"

"Yeah, I guess." Though she didn't feel much like celebrating right now. "I have a ton of work to do, but the house is mine."

"Which means you can't go to Pueblo with Lucas," Darla said, her eyes sobering.

"No. I can't." And he probably wouldn't want that anyway. Too much had happened. How could they possibly reclaim what they'd once had with all of this standing in the way?

"Maybe he'll stay in Topaz Falls."

"I don't think so." Not with the way people treated him. She knew that all too well after the incident with the principal at the play the other night. "I don't blame him for wanting to go. I wouldn't want everyone waiting for me to screw up, either." He deserved more than that.

"There has to be a way to work this out." Darla tapped her fingers against the table. "Especially if he's Gracie's father."

They sipped their wine in thoughtful silence, but nothing came to her.

Darla didn't seem to have any brilliant ideas, either. "Talk to him," her friend finally said. "Once he's had some time to process the whole he-might-have-a-daughter thing. It's pretty obvious there's still unresolved feelings between you two."

Yeah, but if she couldn't even resolve them herself, what was she supposed to say to him? "I loved him." Which meant he'd hurt her on the deepest level possible. "And I don't know if everything I'm feeling now is real." Or whether it was just the memories of who they used to be that drew her to him.

"You'll never know if you don't give it a chance." Darla handed her a chocolate. "Spend time with him. Get to know who he is now. Let him get to know you. Then you'll have your answer."

* * *

Lucas busted through Lance's front door like a bull that'd just had its ass branded.

His brother and Jessa were seated at the table, finishing up their nice romantic dinner. Normally he didn't interrupt their alone time, but this seemed like it counted as a fucking special occasion.

"Hi, Lucas!" Jessa chirped. He swore that woman got more chipper with each day the wedding drew closer. "How was your date with Naomi?" she asked, batting her eyelashes.

That was one hell of a loaded question, so he ignored her and went straight for Lance. "How long have you known?"

Jessa gasped, but his brother simply wiped his mouth with a napkin.

Yep. They both knew. God damnit.

"Um, you know, I need to go check on the animals up at the shelter," Jessa said, easing her chair back from the table and refusing to meet his gaze. "We've got a full house tonight," she babbled, slipping on her coat. "A couple of dogs. A baby bunny with a broken leg..." She rushed the dinner dishes over to the sink and made a break for the front door. "I'll give you boys some time alone. Be back soon!" The door opened and shut in record time.

His brother didn't seem to share her urgency. Lance kicked back in his chair, stretching his legs out in front of him, all casual and relaxed.

Lucas sat across from him. His heart hadn't stopped

racing since he'd heard Naomi inform Mark that Gracie might not be his daughter. *That's what I wanted to talk to you about.* The words were still on repeat in his brain.

"How long have you known?" he said again when his brother didn't speak.

Lance shrugged. "Only since a few nights ago when she told Jessa."

"Why didn't you say something?" To him, that was the kind of information brothers should share with each other.

"Jessa said Naomi was planning to talk to you about it." Lance rose from his chair and went to the refrigerator. He pulled out two beers and set one in front of Lucas. "I figured it wasn't my place."

"Well, a little warning would've been nice," Lucas said, popping the top on his beer. Between swigs, he told his brother about the scene on the street.

"Shit." His calm and collected brother sat straighter now. "Gotta say, I never thought Mark would come back to town."

"Obviously Naomi didn't, either." She never thought she'd have to tell Lucas the truth. He still couldn't believe it. If Mark hadn't come back, he might never have known the possibility that he had a bigger part in Gracie's life...

"So what're you gonna do?" his brother asked.

"She wants a DNA sample. So she can find out for sure." That'd be a fun appointment...

"Well, yeah. Obviously. But what are you going to do about Naomi?"

"What can I do?" He'd thought things were happening—he'd kissed her and she'd agreed to go out with him, but it was all because Mark had forced her hand. "I screwed up. She tried to tell me in those letters she wrote and I ignored them." He'd turned his back on her when she needed him. How would she ever trust him again?

"She let you kiss her," Lance reminded him. "Was she into it? When you kissed her, did she kiss you back?"

"Yes." She most definitely had kissed him back. She'd clung to him. She'd opened herself up to him. "But you should've seen her face tonight. It was cold." After she'd collected herself, she'd looked at him like he was a stranger.

"She's trying to protect herself. Ever think of that?" His brother shook his head.

Oh, sure. Eight months with Jessa and now he thought he was some relationship expert.

"She's afraid you'll leave her behind again," Lance said as though Lucas was an idiot.

"It wasn't exactly my choice to leave in the first place."

"I know, but you didn't have to cut her off from your life. She tried to contact you for months and you rejected her."

"Because I thought it was for the best." He'd never been so wrong about something in his life.

"It wasn't for the best," his brother countered. "You *knew* Mark left. And you could've come back years ago. You didn't."

How could he have come back? Even now, it'd been over ten years since the fire, and everyone still held it against him. They probably would've stoned him if he'd come back any earlier.

"You can't blame her for being scared." Lance leaned into the table as though ready to defend Naomi. "She's always protected Gracie. It's been up to her. She's never even dated anyone. Did you know that? She's always put her daughter first. And she likely doesn't want to set her daughter up to meet her father only to have him take off again."

"I wouldn't take off." If he found out the three of them were connected that way, he couldn't be without them. "If Gracie's my daughter, I'll do anything to be with them. I'll figure out how to make it work." Maybe Naomi would agree to move to the McGowen Ranch. Or they could go somewhere else and start over together.

His brother stood and walked past him, giving his shoulder a hearty pat on the way. "Maybe that's what she needs to hear."

Chapter Eight

By the time Lucas made it down to Naomi's place, evening darkness bruised the sky. Stars flickered overhead, still faint but gaining momentum as twilight took hold.

The porch light glowed pink, which meant either Gracie had picked out the lightbulb or Naomi's favorite color hadn't changed since high school. Despite the painful knot in his throat, he grinned.

These two girly girls could change his life forever.

Before he could make it up the porch steps, the front door banged open. Naomi's backside came through the door first, her body bent as she dragged something onto the porch.

God almighty, the woman made jeans look hotter than a high-end teddy.

Grunting, Naomi tugged an overstuffed chair across the porch, swearing softly when it caught on the doorjamb.

A woman who could swear like a sailor and look that hot in a pair of Levi's? He was sold.

"Can I help you with that?" he finally asked, hoping she wouldn't realize he'd been standing there checking her out for at least a full minute.

Her back went as straight as the column that held up the porch. "I didn't realize anyone was out here." She smoothed her hair away from her face. Perspiration shimmered on her skin, giving her cheeks a hearty glow.

"Yeah. Sorry. I didn't mean to sneak up on you." He couldn't help it. When he'd seen her ass in those jeans, time had stood still. "Looks like you could use a hand with that." He nodded to the chair. It belonged in a living room next to the fireplace, not out on the porch. "You want me to take it somewhere for you?"

"No," she said without a pause. "It's fine. I've got it." Leaning over, she secured her hands to the chair's arms and tugged, shimmying it out of the way. After pushing it aside, she stood upright and mopped her forehead with her sleeve. "I'm glad you're here, actually." Her voice had a wispy, nervous quality, almost as if she was talking to someone she'd never met before. "I feel so awful about what happened earlier—"

"Don't," he broke in before she could finish. "I shouldn't have run out on you like that." Dads didn't do that sort of thing. Not *his* dad, anyway. He'd stuck it out, even when he was all on his own. He'd faced his problems head on. And that's what Lucas would do, too. If he had the privilege of being a dad, he'd make the most of it.

"Do you want to come in?" Naomi asked, shuffling out of the way so he could walk into the house.

"Sure." He eyed the chair. "But first... Where's that thing supposed to go?"

She looked at the chair as if she'd forgotten about it. "I was going to load it into my SUV."

"By yourself?"

She half laughed. "It's no big deal. I do things myself all the time." As if determined to prove it, she nudged the chair to the steps and struggled to maneuver it down to the sidewalk.

"Maybe you should ask for help once in a while," he suggested, following behind her.

"I don't need help." She pushed and pulled and grunted until she had that chair at the edge of the driveway. With a smug look, she opened the hatch of her old SUV. At least she'd been sensible enough to keep it when she'd gone out and bought the yellow beetle.

"You sure you can lift that thing?" he asked, wondering how long it would take her to stop and ask for his help.

"Of course." She stood back, seeming to assess the best way to make it happen and save herself the embarrassment of failing.

Hell, he couldn't watch her try to lift that thing on her own. Before she had a chance to get her hands on it, he swooped in there and hoisted it up, wedging it securely into the back of the SUV.

"I could've managed." Naomi slammed the hatch shut and turned to him, her face all hot and riled. He was pretty damn sure it wasn't anger. She felt it, too—the heat that crackled between them, flaring and retracting like the chaos of a fire.

"I don't doubt you could've managed," he said, letting the flames draw him closer to her. "But why do it alone when

I'm standing right here?" She'd done everything all on her own. He got that. But they were connected—by their past, by the feelings they tried to hide…maybe even by a child. And he wanted to help her. He wanted to be part of her life. Whether Naomi liked it or not.

"We can go in and talk," she said. Judging from the way she dodged him and charged up the walkway to the porch, she didn't like it one bit. "Gracie's already asleep. It's been an intense few days."

Tell him about it. "So where're you taking the chair?" he asked, shrinking the distance she kept trying to inch between them.

"Oh." Her body came to an abrupt stop inside the doorway of the house. She sighed. "I guess it won't matter if I tell you now. I bought the old Porter house."

"You *what?*" Bogart, her faithful German shepherd, trotted over and sniffed his hand.

"I bought it," she said with an unsure smile. "I'd heard the family wanted to sell, so before it went on the market, I made them an offer."

"But…" She had a perfectly good house right here on the ranch. "You're moving?"

"Yeah." Her eyes lit. "I'm planning to open a bed and breakfast." She seemed to be watching for his reaction.

He forced a neutral expression so she couldn't read his shock. The dog bumped his hand like he wanted a scratch behind the ears. Lucas couldn't manage it. Even though he hadn't been in touch with her over the years, they were still connected through his family, through the ranch. Now she was starting a new life on her own…

"It'll take a ton of work of course, but it's something I've always wanted to do."

Then he'd be happy for her. Or at least he'd do his best. "Does Lance know?"

"Not yet. I'm planning to tell him tomorrow. I'll give him plenty of notice," she said quickly. "But this place belongs to him and Jessa. And I'm ready for something new."

Bogart gave up on Lucas and retreated down the hallway.

"Wow." In defiance of the disappointment that sunk into his stomach, he fired up a smile. "Congratulations. I'm sure it'll be a huge success." She had plans. A dream. After all of these years, the heartbreak she'd been through, she was getting what she wanted. Which meant no matter how much he wanted to, he couldn't ask her to move away with him. He couldn't draw her away from everything she'd worked for.

"We'll see," she said, leading him through the living room to the kitchen. She opened the refrigerator. "Can I get you anything? A beer?"

"No, thanks." He took a seat at the small kitchen table, noticing how full her house seemed to be compared to his stark, empty place. The kitchen was small but cozy, with pale green walls, bright white cabinets, and Gracie's artwork everywhere. Paintings and Popsicle-stick sculptures and sweet little scribbled notes. Piles of papers and books were stacked on the countertops, making the place look comfortable. What would it be like to live with that kind of beautiful clutter? His own house always seemed so cold.

"I'm meeting with the contractor tomorrow," Naomi said, coming to sit across from him with a glass of red wine. "So I'll know more after that."

"I'm happy to take a look, if you want another opinion," he offered, even though it was clear she didn't take too kindly to help. He had plenty of experience to offer. In the early days down at the McGowen ranch, he'd earned extra money fixing up the old buildings and even helping to put up new ones. Before he was arrested, he'd planned to major in construction management in college. He'd always been handy and liked manual work. He figured he could be a contractor and come back to Topaz Falls to live with Naomi. That'd been the extent of his dreams. Spending the rest of his life with her while he made a comfortable living to provide for the family they'd build.

That'd been the plan. He'd even known what ring he wanted to buy her. Right before Levi had set the fire, Lucas had taken Naomi to Denver for a special night out. On their way to the restaurant downtown, they'd walked past a jewelry store and he stopped, asking her what she liked the best. He'd expected her to point out one of those big honking solitaire diamonds, but instead, she'd gazed longingly at an understated band. "That one is perfect," she'd said. "It's simple but so artistic." He'd never forgotten it. In fact, he'd planned to go buy it at the end of the next summer so he could give it to her as a promise before he left for college, but he'd never gotten the chance.

Putting those old dreams out of his mind, he tried to focus on the present. "I've done my fair share of projects. I'd be happy to take a look at the bid."

"Oh..." She drew out the word as though buying time. "Um. Thanks. I'll keep that in mind."

Something told him she'd already put it out of her mind.

"Look, Lucas..." The drop in her tone informed him that the small talk was over. They weren't sitting here to chat about her new business venture. "I don't want you to feel like you owe me anything."

"I don't," he said simply.

"This doesn't have to change anything. Even if you are Gracie's father—"

"It would change everything," he put in before she could finish that ridiculous statement.

"I know you don't want to stay in Topaz Falls. And I don't blame you. Even after all you've been through, you've built an incredible life for yourself at the McGowen place."

Exactly. He'd built a life for *himself.* But it didn't include anyone else. It wasn't a life he *wanted.* It was the life he'd thought he had to choose. "Why didn't you tell me when I came back?" he asked as gently as he could. "Why did you wait so long?" He had to know if his past—his record—embarrassed her. If she couldn't see him the same way she had when they were dating.

"I guess...I was afraid to." She looked down. "I mean..." A heavy sigh dropped her shoulders and exposed more of her graceful neck. "I've never had to share Gracie with anyone. You know?" Her eyes squeezed shut. "That sounds horrible."

"It doesn't." It made sense. She hadn't kept it from him because she'd be ashamed to have him as Gracie's father. She'd kept it from him because she was afraid she'd lose her daughter. She was afraid to lose what they'd built together over the years. For the first time, he realized how hard this must be for her. How threatened and scared she must be by Mark coming back. The questions that must plague her. She didn't have to voice them. He could imagine.

What if Gracie chose her father?

"It doesn't matter who comes into her life now," he told her. Though touching her posed more of a risk than grasping a live wire, he reached for her hand over the table and swallowed it in his. "You've shaped her. She's so much a part of you, Naomi. I see it in her. Your tenacity. Your strength." Her flair and sparkle. "Those things aren't inherited. They're taught."

When she opened her eyes they were filled with gratitude. Her hand trembled beneath his, but she didn't pull it away. "One night after Mark left, I was holding Gracie. She was crying…inconsolable…and I held her against my chest and rocked her for hours." Her gaze remained steady on his. For once she didn't seem to fear letting him see a deeper part of her. "I promised her I would always take care of her." Tears brightened her eyes, but they didn't fall. That must've been her stubbornness, years of holding back tears so Gracie wouldn't see them.

"I've done my best to protect her and teach her and give her everything she needs to be happy. And now it feels like everything's about to change. I'll lose control…"

"Change isn't always a bad thing," Lucas murmured, openly staring at her, letting himself indulge in the details of her face. The fair, silken skin that hadn't aged the way his had. Her petite rounded chin. The way her lips naturally curved into that playful pout. He never thought he'd have the luxury of sitting across the table and looking at her again. In prison, he'd longed for it. To simply sit and look at her. "You're an incredible mother. You've done so much for her." But if he was Gracie's father she wouldn't have to do it alone anymore. He would tell her that eventually. When she was ready to hear it.

"I hope it's you," she whispered, and even with her chin dipped low, her eyes glanced up and found his.

"Me too." But he didn't want her to choose him based on her fear. He wanted to earn her.

She'd loved him once; he was sure of it. Then he'd gone and abandoned her. In the years since, she'd lived a lifetime of heartbreak and disappointment. She'd become so independent, refusing to rely on anyone for anything.

And now if he ever wanted her back—if he wanted her to be truly his—he would have to start all over.

Chapter Nine

I can't believe this is *mine*." Naomi ran up the porch steps fully aware that she looked like a little girl, and yet she couldn't stop herself. She *felt* like a little girl, like she was walking into a dollhouse. And it all belonged to her...

"Easy, there." Colton trailed behind her as though he was embarrassed to be seen with her. "You do have a reputation to uphold in this town," he cautioned. "Might want to start acting like a *real* professional."

"Inn owners aren't professional." She unlocked the door with her very own key and pushed it open, that old-fashioned creak making the best kind of music. "Inn owners are *eccentric* and *charming*." She puckered her lips in a goofy smile and led the way inside.

"God, let's hope that's not how you greet patrons at the door," Colton said with a belittling roll of his eyes.

"Watch it. This is *my* house and I can kick your ass out." She stacked her hands on her hips and looked around. Above their heads, a broken antique chandelier hung askew. A few spokes had fallen out of the wooden banister that wound along the staircase in the entryway. Dust clung to every surface, the particles that hadn't settled floating like specks of iridescent glitter. But each one of those dust motes belonged to her. "It's so beautiful," she whispered, picturing exactly how it would look with everything cleaned and polished and restored. Over the years it had been abandoned. No one else had taken care of it. And she could relate to that. "I don't care what anyone thinks about me." She turned to Colton, sure the tears in her eyes were drops of pure happiness. "I'm going to make this place into a *palace*. And that's why people will keep coming back."

"You know I love you, kid." He plunged a hand into his man purse and pulled out a bottle of champagne and two plastic goblets. "And I'm proud of you. Congrats on your new venture."

"Aw, Colton!" She pinched his cheek. "I couldn't have done it without you."

"No shit." He put his grumpy face back on and rubbed at the red mark she'd left on his cheek. Leaving her behind, he stepped into the small parlor. "There's no place to sit and do a toast," he complained.

"I have a chair in my car." The chair Lucas had hauled up into the air all strong and manly, loading it before she had a chance to argue. Even the thought heated her blood. Which, of course, warmed the rest of her right up.

"Oh, and I suppose you expect me to drag that chair in here for you." Colton walked past her and brushed dust off the staircase before sitting down. "Unlike your possible baby-daddy, I don't enjoy manual labor."

"It's fine," she said, sitting next to him. "I'll bring it in later. Right now I want to celebrate."

"Hear, hear." He popped the champagne's cork and poured them each a glass. "So speaking of baby-daddy, have you heard from Lucas yet?"

"Not yet." When she'd explained the process for the paternity test and told him they'd have to mail off the kit, he'd said that wouldn't be necessary. He wanted to drive down to Denver and go straight to the lab to cut down on the wait time for both of them. The gesture still made her heart ache. He hadn't changed at all: take charge, be chivalrous, honorable. She inhaled slowly to battle the intense thrum of desire. "He should be back in a few days. He said he had some errands to run in Denver, anyway."

Colton set his half-empty glass on the stair next to him. "By then you'll probably know the results. If he hand-delivers the sample, it should only take a couple of days."

A couple of days. Naomi planted a hand against the floor to steady herself. Either way, in a couple of days life as she and Gracie knew it would change forever.

"Did you talk about the what-ifs?" Colton asked in the gentle tone he normally reserved for little old ladies.

"No." She couldn't bring herself to discuss that with Lucas last night. It was bad enough she'd admitted she hoped it was him. He didn't say too much after that, and they'd moved on to discussing the logistics of the paternity test.

"So you didn't tell him you still have feelings for him?"

"I couldn't." She sipped the champagne to soothe the burn that tortured her throat. "I can't afford to make any emotional decisions. Not right now." She had to keep her head straight and prepare for everything that was coming. She had to focus on Gracie—on how to prepare *her*.

Colton eased his arm around her, pulling her close. Sometimes there was no safer place to be than in the embrace of a friend. "So I heard back from my guy in Denver."

The private detective. She gasped. "Did he find anything we could use against Mark?"

"Nothing." Her friend's face sobered. "He says Mark is squeaky clean. No police record. Owns a successful landscaping business, has a five-thousand-square-foot house in Cherry Hills." He ticked off each positive point on his fingers. "He's been married to a first-grade teacher for seven years, and they have a five-year-old son. Sounds like a hell of a guy. He even volunteers at his church, the bastard."

"Mark has a son?" She lurched to her feet, trying to absorb the shock. "While I was raising his daughter alone, he was creating the perfect family for himself and buying a *five-thousand-square-foot house* in Cherry Hills?" Fury surged, hot and fierce, forcing her to pace. "It makes no sense," she nearly yelled at Colton. "Why now? Why does he want to see Gracie now?" It'd been *ten* years. He could've contacted them a long time ago…

"Sounds like he had a cancer scare last year." Colton reached over and drained her glass of champagne, too. Which was fine by her. She couldn't stomach it right now.

"Nothing too serious. Just prostate cancer, but they caught it early. My guess is he feels guilty. Gave his life a hard look and realized the only thing missing was his daughter."

Naomi sat back down and bent over, resting her forehead on her knees. What if Gracie fell in love with Mark's wife? With her half-brother? "Maybe I won't have to worry about it," she said, raising her head and grasping hope. "Maybe it's Lucas." *It had to be…*

"What if it's not, honey?" Colton asked, giving her fears a voice.

"Then I'll do whatever Gracie wants me to do," she said, like she was reading it straight from a cue card. What she really wanted to say was that she'd fight Mark forever. That she'd never let him have a part of her daughter, but that was so selfish. "If Gracie wants to know her dad, I can't stand in the way." No matter how much it pierced her. No matter how much it scared her. "I need to know him more. I need to learn more about his life. But once I'm convinced he's a safe and responsible adult, I'll leave it up to her."

"You sure are a hell of a lot wiser than you look, mama," he teased.

"Sometimes I hate being wise." She leaned her head on his shoulder. "Life was so hard after Mark left. But, baby, him coming back into our lives would be ten times harder."

* * *

Well, shit. Lucas didn't know exactly what he'd expected to find when he pulled up in front of Mark's house in Denver, but he sure as hell hadn't predicted it would be a mansion in an upscale neighborhood. Quite the change from how they'd both grown up. Mark had lived with his parents and three siblings in a three-bedroom cabin just outside town. His dad had been a truck driver, which meant he was gone most of the time, and while his mom worked part-time at the gas station, she'd had to keep track of her kids, too, so there wasn't a lot of extra money.

Now it seemed the man was doing pretty well for himself. Lucas parked along the curb in front of an expansive yard that had been landscaped to perfection. A rock retaining wall ran along the perimeter, containing flowerbeds that looked like Martha Stewart herself had planted them. Not that he'd ever seen her work, but he'd heard plenty about her. She was real popular in prison.

He let the truck idle a minute, trying to decide if it was anger or envy that set his stomach to a boil. While he'd been in prison, Mark had obviously been very successful. And yet how could he have purchased this estate while never giving Naomi and Gracie a dime? That was one of only a hundred questions he had for his former friend. It was why he'd come. To get some answers, figure out where they stood.

There was a time he'd considered Mark his best friend, which meant he'd hung out with Naomi, too. When Lance had told Lucas that Naomi was pregnant and she and Mark were getting married, Lucas had practically doubled over. It had felt like the ultimate betrayal, and yet at the same time, he'd hoped Mark would take care of her, that he'd make her happy. But the next time he'd talked to his brother, he'd learned that Mark had left. That was when Lucas had asked Lance to invite her to move to the ranch and give her a job. If he couldn't be there, at least he could help provide for her.

That was all so long ago, but he had to wonder if Naomi had any lingering feelings for Mark. It would appear the man had a lot to offer now, especially in comparison to him.

Lucas had built his own home on the McGowen Ranch. A modest two-bedroom cabin, really. It'd taken him six months to complete, all the way from falling and hewing the logs to finishing off the inside with drywall and fixtures. It wasn't a family home in the suburbs where there were probably any number of choices in schools and sports and friends. And that wasn't the only difference between him Mark: His old friend had never served time. He didn't live with the stigma.

Gracie wouldn't have to explain to her friends that her dad hadn't been around the first years of her life because he'd been in prison.

Fuck it. He didn't care about all that. Maybe he should, but he couldn't make himself. He turned off the truck and climbed out, then marched his ass right up to Mark's fancy rustic walnut front door. The thing seemed to tower above him, casting him in its shadow, but he'd stand tall anyway. Because he might not have a ten-foot front door that looked like something out of a magazine, but he cared about Naomi. And it didn't matter if Gracie was his daughter or not. He'd fight for them both.

He rang the doorbell and the thing sang some cheerful tune. It almost made him laugh. What a picture he must be, standing up on this concrete stoop in his worn jeans, faded T-shirt, and scuffed shit kickers. Hell, he hadn't even bothered to scrape the mud off 'em.

He listened for footsteps or any sign someone had heard the bell but that front door was like a fortress. Before he lost the nerve, he tried the bell again.

This time it opened quickly.

Mark stood there, keeping a grip on the door, likely in case he had to shut it fast. "Hey, Lucas," he said with the same enthusiasm he might use to greet a door-to-door solicitor. "What can I do for you?"

"Just thought we should talk." And yeah, he also wanted to scope things out, see what he was up against. Maybe that had been a mistake.

"You want to come in?" Mark's rigid posture sent a certain message. Lucas had to hand it to the man; he was being relatively diplomatic considering the circumstances.

"Nah, I don't need to come in. Don't have the time." He

had plenty of time seeing as how he'd gotten a hotel room and planned to drive back tomorrow morning, but he didn't need to spend more time here than necessary. "I only wanted to come and tell you that I still love her." Might as well shoot straight. He didn't want to waste either of their time.

Mark seemed to relax. His shoulders softened and a trace of humor pulled at his mouth. "Hell, I know that. I may never have been as smart as you, Cortez, but I knew you loved her. *Love* her," he corrected. "And she always loved you." He shook his head. "I knew it before I married her."

"That why you left?" he asked with more contempt than he'd intended. But he didn't get it—how a man could walk away and not take care of the people who relied on him. How could he stay silent for ten years and then all of a sudden want a place in Gracie's life?

"I left because I was a stupid kid." Mark stepped out and closed the door behind him. Probably didn't want to waste the air conditioning. "I screwed up. At the time, it was panic. I knew we didn't belong together. Couldn't handle all the responsibility. But there obviously would've been a better way to figure it out. I should've gotten in touch with her long before now, but I figured she didn't want to hear from me."

Lucas nodded, the self-righteous judgment being squeezed through the sieve of his own reality. He could say those same words in a different context. "Hindsight is always 20/20."

"Sure is," Mark agreed. He faced Lucas directly. "You've got nothing to worry about. If Gracie's my daughter, I want to do right by her. But I'm not stupid enough to think Naomi would want anything to do with me. I've been married for seven years now. We have a son. Not gonna screw it up this time. Trust me."

Once again, anger reared its head. Mark hadn't lost out on

anything. Even though he'd walked out on his family. Lucas was about to say something, but the words dissolved on his tongue. He had no room to talk. He'd abandoned her, too. "I guess I *am* stupid enough to ask for a second chance." But he'd make a complete ass out of himself if it meant winning her back.

Instead of agreeing with him, Mark shook his head. "You two always had it. Whatever 'it' is. Even in high school." He eyed him. "None of us ever believed you started that fire. After you were sent away, Naomi tried to find out what really happened. We both did. She even questioned the police chief."

"Really?" He had no idea. No one had ever told him…

"Yeah. She was convinced you were covering for someone." He shrugged. "Made sense to me, but people in town had their conviction and wanted to move on."

Lucas said nothing, afraid one word would give him away. The truth wouldn't do him a lot of good now.

"Anyway, I guess we all made mistakes back then," Mark said. "Best thing we can do now is try to make up for them."

"I intend to." Going to prison had cost him everything. Too much. But maybe it wasn't too late for him to reclaim all he'd lost. His place with his dad and brothers at the ranch. A life with the woman he would always love.

Chapter Ten

Family dinners were one of Naomi's favorite things about living and working at the ranch. Technically, she had no blood relation to the Cortez men, but seeing as how her parents and only sister had all moved to Florida when Gracie was two, she felt more at home with this family than her own. And now, with Jessa as part of the package, she looked forward to these gatherings even more.

Outside Jessa and Lance's front door, Naomi paused. Hopefully, after she told them the news about the bed and breakfast they'd still want her to come, even after she moved to the Porter House.

"Let's goooo, Mommy," Gracie said, tugging on her hand. When she didn't budge, her daughter let go and went inside without knocking. Lance wouldn't mind. Ever since the girl was an infant he'd spoiled her, and now it was his own fault she had no boundaries. Naomi only hoped Jessa and Lance were decent. You never knew when you stopped by their house these days.

They wouldn't be expecting anyone for another half hour, but she'd wanted to come and tell them her news before everyone else got there. After the meeting with the contractor yesterday, she'd decided she wanted to work at the ranch through mid-October, then take a month off before opening the Hidden Gem Inn.

Tears misted her eyes. She couldn't wait to start a new chapter, but she'd miss life around here, too. They'd been so good to her…

"There you are." Jessa traipsed out the open door and joined her on the porch. Her pet pig Ilsa trotted behind, occasionally stopping to root her nose around the ground. "Oh God," Jessa gasped. "Are you crying? Is everything okay? Has the lab called?"

"Not yet." They were supposed to call any time now. Lucas had returned earlier that morning, though she hadn't seen him yet. He'd simply sent her a text saying the lab should be calling her today.

But she couldn't think about that now. She had to deal with one life-changing announcement at a time.

Naomi brushed away tears. "Actually I need to talk to you and Lance about something. Before everyone else gets here."

"Of course." Her friend linked their arms together and led her inside. The pig scampered after them, snorting distastefully at the prospect of being left behind.

Gracie was already sitting at the kitchen island trying to catch the M&Ms Lance tossed in her direction.

Jessa shook her head. "I swear. I leave you alone for one minute and you're feeding the princess M&Ms before dinner."

"Eight out of ten," Lance said, kissing his soon-to-be wife. "That's our best record yet."

"Yeah it is!" Gracie squealed, slapping him a high five.

"Well, you'll have to give it a rest." Jessa snatched the bag of M&Ms away from him. "Naomi needs to talk to us."

"Oh." That seemed to get his attention. "Everything all right?"

"Everything's great," she managed. Damn the womanly emotions. Why couldn't she be more like the Cortez men when it came to hiding her feelings? Before she fell apart, she rested her hand on Gracie's shoulder. "Do you want to tell them the good news, honey?"

Without missing a beat, Gracie popped off the stool. "We bought a new house!" she announced, dancing around. "It's so so so pretty. Wait until you see it!"

Ilsa danced around with her until Gracie dropped to a knee and started to pet her. "Hello, Miss Piggy," she crooned. "Aren't you looking beautiful today?"

Her daughter didn't seem to notice that both Lance and Jessa's mouths had dropped open.

"The new house is right on the river and it has so many rooms and we're opening a bed and breakfast there!" Gracie went on, mainly addressing the pig.

"Wow," Jessa finally said.

But Lance didn't even try to hide his disapproval. "You're moving?" he demanded. It seemed having his favorite ten-year-old deliver the news hadn't softened the blow. "When? Why?"

Naomi pulled out a stool and sat, caught between Gracie's excitement and her own sadness. "Because it's time," she said with a smile. "You know I've always dreamed of having a small inn. And now you two are getting married. Everyone's moving on. I want to move on, too."

"We understand," Jessa said quickly, making up for

Lance's stony silence. "Of course you do. This is amazing, Naomi. We're happy for you." She elbowed her fiancé as if prodding him to agree.

He didn't.

"I won't be ready to move out until October." Which would hopefully give them all the transition time they would each need. "So nothing has to change until then. And even after we move, we'll still see you guys all the time."

"That'd better be a promise," her friend said, nudging her future husband again.

His drawn mouth hinted at disappointment but over the years Lance had mastered unreadable expressions. "What about Lucas?" he asked.

That sat her up straighter. "What about him?" She widened her eyes and nodded toward Gracie. She sure as hell didn't intend to discuss anything about her and Lucas in front of her daughter.

"Hey, Gracie," Jessa called. "Guess what I rescued the other day?"

Her daughter spun. "What?" She was a sucker for animals.

"A baby bunny with a broken leg."

"A baby?" Gracie's eyes widened with childlike awe.

"Yep. You wanna see?" Jessa asked. "I can take you up to the shelter."

"Yes! Can I go, Mom? Can I? Pleeeeese?"

"Sure." Naomi matched Lance's glare, counting down the seconds before she could tell him that she and Lucas were none of his damn business.

"Come on." Hand in hand, Jessa and Gracie bounded out the front door with Ilsa running to keep up.

"So you're not even gonna give him a chance," Lance said before the door had closed.

"A chance for what?" she shot back. Lucas hadn't asked her for another chance. He hadn't said anything about the complicated mess between them.

"A chance to be part of your life. To be part of Gracie's life."

She shook her head wearily. "He might not even be her father."

"So?" Lance argued. "He loves you. And that means he'd love Gracie, too."

And how was that supposed to work? "Lucas doesn't want to be here."

"And you won't leave Topaz Falls," he accused. "Even if it means being with the person you've always loved."

She stood and marched over to him. "Don't make me feel guilty for wanting to stay. My life is here. My support system. Don't make me feel guilty for wanting to keep Gracie's life as normal as possible, even with everything that's about to change."

His expression relented. "No. You're right. Sorry. That was out of line."

"I don't even know what Lucas wants." He hadn't told her. He'd kissed her, but they'd been so busy sorting out the whole paternity issue, they hadn't discussed any future plans.

"What do *you* want?" Lance asked.

"I want what's best for my daughter." For the last ten years that had been her guiding principle. The basis for all of her decisions, and it wouldn't change now. She wanted love, too. Real love. That raw, soul-binding masterpiece that broke you and healed you all at the same time. But that couldn't be her focus. Not for herself. Not right now.

"I'll miss you," Lance said, and she'd never heard him sound so sweet.

"We'll still come around. I'll still nag you all the time," she promised. "And Gracie will probably babysit your kids someday."

"That's a crazy thought." A smile reached up and grabbed his eyes. "Bet you never thought you'd see the day—"

The front door opened and cut him off. Lucas walked into his brother's house and the oxygen levels in the room seemed to take a dive. At least for her. A woozy feeling pulled the rug out from under her composure—from dizziness or elation, she couldn't be sure. Whatever it was, she couldn't let anyone else see it, so she forced an easy smile. "Hey," she said casually. "Glad you made it for dinner."

"Yeah. Me too." He strode over to where they sat in that confident gait of his, never taking his eyes off her. "No phone call yet, huh?"

"Not yet." She pulled her phone out of her pocket and looked again, just to be sure.

"I'm gonna go check on the meat." Lance walked away in an obvious ploy to leave them alone. "Threw a few racks of ribs on the smoker this morning. Should be about done," he said as he slipped out the back door.

Even though she was suffering from serious heart palpitations, she turned to Lucas. Without his hat on, his hair was mussed and so sexy. She swallowed. "How was Denver?"

"Good. Easy," he corrected as though he wanted to reassure her.

"Glad to hear that," she said awkwardly. "Thanks again for going all the way down there." As if a simple thanks could make up for all of the trouble he'd gone through.

"No problem. I had some other business to take care of anyway." Lucas slid onto the stool next to her, and she let herself lean over just the slightest bit to smell that manly woodsy scent that always seemed to cling to him. Undercover indulgences were all she could allow herself right now. Even that was enough to tighten her stomach and ignite her cheeks.

Lucas turned to her, his lips jacked into quite the hot little smile, as if he'd noticed the blush.

Down, girl, she told herself. God, it had been way too long since she'd been with a man. Even just his aura was pulling her in.

"How're you feeling about everything?" he asked her, his eyes clear and at ease.

I'm feeling like I want to take you home with me. Let you undress me slowly. Let you kiss my lips and my neck until you earn free rein over my body...

Humiliation pinched her cheeks. What the hell was the matter with her! She'd been watching too much Starz, that was for damn sure.

"You okay?" Lucas asked, studying her like he might a rare sculpture.

"Fine," she squeaked. "Good." Better than good. Her lady parts were playing a seductive tune...

"Everything's gonna be fine," he assured her, covering her hand with his.

Now her body whimpered. Maybe she should just say screw it all. Who cared about being responsible? Who cared about how complicated it could make her life? Something told her sex with Lucas would be worth whatever complications came from it...

Before she could act on her lusty side, doors opened—the front and the back—and all of her favorite people started to file in to Lance and Jessa's kitchen.

Jessa and Gracie, who chattered excitedly about the baby

bunny. Levi. Luis, who looked stronger and healthier, with his special lady friend, Evie Starlington, by his side. Evie was a local stained-glass artist who'd moved to Topaz Falls after her husband had passed away last year. She and Luis seemed to be spending more and more time together.

Even Cassidy and Darla were joining them tonight. Seeing as how the wedding was only two weeks away and Jessa still hadn't found a minister, they were going to have a special meeting to figure things out.

Naomi let out a breath. Saved by the family dinner. Two more minutes alone with Lucas and she may have thrown herself at him.

"Mom!" Gracie exclaimed right in her face. "Jessa says I can help her nurse the baby bunny back to health! Can I? I'll have to check on it every morning before camp."

"Of course you can." She shot her friend a grateful smile. If she needed to justify the tears that had fallen earlier, there you had it. All of the people in this room had been such an important part of Gracie's life. There wasn't a day she'd ever felt like a single mom, because she hadn't done it on her own. They'd been her lifeline.

Oh God. Now she was getting teary again. Before the emotions took over, she stood and worked her way through the group, greeting everyone.

The boisterous talking and laughing crowded the room, but she couldn't quite join in.

From the outside looking in, she had everything. She was in a room with all of her favorite people. Then there was the house, a new adventure waiting for her.

So why did she feel like something was still missing?

* * *

"Dearly beloved..."

Lucas rolled his eyes at his younger brother's audition to play the minister in Lance and Jessa's wedding.

The rest of the room erupted into laughter.

They were all sitting around Lance's living room after one hell of a ranch dinner, and he had to admit, he'd come to appreciate these kinds of evenings. He may have missed out on them for years, but for the last several months it had felt like those years didn't matter so much. Family, friends—community—made him feel a part of something bigger, something more important.

"Sorry. I just can't see you as a wedding officiate," Cassidy Greer said to Levi. Even with his status as a professional bull rider, he didn't seem to impress her much. 'Course she'd known him forever. He'd been her late brother Cash's best friend while they were growing up.

"Maybe if you took off your shirt and tried again," Darla suggested innocently.

"Now, that's something he's good at," Lucas threw in. Every time he turned around there was another picture of his shirtless brother popping up online. The dig drew more laughter, but Levi walked over and threw a punch into his shoulder.

"I could do it," he argued. "You get up there and say a few words. How hard can it be?"

"The point is to keep the attention on the bride and groom," Lucas informed him. "Not to steer it to yourself." He was giving him a hard time, but the truth was, Levi happened to be a pretty good guy. Cocky, sure. But he was also loyal and generous.

"Yeah, I'm not sure you're right for the part," Jessa said thoughtfully. She and Lance were snuggled up on the couch, arms entwined.

A pang of jealousy riffed him. While he'd managed to snag a seat next to Naomi on the other couch, there definitely wasn't any touching. She'd hardly said a word all evening and he could almost see the weight of the unknown pressing down on her.

"I know who should marry you!" Gracie blurted, sprinting across the room and launching herself onto his father's lap. "Papa Luis!" She wrapped her arms around him in a suffocating hug. "You could do it. You even have white hair!"

Lucas cracked up. As if white hair was a prerequisite for officiating a wedding. God, he loved that girl. She was so precocious and full of life. And the way she sat on his father's lap…It was as if he already was her grandfather.

Once again, that feeling rose inside of him, strength and power and conviction. He wanted to be her father. It had to be him…

His dad smoothed his wrinkled hand over Gracie's red curls. "I'm not much for words," he said. "Especially in front of all those people."

Gracie took his cheeks in her hands and brought his face closer to hers. "Your words might be quiet," she said wisely. "But they mean more than most people's."

The tenderness in her eyes sent a jab straight to Lucas's gut. How could Dad turn her down now? Lucas sure as hell wouldn't be able to. She looked at *him* like that and he'd give her whatever she wanted—whatever she asked for. He'd be putty in her hands.

"That's a great idea, Dad," Lance said, squeezing his fiancée's hand.

Jessa was already teary-eyed. "Oh, Luis. It would mean so much to us."

"I think it's a wonderful idea," Evie said shyly. Lucas sure had been seeing a lot more of her lately, though his dad insisted there was nothing going on. She was maybe a few years younger than his father, but her long white hair and flowered clothes made her look youthful. He'd have to remember to tell his dad how much he liked her. Luis could do a lot worse.

"I can help you get ordained online," Levi offered, seeing as how they all knew Luis had likely never been online.

The old man shook his head slowly back and forth the way he always did when he didn't understand something. "I guess I got no choice in the matter," he muttered, but his smile told the truth. He was honored that they'd even ask.

"Oh, this will be so amazing. So perfect!" Jessa dabbed at the corners of her eyes. "Thanks, Luis!" She peeled herself away from Lance and stood. "This calls for dessert. Darla brought a chocolate cake."

A murmur of excitement went around the room.

Naomi stood. "I'll help—"

Before she could finish, some teenybopper song rang out from her pocket.

Lucas winced. Wow, that was quite the ringtone.

Everyone quieted as she dug the phone out and looked at the screen. Her gaze went straight to Lucas.

"I need to take this outside," she nearly whispered.

"Of course." Jessa shooed her along. "We'll dish up dessert and save you a piece, won't we, Gracie?" She tucked the girl under her arm.

Lucas stood, but he wasn't sure how. This phone call could change his life. Change all of their lives. Wordlessly, he followed Naomi out to the back patio, heart thumping the same way it had when he'd kissed her after the play.

As he quietly closed the back door, Naomi stood facing the mountains, murmuring, "Mmm-hmm. Right. Yes."

Lucas turned his eyes up toward the sky, giving her space, but wanting her to know he was right there with her. The sun hovered above Topaz Mountain, its rays cutting the sky. For a minute, he got lost in it—the brilliance and the peace. He'd missed sunsets those three years he spent in prison, and now he never took one for granted. A lot of nights since he'd come home, he'd pack up his fishing gear and head out to the river right when the sunset gave the world that rare lighting. No matter how bad a day had been, the sunset was a reward. It always seemed to set things right.

"Thank you," Naomi seemed to choke out. She hung up the phone and stuffed it into her pocket.

Lucas couldn't bring himself to ask. He simply waited. And when she looked at him, her eyes drawn and sad, he knew. She didn't have to tell him. The flood of disappointment nearly took him down.

"I'm so sorry I dragged you into this," she whispered, tears streaming down her flushed cheeks. "I thought for sure…I'd hoped…"

"Don't be sorry." That would mean he'd lost her, that they'd say goodbye and go their separate ways. He'd never been a betting man, but he gambled with a few steps closer. The stakes were higher than they'd ever been. He'd never wanted anything as much as he wanted her. "This whole thing brought you back to me," he said, refusing to let her look away. Before, she hadn't even let herself see him. She hadn't talked to him or sat next to him. Fear had kept her away.

Now her hand reached for his. "Oh my God, Lucas. I don't know how to do this."

He didn't ask her to clarify. Maybe she meant how to let Mark in to Gracie's life. Or maybe she meant how to open herself to him fully after all of these years. It didn't matter. "You won't do it alone." He pulled her into his arms, sheltering her, holding her up. "I'll help you."

She leaned into him as though giving up the fight. "Okay," she whispered against his chest. "Okay."

Chapter Eleven

Naomi walked back into the house in a daze. How could it be Mark? All these years she'd been so sure. That was the power of hope, though. She'd loved Lucas so much, she'd felt so connected to him, she'd believed Gracie belonged to them both.

With one phone call, that hope had been taken away from her, leaving behind an empty, hollow space.

When she wandered into the kitchen, the laughter died down. But in true Cortez form, everyone tried to act normal, even though they all knew who'd been on the phone. They all knew something had changed.

They just didn't know what.

She wasn't quite sure herself. When Lucas had held her and promised to help her, she'd melted into him, stealing those few moments of comfort and stillness in the face of a descending storm that would whirl through her life and touch everything. Even though his arms felt like the safest place she'd been in a long time, that feeling of needing him, of not wanting him to let go of her, terrified her, too. He'd have to, eventually. He'd have to let go of her and she'd have to let go of him, and she couldn't do it again. Let herself get so close, let her heart knit together dreams of a future with him. It had taken her years to recover. She'd walked around like half of her was missing. And she couldn't fall that way again, not now. Not when Gracie would need all the stability she could give her.

Naomi made her way across the room, not looking at anyone directly.

They were dying to know the test results—she could read the questions in their silence, but she couldn't tell them what she'd learned. Because that would make it real.

On the way to the front door, she snagged her daughter's shoulder. "Come on, Gracie girl," she managed to say without crying. "We should go on home and get you into bed." That was all she wanted to do. Fall into her bed and pull the covers up over her head.

Jessa appeared in front of her, halting her hasty escape. "Actually, we were hoping she could spend the night here." Her friend gave her shoulder a knowing squeeze. "If it's all right with you. Then she and I can go up and visit the baby bunny first thing in the morning."

"Can I, Mom? Please?" her daughter begged, tugging on the hem of her shirt.

"Of course." She gave Jessa a grateful look. Somehow the woman already knew. They'd gotten so close, there was no doubt that Jessa had read the results on Naomi's face. Her friend knew she would need space tonight, time to come up with a plan.

And she had to call Mark.

"You listen good to Uncle Lance and Aunt Jess," she whispered, pulling her daughter in for a hug and a kiss. God, was it possible for her heart to bleed? "I'll be here to pick you up for camp at eight thirty." Or maybe she wouldn't take her tomorrow. Maybe she'd spend the day with her. Take her shopping and out for pedicures.

She hadn't even told Gracie about her father yet, but she already felt like she was losing her.

"I'm always good at listening when I'm at their house," the girl said emphatically.

"You are, honey. You're such a good girl," she murmured, smoothing her daughter's hair, holding her eyes closed until the tears dried.

"Come on, sweet girl." Jessa took Gracie's hand. "Let's get you set up in the guest room."

Briefly, Naomi looked up at the rest of the group. They'd all resumed their conversations, silently giving her permission to leave quietly. Without saying goodbye she let herself out the front door, but before she could get it closed Lucas was there.

"Can I walk you home?"

"Sure." The word stuck in her throat but he didn't seem to notice.

They walked silently side by side down the porch steps, the only sounds the crunching of their footsteps and the occasional chirp of a cricket. Night in the mountains was so still, with the valley tucked in the peaks' shadows quiet and secluded. Moonlight spilled onto the dirt, unhindered by smog and manufactured light. Out here you could see the radiance of the stars. You could hear the wind breathing. Most summer nights, after she put Gracie to bed, she'd go out and sit on the porch, taking in the tranquility of it all. But now, with the chaos inside of her, she felt out of place in the midst of it.

"What can I do?" Lucas finally asked. He stopped at the edge of her driveway. "I want to make this easier for you."

"You can't." She turned to him, hovering closer to the road, intent on keeping distance between them.

"I think I can." He stepped into her space, searching her eyes, her lips. But he didn't touch her. "What are you going to do?"

"I don't know." She folded her arms, trying to ward off the chill. It wasn't so much the brisk mountain air—it was that cold empty feeling that left her exposed. "I have to call Mark. I have to tell him." Right now that was her only clear next step.

"What if you invited him to come to dinner? At Lance and Jessa's? Then everyone could be there. You could introduce him to Gracie. And then you can let her decide what she wants."

It made sense. To bring him to a familiar location. To have her friends and family there for support. "I guess that would be best." She peered at his face, the moonlight softening his cheekbones and sturdy jaw. "What do you think she'll choose?" She hadn't meant to whisper but that was all she had.

His hesitation answered her question. He'd know. He'd grown up without a parent.

"I always wanted to know my mom," he said gently. "Didn't matter how long she'd been gone. If she would've walked back into my life, I would've wanted to know her."

"Of course you would've." A parent was like an anchor. Even though her own parents had moved away, they gave her identity and support. They'd helped her know who she was in the world.

Lucas took her hands and tugged her closer.

His touch reached through her hesitation. Those hands were so strong in hers. Enough to steady her.

"Even if she chooses to have a relationship with Mark, you'll always be the person she turns to," he murmured, his face close enough for her to feel the softness of his breath on her mouth. "You've been everything to her. That won't change."

He touched his fingertips to her cheeks, smoothing away tears she hadn't even realized were falling. "A lot will change," he said. "But no matter where she goes, you'll always be home to Gracie." He spoke it with authority because he'd lived it.

"That was your dad for you."

"Right." His own tears made those gorgeous hazel eyes glisten. "Even when I was away, when I thought of home, it wasn't the house or the land. It was him."

His fingers threaded through hers and held on tighter. That one small touch sent a blinding surge of want. Just screw it all, she thought. Screw being a responsible adult. Screw all of the reasons she couldn't be with him right now. Tonight.

He caught her in his arms. "And when I came back after all of those years and saw him again, it was like nothing had changed. You and Gracie have a bond she can't have with her dad. Because he wasn't there."

Once again, her feet steadied beneath her. How did he do that? Reach into her fears and sort them all out? Make them so insignificant? "I'm glad you came home," she uttered because they were right there. *He* was there. And he made her feel good—younger and freer and fearless. "God, Lucas. Why did you stay away so long?" She breathed the words against his neck, inhaling the wild scent of the woods, before pressing her lips in to taste the salt of his skin.

"I never thought I deserved another chance with you." His chest rose and fell faster. Those large strong hands came to her hips, holding her so tightly against him that she could feel the sheer strength of him, the force of his desire for her.

Lucas pulled her face to his. "You know what?" he whispered against her mouth, his eyes seeing into her very soul. "I might not deserve it, but I want it. Another chance. I want you."

Her breaths came so fast she could only manage a small sound of agreement deep within her throat.

It seemed to be enough, though. He lowered his mouth to hers and completely took her over, tracing her lips with his tongue. The faint taste of chocolate lingered in his mouth, filling her senses. How had she ever thought this would be a bad idea?

She kissed him back harder, wanting to free herself to feel everything, every part of him, every cell that sparked within her. His mouth moving her overs aroused an overwhelming greed that had been dormant for so long. "Take me inside," she murmured between tastes of his lips.

He groaned, too busy thoroughly kissing her to say a thing. His lips moved desperately but in control, as if he couldn't get enough of her, as if he were afraid she might run away. Then they skimmed her jawline, inching their way down her neck, nibbling and sighing against her sensitive skin.

She couldn't run even if she tried. It seemed he'd learned a few tricks in the years they'd been apart. Her legs were already giving out. *Everything* was giving out. Turning her body completely over to him. "Take me inside," she said again, this time with the force of her hunger.

"You're sure?" he asked in her ear.

Her whole left side seized in a shiver. "Don't make me beg." She couldn't stop here. Not now. He'd already brought her too far. He'd already made her want him too much. The years without him had left her with a void, and she hadn't realized how lonely she'd been until this moment. How much she'd neglected a whole part of herself—the sensual part, the passionate part. Slowly he was reawakening the need to be held and touched and completely lost in someone else. Each year that had passed between them only added to the intensity of this bond between them, the desires that gripped her so fiercely. She'd lost him once. And now she had him back.

Easing his lips over hers again, he lifted her against him. She wrapped her legs around his waist as he moved easily across the lawn, up the porch steps.

One of his hands held her backside, caressing in a way that made her hips grind into his, while his other hand fumbled with the doorknob.

Her hair fell into her eyes as he staggered inside, but he smoothed it away from her face and set her feet on the floor, holding his arms around her waist. "You don't know how much I thought about this. About kissing you one more time."

"This kissing is good," she agreed, breathless. "But I can think of something even better." She tugged his T-shirt up and over his head and let it fall to the floor. "Wow," she uttered, awed by the sheer strength of his body. He'd been toned back in high school, but now hard muscle sculpted a ladder up his abdomen, and his broad chest tensed with sheer power. She laid her hands against his tanned skin, sliding them down the front of his body, taking in every bend and curve.

His eyes closed as though he had to gather himself, then he leaned down and pressed his lips to hers, more slowly this time, savoring. His lips held their own power, prying her open—not only her mouth but also her heart, bringing her back to that place when she'd trusted him fully, when she'd given him every part of her.

His lips inched back from hers, but his eyes didn't let her go. "Tell me what you want," he said, low and hoarse.

"I want you to make love to me." She wanted him to remind her what it meant to be cherished. She'd forgotten. It had been years since she'd been with him, since her body had ached in this tantalizing desperation. They were both different people now—both broken in so many ways, both searching for wholeness. She felt that need as strong in him as she did within herself.

"Say it again," he said with a tempting grin, already working his way down the buttons on her shirt.

God, just the feel of his fingers grazing her collarbone made her legs clench tight. "I want you to make love to me, Lucas Cortez." Her voice had gone husky. "I want you to tear off all my clothes, lay me down on that couch, and bury yourself inside of me." She stared at Lucas, wide-eyed. Wow! She might be out of practice, but she could still talk with the best of 'em.

"With pleasure." The raise of his eyes promised plenty of that. His breath seemed to hitch as he undid the last button on her shirt and slid it off her shoulders. His gaze fell to her bra. It definitely wasn't one of her best—boring old white, hardly any lace. But it wasn't like she'd been planning on sleeping with anyone. That wasn't exactly part of her daily schedule. Or even monthly schedule...

"You are so sexy," he growled, cupping her breasts, his eyes fixating on the bra as if it were one of those hot little numbers a woman wore to seduce a man. Which was sweet, considering it was clearly a mom bra.

Kissing her cheek, then her neck, he reached his arms around her back and popped the clasp, sliding his hands around her rib cage and up underneath the bra.

A gasp hit her in the lungs as his fingers scraped her nipples.

"Your body is so damn perfect," he said, dragging the bra straps down her shoulders until he could pull it off.

A self-conscious shudder rattled her shoulders as she stood bare before him. Her body had changed since he'd seen her last. She'd developed quite the chocolate habit, and she'd had a baby...

"You're even more beautiful," Lucas murmured, as if he'd heard her worries. Lowering his head to her breast, he dragged his tongue to her nipple and covered it with his hot mouth, melting her from the inside out.

"This is so much better than Starz." The words trembled through her lips.

Lucas laughed against her skin. "I'll do a hell of a lot more for you than Starz ever could," he promised. Taking her face in his hands he drew her lips to his, kissing her with that soft, bone-melting heat. "I want you so bad I'm in pain," he groaned.

"I can help with that." She ripped open the button fly of his jeans, freeing the impressive erection his boxer shorts couldn't contain. The feel of him throbbing in her hands submerged her in the depths of passion.

Lucas's shoulders caved as though he couldn't hold himself upright. Desire darkened his eyes as they stared into hers. Working on the button of her jeans, he urged her backward toward the couch and lowered her to the cushions. He pulled his body over hers and she shoved his jeans down over his hips. Just as he went to work on hers, her back left pocket started to vibrate.

Naomi froze underneath him. "Oh God. My phone."

"Ignore it," Lucas murmured, kissing his way down her chest again.

"I can't." She was a mom. She *never* had the luxury of ignoring her phone. She wriggled until she could reach it.

Lucas rolled onto his side. "Who is it?" he asked, tracing a finger over her breast.

"Jessa." Which meant something was wrong. Pushing away from him, she sat upright on the couch and cleared the impassioned wheeze out of her throat before swiping the screen. "Hello?"

"Hey, girl," Jessa said with a worried undertone. "I'm so sorry to call, but Gracie threw up."

Her shoulders dropped. "Oh no. I'm sorry." Jessa and Lance didn't have kids. The last thing they needed to deal with was throw-up.

"It's no problem," her friend assured her. "I wouldn't have even called except she's still not feeling well and she's asking for you."

"I'll be right there." Naomi scrambled to stand and put herself back together.

"What is it? What's wrong?" Lucas asked, already by her side.

"Is that *Lucas*?" Jessa asked with a horrified gasp. "Is he still with you?" She didn't give Naomi a chance to answer.

"Oh no! I'm so sorry! I shouldn't have called. Forget I called. Okay?" she pleaded. "Lance and I have got this. We'll take care of her. You two just carry on, and—"

"I can't forget," Naomi interrupted, regret sinking her heart. What had she been thinking? She hadn't. That was the problem when she was with Lucas. She couldn't think straight. And while she was here pretending to be a free and clear woman, Gracie was at someone else's house throwing up and miserable. "I'll be there in a few minutes," she told Jessa before hanging up the phone.

"Everything all right?" Lucas had already dressed, as though anticipating he'd have to run out and save the day.

"Gracie threw up." She avoided his eyes as she buttoned her jeans and slipped her bra and shirt back on.

"Poor girl." He walked to the door and opened it, waiting as if he wanted to go with her. "I'll help you bring her home."

Heartache spilled through her. If she needed a reminder of why she hadn't dated, why she hadn't slept with a man since before Gracie was born, there she had it. "It's okay. You don't have to come," she said carefully, though Lucas wasn't clueless. The sad draw of his mouth proved he'd heard what she hadn't said.

"I don't want her to know we were together." Things would be confusing enough once she introduced Mark into the picture.

"It's okay for you to do things for yourself once in a while." He strode over to her. "You shouldn't feel guilty for letting yourself enjoy the moment."

She couldn't help it. All these years, she'd worked so hard to be everything Gracie needed her to be. She'd had to be as good as two parents all on her own—always there, always available. There was a constant pressure to make sure her daughter never missed out on anything. Now she didn't know how to let go of that.

"Maybe it's better," she said, scooting past him and out the front door.

"What the hell does that mean?" He chased her down and stood in front of her.

"Just that I have no idea where this would go anyway." What good would sex do for either one of them? Besides the instant physical gratification.

Lucas studied her as though trying to figure out what was going on. "Ten minutes ago you asked me to make love to you."

"Obviously that was a bad idea. You're leaving," she pointed out. "And I can't. I just bought a house."

He seemed to know better than to argue.

"Besides that, I have to deal with Mark." She couldn't let her emotions take over all the time. "My daughter needs me to be fully present."

"Your daughter needs you to live, too," he shot back. "She needs to see you taking risks and making the most of every opportunity life throws at you so she will, too."

The words wrecked her defenses.

As if intent on finishing the job, he swept his hand down her arm. "You're right. I don't have it all figured out. I don't know where this'll go. But I'm not afraid to find out. You might be. But I'm not."

He leaned down and kissed her on the lips, then turned around and left.

Chapter Twelve

"You sure Harlan Wellington is gonna be okay with this?" Lance turned off the highway and onto the dirt road that cut through the flat grasslands outside of Casper, Wyoming.

"Nope." But Lucas had learned in this business that sometimes it was best to take initiative and ask for forgiveness later. Or, better yet, make people like you so much that you never had to ask for forgiveness at all. "He'll be surprised to see us, that's for sure." Not only because they were showing up at his ranch two days before the auction, but also because Lucas wasn't there representing Bill McGowen. That alone might make Wellington shit his pants.

It also might give them an advantage. While most players in this game catered to Bill McGowen, the vast majority of them didn't like him, because he was a cutthroat businessman who cared only about the bottom line. These were rural people. Family and values meant something to them.

So while Lucas hadn't asked Wellington for permission to come early and check out Reckoning II, he was sure the man would be open to hearing him out.

"Can't believe how fast the drive went," Lance said, hardly watching the road. Not that he had to. It was straight and flat the whole way. "Remember when we used to go on road trips with Dad?"

Lucas laughed. "Man, those were brutal." Probably a hell of a lot worse for Luis than it was for them, having his three boys wrestling in the backseat the whole way.

"Were you disappointed when Naomi got the test results?" Lance asked.

Lucas automatically gazed out the window, his smile fading fast. He'd managed to avoid talking about this during the whole five-hour drive. They'd filled the silence mostly with discussing logistics for the ranch, but now there was nowhere to hide.

"Because you seemed disappointed," his brother persisted. "And I wouldn't blame you if you were. That's gotta hurt."

"Yeah. It sucks." But he wasn't going to dwell on it. In his mind it didn't matter if Gracie was his biological daughter or not. "I could still be her dad, too." If Naomi would stop pushing him away every time they got close. "I mean, I'd be the best stepdad I could if things worked out between her mom and I."

His brother drove under the modest wooden Wellington sign posted over a wide metal gate. Thankfully the gate was already open.

"You gonna *make* things work out?"

"I'm trying." Wasn't that part of what he was doing here? After Naomi had kicked him out last night, he'd been restless, thinking through every possible way to win her over. But in order to do that, he had to build a life in Topaz Falls. He had to find a way to make a living there, to prove to her he was serious about staying. Which meant they had to make Lance's stock contracting operation more lucrative. So he'd decided they'd drive out to Wellington's to get the jump on any potential buyers. And, wanting to be upfront about it, he'd called Bill McGowen. The man hadn't answered, so Lucas had left him a message telling him they needed to talk. He'd planned to resign, but McGowen hadn't called him back yet.

The truck turned the corner and some of the ranch's outbuildings came into view. Wellington did well selling off the bulls his family had raised for years, but you wouldn't know it from the humble facilities. They were adequate but nothing fancy. "Park over there by that corral," he instructed, confident that Wellington had already heard them coming and was heading outside.

Sure enough, the door to the log house opened and the man himself lumbered down the steps, sizing them up as they got out of the truck. He was in his early fifties, but sun exposure made him seem older. His tanned, leathery face and scraggly graying hair made him look meaner than he was, too.

"Cortez?" he squinted in the sunlight. "What're you doing here? Auction's not for two more days."

"I know," he said, sauntering around the truck to greet the man properly. Lance kind of hung back as though letting him take the lead.

Wellington looked back and forth between them like he wasn't quite sure what to expect.

"I'm sure you recognize my brother. Lance Cortez."

Introductions were a mere formality. Everyone in the bull-riding world knew Lance.

"Yeah. You were a hell of a rider," Wellington said, still looking confused. "Did McGowen send you out here early?"

"Actually, I'm not here on behalf of McGowen." Lucas leaned against the tailgate. "I'm here on behalf of my family. We're starting our own operation and need to purchase the best bulls in the business."

Interest sparked in Wellington's eyes. "McGowen know about this?"

"He will. As soon as I can get ahold of him."

"He's gonna be madder than a bobcat caught in a piss fire." A low laugh growled out. "Wish I could be there to see his face."

Yep. That's what Lucas had been counting on. Secretly, a lot of these people didn't want to see the man succeed. He stood taller and faced Wellington. "You know how I operate. I don't want to waste anyone's time." They'd left Topaz Falls at four o'clock that morning, and he was hoping they'd be home in time for dinner. "We both know the range of bids that'll come in for Reckoning II. And we're willing to pay ten percent more." The words brought on a niggling pain in his gut. He'd had to put up a lot of his own money to make this happen, so it'd better be worth it.

With that in mind, he gestured to the trailer. "We'd like to take him today. We can have the money transferred to your account as soon as you give the okay."

Wellington's eyes narrowed with suspicion. "You're gonna pay ten percent more than what I'd get for the top bid at the auction?"

"Ten percent," he confirmed. "Then you don't have to go to the trouble of doing the auction. You've got a buyer here. And we're ready to pay now."

The man took his sweet time thinking it over, and Lucas didn't push. He had a reputation. People trusted him. That's what he would count on.

Finally, Wellington chuckled and shook his head. "You're one gutsy cowboy, Cortez. I'll give you that."

Gutsy wasn't exactly the best way to describe it. More like determined. He'd stand up to anyone if it meant he could be with Naomi.

"I'll take the deal on one condition," Wellington said, his eyes sly again.

"Sure. Whatever you want." They couldn't swing more cash, but it didn't appear that's what the man was after.

"You make sure to snap a picture of McGowen's face when you tell him about this and send it to me."

"I'll do my best." As long as he was still standing upright and Bill McGowen didn't take him down.

* * *

"Isn't this the sweetest baby bunny-wunny you've ever seen?" Gracie asked, peeking into the baby bunny's kennel.

Naomi leaned down to see inside. "He's pretty cute, all right." The poor thing was all scrunched in a corner, trembling with fear. Probably as a result of her daughter's enthusiasm. Gracie had been waiting all day to see the bunny again. When Naomi picked her up from camp, she begged to go straight back to the ranch instead of running errands so she could go up to the shelter.

"We can take him out and see if he'll hop around," Jessa

said, pulling on some gloves. "But you have to promise not to touch him."

"I won't. I swear I won't," Gracie vowed, her eyes solemn.

"Okay, then." Jessa opened the kennel and carefully lifted the small creature out, glancing over it before setting it on the ground. "There you go, little guy. Let's see how that leg is feeling."

The bunny simply scrunched up as though it was trying to burrow into the floor.

"Let's give him a little time," Jessa suggested. "You keep an eye on him, and your mom and I will go over there and have a chat." She pointed to her desk on the other side of the room.

Shaking her head, Naomi followed Jessa, bracing herself. They hadn't talked since she'd picked up Gracie last night, and her friend was obviously dying to hear details about her and Lucas.

"So Gracie seems fine today, huh?" Jessa asked, pulling another chair over.

"Yes. She begged to go to camp." They were going swimming that day and she hated to miss the swim days. "After I got her home last night, she admitted that she'd had three cookies and two brownies in addition to the M&Ms Lance gave her. So I'm guessing that's what upset her stomach." Normally, she limited her daughter's sugar intake, but she'd been distracted.

"That'll do it." Jessa cleared her throat loudly and leaned closer with a smirk. "So what were you and Lucas doing when I called?"

"Oh, you know..." Naomi kept an eye on Gracie, who was now lying on the floor near the baby bunny, doing her best to coax it into hopping.

"No...I don't know." Her friend lowered her voice. "I can guess, though. If I have to."

She didn't have to guess. It had to be pretty obvious from the way her face flushed. "He was amazing. So supportive. Understanding. He always knows what to say." And yet nothing about their situation was simple.

"So you're telling me you two just *talked*?"

"He kissed me and I lost my mind," she admitted in a whisper. "We were half-naked on the couch when you called."

"I knew it!" Jessa cried, smacking her palm against her thigh.

"What did you know?" Gracie asked, pausing from the hopping lesson.

"I knew you'd be the best doctor for that bunny," her friend said skillfully.

Gracie just grinned and went back to work.

"So are you going to see him again? Tonight?" her friend pestered. "Lance and I will take Gracie. It's okay if she throws up. It's good practice for us."

"No." She let her head fall back to rest against the chair. "I'm not seeing him tonight, and I don't know if I should spend any more time with him."

"What? Why?" Jessa demanded. "He cares about you. And Gracie."

"I care about him, too." She could love him again. So easily. "But right now I have to focus on Gracie. I have to help her through this situation with Mark." It was an easy excuse to hide behind. "Besides, Lucas is planning to go back to the McGowen Ranch. You said so yourself."

"I'm not sure about that." Her smile was all mystery. "He took Lance up to Wyoming today. They went to purchase some bull that's supposed to be the next champion."

"What does that have to do with anything?" And why hadn't Lance mentioned another purchase? They didn't exactly have extra money to throw around.

"Lucas was supposed to purchase the bull for McGowen," Jessa whispered. "But he's helping Lance buy it first."

"Really?" A tendril of hope wrapped itself around her heart. "Won't he lose his job?"

"Maybe that's the idea." Her friend obviously *hoped* that was the idea, judging from the excitement glittering in her eyes. "Maybe he wants to stay. Maybe—"

Jessa's phone chimed from the desk. She rolled her eyes and glanced at the screen. The woman hated to be interrupted when she was romanticizing. "Oh! That's them now. They're up at the corral." She popped out of the chair and reached for Naomi's hand. "Come on. Let's go see our men."

Our men? "Hold on." Naomi tried to dig in her heels, but Jessa nudged her from behind.

While her friend stashed the bunny in its cage and shooed Gracie toward the door, she hung back. She didn't have the space in her heart to entertain any maybes. Not for her daughter and not for herself, either.

As they walked up the road, Gracie chattered about possible names for the baby bunny, but Naomi couldn't focus. Had Lucas really sacrificed his job to help Lance? Or had he done it for her? Nerves sparked in her stomach. He shouldn't give up anything for her. What could she give him in return?

"Uncle Lance! Lucas!" Gracie sprinted up ahead of them to the corral fence.

"Gracie!" Naomi ran after her, afraid she'd hop right over and sprint into the arena. Instead, her daughter stopped where Lance stood on the outside of the gate.

Glancing past them, Naomi caught sight of Lucas in the corral. He walked slowly behind the biggest bull Naomi had ever seen. The beast was white with brown splotches, a massive snout, and lethal-looking horns.

Lucas lightly tapped the bull's backside with a long pointed stick and the creature tossed his head back with a snort.

"Oh my God," she breathed. "He's gonna get himself killed."

"No he's not." Lance grinned. "He's gonna train him."

"That cow is huge!" Gracie climbed on the fence as though she wanted a better look. "Be careful, Lucas!" she called. "Don't let him step on you!"

Lucas sent a quick glance over his shoulder and waved, then went back to stalking the bull.

"Holy moly. That thing must weigh two thousand pounds." Jessa moved to Lance's other side and snuggled under his arm as though looking for protection. Naomi wished Lucas would come over and snuggle with her instead of standing so close to that thing. If it lurched back at all, it'd trample him.

"Ladies, meet Reckoning II. The toughest bad—" Lance caught himself before he swore in front of Gracie. The girl was a stickler. "I mean the toughest son of a gun in the sport of bull riding."

"Looks pretty tough," Naomi agreed, keeping a wary eye on Lucas. He eased along right behind the bull and jabbed its hind end again. Reckoning II tossed his head and let out a vicious grunt, saliva flying from his mouth.

"Oh dear God." She stopped breathing and curled her fingers around the fence railing, trying to steady herself. Lucas didn't seem nervous at all. His eyes were narrow and focused, his stance authoritative. The deep humming that had thrummed through her body last night started again. He was so strong and steady, and God, he looked sexy in worn jeans, a tattered T-shirt, and a black cowboy hat. Heightwise, Lucas was barely as tall as the bull, but his presence held all the control.

"See that?" Lance asked, shaking his head. "The bull whisperer. Reckoning's going exactly where Lucas wants him to go."

"Let's hope he doesn't turn on him," Jessa muttered, sharing a glance with Naomi.

Yes. Let's hope. She knew this was what he did for a living—and from the looks of things, he was good at it—but watching him out there still rattled her.

"Come on, Reckoning," Lucas drawled as though teasing the bull. "Let's see you jump. I know you've got more than this." He prodded the bull a few times and the beast started to trot. "Atta boy." Lucas lightly tapped the stick against the bull's back legs like he wanted to provoke it. Suddenly, it launched into the air, jackknifing its body.

Naomi gasped, but Lucas had anticipated it, and dodged out of the way just before getting kicked.

"There it is." Lucas gave the bull some space while it continued bucking and snorting out its frustration at being pestered.

"This here's a fighting bull," he called over, as though proud of Reckoning's tantrum.

"Are you sure he won't hurt you?" Naomi couldn't help but ask. It was the mother in her.

"Yeah, Lucas!" Gracie yelled, dropping from the fence to stand on the ground. "He looks so mean!"

The bull had settled some. Lucas backed away from it and

sauntered to the fence. He knelt across from Gracie. "Don't you worry. He's not gonna hurt me. He'll tolerate me 'cause I fed him the good stuff a few hours ago."

Her daughter nodded slowly, her eyes open wide with unmistakable awe. Though she guarded her own expression, Naomi could relate. This man was so appealing, with his strength and patient persistence. Why had she cut things off last night, again?

Lucas stood and faced her, those arms and chest so broad.

"Gracie, do you want to help me feed some carrots to the horses?" Jessa asked a little too eagerly.

"I love feeding the horses!" Her daughter was already skipping toward the barn.

"Come on. You too," Jessa told her future husband, nudging him away from the fence.

"What?" he demanded as though put out. "I don't want to feed the horses."

"Yes you do," she countered, widening her eyes in Naomi and Lucas's direction.

"They can talk in front of me," Lance argued.

"We're feeding the horses." With a prim smile, Jessa linked her arm through his and dragged him away.

Lucas watched them go with that same small smile that had revved her up last night. Behind him, the bull was calm as a kitten, now chawing happily on some hay from a trough in the corner of the pen.

"Are you going to lose your job?" Naomi asked, wondering how she could be so comfortable and nervous at the same time.

"It's likely," he said, tipping up his hat as though he wanted to see more of her. The sun made his lustrous eyes glisten.

Her heart thrummed. "What will you do?" she half-whispered.

"Lance said he has an opening. Might fit me just right." The words were casual, but his eyes locked on hers.

"You're staying?" she asked cautiously.

"I'm sure as hell gonna try."

Chapter Thirteen

This was a bad idea." Lucas hung back next to Lance's pickup where no one else could see him.

"What'd you mean?" Levi asked, coming around the other side. "This is perfect. You help out with the fire mitigation for a while, show that you're concerned for citizens of Topaz Falls, and you're back in the fold. Simple as that."

"Yeah. Simple." Sometimes it appeared his younger brother actually grew up in Disneyland. Or maybe all that optimism was the result of everyone jumping in front of him to take on the brunt of the shit storm in his place.

"No one's gonna say anything." His father hauled a chain saw out of the truck bed. Never mind that the man had Parkinson's. He wasn't about to be left at home or leave the heavy lifting to his sons.

Lance took the chain saw away from their father before Lucas could get to it. "This is important work. They know we need all the help we can get."

He had a point. They had a hell of a lot to do. With the dry spring and a hot start to the summer, most of the brush and dead trees on the outskirts of town would make great kindling. One spark and the whole mountain could go up in flames.

"There's only one problem," Lucas said to his brothers as he eyed the group standing near a familiar Land Cruiser. "Marshal Dobbins is here." Didn't make much sense to him why the man still held a grudge, but he'd made it known. In fact, Dobbins had made it known that he hated the entire Cortez family. Lucas suspected that Marshal had somehow discovered Luis had had an affair with his mother years ago. Back in the day, Luis Cortez had made a lot of mistakes, all of which he'd later owned up to.

"Dobbins is harmless," Levi insisted, but Lance glared over at the man, eyes narrowed and dark. He'd been with Lucas a couple of months ago when they'd run into Marshal at the Tumble Inn. The man had been drunk and tried to start something, but in prison, Lucas had learned to walk away.

"That kid had a tough time after his dad left," Luis reminded them, as if that excused him from everything.

"Time for him to get over it." An insinuation hid in Lance's tone. If Marshal didn't get over it on his own, he would obviously be willing to help him out. But Lucas didn't want to cause any trouble in town. Especially not today, when they were supposed to be helping. Especially not after the conversation he'd had with Naomi a few hours ago. The hope in her eyes when she'd asked if he was staying had burned into him. Levi was right—God help him for saying that—he had to get on the town's good side if he wanted to stick around and prove to her they could make it work. Getting into a brawl while they were volunteering wouldn't help his cause.

"Guess we should go over and get our assignment then," Lucas said, heading to where Hank Green sat in a camp chair behind a plastic folding table. The man obviously wasn't dressed to work, if his pressed gray slacks and sweater vest were any indication. Besides that, his wide girth didn't exactly scream manual labor.

Lucas approached the table first, hoping Levi would keep their dad away. Luis and Hank Green had a hard time being civil to each other.

"Good of you to stop by," Hank said, sounding as phony as if he'd suddenly stepped behind a pulpit. "But it would appear we have all the help we need for today." The man's watery eyes settled on Lucas and sent the message behind the words. He wasn't welcome here.

"Bullshit." Lance pushed past him. "You're gonna turn down help that could make a difference for the town?" he demanded. "You're a bigger moron than I thought."

Green's cheeks got all ruddy and it was everything Lucas could do not to laugh. That was exactly the way the man had looked when their father had proven they hadn't stolen from his store in junior high.

"Last I checked this here was public land." Lucas glanced around. Most of the crews were already heading out. Looked like Dobbins was gone. He stepped closer to the table and studied the map. "There's a whole section on the east side that isn't designated." He pointed it out to Green. Likely because it was the steepest terrain. Nothing they couldn't handle, though.

"Fine," the man snipped. "You can take that. Just don't make any trouble."

"When are *you* gonna stop making trouble?" their dad called.

Lucas quickly slung an arm around Luis. "We're here to help," he said to both Green and his dad. "Seems to me when something's threatening the town we can all put aside our differences and work together."

Both men harrumphed. After another glance at the map, Lucas dragged his father back to the truck.

"He has no right to treat you that way," Luis muttered.

"Doesn't seem to stop most people." He'd gotten used to it. Lucas unloaded another chain saw. But he was over it—the glares, the comments. He was done fighting them. The best thing he could do was go about his life. Eventually people would get tired of giving him a hard time and they'd move on to something else. They wouldn't have a choice.

The four of them headed up the hill, crunching through the underbrush, Lucas and Lance carrying the chain saws.

"I'm warning you," Green called after them. "If there's any trouble, I've got Dev on speed dial. You so much as blink wrong I'll have him up here."

Lucas stopped and turned back to him. "I'm here because I want to be part of this town. Same as everyone else." Best if Green knew that now.

The man stood so fast he knocked over his chair. "I heard you're headed back down south."

Of course he had. "Nothing's set in stone yet." He shot the man a nice big grin. "I'm thinking of sticking around for a while." A long while if Naomi would let him.

Green didn't seem to know what to say to that. Words fumbled on his lips, but Lucas didn't give him a chance to get them out. "Anyway, don't worry about a thing. We'll take care of the east slope," he said cheerfully. "You stay out of our way and we'll stay out of yours." With a tip of his hat, he ambled off to join his brothers.

Lance had already fired up the chain saw and was working on a dead plume of scrub oak while Levi piled up the gnarled fallen branches. When they saw him approach, his brother shut off the chain saw.

"He give you any shit?" his dad growled like a dog looking for a fight.

"Nah." Hank Green was the least of his worries. Everyone knew he'd always had it out for their family. "I could give a shit about getting on *his* good side." It was everyone else he had to win over. No one listened to Green anyway. The only reason he'd been elected as mayor last March was because Edward Collins, the man who'd served as mayor for seven years, had met a woman online and moved to Canada, which meant the town had to scramble to elect someone and Green was the only one who'd thrown in his hat.

"So how's Naomi taking the news about Mark?" Lance asked, tossing over an armload of branches.

"She wasn't taking it well." He should've known better than to start kissing her last night. She was still in shock, too emotional.

"Can't say I blame her." Their father dragged over a fallen log, and Lucas quickly scrambled to lift the other side.

"What's she gonna do?" Levi asked, tying a bundle of branches with twine.

"She's gonna call Mark and invite him to the next family dinner so he can meet Gracie." At least he thought so. They hadn't exactly had time to confirm the plan when he'd left her place.

He and Luis set the log up so Lance could cut it.

"And what about you two?" His older brother didn't turn

on the chain saw. "You two get anything sorted out while I was forced to feed the horses?"

"I guess you could say that." Though his brother and Jessa hadn't quite given him enough time to make sure. "I told her I'd like to stick around. Give it my best shot."

And the happiness that lit her eyes solidified his decision.

He didn't care how much Hank Green badgered him. He wasn't about to leave Topaz Falls unless Naomi told him to herself.

* * *

Naomi slipped on a pair of Jackie O sunglasses and pulled the straw fedora lower down over her forehead.

"You look like Lindsay Lohan leaving rehab," Colton said, giving her a critical eye.

"I don't want anyone to recognize me." That was why, when Mark had asked her on the phone where they should meet, she'd picked this little diner an hour outside of town. The rumor buzz had only recently started to die down in Topaz Falls. At least people weren't elbowing each other and whispering when she passed them in the grocery store anymore. She couldn't afford to start it up again.

"A straw fedora and sunglasses is classic code for *I'm hiding something*," Colton insisted, parking the Hummer as far away from the other cars in the parking lot as possible. "Trust me, you're only drawing more attention to yourself."

"Well, hopefully if anyone I know is in there, they won't recognize me," she snapped.

"You'll be as inconspicuous as Elizabeth Taylor," he muttered, getting out of the SUV. She got out, too, her annoyance with Colton somehow distracting her from the nerves that left her feeling fragile. That's why she'd brought him. She needed a smart-ass to rile her up so she wouldn't break down and cry. When she'd told Mark the test results over the phone, the whole situation had suddenly felt real. She would have to share Gracie with a complete stranger. She'd have to give up nights of tucking her in with five rounds of *one more kiss*. She might have to give up holidays...

"You know, you should've worn a trench coat, too," Colton mused. "Preferably zebra print. Hot pink and black."

She punched him in the shoulder and it made her smile.

He smiled back as he held open the door.

"Table for two?" the hostess asked when they stepped inside.

"Oh no," her friend scoffed. "We're not together. I'll just take that table over there by the window. Is that the farthest one from the kitchen?" He leaned in closer to the poor woman. "The smell of grease makes me nauseous."

Naomi moved in front of him and butted him out of the way. "I'm meeting someone else," she said. Then added, "You can just put him at the table closest to the restrooms. He has irritable bowel syndrome."

"Hey," Colton said, feigning shock. But he reached over and squeezed her hand. "My work is done here. Go get 'em, tiger. Hold him to the promise that this is all on your terms."

"Thank you." She squeezed his hand back, then left him standing with the speechless hostess and made her way down the row of tables until she spotted Mark. He sat in a booth by the window.

He stood as she got close, and she still couldn't get over how different he seemed, how the smile lines and the kind crinkles around his eyes made him look like a true gentleman. Instead of beating him down like she'd always assumed they would, the years seemed to have refined him, giving his face a softer quality and his eyes a wiser tint.

"Thanks for calling," he said, standing awkwardly still, as though he wasn't sure if he should shake her hand or lean in for a hug.

"Of course." Without doing either, she sat, leaving the hat and sunglasses in place.

If he noticed the disguise, he didn't mention it.

"I wasn't sure you'd call." He sat down across from her, folding his hands around a steaming mug of coffee. "After Lucas came to see me, I—"

"What?" The surprised gasp nearly throttled her. "Lucas came to see you?"

"Oh." Mark sat up straighter. "I thought you knew."

"Um, no." He definitely hadn't mentioned a meeting with Mark. "I wasn't aware," she said, doing her best to make it sound like it was no big deal.

"He wanted to make sure I didn't get any ideas about being with you again." He half laughed. "I told him not to worry. That wasn't my purpose in coming back. You know that, right?"

Nodding, she tried to picture Lucas walking up to Mark's door. That must've been fun for him. She probably should've mentioned that Mark was married.

"I know you never loved me," Mark said. "We didn't love each other. Not enough to make a lifetime work."

A sad sigh slipped out. "I thought I could love you." She'd been foolish enough to think she could force those feelings to develop.

"I didn't expect you to. Everything happened so fast. And I regret a lot of things, but I don't regret bringing Gracie into this world. I could never regret that."

Yes. That was so true. Every moment of pain Naomi had experienced was worth it because it had given her the most amazing daughter in the world. But if that was how he felt, why hadn't he contacted her sooner? "Why did you wait so long?" She figured she'd earned the right to ask.

A waitress chose that minute to swoop in with a coffee pot. "Hi there! What can I get you?" she asked Naomi, leaning over to refill Mark's mug.

"Oh." Naomi took a glance at the menu, but nothing sounded good. "Just some coffee, please."

The waitress's smile dimmed as she turned over Naomi's mug and filled it. "Let me know if you want anything else." She quickly scurried away, likely in search of bigger tips.

Mark ripped open a sugar packet and dumped the whole thing into his coffee. "I waited to get in touch with you because I was afraid," he said simply.

"That's not an excuse." God, she was glad she'd brought Colton along. The whole ride there he'd built her confidence and now she wasn't about to back down. Mark might be a different person, but that didn't change the fact that he'd walked out on his daughter. She didn't even care so much about him leaving *her*. She simply didn't understand how a parent could abandon his child. "I was scared, too," she reminded him. "But I loved her so much it didn't matter." Love could always trump fear. She'd learned that real fast.

"I know." Mark didn't seem surprised by the challenge in her tone. And he didn't shy away from it, either. "I didn't know how to love anyone. Except myself." He continued to stare back at her as though willing to face up to all of it. "I knew I didn't deserve a place in her life. For the two years after I left, I moved from apartment to apartment barely able to feed myself. Then I started working for a landscaper and he gave me a chance, taught me how to work hard. When he got sick, he let me buy his company and I've spent the last five years building it up."

"I don't care about your job." Didn't he get that? "You could work at a gas station and it wouldn't matter as long as you loved Gracie, as long as you could take care of her." That was it, what wrecked her the most. "I don't trust you, Mark. I don't trust that you won't work your way back into her life just to make yourself feel like a good person and then abandon her again. I have to protect her from that. Before you spend one minute with her, you'll have to convince me that you won't walk away again." Because it would destroy her.

"That's fair." He leaned in with a look of complete sincerity. "I already told you I'll do anything. This can be on your terms. When I get to spend time with Gracie—"

"*If*," she corrected. "If you get to spend time with her."

He nodded. "If I get to spend time with her, I promise you I won't take it for granted. I'll be there for as long as she'll let me."

Naomi didn't acknowledge the emotion behind his words. Right now, this wasn't about emotion for her. It was about protecting Gracie.

"I'm going to leave this decision up to her." She lifted the mug to her lips and took a long sip of coffee. "I want her to meet you. We can schedule a big dinner at Lance and Jessa's place so she's comfortable. And after that, she'll be the one to decide if she wants to have anything to do with you."

"Understood," Mark said automatically. "I think that's a great idea. Name the day and I'll be there."

Naomi set down her mug, but she couldn't seem to let go of it. The warmth brought comfort in the midst of uncertainty. Mark seemed so nice and accommodating, but she still had to find a way to help Gracie understand all of this. She still had to help her navigate this monumental change in their lives. She couldn't plan the dinner until she'd told her. "I'll let you know." She'd have to tell Gracie about Mark, then schedule something with Jessa. "I'd like to do it within the next couple of weeks." As tempting as it was, she couldn't drag this out.

"Sounds good." Mark's head tilted as he looked at her. "I hope I didn't mess anything up by telling you Lucas came to see me."

"Oh. No." She wasn't sure there was something to mess up. "Things with Lucas are a little complicated right now."

"Doesn't seem too complicated to me," he offered. "It's so crazy. After all these years, all you two have been through, the man would still do anything for you. Don't hear that too often. High school sweethearts making it through all that."

They hadn't made it through anything, yet. She was still trying to process what it meant that he wanted to stay in Topaz Falls. And even though she was thrilled at the prospect, she also feared how Gracie would handle all of these changes. No matter what, she had to make her daughter her first priority. Which meant she and Lucas would have to take things slow. Not that she wanted to have this conversation with Mark, of all people. "I should get going." She stood and threw a few dollars on the table to cover the coffee. "Thanks for coming up," she said distantly. "I'll let you know when we can schedule a dinner."

"Okay. Sure." He stood, too. "Thanks again, Naomi. I really appreciate all of this."

Technically he shouldn't be thanking her for anything

yet. "We'll be in touch," she said, then turned away and walked calmly to Colton's table.

He was busy picking at a pile of lettuce greens with a fork. "I thought I ordered a chef's salad, not what they fed the barnyard animals yesterday."

She shook her head. "Come on. Let's go get you some real food."

He threw down a twenty and bolted out of the booth as if he'd been waiting for that invitation for an hour. "So how'd it go?" he asked as they walked out the door.

"Good." She realized how much lighter she felt now. Almost buoyant. It hadn't been nearly as hard as she'd thought it would be to face Mark. "I told him there was no excuse for walking out on his daughter. And then I told him I didn't trust him."

Colton raised his hand for a high five. "You're a total badass."

"Ha," she said, but slapped his hand anyway. She didn't care about being a badass. But somehow in the midst of the confusion and uncertainty of the past few days, she was finding herself—rediscovering her courage and her confidence. Maybe she really could be the brave girl Lucas had once loved. Only older and wiser and ready for something far more than she would've been at eighteen. The thought chased out a smile.

Maybe this really was their time.

Chapter Fourteen

Even with the dust and debris scattered about, walking into the new house was like walking into her dreams. With the demo work nearly done, it was now a clean slate. Light and airy, uncluttered. Brimming with potential. Naomi inhaled a deep, deep breath, holding it, letting it fill her. In here her problems didn't seem so important.

Taking Gracie by the hand, she led her from room to room, pointing out where everything was going to go. Her daughter *oohh*ed and *ahhh*ed over the plan. Four suites upstairs and their two-bedroom apartment attached to the main level, but also completely closed off as its own unit. After they'd walked around the entire place, they sat out on the front porch eating Gracie's favorite snack—peanut butter and banana sandwiches.

Right after she and Colton had arrived back in Topaz Falls, she'd gone straight to the school to pick Gracie up from camp early. It was time to tell her everything. Time for them to move forward together. That's why she'd brought her to the Hidden Gem. The bed and breakfast was a change, too. An exciting change, and she hoped it would help Gracie get excited about the prospect of meeting her dad.

As soon as her daughter finished telling her about the game they'd played at camp, Naomi set her sandwich on a paper plate. "Gracie, honey. There's something I need to talk to you about."

"Okaaayyyy." A guilty look stretched her mouth. "It's not about the cookies and brownies I ate at Lance and Jessa's that one time. Right? Because, trust me. I learned my lesson."

Naomi laughed softly, wishing it was that simple. "No. But that was a good lesson to learn." A lesson in forgiveness would be much harder. "This is actually about your dad."

The girl stopped eating mid-bite. "My *dad*?" she repeated with a full mouth.

"Yes." Naomi inhaled slowly and deeply. She'd never told her much about Mark, simply that he had to leave because he couldn't take care of a family. And whenever Gracie had asked any questions, she'd always quickly steered her toward remembering everyone who *was* there—Lance and Luis. Jessa. Darla and Cassidy. In the years since Gracie was born, Naomi had learned it took a village to raise a child, and she didn't know how she'd survive without hers.

"What about my dad?" her daughter asked, dropping the sandwich to the porch.

"Well…he'd like to meet you." She paused to regain strength. If Gracie detected any hint of sadness, she'd get worried.

But her daughter simply stared at her, eyes scrunched like she didn't understand.

"He called me last week," Naomi explained, keeping her tone even and neutral. "And he's changed a lot. He has a good job and a nice house and he said he was very sorry he had to leave. He's sad he never got to know you." Even to her it sounded lame. One small part of her wanted to roll her eyes and call the whole thing ridiculous. But she couldn't blame everything on Mark. She'd made choices, too. And back then they were both only eight years older than her daughter was right now.

"What did you tell him?" Gracie asked, picking at the crust of her sandwich.

"I told him I would talk to you. I'd like you to meet him, honey. Because if you don't, you might always wonder." Lucas was right. Gracie should know where she came from. As she got older, she'd want to know. Even if she wasn't so sure right now. "So I thought maybe he could come to the ranch and have dinner with all of us." She tried to make it sound exciting, like a party. "Then you could meet him and make up your own mind about whether you'd like to know him."

The girl's lips bunched like they always did when she wasn't sure about something. "Do *you* like him?"

"I don't know him all that well," she admitted. Yes, it was the easy way out, but that was all she could offer at the moment. "We have to get to know him." She patted her daughter's leg, wishing she could offer her more reassurance. Wishing she could find it herself. They didn't have a choice except to get to know him.

"Would he come to live with us?" the girl asked warily.

"No, honey." God, how could she explain all of this? "We were already married once and it didn't work out. He's married to someone else. A very nice woman," she said, even though she had no idea. Her heart lurched at the prospect of Gracie someday having another mom.

A strong breeze picked up, scattering her daughter's hair. Naomi studied her, unable to believe how old she looked. Most days, she still saw her as a plump toddler who needed her to be everything—her whole world. But she was growing up.

"I don't understand why he had to leave." The first hint of anger broke through her words.

Naomi took her hand and squeezed it. "It wasn't because he didn't love you." Whatever else she thought, she had to believe that. "I think he didn't know what to do. We were very young. And that wasn't what he thought his life would be like." It was impossible to explain the mind and motivation of eighteen-year-old kids who were pretending to be adults.

"But *you* didn't leave."

She wanted to throw her arms around her daughter and tell her to always remember that, no matter how much they fought, no matter how much drama entered their lives. She leaned in closer. "The second you were born, I knew I could never leave. I couldn't be apart from you," she murmured. "A lot of things might change, Gracie. But that'll always stay true."

Her daughter climbed over the sandwiches and wedged herself into her lap. Naomi couldn't see over Gracie's head anymore—she was much too tall—but she snuggled her and held her tight the same way she always did when she had a nightmare.

"What if I don't like him?" she asked.

"Then you don't have to see him again." Naomi smoothed her hand over that lovely red hair. "But you know what?"

She tilted her head to see into her daughter's eyes. "I think you'll like him. He's very nice."

"Was he ever mean to you?" she asked as though afraid to know.

"No, honey. He was never mean. We just weren't right for each other." Because her heart had already belonged to someone else and she was never able to reclaim it. That was the sad truth.

Speaking of that someone else…His truck came lumbering down the street and pulled up in front of her house. How did Lucas always seem to know when her thoughts turned to him?

Gracie scrambled out of her lap as though embarrassed to be caught hugging her mother. "Hi, Lucas!" she greeted cheerfully as he got out of the truck. The girl was remarkably resilient, considering what she'd just learned. But that was the best thing about kids. They were much better at compartmentalizing than adults.

He strode up the front walkway. "How're you two lovely ladies this afternoon?"

"Great!" Gracie answered for her.

Naomi stood and brushed herself off. "We're good." She tried to say it casually, but her voice caught. He always had to look so sexy, wearing those tight jeans, and those T-shirts that fit snug against his broad shoulders.

"Guess what?" Gracie asked, hands on hips and eyes wide.

"What?" Lucas asked as if the anticipation was killing him. For someone who had not been around kids much, he had a gift. Once again Naomi felt a stab of regret that he wasn't Gracie's father. That they couldn't simply pick up where they'd left off last night. But he deserved more than to be her escape from reality.

"My dad called my mom," Gracie informed him. "And he wants to meet me."

Naomi thought she saw a flash of pain behind his smile, but then it was gone.

"Wow." He took a knee, lowering himself to her level. "What do *you* think about that?"

"Dunno yet." Gracie gave a shrug. "But Mom says I don't have to see him if I don't like him."

"I doubt that'll be a problem." Lucas stood. His eyes met Naomi's and that one meaningful glance was enough to loosen her knees.

Everything she'd felt when they'd made out in her living room came boiling back up to the surface—the zinging hormones, the greedy hunger, the exquisite vertigo. Clearing her throat, she steadied a hand on the porch rail. "Gracie, why don't you go pick some of those flowers?" She pointed to the gardens that had been overtaken by alpine sunflowers, blackfoot daisies, and purple aster.

"Really?" her daughter gasped. When they were out hiking, Naomi never let Gracie pick anything—*we have to leave the wilderness like we found it*, she always said. "Picking from a garden is different. You can get as many as you want." They'd have to redo it anyway with how overrun it had gotten.

"Wow!" Her daughter shot off the porch and sprinted all the way to the flowerbed at the edge of the expansive lawn.

"She seems to be taking it well," Lucas observed with a smile. God, she loved that smile, the way his lips curved all sexy and delicious. She knew for a fact they were delicious.

She looked away. Now was not the best time to be considering how delicious his lips tasted.

"She seems okay so far." She sighed. "I don't know how to prepare her for what it'll be like to see him." What would that feel like for a kid? To have a strange man walk into the room and say, "Hey, I'm your father." Gracie was usually pretty easygoing, but that would be a shock for anyone.

Lucas rested his hand on her arm, making her quiver with a deep sense of longing. "We'll all be there when she meets him. Hopefully that'll make her more comfortable."

He might have been talking about Gracie, but the way his kind eyes held hers so tenderly made it clear he wanted to be there for her, too. And who was she to argue? "Jessa said we could do dinner on Sunday," she said, hoping he could make it. "I called Mark and he already said he'll be there."

"Sounds good." He stared down at her, seeming to focus on her lips.

It was a good thing Gracie was right over there or she might drag him inside to pick up where they'd left off on the couch. "I feel so bad making them host a dinner with their wedding coming up, but Jessa insisted it wasn't a problem," she babbled, feeling shaky all the way to her bones. Her body was literally crying out to him. He could probably hear it. She could still hear the echoes from the other night—*Make love to me, Lucas...*

"Sorry for just showing up like this" His little smirk didn't make him look sorry. It made him look like he knew exactly what his presence did to her. "But I got you something and I wanted to drop it off."

"Oh." Her cheeks got all warm and tingly. Much like other regions of her body...

"It's in the truck," he said, turning and swaggering that hot ass of his down the steps.

She watched him intently until he glanced over his shoulder. *Busted.*

"I'm coming." She hurried down the steps after him, pretending she'd been watching Gracie pick flowers all along.

Lucas waited for her halfway down the front walk, standing there looking close to perfect the way he filled out those snug jeans. But she shouldn't look at his jeans. Or his shoulders, she realized when the sight of his broad shoulders and muscular arms brought on another hopeful exhale. She raised her gaze to his face, but that proved to be dangerous, too. He seemed to know *exactly* what she was thinking.

"You didn't have to get me anything." What could it possibly be? And why would he buy her a present after she'd run him off?

"I know I didn't have to," Lucas said, leading her to the truck. "I *wanted* to." He leaned over the tailgate and lifted out a large, flat cardboard square. "Think of it as a congratulations gift. Something to help get this place started." After setting it carefully on the ground, he ripped off strips of tape, then slowly opened the box.

"Oh." A punch of surprise hit her beneath the ribs. She lowered to her knees, hovering to get a better look.

It was a sign. A beautiful custom sign made from an antique stained glass window. "God," she breathed. "Lucas..." It was incredible. She touched the pattern of colorful Colorado wildflowers pieced together from different colors of glass. On the wide white molding that framed the sign, someone had hand carved the name of her new bed and breakfast in wooden letters.

Hidden Gem Inn.

She peered up at him, tears making the world look more

like a watercolor painting. "Where did you get this?" She never could've even dreamed up something so wonderful.

"I know a guy in Denver," he said, kneeling next to her. "From prison, actually," he added, as if that made any difference to her. "He's an artist now." Lucas admired the sign. "I mean, I came up with a general idea, but I had no clue how to make it work."

"I can't accept this." But she was desperate to. It could hang on the front porch—right above the steps. But... "It must've cost you a fortune."

"My friend owed me a couple of favors, anyway." He stood, not expanding on why an old prison buddy had owed Lucas something. Though she suspected he'd somehow gotten him out of trouble. He seemed to be good at that.

"I don't even know how to say thank you." The wobble in her knees made it difficult to stand.

Lucas reached for her hand and pulled her up, hanging on to her longer than necessary.

"You don't have to say thank you." He leaned against the bed of his truck, looking over at her house. "I think it's great what you're doing. Starting something new. Making your dream come true." He focused on her, lips quirked with a secret. "It's inspiring."

"What d'you mean?" She couldn't *not* smile back at him.

His fingers brushed her hair back, skimming her neck. "You're going after what you want. Not letting anything stop you. Makes me want to do the same."

She didn't ask what he wanted. She feared the answer too much. What if she couldn't give it to him? She had so much pulling at her already—with Gracie and Mark and the inn.

"Come on." Lucas bent to pick up the sign. "Why don't you show me where you want to hang this?"

He started to walk away, but in a move of desperation, she reached for him, clasping her hand on his solid bicep and towing him back to her. “Thank you,” she whispered. “Not just for the sign, but for believing in me.” For thinking she could actually do this.

It made her believe, too.

Chapter Fifteen

You got the shotguns loaded?" Levi passed Lucas on his way to the fridge to get a beer.

"I don't think that'll be necessary." He continued stirring Jessa's baked beans on the stove. If he let those things burn on the bottom she'd be after *him* with a shotgun. She'd been scurrying around the kitchen getting things ready for dinner for the last hour. You'd have thought they were welcoming the president the way she was carrying on.

"Mark's harmless," Lucas said, turning down the burner. He should know. When he showed up at the man's doorstep he could've gotten all pissed off, but instead Mark had invited him in for a beer.

"Still don't make much sense to me," his dad grumbled from a stool at the kitchen island where he was shelling fresh peas. "You ask me, a man who walked out shouldn't be allowed to walk back in."

"It's not up to us," Lance reminded him, carving up the smoked brisket with a honed precision.

Lucas inhaled. Damn, it smelled good—like coriander and brown sugar.

Dad huffed. "Well, we sure as hell didn't have to use the good beef."

"The cheap stuff isn't allowed in this house," Jessa said, aiming a playful glare at Lance. "I tried to buy the brand on sale and you would've thought I'd bought a pint of cocaine."

Lucas busted out a laugh. "Nice try." A pint? Seriously? Sadly he knew the lingo a little too well. He'd heard it enough. No sense in educating her, though. She didn't need to know.

"Anyway," Jessa went on, smoothing out her frilly apron. "We're using the best beef because that's the right thing to do." She rested her hands on Luis's shoulders and leaned in with a smile. "And we're all going to be polite and civil the whole evening. If you want a taste of my berry pie, that is."

"I'm always polite and civil," Luis muttered, but he reached back and patted her hand.

Lucas gave the pot another stir. Even though he'd been back eight months, there were times he still felt like an outsider in his own family. Though he and his father had come a long way, they hadn't reached the point of bantering back and forth. And Jessa was always kind to him, but she didn't tease him the way she did Levi and Luis. They all still seemed cautious around him. Building relationships took time.

"How're those beans looking?" Jessa asked, scooting over to glance into the pot.

"Look good to me." He kept right on stirring. "Smell good, too."

A smile flickered. "They need about ten more minutes

to simmer," she said, hauling ass back to the kitchen table. "Keep stirring!"

"Will do—"

The phone rang, momentarily distracting him from his mission. Since he was closest, he picked up with his free hand. "Hello?"

"Lucas?" Naomi's voice sounded as sullen as it had when she'd kicked him out of her house the other night, only this time he couldn't be the source of her frustration. He hadn't seen her since he'd brought over the sign. When he wasn't in the corral with Reckoning, he was out cutting trees, trying to convince everyone in town he wasn't the villain they wanted him to be. In between all of that, he'd been trying to get ahold of McGowen for days, but the man wouldn't call him back.

"Hey, everything okay?" he asked, glancing at the clock. She and Gracie should've been up twenty minutes ago.

"Is Jessa there?" she asked without answering his question.

He glanced to the dining table where Jessa was fussing over the napkins again, all the while muttering to herself.

"She's pretty busy." He turned around so the rest of them wouldn't hear. "Anything I can help with?"

"No." She sighed. "I don't know. It's Gracie. She doesn't want to come to dinner. I can't even get her out of her room."

He glanced over his shoulder. Levi happened to be headed to the fridge again, so he caught his arm and handed him the stirring spoon. "I'll be right down. Okay?"

There was a pause on the phone. "Um. Okay," Naomi finally said.

"See you in a few." He hung up the phone before she could change her mind and tell him to send Jessa instead.

Levi held up the spoon and stared at it like he didn't know what to do with it. "What the hell?"

It was high time the man learned how to stir a pot of beans instead of sitting around and drinking beer while everyone else worked. "Make sure they don't burn or Jessa might be serving your head on that platter," he called to his brother on his way out the door.

Outside, he took the porch steps two at a time and jogged down the hill.

Naomi stood out on her front stoop, arms crossed, face flushed with a tinge of color. She wore jeans and a white tank top that stretched over her curves.

"Hey," he said, letting his gaze travel all the way down to her manicured red toes, aching at the memory of holding those perfect curves in his hands. God, the woman even made flip-flops sexy.

That impulse to pull her into his arms flashed stronger every time he saw her.

"Hi," she murmured, slightly breathless.

He would've loved to completely take her breath away, but that wasn't why he'd rushed down. "Can I talk to her?" he asked, keeping a safe distance.

"Be my guest." She shook her head, her sleek red hair falling around her shoulders. "I don't understand. She's never difficult. *Never.*" She opened the door and he followed her into the house.

Bogart trotted around the corner, greeting him with a gruff bark.

"I know this is hard for her, but we've been talking about it all week," Naomi said, scratching behind the dog's ears. "I've told her everything I can. I've answered all of her questions. I don't know what else to do."

"Let me try." He'd never had a heart-to-heart with a kid before, but he knew something about being abandoned by a parent. Maybe that would make a difference.

With a doubting lift of her eyebrows, Naomi pointed down the hallway.

It was pretty obvious which door belonged to Gracie. She'd decorated it with glittered stickers—hearts and flowers and horses. Smiling to himself, he knocked quietly.

"Go away, Mom. I'm not going to dinner," came a muffled, grouchy voice.

He leaned close to the door. "Actually, it's Lucas."

There was a rustling sound, the thump of footsteps, and then the door creaked open. Gracie stared up at him. "What're you doing here?"

"I came to check on you," he said casually, like that was something he did every day. "I know it's a big deal to meet your dad for the first time, and I wanted to see how you were doing."

"I'm *not* meeting my dad." Stubbornness gripped her delicate face. "I'm not going to dinner."

Lucas leaned against the door frame, pressing his lips into a frown. "Now, that's a real shame because you should see all the food Jessa and Lance have made." He rolled his gaze up to the ceiling as though trying to recall everything. "Brisket with a tangy sauce, Jessa's baked beans with brown sugar, fresh sweet peas. And the pie..." He whistled low. "Well, I don't even think it's gonna need the ice cream she bought to go with it."

A panicked look flared in the girl's eyes. Jessa had informed him earlier that berry pie was one of Gracie's favorites. That's why she'd made it.

"I can't go." Her voice got smaller. "I can't meet my dad."

"Mind if I ask why not?"

Leaving the door open, she crept to a fuzzy pink reading chair in the corner of the room.

Bogart slunk past him, curling up at her feet. The dog stretched his head and laid it in Gracie's lap.

Though she didn't invite him in, Lucas ventured as far as the end of her small twin bed and sat on the edge patiently. Two weeks ago, he'd never envisioned himself sitting on a frilly pink bedspread having a heart-to-heart with a ten-year-old girl. That was before he'd thought he might be a father. Before he knew he wanted to be a father so badly.

"What if he doesn't like me?" Gracie finally asked, tears streaming down her cheeks.

The words gouged at his heart like a dull spoon. They were an echo from his own past. To a child, that was the only logical explanation for why a parent would ever leave.

Lucas eased himself off her bed and knelt in front of her, holding her tear-laden gaze firmly in his. If she never heard anything else he said—if she never remembered him at all—she needed to hold onto this. "If he doesn't like you, it's because *he* has a problem, Gracie." That truth had taken him years to understand. For a long time he'd thought he could earn back his mom. That maybe somehow she was still watching, and if he did everything right and took care of everyone else and didn't get into any trouble, she'd come back. That was why he'd always followed the rules; that was why he'd taken his brother's punishment. Somewhere in his subconscious he'd believed that once he was good enough, she'd come back for him.

He wished someone would've told him it wouldn't matter. That he was already good enough. That he didn't deserve to be abandoned. That he could never be perfect enough to fix all of his mother's problems. And that was okay. Because it wasn't up to him.

"You are funny and brave and smart and pretty much amazing," he told Gracie. "Your dad didn't leave because you weren't worth sticking around for. He left because he had a lot of problems."

"He did?" Her eyes were wide.

"He did," Lucas assured her. "But he's trying to get them all sorted out now. He wants to be a better person." Much as he hated not being Gracie's father, he had to hand it to Mark. It took courage to come back and try to make things right. It was something he was still waiting for his own mother to do.

"My mom left when I was your age," he said, wondering how it could still hurt to say it after all these years.

"Your *mom* left?" she asked, as though completely astonished. That was a testament to the safe and secure life Naomi had built for her. She didn't even think that was within the realm of possibility.

"She did. And you know what?"

"What?" Gracie asked, completely transfixed.

"I still wish she'd come back." He knew now that she'd struggled with anxiety and depression. And he didn't need her anymore, but… "I'd like to know her."

"Do you think she'll *ever* come back?" Gracie asked, showing sweet concern for him.

"I don't think so." Though he wouldn't give up hope altogether. He couldn't.

The girl reached into a pile of stuffed animals next to the chair and pulled out a tiny owl. "I used to pretend this was my dad." She handed it Lucas. He looked it over—the large, wise eyes, the tufts of feathers sticking out around its ears.

"I'd set him right over there." She pointed to the bookshelf next to the bed. "And pretend he was always watching over me."

"That's a good idea," Lucas said, marveling at her openness, her ability to trust him with something so personal. Hell, he was still working on that.

He went to hand the owl back to her, but she pushed it toward him.

"I want you to have it." Her big grin was all confidence. "My dad's back. But your mom's still on her way."

"Thank you," he murmured, the back of his throat all mucked up with emotion. Hadn't he come in here to help *her*?

Standing, Gracie threw her arms around his neck. "I'm glad you came."

He hugged her back. "Me too." More than she knew.

She pulled away and he stuck that owl in the pocket of his shirt. He didn't care about the razzing he'd get from Lance and Levi; he planned to leave it there all night.

"Come on, let's go meet my dad." She stuck her hand in his and led him out the door.

In the hallway, they nearly ran over Naomi. Her eyes were red and watery. "What's going on?" she asked, though if her teary eyes were any indication, she'd been eavesdropping.

"We're going to meet my dad," Gracie said, still clutching his hand as though it gave her courage.

"All right, then." Smiling, she grabbed his other hand and held it all the way out to the porch.

Chapter Sixteen

She should be happy. Considering Naomi hadn't thought they'd even get Gracie to come to dinner, she should be glad things were going so well between Mark and her daughter. *Their* daughter. So why did her eyes tear up every time she looked at the two of them?

"He's really good with her," Jessa said quietly, coming up behind her. They were in the kitchen getting dessert set out.

"He is." From across the room, she watched the two of them chat at the dinner table. Gracie was telling Mark about her Cinderella performance and all of the men at the table were *ooh*ing and *aah*ing over her theatrical details.

Lucas sat across from Gracie, and Naomi couldn't help but notice that her daughter seemed to pay him special attention, as though they had a bond. And they did. When she'd stood outside that room listening to the two of them talk, it had hit her that they had something in common she could never understand. She hadn't even known about the owl that was now stuffed into the pocket of his shirt.

"Gracie sure seems enamored with Lucas all of a sudden," Jessa commented with an airy nonchalance.

"Yeah." She sighed, unable to take her eyes off the man so she could focus on cutting the pie.

"Almost as enamored as someone else," her friend murmured, sliding the pie away and cutting it herself.

"You should've heard him talking to her, Jess," she whispered. "He was perfect. So empathetic. He knew exactly what to say."

"So remind me again why it won't work with you two." Her friend started to dish generous slices of pie onto delicate china plates.

She had to remind herself, too. "I can't add more change to Gracie's life right now." She picked up the ice cream scoop and plopped oversized helpings right on top of the pie slices. "And I have to protect her." That was why she'd never dated anyone seriously, why she'd never brought a man home. "What if Gracie got attached to him and things didn't work out?"

Jessa turned to her, those expressive brown eyes calling her out. "Are you sure it's Gracie you're worried about?"

The question silenced her. No. She wasn't sure. Not at all.

"Your life will likely look different in a year," her friend reminded her. "I know it won't happen now, but eventually Gracie might want to go visit Mark on the weekends. And she might want to spend a couple of weeks with him in the summer."

An itch scraped at the back of Naomi's throat, but she cleared the sadness away. Jessa was right. Gracie would want to know her father. She'd want to know her half-brother.

Jessa took the ice cream scoop out of her hand and finished filling everyone's plates. "You've put your life on hold for a long time, hon," she said gently. "But I'm not so sure you have to do that anymore. Gracie wouldn't want to be the reason you won't let yourself find happiness with Lucas."

"It's not that simple." Jessa made it sound like all you had to do was flip over a rock and there they would be—the dreams you'd buried a long time ago. A lifetime ago. "I was a different person when he loved me." She'd been more carefree and less stressed and skinnier and lighter and more fun. Now she was a mom, and she didn't know how to be that girl anymore.

Jessa took both of her hands in hers, squeezing them tightly. "Darlin', that man *still* loves you. Seems to me that's all that matters." She let her hands go and gathered up as many plates as she could carry. "Dessert's on!" she called, sashaying across the room.

Naomi followed, somehow balancing two plates in each hand. She served Gracie, then Mark, then Lucas, who laid a hand on the small of her back and said, "Thanks."

Such a simple touch, yet it reached all the way to her heart. "You're welcome," she murmured, setting the last plate at her spot. Somehow, she managed to get herself in the chair without stumbling.

"This was one amazing meal," Mark said, sawing his fork into the pie. "Seriously, everyone. Thanks for letting me share it with you."

"Of course," Jessa said in her usual polite way.

Naomi thought she saw her kick Lance under the table.

He sat up straighter. "Yeah. Glad you could be here," he said as though his fiancée had made him rehearse ahead of time.

Luis, however, remained stonily silent, just as he had all through dinner. It would take more than polite talk for Mark to earn his way back into that man's good graces.

"How long are you staying, Dad?" Gracie asked.

Dad? The easy way she said it almost made Naomi drop her fork.

"Well..." He looked at Naomi as though summoning her approval. "I thought I'd stay through Tuesday, if that's okay with everyone. I took a few days off."

"Of course." Naomi forced out the words as she cut into her pie. Not that she'd be able to eat one damn bite.

"There's a concert in the park tomorrow night," he went on. "I'd love it if you two would join me."

"A concert! I love concerts in the park," Gracie squealed.

The rest of the room quieted and Naomi felt the weight of all of their stares. Especially Lucas's.

"Can we go, Mom?" Gracie pulled on her arm.

Easing out a breath, she dropped her hands into her lap, pinching them into fists. That was the only way she could keep them still. "Um, I don't think I'll be able to make it," she croaked out. She couldn't give Gracie the wrong idea. If the three of them spent time together, Gracie might read too much into it. She might think there was a chance they'd end up together...

"Lance and I were planning to go," Jessa piped up.

Her fiancé's jaw dropped. "Wha—?"

"Maybe we can sit together," she offered before Lance could ask too many questions.

Naomi cast her a grateful look. Jessa would drag Lance to the concert and they'd keep an eye on Gracie for her.

"So I can go, Mom? I can go with Dad?" Gracie asked, a smear of berry pie on her chin.

"You can go," she managed, pinching her hands harder.

"Great. That's great." Mark's eyes crinkled with gratitude. "We'll be gone two hours, tops," he promised. "I'll pick her up at six thirty and have her back by eight thirty."

"That sounds fine." As long as Jessa and Lance were there to keep an eye on her. Underneath the table, Lucas's boot brushed her foot lightly, just a small, slight touch as though he knew she needed it.

The conversation then veered into talk of the stock operation—mainly about Reckoning II. Mark asked questions and Lance even invited him to take a look at the bull after they all finished their pie. Naomi shoved in a few bites, just to keep up appearances, then she quickly stood and stacked the empty plates. The conversation didn't seem to lull as she rinsed them and filled the dishwasher. Needing a few seconds of quiet, cold space, she slipped out onto the back patio.

The sun had already set, leaving behind only the watery cerulean marks of the day. A cool breeze washed over her, fanning her hair and purging the anxious perspiration from her skin. Jessa was right. Her life could look so different in a year. And what would she have if Gracie started to spend more time with Mark and his family? She'd have the inn. But no one to share it with…

The creaking of the back door forced her eyes closed. She didn't have to turn around. Lucas's presence always managed to overpower her.

For a few moments she simply tried to breathe, but the fast pounding of her heart weakened her lungs. There was no meditative breathing when Lucas Cortez was around.

"I'm proud of you," he finally said in that ruggedly low tenor. "That couldn't have been easy."

"It hurt like hell," she admitted, turning to face him. She expected him to say something else, but he didn't. Instead he simply opened his arms, making a place for her as though he knew she simply needed to be held.

She wobbled into his embrace and his arms closed around her, shutting out the rest of the world—all the hard stuff, the ugly stuff. He was warmth and strength and peace, but fire, too. All-consuming. And her body fit so perfectly against his, sinking into his powerful chest. "I need you to remind me who I am," she uttered, knowing he wouldn't think she sounded crazy. He'd known that brave, sure girl who didn't shy away from risks. "I think maybe I've forgotten."

"That's okay," Lucas said, leaning down to kiss her lips. "Because I remember." And when his mouth moved over hers in that seductive rhythm, she knew he could help her remember, too.

* * *

Lucas believed in volunteerism. Ever since he'd gotten out of prison, he'd done his best to "contribute to society" and "focus on the greater good." Those phrases had been a part of his early release agreement, but he liked doing so, too. For a while he'd volunteered at a homeless shelter down in Pueblo. And while he'd had a shitty couple of years, they were nothing compared to what those men and women were facing. Compared to living on the streets, prison had been like a hotel—free meals, shelter. Hell, they even got to lift in a gym. Sitting across the table from a homeless man who'd lost all of his teeth from malnutrition only proved that things could always be worse. It'd given him a different perspective, made him appreciate what he'd managed to build after walking out of his cell. A lot of his comrades had ended up back in the cycle, then eventually like the man with no teeth.

While he'd *had* to volunteer, it really did make him feel like he was part of something bigger, something more important.

But today, his volunteerism definitely had ulterior motives. Mo*tive*, he should say. And her name was Naomi. He hadn't seen much of her since Mark had come for dinner. They were both busy—he got that—but it seemed she was still avoiding him. The next time he saw her, he wanted to talk through the future, tell her he was committed to being here. It'd sure help if Bill McGowen would get back to him so he could officially resign.

Lucas sliced the whirring chain saw through a small ten-foot tree that'd been riddled with pine beetles. Those damn bugs had killed a fourth of the trees in this forest, leaving behind empty, blackened shells. All it would take was one spark and those trees would become instant torches, shooting flames fifty feet into the air.

The tree fell easily, collapsing in a heap of dead wood and dust. Lucas moved down the trunk, slicing it into sections like a tenderloin, then stacking the logs neatly in a pile.

The town had been sending in other teams to collect the fallen wood and store it out on the edge of City Park, planning to offer it free to families who needed extra help heating their homes when winter came. The cutting crew had gotten up here about six o'clock that morning, and Lucas had silently joined them. Both Lance and Levi had had plans for the day, so he was on his own. So far, he'd managed to avoid any trouble, but he'd seen Marshal Dobbins farther up the mountain twenty minutes ago and he figured he wouldn't be able to avoid him forever.

In fact, it might be time to get the confrontation over with. Something told him Dobbins was fueling the town's anger against him. He wouldn't be shocked if Marshal was the one who'd vandalized his truck. But they weren't in high school anymore, and it was high time he stopped acting like it.

Lucas worked his way up the slope, sawing through the small dead trees he could take care of by himself, then stopped to glug some of the water he'd thrown in his backpack earlier.

As he leaned against a tree stump, footsteps thrashed through the brush behind him. He turned.

Marshal Dobbins was hiking down the slope, dragging his chain saw behind him.

"Hey," Lucas said, standing upright. "Tough work up here today, huh?" He figured it didn't hurt to try and make conversation.

Dobbins stopped, his glare darker than a black hole. "What the hell are you doing here?"

"Same thing you are," he said before casually taking another sip of water. What else would he be doing out here with a chain saw? Marshal had never been the sharpest tool in the shed.

The man stomped down the hill until he stood across from him. The years seemed to have worn down his face. His brown eyes were bloodshot and miserable. "When are you gonna figure it out, Cortez? You're not wanted here."

There were plenty of people who'd argue that. "I grew up here," he reminded him. "My family's here." The woman he loved was here. And she seemed to like the idea of him sticking around when he'd mentioned it, albeit briefly. Which meant no one would drive him away. Especially not Marshal

Dobbins. "Actually, I'm thinking about moving back." So Marshal might as well get used to seeing him around.

"And why would you want to do that when everyone in town thinks you belong in prison?" the man asked, his face a mask of hatred.

"Already served my time." Lucas didn't look away. He'd even written the Dobbins family an apology, though he hadn't committed the crime. "It's time to put the past behind us. Don't you think?" Moving on didn't seem to be Marshal's specialty. He was pretty sure the man had worn that same Metallica shirt in high school.

"No one wants you around. Understand?" Dobbins stepped up to Lucas, raising his shoulders as though trying to intimidate him.

It was all Lucas could do not to laugh.

"No one wants a felon hanging around Topaz Falls."

"Guess it's not your decision." It wasn't like Marshal was revered in town or anything. He owned the auto body shop and was the best mechanic in a fifty-mile radius, so people had to put up with him, but Lucas wouldn't say he was well-liked. "I've already done my time. I've apologized to your family. What else do you want from me?"

The man's face was strangely expressionless. "I want you gone." His grip tightened on the chain saw he held in his hand. Instead of making him look intimidating, the whole thing was starting to border on pathetic.

"Like I said, not your decision." He went to walk away. Obviously, Dobbins wasn't going to let it go, which meant Lucas wasn't going to waste any more time apologizing.

"You know my dad's dead?" Marshal barked after him. "He lost everything because of what you did."

He turned back to Marshal. The fallout from the fire

hadn't caused all of George Dobbins's issues. He'd had a gambling problem to go along with his drinking problem ever since Lucas could remember. "I'm sorry about your dad." He was. Genuinely. "But it's not my fault he left. And I already paid for my crime." For Levi's crime. He'd given up the girl he loved, abandoned her for too many years. And he was done. He was done doing penance for something that had already been paid for. He was done worrying about how people saw him. He was done sacrificing time with Naomi. And he planned to prove it to her tonight.

"I swear to God you're gonna regret coming back, Cortez."

Lucas didn't even acknowledge him. Instead, he picked up his chain saw and walked away. Kept right on walking down the slope. In a clearing below, he caught sight of Dev stacking wood. Just the person he wanted to see.

"Hey there," Dev said as Lucas approached. He wiped his forehead with a bandana. It might have only been eight o'clock in the morning, but the temperature was already rising. "It's good to see you out here, Cortez."

"Not everyone thinks so." Lucas checked over his shoulder but Dobbins had disappeared into the trees. "What's up with Marshal?"

"He's been in a bad mood for months now." The deputy seemed to shrug it off. "Heard he and Jen are separated. Sounds pretty bad. Besides that, the man knows how to hold a grudge. I wouldn't worry about it too much. People in town don't exactly listen to Marshal Dobbins."

"That's good to hear." He dropped the chain saw so he could give Dev a hand with the pile of logs. "'Cause I'm thinking about sticking around a while."

"Yeah?" Dev looked surprised. "I thought you were some big rock star down at the McGowen place."

"Thinking about making a change. Lance needs some help getting his operation going." He peered over to gauge Dev's reaction. The man didn't seem to think it was a bad idea at all.

"It'd be great to have you back," he said. "From what I hear, your family could use the help. It's a competitive business. You seem to have a good handle on it."

"I like to think so." He'd been studying it for seven years. Considering he'd had nothing else in his life, he bordered on being a workaholic. Something told him he'd find a better work and life balance in Topaz Falls. Though he'd definitely have other challenges. "So do you have any leads on who might've messed up my truck?" he asked, stacking another log.

"Nothing conclusive." Dev shot him a dry smile. "Though I have some suspicions."

Yeah. He wasn't the only one. "Have you asked Dobbins?"

"He's the first person I talked to." Dev dropped another log onto the stack with a grunt. "He was shocked. Knew nothing about it." The man had always excelled in the art of sarcasm.

"Of course not." Didn't appear that he had to tell Dev he was ninety-nine percent sure Marshal had slashed his tires. Other folks in town might not take too kindly to him, but in his estimation few were as vindictive as Dobbins.

"I've got my eye on him," Dev said. "Don't worry. I'm on your side in this thing."

"That means a lot." If he had Dev on his side, he had a better chance at winning over everyone else, too.

Chapter Seventeen

It'd been a while since he'd pulled a twelve-hour day, but he hadn't had this much to work for, either. Lucas tipped up his hat and wiped away the sweat caked on his forehead. He'd watched the sun rise over those mountains this morning while he was training Reckoning II. After the brief fire mitigation stint, he'd gone right back to the corral, and now, at five o'clock in the evening, he was ready to call it a day. "You're not exactly my first choice for a date tonight," he informed the bull, tightening the strap that held the remote dummy in place. But that was okay. He'd put in a few more hours of training, then he had plans that involved sweeping a certain single mom off her feet.

Reckoning II stomped and swayed listlessly, already trying to throw the dummy, even though Lucas hadn't opened up the chute yet.

"Atta boy." The desire to throw a rider had to be innate

for a bull, and Reckoning here seemed to have it. After letting the agitation build for a few minutes, he threw open the chute and Reckoning tore into the corral snorting and tossing his head while he launched his hind end into the air. Lucas walked along the fence watching carefully, his finger over the button that would eject the dummy rider. But he couldn't reward the bull and launch the thing until Reckoning put up a serious fight.

"That's it," he called as Reckoning jerked his back end into a spin. The bull lunged and turned and twisted its body, all the while catching some serious air. Reckoning's back arched, sending him flying even higher, and Lucas hit the trigger.

Instantly, the thirty-pound dummy was released and went sprawling into the dirt.

Snorting an insult the dummy's direction, Reckoning bucked a few more times then settled.

Lucas glanced at his watch. "Damn. You had that thing off in three seconds. Not bad. Not bad at—"

A truck rolled up the gravel drive and parked next to the fence.

Well, shit. The only person he knew who drove a F-350 XL diesel super cab was Bill McGowen. Sure enough, the man himself climbed out of the cab. Seemed he couldn't manage a phone call, but he could easily ambush Lucas with a visit. That was definitely more McGowen's style. Lucas should've anticipated it.

Bracing himself, he left Reckoning behind and strode over to meet Bill. This would be a fun conversation…

"That's my bull," the man said as he approached the fence. Much like Reckoning, McGowen was a behemoth: at least six-three and as wide as a linebacker, which was why he'd never been a bull rider himself. He was too bulky. Too genteel also, as showcased by his black jeans, white starched shirt, sterling silver bolo tie, and shiny cowboy boots.

Lucas looked the man square in the face. McGowen was in his early sixties but he could've easily passed for fifty. His face was hard, his dull gray eyes iced over.

Lucas ducked under the fence so they could do this face to face. "Actually this here is Lance's bull," he said evenly. "He paid a steep price, too." Likely more than McGowen would've had to pay, but if today's training was any indication, it would be worth it.

McGowen glared past him at the bull, but he said nothing.

Which meant it was up to Lucas to break the ice. "I've been trying to call," he said, snagging Bill's attention back to him.

"So I've heard." The man made no excuses for not calling back. He never made excuses for anything. He was always straightforward and direct. Which meant they'd best get on with this.

"I appreciate everything you've done for me." If only that didn't sound so trivial. "And I don't take it for granted. But it's time for me to step up and help my family. So you can consider this my official notice."

McGowen didn't flinch. He simply gazed down at Lucas as though completely unfazed. "You remember what I asked you when I hired you?"

God, that was so long ago. He didn't remember much about that time. It was all a blur. Walking out of prison, trying to figure out where to go and what to do next. "No," he admitted. He'd just been relieved to find a job.

"I asked why you didn't go on home. Be with your dad and brothers. You remember what you said?"

The question brought it all back. "That I had nothing to go back to."

"And that no one would want you back," Bill reminded him. "Has that changed? People in this town welcomed you back?"

Lucas didn't answer. He was still working on that.

"Here's the thing, Cortez," McGowen said, all business. "I'm lookin' to cut back my time some. The wife wants trips and weeks with the grandkids and shit like that."

He tamed a smile. That was about as much sentimentality as he'd ever heard come out of the man's mouth.

"So I need someone to take the reins," Bill went on. "Someone good. Someone I trust. Someone who's proven himself." He paused as though he wanted to let that sink in.

But Lucas was having a hard time believing it. He couldn't be serious. "I just helped my brother swipe a bull right out from under you and you want me to take over your entire operation?"

"You know I don't need Reckoning." His boss's mouth fumbled between a grin and smirk. "If I'd needed him, you wouldn't have helped Lance get him. You're too loyal for that."

It was true. If he'd thought it would've hurt Bill's operation, he never would've gone after the bull for Lance.

"I need that loyalty." McGowen stepped closer and clapped him on the shoulder like they were old friends. "You're smart. You've got a good eye. And I taught you everything you know."

In other words, Bill felt he'd earned Lucas's loyalty.

"This is one hell of an opportunity," the man added. "You can name your price. I'll double your salary if you want."

"Wow." He was too stunned to say anything else. This

kind of opportunity was beyond anything he'd ever dreamed for himself when he'd walked out of that prison cell. He'd thought he'd be a day laborer for the rest of his life. Bill was right. It was a hell of an opportunity. But if he took it, he'd have to live on the ranch. And he'd be on the road half the year, easy. That wasn't the life he'd started to envision for Naomi and Gracie and him. Their lives were here and if he wanted to be with them, he'd have to stay, too. "Sorry." He shook his head. "It's a generous offer, but I can't take it. I'm planning to build a life here." He was committed to it, to doing the tough work of atoning for his mistakes.

McGowen nodded as though that was what he'd expected to hear. "Offer's open for a while. Don't answer now. Take your time. Think about it," he said as though confident Lucas would change his mind.

When Bill McGowen wanted something, he rarely took no for an answer.

* * *

"Okay, honey." Naomi stooped in front of Gracie, swallowing back yet another round of threatening tears. "You remember to listen good. And if you need anything—anything at all—Jessa and Lance will be right nearby."

"I *know*, Mom," the girl said as though she'd gotten tired of hearing it. "You've told me five times."

"I can't help it." Naomi rose, peeking out the window next to the door. Mark stood on the porch waiting. They'd talked a lot while Gracie was getting ready to go to the concert. He'd told her he didn't intend to take over. He was happy to come up to Topaz Falls and visit Gracie for a day here and there while they built a relationship.

But God, a *relationship*. That was the word that made all of this real. It wasn't like this would be the first time her daughter had been out of her sight, but it felt so different. She wouldn't be at one of her friend's houses. She'd be out building a relationship with another parent.

"You have to prepare yourself to give up some control," Colton had told her when they'd driven back to Topaz Falls after she'd met Mark. And wasn't control always the hardest thing to give up? For ten years, no one else had had any say in Gracie's life except for her. But that wouldn't be the case anymore. She might make most of the day-to-day decisions, but a relationship with her dad meant Gracie would have another voice speaking into her life.

"Mom..." Her daughter tugged on her hand. "Are *you* gonna be okay?"

"Of course." Naomi forced a confident smile. "I have a ton to do around here. And I know you'll be in good hands." Especially with her spies out on assignment. "You have a great time, Gracie girl. Don't worry about me." She pulled her daughter into a tight hug. "I'll see you in a couple of hours." Which should be nothing. The girl was in day camp six hours a day all summer long. Naomi could survive two hours. She shook her head at herself and opened the door to walk Gracie out onto the porch.

Mark always looked nice. A lot more preppy in those khakis and a blue polo shirt than he'd ever dressed in high school, but she guessed that's what happened when you moved to the suburbs.

"Ready?" he asked Gracie.

"Ready!" She bounded down the steps, but Mark hung back.

He gave Naomi a sympathetic look, like he understood

how hard this was for her. "You sure you don't want to come?"

She almost said yes. But that wouldn't be fair to any of them. Mark had rights. He had the right to get to know his daughter without her hovering. "I can't," she said apologetically. "I have a lot to do around here tonight." It wasn't a lie. She had to go over the budget for the inn and look into getting some marketing started in various publications.

"All right, then." He gave her a friendly smile. "I'll have her home by eight thirty. No later."

"Perfect." She walked him down the steps and watched as the two of them climbed into his very nice, very safe-looking Volvo SUV.

The house felt lonelier and quieter than it ever had. Bogart seemed to think so, too. The second Gracie left, he became Naomi's shadow, following so closely she almost stepped on him. "It's okay, Bogy," she said, trying to convince herself, too. "She'll be back soon." But the minutes seemed to crawl by as she turned on some Carrie Underwood and finished up the dinner dishes.

After she'd put the last one in the dishwasher, she looked at the clock. It hadn't even been ten minutes since Gracie had left.

This was going to be the longest two hours of her life.

In search of a longer distraction, she dug through the messenger bag where she'd stuffed all of the papers for the inn—the estimates and the permits and the lengthy to-do lists. But they seemed just as disordered as her mind. Pulling out a stool, she sorted them into piles. She needed to develop a filling system—

The doorbell rang and cut off all of her thoughts about organization. Which was fine with her because she wasn't in the mood to focus on business anyway. Shoving the mess of papers aside, she stood and hurried through the living room.

On her way to the door, she caught sight of Lucas standing on the porch. That one quick flash of him sent hope and happiness brimming over. After he'd kissed her on Jessa's porch last night she'd figured she'd see him earlier today, but he hadn't been around. In an effort to run into him, she *may* have gone up to Lance and Jessa's house to borrow a cup of sugar, then four tablespoons of butter, then a half cup of milk. Jessa finally told her he was out on fire mitigation duty.

Now he was at her house…

She paused to quickly glance at herself in the mirror. Since she'd been stalking him all day, she'd dressed a little nicer—in shorts and a green cashmere camisole that matched her eyes. Just in case.

Smoothing down her hair, she lightly pinched her cheeks to plump them up. That would have to do. She didn't have time to run into her bedroom and find her lucky lipstick.

Bogart pawed at the door as though growing impatient. "All right, all right." She gently nudged the dog aside and opened the door.

"Hi." The word floated away from her as a rush of blood charged through her heart.

"Hey." Lucas always seemed to take his time looking at her. All of her. And judging from the raw hunger glistening in his eyes, he liked what he saw. "I thought maybe you could use some company tonight."

She could use more than company but she didn't want to sound desperate. "That'd be great," she said, stepping aside so he could come in.

He stayed put. "Actually, I thought we could go out."

"Out?" She tried not to look disappointed, but she'd

envisioned picking up where they'd left off on the couch the other night…

"I don't feel much like going to a restaurant or anything." And there wasn't much else to do in Topaz Falls. Minus the concert in the park.

"What I have in mind has nothing to do with food." God, that smile of his. It made every word that came out of his mouth seem dirty. Which was enough to pique her interest.

"What *did* you have in mind?" she asked, fingering the edge of her hair, hoping it hadn't started to frizz from the heat rising off her body.

"You'll see." He reached for her hand as if he were her own personal Aladdin, preparing to take her on a magic carpet ride. Except he wore a cowboy hat and sexy tight jeans. Okay, he was nothing like Aladdin. Though when she put her hand in his, she swore her insides sparkled.

Good lord, she watched too many Disney movies.

"Where are we going?" she asked as she shut the door behind her and they moved easily down the steps together.

"You'll see." He wore a mysterious grin while he helped her climb into his truck, brushing his hand against her ass—on purpose, she was pretty sure.

When he slid into the driver's seat and started the engine, she laid a hand on his arm. "I have to be back by eight fifteen. No, eight," she corrected. Just in case Gracie wanted to come home a little early. She had her cell phone securely in her back pocket, but she wanted to be home, too. Just in case.

"I know." Lucas patted her hand, then moved his to the steering wheel, guiding the truck down the winding drive.

The evening was hot but soft, too, the sun dimmed by the puffy cumulous clouds billowing overhead. They did that every night—built large white cottony mountains in the sky—but they never seemed to bring the rain the region so desperately needed.

"So Jessa said you were out all day. Cutting down trees and stuff." She noticed a deep gash in his forearm.

"Yeah. The situation's bad up there." He turned the truck out onto the highway. "We're making progress, though. It's hard work."

"It's so great of you to help." Considering he wasn't necessarily a full-time resident. "I'm sure everyone appreciates it."

"Not everyone, but most people." He glanced over at her. "Talked to Dev out there for a while. Told him I'm thinking of staying."

"What did he say?" She was almost afraid to ask. Ever since he'd told her he was going to try to stay, she'd guarded herself from holding onto him too tightly. He hadn't said he would stay for sure. He said he'd *try*.

"He thought it was great." His gaze found hers again before darting back to the highway. "What do *you* think?"

That had to be obvious. She was pretty sure her smile could've bridged the Pacific. It was much harder to guard herself when he sat right next to her. "I think it's great, too," she said, inching closer to him. If the damn console hadn't been in the way, she'd sit right next to him, like she used to, in his old truck. "Have you told Bill McGowen yet?"

Lucas's easy smile fell away. "We've talked." He turned the truck off onto a dirt road.

Naomi looked around. She hadn't even realized where they were going, but now she saw… "This is where I almost hit you." Right back there on the highway…

"Yeah. Won't be able to forget that anytime soon." He grinned and snuck a hand onto her thigh.

The sensation rolled all the way up her body, bringing a slow, burning throb. Any chance he was driving her to some secluded backwoods make-out spot? God, she hoped so. "Um...are we there yet?" she asked, ready to slide over into his lap.

"Just about." He drove up a rough switchback, then parked the truck next to the river.

She glanced around. It was a little open for making out, but hey, she wasn't picky. "So what are we doing?"

Cutting the engine, Lucas turned to her. "I'm taking you fly fishing," he said as though that was as fun as staying in the truck to make out.

"Fly fishing," she repeated. "Hmm. Well. Um..." How could she put this delicately? "That wasn't exactly what I had in mind." She added an insinuating bounce of her eyebrows so he wouldn't miss her meaning.

"Trust me. You'll love this," he murmured, leaning in to give her a long, heated kiss. So unfair! The man was such a tease.

"I liked *that*," she sighed. As far as she was concerned, they could stay in the truck for the next hour doing that exact same thing over and over and over...

"I liked it, too." His lips were still so close. "But once that starts, I'm not gonna want to stop this time."

"That's okay," she whispered. That was *really* okay.

"Except we only have..." He glanced at his watch. "Forty-five minutes."

"Plenty of time." Heck, he'd already started some serious foreplay...

He traced his finger down her cheek. "Not nearly enough

time for what I want to do to you." His gaze dropped to the low-cut neckline of her camisole. "We have years to make up for, Naomi. That's going to take *hours*." He made that word sound so fun...

"And it's not gonna happen in my pickup," he added. "We're not in high school anymore, baby."

And yet he made her feel like that girl again. The same one who'd chased adventure, who'd feared nothing, who'd sneak off with him whenever she had the opportunity.

"We only did it in your truck once," she reminded him. "And it wasn't half bad." They'd pulled over on an old jeep road halfway up Topaz Mountain and started kissing. Even back then, he'd made her lose control faster than she knew was possible. In all of three minutes, she'd stripped her pants down, undid his zipper, and climbed right into his lap. By then he'd learned to carry condoms in his wallet.

The memory combined with his low laugh made her quake with the desire to do that again. Lose control. Let everything go except the sensation of his skin against hers...

"Come on." Lucas broke away from her and got out of the truck.

Pouting, she did the same. "I'm pretty sure I'm not going to like fly fishing as much as I liked having sex in your truck that day," she informed him.

"Good." He ruffled her hair. "I'd hope not." He pulled a backpack out of the truck bed and strapped it on, then gathered her against his side before leading her toward the river. "When I finally get your clothes off, once won't be enough. I won't want to take you home in time to be there when Gracie returns." They reached the river and he knelt to unpack the backpack—a fishing pole in three pieces, a tackle box and...*two* pairs of waders?

"Besides that, I figure there's a good chance she might call. Seeing as how this is her first time out with Mark and everything."

"You're right." She sighed. "I know you're right." And yet she also knew she couldn't wait much longer. She'd already waited too long.

Lucas screwed the pole together, then laid it carefully on the ground. "Trust me. Fly fishing is definitely the next best thing," he teased. "I haven't dated much since I got out of prison."

For the life of her, she couldn't figure out why. He likely could've had any woman he aimed those charismatic hazel eyes at. Though she couldn't say she was disappointed to hear he hadn't been with many other women. She hadn't been with many other men after Mark left, either. It seemed to level the playing field.

"So in the absence of good sex, this is what I learned to do for therapy," he said, focused on tying a fuzzy little fly to the end of the fishing line. "I come here to think. To find some peace."

She granted him a soft smile. "Then I'm glad you're sharing it with me." Since it meant something to him, she'd *try* to like it.

Especially if it helped her know him again.

Chapter Eighteen

Good thing she had those waders on. Lucas eyed Naomi. Waders made it a lot harder to get into her pants. A nice solid barrier, that's what he needed. *Damn.* He couldn't remember the last time he hadn't felt like fishing. But once Naomi had started talking about sex, he couldn't stop thinking about it.

"So these are real attractive," she said, pulling on the suspender straps.

They shouldn't have been. There shouldn't be anything sexy about brown rubber waders, but tonight they were quite the turn-on. "You could make a snowsuit look attractive," he complained, snatching up the fishing pole, then plodding over to where she stood on the riverbank.

She turned to face him, her hands seductively placed low on her hips. "You make it sound like you're having a hard time keeping your hands off of me."

"Oh, my hands will be all over you," he assured her. "I plan to make this lesson a *hands-on* learning experience."

Might not be as satisfying as a roll in the hay, but he'd still make sure to get plenty of touching in.

Naomi's fair skin turned a dangerous shade of red. She hadn't outgrown the blushing. He hooked an arm around her waist and urged her closer to the water. "Normally you'd have on big clunky boots along with those hot waders," he told her, shifting into teacher mode. "But this section of the river isn't too rocky. And I couldn't find any boots in your size."

"Okaaayyy..." She looked down at the neoprene booties connected to the waders.

"Those'll keep your feet nice and warm, and I'm gonna help you stay balanced in the current."

"Good luck with that," she said with a telltale smirk.

Yeah, he wasn't feeling particularly balanced either. But still, someone had to be the stable one.

Slipping behind her, he prodded her down the riverbank and helped her step into the water.

"Oh, wow." She shuffled her feet slowly, finding her footing, wading deeper. "The current's so much faster than it looks." Reaching back, she patted his body until her hand found his arm and held on.

"Once you get used to it you won't feel so off balance." He secured his arm around her waist as they moved deeper into the water. When it was up to their hips, he stopped her.

"Don't let go," she gasped, tightening her grip on his arm.

"I won't." Now that he had her body against his, it'd take a crowbar to pry his hands off her. "But I have to move a little, so I can hand you the fishing pole."

Her breathing deepened, but she nodded.

Shifting his weight, he secured the pole in her free hand,

showing her how to hold it with four fingers wrapped around the handle, her thumb on top and reel facing down, while he kept his body behind hers to hold her steady.

"The key to fly fishing is the motion." He clasped his hand over hers and kept his chest against her back. "It's all in the elbow. Not the wrist."

"Elbow. Okay. Got it."

He loved the solid confidence in her voice. She was so much braver and stronger than she realized. He would help her remember that. Maybe they'd help each other.

He lowered his lips to her ear. "Now, the most basic cast is the back cast." He started to pull out line to give them plenty to work with and waited until the current had dragged it out straight. Molding his arm over hers, he prompted her to accelerate the rod up and back in one smooth motion. "See how the line arcs when you pull back?" he asked low against her hair.

"Um. Mmm-hmm," she murmured, snuggling in closer to him.

Yeah, his heart was pounding pretty hard, too, having her body against his this way. He held up her arm as she gripped the pole. "You don't want to bring it back too far. Just past the point where it's vertical."

Naomi snuck a peek back at him and he took the opportunity to lay a sensual kiss on her lips.

"What technique is that?" she whispered.

"It's called hooking 'em," he told her seriously.

"Very effective." She turned to face the river again.

He inched closer to her so there was no space between their bodies. "When the line is straight behind you, bring the rod forward in a smooth, accelerating stroke." He demonstrated the motion so she could get the feel for it.

The line snapped over their heads and straightened, pitching the fly out to land on the water's surface before the rest of the line settled.

"Make sure the power in the cast comes from your bicep and shoulder," he instructed, giving that area of her body a nice suggestive caress.

She shot him a brassy look.

"Told you it'd be a hands-on lesson," he said with a grin. If he couldn't sleep with her tonight, at least he could still be all over her.

"I'm not complaining," she muttered. "You'll recall *I* didn't even want to get out of the truck."

He secured his arms around her waist and rested his chin on her shoulder. "But aren't you glad you did?"

Her face relaxed into a smile. "Yes, actually. I am."

"So am I." He kissed his way down her neck. Holy hell, she smelled so good. Like a tropical vacation—coconut and sunshine. The scent took him right to a secluded beach, making love while the waves crashed over them…

"I'm about to drop the pole," Naomi said in a panic.

He almost let her, but he'd had that pole custom-made. So he forced his lips away from her neck and secured his hand against hers again. Best find something else to focus on instead of picturing her in a string bikini. "Let's try casting again." He pulled back his forearm. "Maybe we'll actually catch something this time."

Naomi shuddered against him. "I hope not. I want nothing to do with a slimy fish."

"You'll love it. Trust me." He brought her arm back and jerked it forward, sending the line bowing into the sky before it struck the fly against the water's surface.

"It *is* kind of relaxing." Naomi smiled at him over her

shoulder. "The motion and the water and everything." She looked up through those long eyelashes. "And having you this close."

"Relaxing?" Having her this close didn't exactly make him feel relaxed. He felt ready to go. But they only had a few minutes until she'd wanted to leave to be back home. So instead of hauling her to the riverbank, they casted a few more times.

"You're sure the fish can see that tiny fly?" she asked skeptically.

"Oh, I'm sure. But fly fishing also takes a lot of patience."

"Not my strong suit."

"After a while, you lose yourself in the motion. It's almost like dancing, I guess." Not that he had much experience.

"Is that why you love it so much?"

"I love it because I can be alone." That didn't sound good. "I mean, it was kind of an escape for me. A place where my past didn't matter. No one judging me."

She let go of the rod, leaving it in his hand, and turned to him fully, reaching her arms up around his neck. "You know I don't, right? I'd never hold your past against you."

"I know." He let his concerns show on his face. "But that doesn't mean it would always be easy for you. If I stayed here." People might give her a hard time. He knew she could handle it, but what if things moved along with them and then people started giving Gracie a hard time?

"I don't care what people think." She stood on her tiptoes to kiss him. "They'll get over it."

"And if they don't?" he asked, already winded from one small peck on the lips. Their bodies generated so much power together. It was getting harder to fight it.

"It won't matter." Tears brightened her eyes. "I'd want to be with you anyway."

He'd waited eight agonizing months to hear her say those words. Eight months of watching her walk by without a glance, of holding his breath whenever he saw her so it wouldn't hurt that bad. Eight months of believing she'd really given up on him.

But she hadn't. And her forgiveness was the best gift he'd ever been given.

"Thank you." He leaned down to kiss her again, unable to fend off desire any longer.

Wrapping an arm around her waist, he hauled her to the riverbank.

He didn't want to fish anymore. He only wanted her.

* * *

They made it to the truck, leaving a trail behind—Lucas's boots, both pairs of waders. Naomi had no idea how they'd gotten them off. She was too busy clutching him and letting her hands wander all over him while they kissed to focus on the details. It was so freeing to tell him how badly she wanted him, to let herself fall without worrying that he would leave again. Every last barrier between them had been torn down, and she couldn't get enough of him.

He was just as insistent, cupping his hands around her backside and doing the most wonderful things in her mouth with his tongue. He pinned her against the truck and lowered his lips down her neck, sending her hands frantically grasping at his shirt.

"It's eight o'clock," he murmured against her skin. "We have to go."

"Right. Yes." She kissed his mouth, devouring him.

He pulled back. "You wanted to be home by now."

She tried to catch her breath. "I did?"

Smiling, he pulled her into a hug. "You did. You wanted to be home for Gracie."

"You're *sure* it's already eight?" she asked, smoothing her hands down his muscular shoulders.

He nodded with a sad frown.

"I guess we should go, then." She took his hands in hers, holding them tightly. "Thank you. For making the time pass so quickly. For getting my mind off everything else." It had made it so much easier. If she'd been at home, she would've sat there counting the minutes until Mark brought Gracie back.

"I'm happy to be your distraction." He opened the passenger's door for her and then hurried back to the riverbank, picking up all the gear they'd left behind.

She buckled herself in, unable to stop smiling. It'd been so long since she'd felt like this, so carefree, so full of hope. Although it seemed things hadn't exactly changed much since high school. "Funny, we still have a curfew," she commented when Lucas got into the truck.

Laughing, he started the engine and sped back down the dirt road. "And that we have to sneak around."

"Yeah. Sorry about that." But she'd never had a man spend the night. She'd never even kissed anyone in front of Gracie.

"It's okay." He caressed her thigh. "It makes it exciting."

"And frustrating." Because if she was truly free, she'd invite him to spend the night with her.

"It builds anticipation," Lucas said, eyeing her like he was picturing her naked.

That it did. He drove over the speed limit, and she loved

him for trying to make sure she made it home on time for her daughter.

When they came up the drive, Mark's car already sat in front of her house. He and Gracie were sitting on the porch.

"Uh-oh." Had something gone wrong? "Why would he have her back early?" The selfish person inside of her hoped Gracie hadn't had a good time, that she wouldn't want to go anywhere with him again.

"They look happy," Lucas said cautiously. "Maybe she's just tired."

"Right. Of course." That had to be it. They did seem happy, heads tilted together while they chatted and smiled.

Lucas parked on the road in front of the house and left the engine running.

"You're not coming in?" The question surprised her as much as it seemed to surprise him. But she didn't want him to go home. She wanted him to stay. To see Gracie. To sit with her awhile.

Relief seemed to well up in his eyes. "I'd love to come in." They both got out of the truck and walked across the lawn together.

"Mom!" Gracie came sprinting over. "Where were you guys?" she demanded, as though she'd been worried.

The panic on her daughter's face flustered her.

"Sorry," Lucas said before she could think up a response. "It was my fault. I took your mom fly fishing."

"Fishing?" Gracie repeated, horrified. "Did you *touch* a fish?"

Naomi laughed. "Nope. We didn't catch anything." They hadn't exactly had time to, what with all the touching and making out…

"Not even a bite," Lucas said, exaggerating a distraught

expression that made her heart melt and her daughter giggle.

Mark walked over and joined them. "Sorry I brought her back so early. I wanted to make sure we weren't late. And I thought you might be missing her."

"Don't apologize." Naomi squeezed her daughter into a hug. "I didn't think we'd be gone so long. And I was definitely missing her." Though it hadn't been as painful as she'd thought it would be, thanks to Lucas.

"Next time I'll call." Mark gave Lucas some bro-code look.

Lucas smiled in that laid-back way of his, but Naomi's cheeks flamed.

"Guess what, Mom?" Gracie tugged on her hand. "Dad has a swimming pool at his house."

"Oh. Wow." She raised her eyes to Mark's. Why would he have told her that? Had he been trying to entice Gracie to visit him in Denver?

"Gracie asked a lot questions about my life," he explained quickly, as though he'd picked up on her uneasiness.

"I want to go there, Mom! I want go to Dad's house and I want to meet my brother and I want to swim in the pool!" She gazed at Mark with a grin. "Dad said I could! He said I could visit whenever I want!"

All of the warmth and delicate feelings of contentment spilled out of her, leaving a cold, empty blackness.

"Can I go? Pleeeeaaaasssse?" her daughter begged.

"No." Naomi gaped at Mark. "God. You can't go to Denver..."

"I'm sorry," Mark said quietly. "I was just trying to answer her questions."

"You told me it was up to me." Gracie posted her hands

on her hips in outrage. "You said I could choose if I wanted to see him. And I do! I want to see the swimming pool!"

"Gracie..." Naomi struggled to find her voice. "Honey, we'll talk about this later."

"But—"

"Hey, Gracie..." Giving Naomi's hand a quick squeeze, Lucas knelt in front of her daughter. "Do you wanna see all of my fishing stuff?"

The girl shrugged as though she was still put out. "Okay. But I don't want to touch a fish. I *never* want to touch a fish."

"Lucky for you we didn't catch one," Lucas reminded her while the two of them walked away.

As soon as they were out of earshot, Naomi turned to face Mark. "How could you do this?"

"What was I supposed to do?" he shot back. "Not answer any of her questions? Not tell her anything about myself?" His eyes softened. "She's my daughter, Naomi. She wants to know who I am."

"Well, you could've left out the swimming pool." Gracie loved to swim. This was exactly what she'd been worried about. That Mark would show up and become Disneyland Dad—the fun one who made sure he got the perks of parenting with none of the responsibilities. He'd charm his daughter and buy her things and then someday when she was a teenager and angry with her mother for grounding her when she broke curfew, Gracie would choose him. She'd want to go live with her dad.

Mark stepped closer, an arm outstretched as though he wanted to calm her. "I know how hard this is for you."

"No. You don't." The tears burning in her eyes only made her angrier. "She's all I've had for ten years." And Naomi wasn't about to give her up that easily. "You said this would be on my terms. Going to Denver was never part of the deal."

"You're right." He sighed. "I'm sorry. I should've been more discerning in what I said to her."

"Yes, you should've." She breathed deeply, trying to regain control over her emotions, but that damn ache in her heart…

"I'll talk to her. Tell her the timing's not right yet," Mark promised. "But I'd like to come back next weekend, if that's okay with you." Fear weighted his words as though he worried she wouldn't give him another chance.

But she had to. Gracie had obviously had a good time with him. He'd taken care of her, had her back early. And he was right. He had to tell her things about his life in order for his daughter to get to know him. He was her father, whether Naomi liked it or not. The mass of anger that had tightened her stomach broke apart. "Of course you can come up. You can spend as much time as you want with her here." So she'd be close by if Gracie needed anything. So they could both continue to learn more about him.

"Thank you." Mark reached over to squeeze her hand. The warmth of the gesture wiped out the rest of her animosity toward him. He'd obviously changed as much as she had over the years.

"Maybe I could take her on a hike up to the falls Saturday," he suggested. "I always loved doing that as a kid, and I haven't been up there in years."

Gracie loved it, too. They made it up there about once a month in the summer. It was an easy four miles round trip.

"I could bring a picnic lunch. I'd have her back in the afternoon." His gaze was still unsure as he looked at Naomi. "You can come, too, if you'd like."

"That's okay. I don't want her to get the wrong idea about you and me." Especially with him being married and everything.

"I get it." Mark glanced at Gracie, who was practicing a cast with Lucas's fishing pole. His smile spoke for him. He may have missed out on years of her childhood, but he was already crazy about her.

Naomi smiled, too. Who wouldn't be?

Mark turned to her. "You think she'd want to go on a hike? With me?"

"I bet she would." She started making a mental list of potential spies she could send this time. Cassidy? She loved to mountain bike. Maybe she could send her up the trail...

"Great. That's great." Mark looked over at their daughter again, joy beaming from his face.

Guilt fell on her shoulders. She was being ridiculous. Since he'd come back into their lives, Mark had done everything right. And like Colton had said, she had to learn to give up some control. Gracie wasn't five anymore. "It's a plan, then," she said, beating down the pain with another smile.

"Thank you." The words were feeble, as if he knew they weren't enough. "I know this isn't easy."

"It's not easy for any of us," she acknowledged. He didn't have a guidebook for this, either, for how to reunite with his daughter after ten years. "But we'll figure it out as we go. Gracie's well-being always has to be the priority." She said it to remind herself, too. If only she could shut off her own emotions.

Mark nodded. "I'd like to make it as easy on her as possible. And on you, too," he added.

She didn't bother telling him it would never be easy. It would likely hurt every time she sent Gracie off with him.

But she'd do it, and she'd never let her daughter see how hard it was.

Wrapped in an easy silence, the two of them walked over to where Gracie was fussing over Lucas's fishing gear.

"I have to get going," Mark told their daughter. "Denver won't work out quite yet, but I'd like to come and see you next weekend. Maybe we could hike up to the falls?"

"I love the falls!" She hugged him as if she'd known him her whole life. "Thanks for the ice cream. And the concert. You're really nice and I'm glad you came."

Naomi thought she saw tears in Mark's eyes. "So are you," he said, hugging her back. "I'll see you next week, then." He shook hands with Lucas before getting in his car to leave.

After his car disappeared down the drive, Gracie attached herself to the fine cowboy standing next to Naomi. "Do you wanna watch *The Little Mermaid*? Can we, Mom?"

"I'd love to." Lucas glanced at Naomi as though waiting for confirmation.

Like she'd say no to spending more time with him. After that little scene, she could use his steadying presence. "Of course we can."

"Sweet!" Her daughter took both of their hands and led the way back to the house.

When they were all comfortable on the couch, with Bogart snuggled between Gracie and Lucas, her daughter turned to him. "Do you *like* my mom?"

If the question caught him off guard, he didn't let on. "I've always *liked* your mom," he said, as though it was a simple fact.

Naomi subtly brushed her hand across his thigh. She *liked* him, too. A whole lot.

Skepticism scrunched Gracie's face. She got the same

look whenever Naomi tried to convince her vegetables were delicious. "How come you were gone for such a long time, then?"

He glanced at Naomi. A warning flared inside of her. He was asking a silent question. Should he tell Gracie where he'd been? She shook her head.

Lucas turned back to Gracie. "I had to go away for a while."

"Where did you go?" she demanded.

"Away," Naomi said, before he could answer. "He just had to go away. But now he's back. And he's not going away again."

Lucas studied her, but said nothing. She reached for his hand and took it in hers as the movie started. She'd explain it to him later. He didn't understand. Kids could be so black and white. And she didn't want Gracie to think anything terrible about him before she could explain things, before she could make her understand that he was a safe, wonderful man.

The movie started with a chorus of dramatic music. Gracie gave her usual running commentary, but after twenty minutes, she seemed to run out of steam. She fell asleep with her head on Lucas's shoulder.

Naomi shut off the movie.

Carefully, Lucas shifted and pulled Gracie into his arms. She stirred, looked up at him, and gave a sleepy smile before drifting off again. Silently, he carried her to her room and laid her on her bed. Naomi slipped off her shoes and covered her with the blanket.

"I should go," Lucas said once they were back in the hallway.

He didn't give her a chance to answer before heading for

the front porch. She followed him, quietly closing the door behind them.

"We'll have to tell her I was in prison eventually." His eyes lowered as though he didn't want to any more than she did.

"I know. But I want her to know you first. There's so much she won't understand." In Gracie's world, only bad guys went to jail. "Right now she doesn't need to know." She only needed to know that Lucas was good. So, so, so good. Naomi wrapped herself into him, pressing her body to his. "I don't want you to go."

"But you don't want me to stay, either," he reminded her, running his hands down her back.

The touch made her seriously reconsider her "no men in the house overnight" policy. But what if Gracie woke in the middle of the night? What if they overslept and she found Lucas in Naomi's bed the next morning? A sigh drained the air from her lungs. "We'll find a way to be alone soon." Maybe during the day while Gracie was at camp...

"I'll hold you to that promise." He leaned down and kissed her deeply, spreading that throbbing sensation through her body again. Then his hands fell away from her and he pulled back. "I'd better go before I can't."

Aching, she watched him leave.

Chapter Nineteen

Lucas must've stood at the end of Naomi's driveway for a good five minutes trying to pull back the reins on his body. He wanted Naomi with an intensity that was getting harder to control, but he knew he damn well better learn to control it because the woman had a ten-year-old daughter, which meant he couldn't haul her back into the house, strip off her clothes, and do what he'd been waiting a long time to do.

With a last look at the brightly lit living room window, Lucas trudged toward Lance's place, fully aware that was also a risky prospect. He might interrupt something between Lance and Jessa, but tonight he was willing to risk it. He was too buzzed to head back to Dad's place. Especially alone.

Gravel crunched under his solitary footsteps—a lonely serenade for the trek up the road. Evenings in the mountains were so still. Heavy and dark. Perfect for reflecting on all the ways things had gotten fucked up over the years. Damn the time that had passed, the things that had changed.

For the first time, he let himself consider what his life might be like if he hadn't covered for Levi. He wouldn't have completely lost three years. He wouldn't have had to start over. He'd likely be in that house right there down at the end of the road holding the only woman he'd ever loved while they made good use of *their* bed.

Instead, he was walking on a gravel road. Alone.

"I don't regret it." He had to say it out loud, to hear it. The truth was, he *couldn't* let himself regret it because that would mean his sacrifice had been a waste, that it was all for nothing, and that just might break him.

Like always, he did his best to stifle the uncertainties as he hiked up the porch steps and strode through Lance's front door. It wasn't locked, which meant his brother and Jessa were likely decent.

But instead of finding Jessa inside, he found his two brothers hanging out at the kitchen table drinking a beer.

"You look like someone pissed in your punch." Levi hopped up and hurried to the refrigerator to retrieve another beer.

He didn't take the bait. "Where's Jessa?" he asked Lance, taking the seat next to him.

"Evening call," his brother whined. "Some lost ferret wandering down Main Street. Then she's headed to Naomi's for"—he made quotation marks with his fingers—"an emergency book club meeting. Which means I won't get laid tonight."

Lucas tried to keep his expression even but he must've winced, because Levi whapped him on his way back to his seat. "Why aren't *you* getting laid right now? Didn't you take Naomi out? You've got time before all of those women show up at her house."

"I took her fishing. And I'm not trying to get laid," he informed him. "Unlike you, some of us actually think of it as more than that."

"If that's the case, why didn't you stay at her place for a while?" his younger brother teased.

"Because she has Gracie." And he completely supported her decision to spare her daughter the questions of what Naomi and he were up to. Didn't need to have that conversation with a ten-year-old.

"I'll babysit the kid," Levi offered. "Give you two some alone time."

Lance and Lucas shared a look. There were so many things their younger brother didn't seem to understand about relationships. Understandable, given he'd never actually had one. "It's not that simple." Things had been simple when they were sixteen. But now...

She had a daughter. And he had a history. Naomi might insist his past was no big deal, but the panicked look on her face when her daughter had asked where he'd been all these years proved she didn't want Gracie to know. And he got it. Prison time wasn't an easy thing to explain to other adults, let alone to a child. Gracie would see him differently, just like everyone else did.

"A relationship with Naomi means a relationship with Gracie." He eyed his brother. God help the woman *he* fell in love with. Wouldn't be easy to break a wild stallion. "And I've got work to do on that front. She doesn't even want Gracie to know I was in prison. Not yet. And I don't blame her."

Levi's cheeks hollowed with a hard look. "That's bullshit.

You didn't do anything wrong. You didn't even belong in prison."

"But I was there." It'd changed him, too. He wouldn't try to deny that. "I served time for a crime. Imagine trying to explain that to a ten-year-old girl." Actually, he didn't want to. He'd already earned Gracie's trust, but once she learned the truth about him, he'd likely have to start all over. "It'll freak her out. I don't want her to be scared of me." If it were up to him, they'd wait until she was twenty to tell her anything about it. Until she could understand a label didn't have to define someone.

"It's not fair." Levi pushed back from the table and stood. He was the tallest out of all three of them, which wasn't saying much. "You can't even live your god damn life because of something I did."

Lucas exchanged another look with Lance. Not only was he the tallest, he also had the shortest fuse on his temper.

Lucas pushed away his nearly full bottle of beer. "It's all behind us now," he said firmly, so Levi wouldn't get any grand ideas about dredging up the finer points of their past. They'd had that discussion and he knew where Lucas stood.

"It's not behind us," his younger brother argued. The man had always loved to argue. "It's not behind *you*."

Couldn't deny that. He'd thought it was behind him until he came back to Topaz Falls. Down in Pueblo, no one gave a damn where he'd been. If anything, his stint in prison made him a "tougher son of a bitch."

Levi ripped the chair away from the table and sat across from him again.

Lucas had to blink. He saw so much of their mother in that lost, dejected look on his face.

"You saved my life."

He went to share another eye roll with Lance, but his older brother simply nodded.

"You saved all of us," he said grimly. "It woke Dad up. Woke us all up."

Lucas looked away from both of them, searching for a way to change the subject, but nothing came to him. "I'm not some savior." He'd simply wanted to protect them. Protect Dad.

Levi waited until he looked at him. "I was already drinking. Experimenting with drugs. There's no telling where I would've ended up if you hadn't done that for me."

That was what he'd been worried about. Levi had always been extreme, never knew how to manage his anger.

"After they took you away, I got my shit together."

This time Lucas pushed back from the table. He didn't do this well. The sentimental stuff. The gratitude party. "You turned out all right," he said, carting their beer bottles to the sink. Considering those rough few years after their mother had left, Levi could've done a hell of a lot worse.

His brother came over and stood in front of him. "I want to fix it."

"I appreciate that. Really." But he didn't need him to. "There's nothing you can do. I'll always have a record. You can tell everyone what really happened and it won't matter. Won't change the fact that I spent three years in prison." He sidestepped his brother and glanced at Lance before Levi pushed any harder. "You guys want to get out of here? Go for a beer or something? Maybe I'll kick your ass in a game of pool..." It might've been almost nine o'clock, but he had a lot more energy to burn and sitting around the table talking about the past with his brothers wasn't cutting it.

"Yeah, sure. We can do that." Lance didn't like the sentimental stuff any more than Lucas did.

"Kick our asses?" Levi demanded. It was almost too easy to distract him. "You're not gonna kick *my* ass," their younger brother said, leading the charge out the door. "I was reigning champ at the Low Country Pool Hall back in Tulsa."

"Nice to be reigning champ in something, huh?" Lance insulted, acknowledging the fact that Levi hadn't won many sizeable purses.

"Oh, it's on." Their younger brother stomped out the door.

And just like that, the Cortez brothers, who'd grown up avoiding every heart-to-heart chat, were back.

* * *

The nine o'clock crowd at the Tumble Inn happened to be on the rougher side than the Happy Hour crowd. Hence the reason Lucas didn't frequent the place after a certain time of night. These days, he did his best to stay out of trouble.

Tonight, the risk didn't seem too great. Only a few stragglers sat at the bar, their eyes tuned into a Rockies game. No one he recognized, so that was good. Maybe they were new to town since he'd been gone or maybe they were part of that big construction crew working on the pass outside of town. Didn't matter. At least they weren't glaring at him with a silent message to walk his ass back out the door.

Shoulders relaxing, he chalked up his pool cue. He had to admit, it was good to get out. Hanging with Levi and Lance, shooting some pool, sharing some laughs. He was actually enjoying himself more than he'd thought he would.

Even with the good beating his brother was currently handing him.

"Who's kicking whose ass?" Levi asked, giving him a shot to the shoulder with his pool cue.

"Game's not over yet," Lucas reminded him, though he didn't have a prayer. Levi had already schooled Lance in the first game and now he was about to prove he really had been the reigning champ somewhere down in Podunk, Oklahoma, whereas Lucas hadn't played a game of pool since prison.

"Come on, man," Lance muttered. "Knock his ego down a few hundred notches."

That wasn't gonna happen. "Doin' my best," he said, keeping up the façade. Maybe a hot woman looking for a good time would come along to distract their brother and give him a break.

Sizing up his next shot, Lucas bent to study the right angle. He had to put that solid four in the corner pocket. Shouldn't be a tough one...

Leaning down, he lined up his cue and popped it lightly. The damn ball ricocheted off the side and headed in the opposite direction.

"Nice shot." Grinning, Levi bumped his shoulder as he skirted past him.

"Just trying to make you look good." He took a swig of his beer. At least there weren't many people around to watch him get schooled by his younger brother. "Maybe we should arm wrestle next," he suggested, knowing that, while Levi worked hard on his abs, he didn't do much heavy lifting.

Sure enough, his brother ignored the challenge and leaned over to line up his next shot. "Eight ball. Right corner pocket," he said smugly. And what do you know? He popped the cue ball and knocked that damn eight ball right in.

"Looks like that's it, boys," his brother said, strutting over to give Lucas's shoulder a nudge. "Pay up—"

"I didn't know it was felon night."

Lucas didn't have to turn around to see who'd just ruined his evening. Damn. He should've been paying attention to what kind of trash was walking through that door, but he'd been too busy enjoying himself. That's what he got.

Levi pushed past him, a recognizable fire in his eyes. "What the fuck is your problem, Dobbins?"

Slowly Lucas turned to the man, taking his time to snuff the fuse of his temper. He'd had plenty of practice. And this man was not worth it.

On the other side of the pool table, Lance stood nice and straight, keeping a watchful eye on Dobbins and his two friends.

"My problem is there's a felon in town. People have to start locking doors," Dobbins slurred. He must've come to the Tumble Inn after getting kicked out of another establishment because the man could hardly stand up straight. His two friends seemed somewhat better off.

"You know what you need?" Levi asked, his jaw locked. "A good ass-kicking." He lunged a step closer as though he planned to make good on the threat.

Lucas hooked his brother's arm and reeled him back. "Not worth it. Ignore him."

Marshal obviously wasn't about to let that happen, though. He wasn't about to let any of them ignore him. He strutted closer to Levi with a smirk that could've provoked a lamb. "Your brother shouldn't be here."

"Neither should you," Lance said politely. "Why don't you go on home? Sleep off the booze before it gets you in trouble."

Dobbins steadied a hand on the pool table, his face crimson. He'd always been a mean drunk. And he'd always gone looking for trouble, too. The fact that he kept harassing Lucas only proved he was the guy who'd messed up his truck. That or he'd sent one of his kids to do it. His oldest had to be fourteen. Plenty mature enough to be vandalizing.

Lucas tossed his pool cue on the table. He'd better give Dev a heads-up. "Think it's time to go." He turned away, hoping like hell his brothers would follow.

"You're trash. You know that, Cortez?" Dobbins spat behind him. "You *and* that whore of yours."

The room blurred with a sudden invasion of pure, unsuppressed rage. It spilled out past the barriers he'd put in place. He whirled back to the man, fingertips already digging into palms. He hadn't used his fists for a damn long time, but he hadn't forgotten how.

Seeing that he'd gotten Lucas's attention, Dobbins laughed and elbowed his idiot friend. "She don't even know who knocked her up."

Before he knew what was happening, Lucas's body had lurched into motion and his arm had wound back, ready to let a punch fly. But before he could knock the teeth out of Dobbins's grin, Levi shoved him out of the way and took it upon himself to throw the first blow.

His brother's fist connected with Marshal's jaw in a crack that sent the man reeling backward.

Shaking out his hand, Levi turned to Lucas. "Don't want you to get busted. Besides, I've wanted to do that for a long—"

Dobbins plowed into his brother and sent him stumbling backward into a table. Lucas lunged into the scuffle, trying to get that lunatic off his brother, but the two morons

Marshal had brought with him attacked, ripping him away and taking clumsy swings at his face. He ducked easily, knocking one aside with his elbow as Lance jumped into the fray, taking out the other one.

Dobbins, meanwhile, had completely lost it, and was swinging furiously at Levi, spit flying from his mouth as he mumbled insults. Lucas went for him again, but those two other bastards had come back for more.

"Fight!" someone yelled from the outskirts, and he distantly realized this would not end well but there was no stopping it now. Ripping out of one of the thugs' grasps, he hauled off and shoved him hard. The man went reeling backward, slamming into a chair and breaking it into kindling. Blinded by the pumping adrenaline, Lucas made his way to Marshal. "Get off him." He tore Dobbins away from Levi and stood him up straight. "This is between you and me."

With an enraged grunt, Marshal ripped free and socked him in the stomach, which would've hurt if the man wasn't so damn drunk. Still, Lucas hit back, sinking his fist into the man's gut, which caused Marshal to double over.

There was more yelling from the outskirts, chants and shouts to stop, but Dobbins's thugs kept right on swinging at his brothers and Lucas couldn't let that go. He went for the shorter one, plowing into him until they were both on the floor vying for the best angle to land a solid punch. He got one in, then jumped up to go after the other one.

"Enough!" The voice of authority rang out. Officer Dev Jenkins had arrived.

Everything came to a screeching halt. Holding up his hands, Lucas backed away from the man. For the first time, he glanced around at the mess—broken chairs, glass scattered around the floor from their beer bottles.

Shit.

At some point Gil Wilson, the owner of the bar, had come over. “Get ’em outta here,” he said to Dev, looking truly pissed off. Which also meant he was likely to press charges.

Standing right where he was, Lucas waited for Dev to cuff him. Looked like he’d get to see the inside of a cell again after all.

Chapter Twenty

There wasn't enough sex," Darla complained, leafing through the pages of their latest book club selection.

"Of course there wasn't." Jessa sighed, sharing a martyred look with Cassidy. "Because it's a historical thriller. Not erotica."

"Well, it lost my attention around page twenty." Darla set the book on the table and folded her hands primly.

Everyone glanced at Naomi, as if waiting to hear her thoughts, but she'd busied herself with refilling wineglasses. Given everything that had been going on lately, she hadn't exactly had a chance to read the book. Not to mention . . . she had other things on her mind. Big things. Like how do you explain to your ten-year-old daughter that the man you love spent time in prison?

"Can I get anyone another brownie?" she offered, deflecting the curious stares with a smile. It was a futile attempt to derail the questions rising in their eyes. She loved hosting book club, even on a Monday night. Loved having these women sit around her dining room table sipping wine and eating chocolate while they talked books with the low hum of Adele in the background. When Naomi hosted, they always waited until after Gracie was in bed to gather, seeing as how Darla like to discuss sex scenes in great detail.

But tonight Naomi had nothing to contribute. She wished things were different. Less complicated. She wished Lucas could've stayed; that they could've made out on the couch and then gone into her bedroom. She wished he could've spent the night…

"Something happened with Lucas." Cassidy tossed her book down on the table, as though she'd much rather discuss that. "Something big."

That woman's intuition was otherworldly.

"Ohhhhh…something sexual?" asked Darla. "Because it's about damn time."

"No." Naomi infused the word with a desperate shush. "Nothing sexual." Unfortunately.

Everyone scooted their chairs closer to the table and leaned in as if they'd just remembered there was a child in the house. Each of their eyebrows raised in a silent demand for her to continue.

"I mean, it's not for lack of desire." Nope, that was definitely not the problem. Her body was revving just recalling the fishing experience. She'd never thought she could like fly fishing so much…

"So what is it, then?" Jessa prompted.

A sigh gave her up. "I don't know how to do this. With Gracie. Especially now. With Mark coming back and so many changes." The enormity of it all rattled her again, bringing a familiar tremble of fear. She'd always been so careful, so guarded, and everything about Lucas made her want to kick in those walls. But there was a lot at stake. And not only for her, either.

"Honey." Darla reached across the table and covered her hand with her graceful, slender fingers. "That girl is more resilient than you give her credit for."

"Yeah," Cass agreed. "She's got you for a mom. And you're the most resilient woman I know."

Warm tears seeped into her eyes. "Tonight she asked Lucas where he's been all these years, and I wouldn't let him answer." She wanted to protect him, too, but still. He probably thought she was embarrassed by him.

"What are you afraid of?" Jessa asked. "If you tell her the truth?"

"That she won't accept him. That she'll be scared of him." That she wouldn't want him to be a part of their lives. Naomi didn't think she could bear that. Because Gracie deserved to have some say in who she let into their lives.

"But you love him," Darla said. It wasn't a question. "And if there's one thing I do know about love, it's that you can't wait." She leaned over the table, her eyes emphatic. "You've already lost too many years with him, Naomi. Don't lose any more time."

The urgency in her friend's wise eyes tempted her to dig out her phone and call him right then. She didn't *want* to wait. Couldn't stand the thought of losing more time. "I want to be careful. To give Gracie time to adjust." Her daughter deserved that.

"You don't have to have everything figured out this minute," Jessa said gently. "Most of us are figuring things out as we go."

"Besides," Cass added. "It seems to me Lucas has already won Gracie over."

"You're right." Of course they were right. She'd handled the news about Mark so well. If she could forgive Mark for being gone ten years, surely she could forgive Lucas for making a mistake when he was high school "I'll find a way to tell her soo—"

Jessa's phone started blaring a Madonna concert. Humming along to "Like a Prayer," her friend held up a finger, signaling for them to give her a minute. "This is Jessa," she said politely.

The woman was the only person Naomi knew who answered her phone even when she didn't recognize the number, but in a way she was always on call. No one ever knew when there'd be an animal emergency.

This time instead of her calm, professional response, a sharp gasp made her eyes bulge. "I'm sorry. What?"

Naomi exchanged looks with Cassidy and Darla.

"What did they *do*?" Jessa squawked, clearly taken aback.

"Uh-oh," Darla muttered. "That can't be good."

"Of course," their friend murmured into the phone. Her face was flushed. "Yes, I understand. I'll be right there."

She clicked off the phone and stared at it.

"I take it that wasn't an animal emergency?" Cassidy asked.

"Um. Not exactly." Jessa glanced at Naomi. "It was Dev Jenkins. Lance and his brothers are down at the station."

Naomi choked on a sip of wine. "Station as in *police* station?"

"That'd be the one." Jessa rose from her chair. "There was some kind of fight at the Tumble Inn. He didn't say much, just that I could come and pick them up."

"Hot damn!" Darla popped out of her chair. "What're we waiting for? Field trip! Not that discussing historical thrillers isn't interesting," she quickly added. "But I *do* love the sight of a man in uniform." And she also loved teasing poor Dev about how much she loved the sight of a man in uniform.

Cassidy stood, too, gathering her purse.

"We're all going?" Jessa asked, as though that might not be the best idea.

"Hell yeah." Cass led the way down the hall. "I wouldn't miss a chance to see Levi Cortez behind bars."

Naomi followed behind them all, swallowing against the nausea that was brewing. How had this happened? "Is Lucas okay?" she asked, shoving her shoes onto her feet.

"I don't know." Jessa opened the front door in a hurry. "I assume they're okay or we'd be picking them up at the hospital."

"I'm sure they're fine. Just men being boys." Darla sped past them. "Cass and I'll meet you there," she called happily.

"You okay?" Jessa asked Naomi as they made their way down the porch steps.

No. She wasn't okay. Lucas would hate this. Instead of following Jessa to her car, she headed in the opposite direction. "I'll be right behind you. I have to ask Luis if he can sit with Gracie."

Without mentioning to the man why.

* * *

Naomi made it to the station just as Jessa led a silent sulking parade out the doors.

"Hey." She hurried over to Lucas, taking both of his hands in hers, not caring that they had an audience.

"Hey." His face was stone, but everything looked intact, minus a slight red swelling in his bottom lip.

"Everything okay?" she asked cautiously while the others spread out, farther down the sidewalk.

"Gil decided not to press charges." His flat response didn't answer the question.

Darla and Cassidy broke away from the group. "Well, folks, it's been fun, but we have to say good night."

"Thanks for the entertainment," Cass said sweetly to Levi.

"I'll provide you entertainment anytime." A lift of his eyebrows added an innuendo, but Cassidy had already turned her back on him, likely pretending she hadn't heard.

"You boys." Jessa shook her head like a disappointed mother, but she still held Lance's hand. "I'll take you back to your car," she muttered to Levi, likely blaming the whole thing on him. She turned to Naomi. "I'm guessing you'll bring Lucas home?"

"Of course."

Lucas stayed quiet as they all parted ways.

Though she walked more slowly than normal, he followed her to the car at a distance. She unlocked the doors and they both climbed in.

When he still said nothing, she turned to face him, holding the keys tightly in her fist. "So what happened?"

He stared out the windshield. "Got into it with Marshal Dobbins."

"Why?" she asked, shoving the keys into the ignition. The engine started up, but she didn't pull away from the curb. "Why did you let him get to you?" Lucas was always so steady. So mellow. He didn't go after someone for no reason.

"He knew what to say."

She carefully studied his face. "He said something about

me." She didn't have to ask. Of course he had. He knew that was the only way to get a reaction out of Lucas.

"Did you hurt him bad?" she asked, hoping the answer was no. Not that the man didn't deserve it, but she didn't want Lucas to get in trouble on her account. Dobbins wasn't worth that.

"Nah. He's not hurt. Dev's making him spend the night to sober up, though." His jaw seemed to loosen. "At least the witnesses vouched for us."

"I'm sorry." She covered his hand with hers, entranced by the feel of his skin. "It doesn't matter what he says about me, you know. I don't care."

"He was looking for a fight and he got one." Lucas pulled his hand away. "And it won't be the last time, either." He gazed down at her, worried and angry. "He's only gonna make it harder for me. And for you, too."

"I'm not worried about it." She didn't need him to protect her or defend her honor. She only needed him to love her.

"The last thing I want is for him to mess up your life." Lucas's voice had softened the way it always did when he talked to her.

"He can't." She placed her hands on his cheeks and tugged his face closer to hers. "No one will mess this up for us. Not this time," she whispered, her breath on his lips. "We won't let them." She kissed him, light and sweet, to remind him what they were fighting for, and immediately lost herself in the rhythm of their lips moving together. He pulled her closer against him, deepening the kiss, brushing his tongue over hers in that electrifying heat. God, she'd always been so afraid to let herself think about him, about this...It was so new and exhilarating but familiar and comfortable at the same time.

His body seemed to thaw against her, that rigid tension from earlier falling away. "Your car is so small," he complained, sneaking his hands up her shirt.

"So small," she echoed, slumping over as his fingers moved over her bra. "We could always go to a hotel."

His head tilted as he looked her over. "Who's watching Gracie?"

"Your dad." And she'd told him she'd be right back.

"We'll do it another time," he promised. "Another time when no one's expecting us and we can just be together for hours." He kissed her. "Or days." Another kiss. "Or weeks."

Pulling back, he withdrew his hands and searched her eyes. "You're sure? About all of this? About us? Because it's not gonna be easy in this town."

Who wanted easy anyway? "I love you, Lucas." She'd told him that in high school more than once, but she hadn't known then what it meant. Not really. She hadn't known until she'd lived so many years without him. Years of learning about life and heartbreak, and depths of joy and pain she hadn't known existed. Now she could say it and mean it and know it was true.

"I love you, too," Lucas uttered, resting his forehead against hers. "I've always loved you." Concern still lingered in the soft tenderness of his eyes. "I just hope that's enough."

Chapter Twenty-one

Naomi traipsed across the porch, smiling as she admired the beautiful sign hanging above the arched entry. *Hidden Gem Inn*. It still baffled her that Lucas knew her so well. That he'd picked out the perfect piece of art to welcome people, to reflect the character and details of the old house.

Once again, her heart melted through the interior walls of her chest at the thought of him. In less than fifteen minutes, he'd be here to pick her up so they could go antique shopping to search for a few authentic pieces for the inn. She'd called him this morning after she'd dropped off Gracie and told him she needed some brawn to help her lug furniture home. *I've got brawn*, he'd told her with an insinuation in his voice. The memory made her warm all over.

Humming to herself, she scooted through the brand-new door that Emilia, her contractor, must've just installed. It, too, happened to be a work of art. The restored antique inset-glass door, all painted and new and shiny, gave the whole porch a charming Old World feel.

Inside the house, the whir of the saw drew her into the kitchen. Much of the main level had already been gutted, leaving the studs exposed. It resembled a blank slate—a canvas of possibility...kind of like her future.

She stepped into the kitchen and Emilia shut off the saw, greeting her with that effortlessly exotic smile. Her long, silky black hair, perfect olive skin, and graceful manner made her look more like she belonged on the runway instead of standing in front of a table saw. Emilia even managed to make work clothes look elegant. Today, she wore ripped jeans rolled halfway up her calves, an oversized blue T-shirt with the straps of the camisole beneath it visible, and a brightly colored scarf tied around her head like a headband. It wasn't fair. The woman didn't even have to try. But it was impossible to dislike her. She was brassy and funny and also kind.

"I can't believe how much progress you've made," Naomi said, taking in the new farmhouse gray kitchen cabinets already mounted on the wall. "You're amazing." *She* could hardly even hammer in a nail, let alone gut and install an entire kitchen.

Emilia grinned. "She's coming along, that's for sure." The woman patted the wall fondly. "I have to say, this has been my favorite project lately. Don't usually get to work on an antique."

"Well, you're doing a beautiful job." Naomi knew using Emilia would mean a slower process than if she'd hired a whole construction company, but Emilia was an artisan. She'd only been in town a couple of months, but had already earned a reputation as a skilled woodworker. Around Topaz

Falls, Emilia mainly did maintenance for homes in the exclusive neighborhoods up near the ski resort, but when Naomi had met her at Darla's place a few months ago, she'd jumped at the possibility of working on a Victorian. As soon as she'd closed on the house, Naomi had called her, and now, what she saw around her was exactly why. "I brought the checkbook," she said, holding it up. "So I can pay you for the materials and hours you've worked up until now." She still marveled at the thought of having her own business account.

"Speaking of..." Emilia walked to her messenger bag, which was slung over the stuffed chair Naomi had brought from the ranch. It was still the only piece of furniture in the room. "I've been looking at ways to save you money. I think you could easily tear out the wood paneling in the den yourself."

"Me?" She laughed. "I'm not sure you want me to do that." How would she even do that?

"It's nothing," the woman insisted, waving her off. "Just use a crowbar to rip it off the wall. Think of it as therapy." A mischievous glow lit her eyes. "And I'm sure a certain Cortez brother would be happy to assist if you asked him nicely."

"Wow, word gets around fast." It seemed the whole town knew about her and Lucas before things were even official. But she likely had that scene on the street with Mark to thank for that.

"Is it true he's planning to stick around?" Emilia asked with a probing grin.

The question brought out Naomi's sappiest smile. "It sounds like it."

"Good. Then he can help you knock out this list." Emilia

handed over a paper. "Next couple of days I'll be finishing up a job for the Bartletts, but I'll get back on yours next week." She gave Naomi a sturdy pat on the shoulder. "That should give you two plenty of time to get this done."

"Sounds great." Manuel labor had never been her thing but something told her it would be a whole lot more fun with Lucas. She snuck a quick glance at her watch. Eight minutes. Her heart did a little flip.

"Here's where we're at so far." Emilia handed her another paper with the total for hours and materials.

"Not bad." Naomi scrawled out a quick check and happily handed it over. She still couldn't believe this was happening, that she was actually—

Her phone rang. "Thanks so much," she told Emilia as she dug it out. "You're doing such a great job."

"I'm enjoying it," Emilia assured her. "Trust me."

Naomi glanced at the phone's glowing screen, instantly recognizing the school's number. That usually wasn't good news. "I'll see you later," she murmured to Emilia as she made her way to the porch. "Hello?" She stepped outside where the reception was better.

"Naomi? This is Eleanor Bradley." In addition to being the school principal, Eleanor ran the school's summer camps, too.

"Hi, Eleanor. Everything okay?" she asked nervously.

Lucas's truck had pulled up in front of the house, but she didn't want to move and risk losing reception.

"There's been an incident and I need you to come to the school right away."

She steeled herself against an outburst of mom panic. *Remain calm*... "An incident?"

"Gracie got into a fight," the woman said in a clipped

tone. "Everyone is fine, but I'm sure you'll understand the need to discuss this as soon as possible."

"A fight?" She didn't mean to keep repeating the woman, but she couldn't be serious. "Gracie has never been in a fight..."

Lucas bounded up the steps, but stopped quickly when he saw her face. *Everything okay?* he mouthed.

She shook her head.

"Well, I can assure you she got into a fight today. And she started it. We'll discuss the details when you get here." The line went dead as though Mrs. Bradley didn't want to leave her more room to repeat anything.

"Oh my God." She stuffed the phone back in her purse.

"What happened?" Lucas asked, taking her into his arms.

"That was the principal. She said Gracie got into a fight." She couldn't even picture it. Her sweet daughter—who'd never once gotten in trouble for hitting or kicking or biting, even when she was a toddler—had gotten into a physical altercation with someone?

"Maybe it's a misunderstanding," Lucas suggested. "Want me to drive you over there?"

"Please." He was right. It had to be a misunderstanding. But her heart hammered her ribs and she held his hand all the way to the truck.

Thankfully, it only took five minutes to get to the school. That was the benefit of being in town instead of out at the ranch.

"I'll wait here," Lucas said, helping her out of the truck. She didn't want him to, but given Eleanor's reaction the last time she'd seen him, it was probably best. "Hopefully we'll be quick." Leaving him standing near the truck, she hurried to the doors and used her keycard to buzz herself in. Surely it would be quick. She could talk to Gracie and get the whole story of what happened and clear up this craziness.

She marched down the hall and turned the corner to go to the office. Gracie sat on a bench just outside Mrs. Bradley's door.

Her daughter looked up with a sullen, tear-stained face. "Gracie." Naomi rushed over and sat next to her. "Honey, what happened?"

Before her daughter could answer, Mrs. Bradley poked her head out into the hall. "Why don't you both come in and sit down?" It was more of a command than an invitation.

Gracie's scowl tightened, but she followed Naomi into the office. They both sat on hard chairs facing Mrs. Bradley's desk.

"Gracie, tell your mom what happened," Eleanor said without greeting Naomi.

Her daughter stared at her scabbed knees. "I pushed Timothy. And then I punched him in the face."

Naomi almost burst out laughing it was so absurd. "Was it an accident?" Maybe she'd tripped and lost her balance...

"No," her daughter snapped. "I did it on purpose."

"On purpose?" She blinked at her. She had no idea what else to say. This was new territory. Fighting at school?

"Timothy had a bloody nose," Mrs. Bradley added. "His mother has already taken him home."

"Oh my God. Gracie..." She turned to her daughter. "Why would you do something like that?" How could her sweet, innocent girl have punched a boy in the face hard enough to make him bleed?

"He said my mom was gonna marry a bad guy," she huffed. "So I told him, my mom's not getting married, you big fat stupid head. And then he said everyone's talking about it. He said you're going on dates with the bad guy who started the fire." Her daughter's face had flushed with embarrassment. "So I pushed him and hit him and I'm *not* sorry."

Naomi's eyes stung so badly, she had to close them. "Oh, honey," she murmured, forcing herself to look at Gracie. She should've told her before now. She should've let Lucas tell her last night.

"Is he a bad guy?" Gracie asked, her voice wobbling as though she was trying not to cry. "Is Lucas a bad guy?"

"No," Naomi said firmly. "No."

Eleanor shifted in her chair. "Gracie, why don't you go sit on the bench and give your mom and me a chance to discuss things?"

Gracie did what she was told, just like always. That was her girl. Obedient and respectful.

"I'm sure I don't have to tell you how serious this is," Mrs. Bradley said as soon as the door closed. "I have to suspend her from camp this week. We have to set an example here."

An example? She thought of her daughter standing there while that boy had humiliated her in front of everyone. She would've wanted to punch him, too. Her throat burned. "What about Timothy? What'll happen to him?"

"He's already been reprimanded appropriately." Mrs. Bradley pushed over a written apology.

Gracie, Sorry for making fun of you or whatever. —Timothy

"How heartfelt," Naomi said drily.

Eleanor seemed to ignore her sarcasm. "Poking fun at someone is vastly different from physically attacking them."

Naomi rolled her eyes so the woman could see what she thought of that statement. "It was hardly an attack. She pushed him and hit him. And she's never done anything like that before. You know her. She's gotten eight citizenship awards, for crying out loud."

"That's what concerns me." The woman glanced at the door and lowered her voice. "I'm sure I don't have to tell you how much children are influenced by the adults they spend time with."

The burning sensation in her throat reached for her stomach. Surely Mrs. Bradley wasn't alluding to Lucas. "I'm sorry, what?" The words were as clipped as her heart rate.

"From the sound of things, you and Gracie have been spending a lot of time with Lucas Cortez." Eleanor said his name like a curse word. "Obviously, it's having a negative impact on your daughter."

"No." Naomi lurched to her feet, the fiery anger now consuming all of her. "I will talk to her about the fight. And there will be a consequence." She paused to regain her composure. "But who we spend time with is none of your business." She ripped open the door and escaped into the hallway. "Come on, Gracie," she said, taking her daughter by the hand. "Let's go home."

"Am I in big trouble, Mommy?" Gracie asked as they hurried down the hall.

"Yes, honey." She tried to say it with conviction. Though the other kid probably deserved it, she'd have to punish Gracie. "You know better than to hit someone. It doesn't matter what they do or say to you. It's never okay."

"I know." Her daughter started to cry. "I know, but he wouldn't stop. He and his friend Tyler Dobbins kept yelling stuff and everyone was laughing at me."

Tyler Dobbins. As in Marshal Dobbins's son. Of course.

She should've known. "Oh, Gracie girl." Naomi sank to her knees and pulled her daughter close. "I'm so sorry that happened. I'm so sorry they were mean to you."

"And I'm sorry I punched Timothy," her daughter sobbed. "I was just so mad."

Mad and hurt. Deeply, deeply hurt. Naomi gave her a kiss on the forehead. "It's okay. Everything'll be okay."

Even as she said it, she wondered if that were true.

* * *

Lucas paced the sidewalk outside the school. It seemed to be taking an awful long time to simply clear up a misunderstanding. He stopped, watching the doors again. If only he could've gone in there. Could've made sure Gracie was okay. If only he could've comforted her and promised to protect her, to punish anyone who'd laid a hand on her…

The doors busted open and the two of them charged out, Gracie crying and Naomi's face hardened with fury.

He may have been out of practice when it came to reading women, but something was very, very wrong.

"Everything okay?" It was a dumb question but he didn't know what else to say.

Neither of them responded. They simply slipped past him and climbed into the truck.

He got in, too, but didn't start up the engine. "What happened?" he demanded. Why the hell was Gracie being sent home?

"Some boys were teasing Gracie," Naomi said. He wasn't sure he'd ever seen her face so red. "So she got upset and made a mistake."

Lucas didn't like the way she refused to look at him.

"What were they teasing you about?" he asked Gracie, not sure he wanted to hear the answer.

"They said my mom was gonna marry a bad guy." Her voice was so small, barely audible. It wasn't the words that slashed through him. It was her eyes. They mirrored a heartbreak that only came from the pain of betrayal.

Drawing in a stabilizing breath, he shared a long look with Naomi.

"But we've already talked about it. I told her you're not a bad guy." Naomi's eyes filled with tears. She snuck her hand into his.

"Why did they say that, then?" Gracie asked Lucas suspiciously. "Why would they say you're a bad guy?"

"Because they're mean." Naomi didn't give him a chance to answer, but he had to. She had to know the truth.

He turned to face the girl fully so she could see into his eyes. "It's because I went to prison," he said, looking at her over the seat. "That's why I had to leave all those years ago. That's why I didn't come back for a long time."

"Prison?" Gracie whispered. "Like jail?"

"Yes." He hated the way she was looking at him, like she didn't know him anymore. "There was a fire at the rodeo grounds and I got arrested." He chose the words carefully. He wanted to be honest, but he couldn't tell them the whole truth either.

"You lied to me." Tears ran down Gracie's cheeks again. "I asked you where you went all those years…"

"We didn't lie," Naomi said gently. "We didn't tell you because Lucas is a different person now. The past doesn't matter."

If only that were true. It may not matter to Naomi, or to his family, but it mattered to Gracie. It mattered to Eleanor

Bradley. It mattered to Marshal Dobbins. It mattered to those kids who'd used it to torment a sweet, fun-loving girl.

"But everyone else knew. And I didn't," Gracie whimpered. "I looked so dumb. That's why they were laughing at me."

Because of him. This was exactly what he'd worried about. Naomi might be able to handle herself in the face of scrutiny, but Gracie shouldn't have had to defend herself at school on account of him. "I'm sorry," he said. What else could he offer her? "We should've told you." At least then she would've been prepared.

"Would you like to get some lunch?" Naomi suggested. "Then we can talk about it and answer any more questions you have about what happened back then."

"No." Gracie turned her head to stare out the window, as though she wanted to shut them both out. "I want to go home."

"But—" Naomi started.

"It's okay," Lucas interrupted. "I'll take you home." She needed time, space. And so did he. When he looked at Gracie, his own selfishness stared him in the face. She deserved more than this. More than him.

As he started the truck, Bill McGowen's offer rang in his ears.

No matter how much he wanted to stay and force people to accept him, he had to do what was best for everyone.

Chapter Twenty-two

Lucas stretched the kinks out of his back and wound up his arm for another perfect cast over the wide river.

The dim, early morning light made the water black and inky, but the old adage was true... fish tended to bite early.

"I bet fishing with Naomi was a hell of a lot more fun than fishing with me," Levi muttered, standing next to him, sullen and waist deep in the river.

"It was a different kind of fun." He watched the fly for a possible strike. "This is fun because I'm kicking your ass at something." He'd already caught four solid rainbows to his brother's zero. After the pool fiasco, he figured it was time to put his little brother in his place, so he'd dragged Levi's ass out of bed before the sun was even up.

"Let's step into the corral when we get back," Levi suggested. "Have a little competition to see who can get the best of Reckoning II. How would you like that? What's it been since you've ridden a bull? Ten years?"

"I ride occasionally." When he wanted to give a possible purchase a test drive. But there was no way he'd beat Levi in a bull-riding competition. Especially on Reckoning II. He wasn't stupid enough to try. "I'm not in a hurry to get back to the ranch." He needed to be out here—hadn't worked everything out in his head yet.

After he'd dropped off Naomi and Gracie yesterday, he'd spent the whole day with Reckoning II, working late, until the sun started to dip and the bull wanted to kill him in the most painful way possible. Naomi had called him after that, admitting that Gracie was still in her room pouting. But Lucas knew it was more than that. He'd betrayed her trust. He didn't blame her for not wanting to talk to him.

"Gotta say…I'm impressed," his brother said, reeling in yet another empty line. "Thought you would've knocked out Marshal's teeth by now." He shook his head. "His kid teasing Gracie like that? You're showing serious restraint."

"I don't have a choice." Going after Dobbins would only rile him up more. Who knew what he'd do then?

"I'll do it for you if you want." Levi sounded more serious than Lucas was comfortable with. "I'd kick the shit out of him for you."

"Kicking the shit out of him won't do any good." He'd thought about it all night. What would happen if he said *screw it all* and went and paid Dobbins a visit? "It'd only fuel him. Give him another reason to make my life and the lives of everyone around me hard."

All that mattered to him in this whole thing was protecting Gracie. And he was afraid there was only one way to do it. "He won't be happy until I'm gone."

Levi fumbled with his fishing rod, almost dropping it in the river. "You're not thinking of leaving."

"Not sure I have a choice. At least for a while." All his life, he'd been solution-oriented. When a problem presented itself, he took action. He didn't wait around for it to get worse. "McGowen came to see me." He'd neglected to mention his boss's visit to his father and brothers. Hadn't told anyone, actually. "He made me a tempting offer."

Levi spun to face him. "You leave her again, she won't let you come back."

"Trust me. I'm well aware of the potential risks." He'd spent hours thinking through worst-case scenarios. "But if I'm gone, she and Gracie won't have targets on their backs." And yes, she might be mad at him. She might not forgive him, but he had to accept that possibility. It wasn't so much the teasing Gracie had taken that got to him; it was the fact that Marshal's son had been involved. When Naomi'd told him that on the phone last night, he'd realized how serious Dobbins was about ruining his life. And it scared him. What kind of man would use his kid that way? Dev had already alluded to the fact that Marshal wasn't exactly stable. "I'm worried about what he'll do next," he admitted. Especially since Dobbins had taken the fall for the whole bar brawl. "Something's not right with him." Maybe it was drugs or some kind of illness, but Marshal didn't appear to be playing with a full deck.

"Wish I could argue, but the guy is definitely not normal." Levi slogged over to the riverbank. Seemed he was done fishing.

Lucas wasn't. He'd be glad to delay the inevitable a little bit longer.

"I could tell everyone the truth about the fire." His brother tossed the fishing rod to the grass and peeled off his waders.

"Won't make a difference." Lucas made another arching

cast. The fly settled on the water a few feet in front of him. "Dobbins hates our family. It's not only me. And it wouldn't be only you, either. Especially after what happened at the bar."

They'd made Marshal look like the ass he was, and now he wanted revenge.

* * *

"Do you have your water bottle? Rain jacket?" Naomi asked, fiddling with the zipper on Gracie's backpack.

"*Yes,* Mom." Her daughter sighed. "I have *everything*." She counted out the items on her fingers. "Snacks, raincoat, water bottle, emergency first-aid kit, sunscreen, and my hat. Oh, and that whistle you made me pack," she finished with a dramatic roll of her eyes.

"Hey, missy. Whistles can save your life out there." Back in high school, she'd done some wilderness training and she'd never forgotten the stories about kids getting lost in the backcountry. "I guess you're ready, then." Naomi sighed, too, but it wasn't exasperation. It was a heart sigh. A release to ease the ache. Mark would be there any minute to pick up her daughter and she'd likely be gone the whole day. "You remember to drink plenty of water. It's a long hike."

"I've done it tons of times," Gracie reminded her. "I could do it with my eyes closed."

No one could do it with their eyes closed. Not with all of the rocks on the trail. "Still, you need to be careful." Naomi knelt in front of her. "I put the phone in the small pocket of your backpack, just in case you need me for *anything*." She always kept a prepaid phone in the house so Gracie could get in touch with her when they weren't together.

"*Okay*," Gracie said again. She smooshed her lips against Naomi's cheek. "I'll be *fine*, Mom. Dad and I are gonna have tons of fun."

"I know you will." But that didn't mean she wouldn't fuss over her until the second she walked out the door. That was every mother's right, and she happened to be very good at it.

The fussing had started this morning when Gracie was getting dressed. Naomi had to make sure she was wearing her hiking socks and a light sweatshirt, even though it was supposed to be in the eighties. Then she'd taken Gracie out for breakfast on the way over to meet Mark at the inn, making sure her daughter got plenty of protein so she'd have enough energy to make the hike.

Energy didn't seem to be an issue for her daughter, though. Gracie traipsed over to where Bogart lay on his plush dog bed underneath the large bow window and knelt down next to him, squeezing his neck.

Bogy licked her face.

"Almost ready, boy?" she asked the dog. "You'll love Dad. He's so great," she chattered.

Naomi tried not to wince. Mark seemed great. So why couldn't she make herself trust him? "Make sure to bring Bogy's leash," she said to distract herself from the question. "Just in case it's crowded and he bothers anyone." It might've been silly, but she was relieved Bogy was joining Mark and Gracie on the hike.

"Bogy won't need a leash." Gracie smothered the dog with kisses. "Will you? You're always a good boy."

Naomi knelt down and joined them on the floor.

"What are *you* doing today?" her daughter asked, patting the dog's head.

A sweltering blush crept up her cheeks. "Um..." She cleared her throat. "I think I'm going to spend some time with Lucas." Her tone was guarded. Gracie still hadn't forgiven him for hiding his past from her. But she would. Naomi had told Lucas as much on the phone last night. They just needed to give her some time. "He's going to help me tear down some wood paneling so we can keep this project moving." Hopefully Gracie didn't detect the high wisp in her voice. She couldn't help it. Even as hard as it was to know Gracie would be with her other parent, the thought of spending a whole day alone with Lucas had her heart twirling.

Her daughter turned, gazing at her curiously. "Don't you care that he was in jail?" she asked bluntly. "Don't you care that he started a fire and hurt animals?"

Naomi took her time gathering a response. This was the most Gracie had wanted to talk about it, and she didn't want to mess it up. "At the time, I was very hurt," she finally said. "I never thought Lucas would do something like that." There was still a part of her that didn't believe it. "But, honey, he was seventeen. Still a kid. He made a big mistake and he was very sorry for it." She smoothed her hand over her daughter's hair, patting down the unruly curls. "You know what, though? Even though it hurt me, I've forgiven him. Because I see who he is now. A good man with a good heart. Someone who only wants the best for the people he cares about." It was what she loved about him and also what she feared most about him. The way he always tried to sacrifice his own happiness for the sake of everyone else's.

Gracie bit her lip thoughtfully. "Papa Luis always says you should forgive everyone or it'll only end up making you sad."

Naomi smiled at that. "Papa Luis is a wise man, isn't he?"

"He sure is," she agreed. Those luminous green eyes narrowed. "Lucas doesn't make mistakes like that anymore?"

"Well, no one is perfect." But her daughter already knew that. Naomi had always been the first to admit her failings and apologize. "But he does his best not to make mistakes. And he'd never do anything that would put him in jail again." She was sure of that.

"If you forgave him, then maybe I will, too," Gracie said cautiously. "At least I'll try."

"That would mean so much to him." She squeezed her daughter just as a knock at the door announced Mark's on-time arrival.

Gracie took off to answer it with Bogy barking and bounding behind her. "Dad's here! Dad's here!"

Brushing the tears from her eyes, Naomi followed behind her.

"Hey, kiddo." Mark leaned down to give her a hug. "Wow." He walked into the foyer as he took everything in. "This place looks amazing."

"Thanks," Naomi said politely. "It's coming along."

"We're gonna open the inn right after Thanksgiving," Gracie informed him as though the whole thing had been her idea.

"That sounds like the perfect time of year. Right before the holidays."

"Maybe you could come to Thanksgiving dinner," her daughter said hopefully. "And bring your whole family."

"Oh..." Mark glanced at Naomi apologetically, as though he was worried she wouldn't approve.

She didn't know if she approved. "Um. Well. Maybe." The words stumbled all over each other. "We'll see. I mean hopefully there are no delays or anything..."

"It's okay," Mark interrupted. "We'll have to play it by ear," he told Gracie.

Thankfully, the answer seemed to satisfy her. Instead of begging, Gracie pulled on his hand. "Okay. Let's go hiking now."

Bogy whined as though worried he would be left behind.

"Come on, Bogy." Gracie snapped on his leash. "He's a really good hiker," she said to Mark. "Most of the time he won't need his leash."

"It'll be fun to have him along." Mark walked her out the door. "I brought some cookies if we make it all the way to the top."

"Cookies!" she cheered.

He turned to Naomi. "I'll have them back by three."

"That's fine." She bent to kiss Gracie's head. "Listen good. Okay? And don't hike too fast. You don't want your dad to get lost."

Gracie giggled. "I promise."

As Mark and Gracie made their way down the porch, Lucas drove up and parked his truck in the driveway.

Just. In. Time.

She waved once more at Gracie and waited for him on the porch.

Lucas seemed to take his time climbing out of the truck. He lugged along an old metal toolbox, making him look all rugged and strong. He *was* rugged and strong. She couldn't take her eyes off him as he made his way across the lawn. The jeans he had on were more worn and tattered than the ones he usually wore, and his faded T-shirt showcased every sculpted muscle. Her heart clenched with an expectant yearning.

"Hey." He bounded up the steps, but instead of pulling

her into his arms like she'd assumed he would, he hung back. In fact, he hardly even looked at her. "Ready to get started?"

The abrupt question made her flinch. "Uh . . . sure." Stiffly, she stepped aside so he could get past her.

He moved like he was on a mission and didn't want anyone or anything to slow him down. She followed at a distance through the foyer and sitting room and finally he paused in the kitchen.

"It's looking good," Lucas said, glancing around. "Emilia's done a lot of work."

"Um, yeah." Naomi skirted the skeleton of the kitchen island so she could face him, so she could see past the façade he was putting on.

"She's been working hard." The flatness in her tone brought on a roll of her eyes. What the hell had happened? They were talking like two strangers, when only days ago they hadn't been able to keep their hands off each other. Didn't he want to be with her today? She tested out the answer by taking a step closer.

Lucas turned away. "Where's the den?" he asked, leaving her behind again. "Back here?" He ventured through the door off the kitchen, and by the time Naomi had made it to the den herself, he was already holding one of the crowbars Emilia had left out for her.

"This shouldn't take long," he said, running a hand down the hideous dark wood paneling that dimmed the room. Eventually this area would be part of her and Gracie's apartment, once a couple of walls were knocked out.

With his back to her, Lucas began to work, shimmying the crowbar into the seams between the panels, monotonously ripping them off the wall and tossing them into a pile on a tarp. He didn't look behind him. Didn't acknowledge her presence in the room at all. Just kept prying and ripping and tossing as if he needed that artless, repetitive movement to give him something to focus on.

She watched, unblinking, until her eyes blurred, until the hurt and confusion swarmed into something fierce, until she couldn't stand it anymore.

"Stop," she demanded, stalking across the room. She ripped the crowbar out of his hands. "Just stop."

He stared through her, face hard and conflicted, his eyes unwilling to meet hers.

She glared at him, channeling every raw emotion that coursed through her. She'd waited so many years for this man to come back. Even though she hadn't known it, hadn't let herself think about it, he was what she'd always wanted. Now he stood right here and he wouldn't even look at her directly. "I'm not doing this," she told him. "I'm not going to stand here and wonder why you're suddenly ignoring me." Too much time had already been wasted. Too many years of silence. And she wasn't about to let it stand between them anymore. "So you can either tell me what the hell is going on, or you can leave." Because she'd already made her decision. She'd let herself love him again. And she didn't deserve uncertainty.

Lucas's shoulders seemed to cave. His eyes finally raised to hers, sad but steeled, too. That stubborn cowboy look. He'd made up his mind on something and come hell or high water he was going to do it.

"I have to go back to the McGowen place," he said. His voice had that empty quality, and if it hadn't been for the flicker of pain in his eyes, she would've been sure he didn't care.

"It's better for you. It's better for Gracie." The hard clench of his jaw told her he believed that. "Kids were taunting her at school. She got into a fight because of me," he went on, as though that would haunt him forever. "I don't want to wait around to find out what Marshal Dobbins will do next."

As she looked back at him her face steeled, too. She felt it—her eyes narrowing, her cheeks pulling tight. "Who cares?" Was he seriously going to let Marshal Dobbins ruin his life? And why would he go back to the McGowen Ranch? "I thought you quit. I thought you told Bill McGowen you were done."

He looked away. "I tried, but he made me an offer."

"An offer?" A sudden assault of emotions made the room spin. "So you were keeping that in your back pocket? Just in case this didn't work out?"

He rushed over and took her shoulders in his hands. "No. But I can't let anything happen to you. Or to Gracie. Don't you understand that? If I'm gone, he'll leave you alone."

"Stop pretending to be noble." She jerked away from him. "I'm scared, too. Okay? But I don't have a plan B." She hadn't given herself a safety net. "I'm all in, Lucas. Even with the risks and the unknowns and the potential trouble it might bring, my life would be more complete with you in it."

His eyes closed.

"I've never loved anyone else," she whispered, touching her fingers to his lips. "I don't think it's possible." It had always been him. Only him. "No matter what you think is best, you belong here. You belong to me. And I don't want to waste any more time." Life had more power when you took risks, when you embraced the uncertainties. Since he'd kissed her that night, she'd been more alive. Terrified, but also expectant and hopeful and passionate.

Lucas's eyes opened and she knew she'd brought his earlier conviction to its knees. Greed and hunger darkened his gaze. She felt it, too, stirring powerfully in her own chest.

"God, I love you," he uttered helplessly as he pulled her close.

"Then don't leave." She let her lips do the begging, brushing them against his in a hot, pleading caress.

His lustful groan filled her mouth while his hands pressed into the small of her back, urging her closer. She didn't need his help. Breathlessly, she pressed her body against his, feeling small against the sheer strength of him.

Kissing her thoroughly, he wrapped her up in his arms. She freed herself to him—to all of it—to the beautiful weakness melting her joints, to the quick pound of adrenaline rushing through her. The energy charging between them drove into her, filling her with an urgency to unite with him, to give him everything before it was too late.

Trembling with the intensity of it, her hands slipped under his T-shirt, inching it up until she could pull it off over his head. She stopped kissing him long enough to admire the lean, sculpted muscle mass that was his upper body. Since high school, he'd gained breadth, and dark hair was scattered across his pecs. The sight almost shocked her but intrigued her, too, setting her aflame with anticipation. Lucas was not an inexperienced teenager anymore. And they were not fooling around in his truck.

With the authority and single focus of a man, Lucas peeled off her shirt and let it drop to the floor. Eyes fixated to her chest, he reached around her back and popped the clasp on her bra with one hand, slowly dragging the straps down her shoulders before he pulled the lacy satin away from her body.

She didn't have time to wonder what he thought before his mouth was on her skin, tasting and kissing and stroking her with his tongue. Unable to hold back a moan of pleasure, she raised her hands to his thick hair, tangling her fingers into it as he buried his face into her chest. The feel of his tongue on her nipples brought on a surge of exquisite tingling. She staggered back a few steps until the paneled wall supported her weakening body.

Lucas kissed his way up her neck, hands covering her breasts, fingers slowly moving over her as though memorizing every detail. "I used to dream about this," he said, gazing down into her eyes. "About touching you like this. About making love to you." His lips grazed her jaw and her head tipped back, resting against the wall while she watched his eyes.

"And I wouldn't want to wake up. I'd fight it, try to stay asleep so you'd still be there."

"I'm here now." And there was nothing else. No other distractions. No threats to pull them away. Just the two of them in this barren room, alone in the house of her dreams. "Make love to me, Lucas," she murmured, wrapping her arms around his neck.

"Oh, I intend to." He lowered those warm skilled lips to hers again.

Judging from the slow seduction of his mouth, he intended to draw it out, make it last as long as possible.

But she wasn't sure she could wait.

Lips still fused to his, she went to work on the button fly of his jeans, clumsily tugging and fumbling until they'd all popped open. She slid them down his hips, taking his boxers with them.

"You're not being very patient," he accused, unbuttoning her jeans and sliding his hands around to her backside.

"I've already been too patient," she gasped. Now she couldn't wait another second. "It's highly overrated."

Laughing, Lucas wriggled out of his jeans and kicked them aside along with his shoes. Then he took hers down to the floor slowly, lowering to his knees as though he wanted to get a better look.

Legs shaking, she stepped out of the jeans, shoving them out of the way with her foot.

Lucas's hands caressed their way up her legs, stroking her thighs until her lower stomach pulsed. Still on his knees, he kissed one thigh then the other, gliding his tongue higher while his hands gently widened her stance.

Blood rushed through her, heightening every sense, wrapping her in the lovely warmth of desire. "I can't stand," she whispered, unable to muster any power. Her legs faltered. "God, Lucas, I can't even stand up."

"You don't have to stand." He took her hands and gently tugged until she sank to the floor with him, face to face, both on their knees on the sheets Emilia had put down to protect the refurbished wood.

He kissed her again and she couldn't keep her hands still. She had to feel him, to touch him, to make him want her even more. Taking the hard length of him in both hands, she pressed her lips to the coarse skin of his jaw, loving the burn it gave her.

Now Lucas was the one faltering. His upper body slumped slightly as her hands slid up and down his pulsing erection. Under her influence, his body trembled noticeably.

"I love the feel of your hands on my body," he uttered between ragged breaths.

The feeling was mutual, but she wanted more than his hands and touching. "I want you inside of me." She pushed him back until he shifted to sit on the floor. "Now. Don't make me wait." She inched forward to straddle him.

"Yes, ma'am," he drawled, fastening his hands on her hips. With a tug, he guided her to slide down onto him.

A sharp gasp escaped her lungs and stilled her body. "God," she breathed. "Oh God. Lucas..." He filled her—not just her body, but her heart, her soul. Being locked together with him, everything was right and good and so... powerful.

"Tell me if it's too much," he murmured. "I don't want to hurt you."

She understood what he meant—the tightness; he must've felt it. Sex hadn't been part of her life for so long. But now she was glad for that. Because it wouldn't have meant anything with someone else. She'd saved all of herself for him.

"It doesn't hurt," she whispered, kissing him lightly. "Not at all. It feels..." Shyness almost took over but she fought it back. "It feels so good, Lucas." So good she couldn't see clearly. So good she couldn't be still anymore. She arched her back, inviting him in deeper.

His head fell back with a low moan and his hips strained upward as though he wanted to get closer, deeper.

She thrust down onto him again, the tantalizing sensation blinding her to everything except his face, his intense gaze focused on hers.

He smoothed her hair away from her face and kissed her as though he couldn't get enough of the taste of her lips.

"This is so much better than my dream," he said through that sexy crooked grin.

"I think it's about to get way better," she managed, rocking her hips into a rhythm that gained momentum with each thrust.

Every time she arched her back, Lucas lifted his hips, plunging so deep into her that she lost her breath again and again. The cord of her desire wound tighter and tighter, flowing out of her in pants and soft moans and pleas.

Lucas slowed things down, pulling out the whole length of her and slowly—torturously—pushing back in. She gave up control, letting him tease her, reveling in the game he was playing, bringing her so close, then drawing it out. But impatience flared again and she ground her hips into his, pulsing against him, contracting every muscle until he was moving faster, gasping and moaning and pleading as much as she was.

"I want to see you let go," he groaned.

She couldn't even answer. The explosion loomed over her, tempting her body to give in, but she fought because she didn't want it to end. She didn't want this to be over.

Thrusting her higher, Lucas took her breast in his mouth, nibbling on her nipple as though he knew that would make her lose her grip. The shuddering rush gripped her, starting deep within and spreading until she trembled with wave after wave of bone-melting pleasure.

He quickened the pace—the friction, the heat prolonging the sensations until he was shuddering and saying her name. Crying out again, she slumped over him, unable to hold herself up or breathe or think.

Lucas's chest heaved against hers. Though he seemed satiated, he held her tightly against him, his arms strong and sturdy.

She turned her head, resting her cheek on his shoulder, gazing up at his mouth. She couldn't even lift her head. "So that's a first." Her voice still had that breathless quality of passion.

He lowered his head and peered into her eyes. "What was?"

"Multiple orgasms," she said with a lazy smile. "I'd heard they existed but I always thought it was an urban legend. Darla always talks about it. I used to wish I knew what it was like."

He laughed and directed her lips toward his. "Baby, I'm here to make all your wishes come true."

Chapter Twenty-three

Lucas couldn't take his eyes off Naomi. She lay on her back on the floor next to him, gazing into his eyes as though she couldn't look away, either. Her pale, soft skin was still flushed, the pink of her cheeks bringing her eyes to life. That silken red hair of hers was sprawled around her head in a soft halo. He was still trying to convince himself this wasn't just one of his hot dreams. That they were really here. Together. In an empty room of this old house. Naked and satisfied.

"What?" she asked him lazily. "Why are you looking at me like that?"

"You're the most beautiful thing I've ever seen." Especially like this. Disheveled and carefree. Unclothed. Fully his. After all of those months of looking at her without being able to touch her, this was the richest indulgence he could ever imagine.

Turning on her side, she wrapped her leg around him,

pressing that lean body against his, fitting her curves into him. God, her skin felt like velvet.

Right on cue, his body fired up, and all of a sudden he wasn't tired anymore.

Naomi ran her tongue over her lips, then kissed him, hijacking his consciousness. "I can't get enough of you, Lucas Cortez." She pulled back, eyeing him in a way that charged his body. That made him feel like he could live for that look in her eyes—like he could live for her.

"You can have as much of me as you want," he murmured in her ear. "I'll give you everything." All of him. All of her dreams. He would make them happen.

Tears brightened the deep hues of her eyes. "Just you is enough." She wriggled her hips until he was inside of her again, until he was pulsing with the feel of her tight wetness enclosing him.

Holding her gaze, he slid his hand up and over her hip until it cradled the curve of her ass, urging her closer, forging their connection deeper. She writhed against him, closing her eyes, letting her head fall back, and those desperate, greedy moans escaping her lips were almost enough to push him over the edge again.

"I forgot how amazing this was," she gasped, bearing her hips down into his.

"Want me to remind you again?" Wrapping her in his arms, he shifted her to her back and kissed his way down her chest as he plunged into her again and again, making sure he hit every sensitive spot.

Her breathing grew ragged and she cried out, then slapped a hand over her mouth.

"You can be as loud as you want," he said, pulling her hand away and pinning it under his against the floor.

She moaned.

"Louder," he encouraged. "Tell me what you like."

"All of it," she gasped. "Everything. I never want this to stop."

He grinned down at her. He wouldn't be able to hold it together much longer. Not while he watched how much she was enjoying herself. That brought his own gratification to a whole new level.

Restraining himself, he kept the rhythm that seemed to bring her outside of herself. Her fingernails dug into his back and her body seized with a soft series of helpless whimpers. Letting go, he gave another good thrust and erupted inside of her, feeling the release flow out of him until he was dead weight, covering her body with his.

Their heavy breaths mingled as he turned his head to rest it on her shoulder, kissing her forehead on the way. They lay like that for a while, quiet and breathing, him stroking her arm with his fingers, a peaceful contentment ebbing and flowing within him. He wasn't sure he'd ever felt this way before. It was so powerful, it was like a drug.

"You're not leaving," Naomi finally said. A note of insecurity barely hid inside the words.

"I'll call McGowen tonight," he murmured, covering her mouth with another kiss. "And tell him everything I want is here. You. And Gracie, too, if she'd ever have me." He didn't know how it would all work, or what he could do to change things with Dobbins. But they would figure it out.

Naomi moved to her side. "Gracie and I had a talk. I think the shock has worn off. She'll forgive you."

"I'll do whatever it takes." He intended to earn her forgiveness, to prove to her that he'd never intentionally hurt her.

Rolling to his side, he glanced at his watch. "Speaking of Gracie, I guess we should get some work done. Or she's gonna wonder what we did all day."

"I guess," Naomi said in a sulk. "But if we get everything done fast, maybe we can take a shower." She propped herself up on her elbow. "There *is* one working bathroom, you know. At least I think it works."

"We'll make sure to test it out," he promised.

* * *

Lucas preferred the naked thing to being fully clothed with this woman, but he had to admit it felt good to help Naomi work on her dream. "I guess that's it," he said, handing her a bottle of water. In a little over an hour, they'd torn down every scrap of wood paneling and had it piled on a tarp ready to be hauled out to the dumpster.

"We make a good team." She uncapped the water and took a swig, her eyes on his the whole time. Energy hummed through him at that desire coloring her face. They were both dusty and sweaty. Seemed to him like the perfect time to test out that shower.

With that in mind, he bundled up the tarp, making sure to seal in all the debris, and dragged it to the doorway.

"Here, I can help." Naomi set down her water bottle and rushed over, picking up the other side.

His gaze traveled down her body. "So how big is the shower?" he couldn't resist asking as they maneuvered their bundle through the kitchen to the front door.

"It's small." She shot him the smile she seemed to save just for him—shy, tempting, and brassy all at the same time. "Could be a tight fit."

"Sounds perfect to me." Moving faster, Lucas opened the front door. They made their way down the porch steps, hoisting the full tarp over to the driveway, where they chucked it into the dumpster.

Clapping the dust from his hands, he sidled up to Naomi, sweeping her under his arm and drawing her close. "I'm so ready for a shower," he said, unable to resist leaning down for a kiss.

But Naomi was staring at something across the street. "What's going on? What're the neighbors doing?" she asked, pulling away from him.

He turned to look. A group of people were huddled together, engaged in some serious discussion, in the driveway across from the inn. He recognized a few of them: Betty Osterman, who'd taught English at Topaz High, and Gus Hubbard, who'd written for the *Topaz Falls Herald* since God was a boy.

"Hey," Naomi called, heading over to join them. "Is everything okay?"

Lucas trotted over, too.

"Didn't you hear the sirens?" Betty asked when they'd joined them. "There were so many fire trucks blazing down the street, my cat's fur was standing on end."

Naomi glanced back at him, her face flaming with panic. "Sirens? No. We didn't hear anything. We were…um… doing some work in the house. Loud work."

Loud, hot work, Lucas thought. Work he'd like to do again. Which meant they should speed up the neighborly chitchat. "What's going on?" he asked.

Gus directed his gaze toward the mountains on the west side of town. "Wildfire," he said, pointing. "Up near the falls. Heard all the commotion about an hour ago."

Wildfire. Lucas squinted at the horizon, noticing for the first time an ominous plume of smoke hovering over the trees. "Near Topaz Falls?" he choked out, shifting his gaze to Naomi.

Her face had gone white.

"Far as I've heard, they're settin' up the command center at the trailhead," the man answered. "They're callin' out all the volunteers. Already got people from the county up there. Sounds like it's spreadin' fast."

"Oh my God." Naomi staggered backward, grasping at his arm. "Gracie's up there. She's hiking."

Betty's hand flew to her chest. "Oh dear."

"I'm sure everything's fine." Lucas took ahold of Naomi, dread churning in his gut. He couldn't be sure. Not until he saw Gracie's face. "We'd better get up there," he said, leading her away from the neighbors. "Make sure they're off the trail."

Naomi stumbled. She clutched his arm as though she'd forgotten how to walk.

Clumsily he led her to the truck. Every motion was a blur. Somehow he got the door open and helped her climb in. "I'm sure they're safe," he murmured. They had to be safe.

A hit of adrenaline carried him around the truck. He jumped into the driver's seat and gunned the engine before peeling out.

"Oh God," Naomi cried, her face in her hands. "I can't believe this. I can't believe I let Mark take her up there."

"You couldn't have known." They'd had the perfect morning. The most perfect morning he'd had in years. "There hasn't been lightning or anything." Nothing was off. Nothing could've indicated that the bottom was about to fall out of their lives. "Must've been a campfire that got away or something," he said, still trying to cut through the fog of shock.

Naomi's hands shook violently as she dug her phone out of her pocket. "Mark hasn't called." She tapped the screen and held it up to her ear. "And his phone goes straight to voicemail."

"There's hardly any reception up there," he assured her, doing his best to override the panic trying to sneak into his tone. He never got service around there. The trailhead wasn't that far from his favorite fishing spot, so he knew. But his heart still raced with movement of the truck's speedometer. "I bet they're waiting for us at the trailhead." He ran his hand up and down her arm. "Maybe Mark wanted to stick around and see if there was anything he could do to help out."

"I hope so," she whimpered. "Please."

The whispered prayer drilled into his heart, echoing over and over. *Please.*

The speedometer inched up until they were traveling well over the town's thirty-mile-per-hour limit. He avoided Main Street, taking the neighborhood avenues instead, and sure enough, once they'd made it to the west side of town, they saw a cloud of thick, ugly smoke mushroom over the mountain.

"Oh my God," Naomi gasped, digging her fingers into his arm.

The sight shattered his breath. That wasn't smoke from a couple of trees burning. It looked like the whole damn forest was on fire.

He blitzed out onto the highway and veered off onto the county road that switchbacked up into the trees.

The small parking lot at the Topaz Falls trailhead was crowded with fire trucks and police cars and SUVs, all in a flurry of activity. Lucas parked on the road and helped Naomi climb out of the truck. In the chaos, he spotted Dev standing near Mark's car.

Hand in hand, they raced in that direction. "Has anyone come off the trail?" he yelled even before they'd reached Dev.

"No." Dev glanced at the car. "I was just getting ready to run the plates, figure out who it belongs to."

"Mark and Gracie," Naomi wheezed, her hand clutching her chest. "They left a few hours ago. Around nine."

The deputy's mouth formed a grim frown. "And you haven't heard from them since?"

"No," she whispered, tears sliding down her cheeks.

Lucas gathered her against his side.

"I'll call up search and rescue, get a team out there." Dev gave Naomi's shoulder a squeeze. "I'm sure they're all right. Maybe they came down a different way because of the smoke." He stepped away and barked into a radio.

Naomi wriggled out of Lucas's grasp and turned to stare up at the mountain. He looked, too. The acrid scent of burning wood made his eyes water.

"Lucas," she whispered. "Where are they?"

He didn't know. He didn't know if they were up there. Or down at the road. Or lost somewhere in between. But he couldn't stand here and do nothing. He couldn't be helpless. "I want to go," he said, turning to Dev. "I want to be on the team."

"Too dangerous." The deputy shook his head. "We've got plenty of trained volunteers."

Where were they? Lucas scanned the parking lot. People were running back and forth, talking, looking at maps, but no one was heading up the damn trail. "Where are the volunteers?" he demanded. "Are they here yet?"

"Not yet. Still getting mobilized."

He released his hold on Naomi, blood pounding in his head. "Then I'm going up. Now."

"I can't let you go, man." Dev shifted as though he wanted to block his way. "Sorry. The situation is too volatile. You know how dry it's been. Wind's shifting all over the place. No way to tell which way this thing is moving."

Lucas had never wanted to deck a police officer. Ever. Until right now. "You can't stop me."

"I can cuff you," Dev threatened. "Lock you in the back of my cruiser."

Lucas stared the man square in the face. "Just give me twenty minutes. I'll run up and see how things look, see if there's any sign of them."

The deputy hesitated, glancing around like he wanted to assess the possibility of anyone overhearing.

"You'd do the same thing," Lucas persisted. "You know you would."

"Fucking hell," the deputy growled out. "Fine." He reached into his patrol car and pulled out a radio, shoving it into Lucas's hands. "Take this, you stubborn bastard. You keep in touch or I'll come up there myself and pull you off the trail."

Lucas clipped the radio to his belt. "I will. I promise."

"I'm coming, too." Naomi grabbed ahold of his shirt.

"No." He lifted her chin, looked down at her. "You have to stay." Across the parking lot, he saw Darla drive up. She'd been on the volunteer force for years. Hooking his arm through Naomi's, he pulled her over to Darla's car. Right as the woman stepped out, he ambushed her. "Mark and Gracie are up there. I need you to stay with Naomi."

"Shit." Darla's eyes went wide. "You're going after them?"

"I have to." He couldn't watch Naomi suffer this way. The smoke was getting so thick. So black. What if they'd passed out from smoke inhalation? "I don't want Naomi to be alone."

Judging from the way she clung to him, she didn't want him to go. Her eyes were wide, glazed with a look of shock.

Darla nodded briskly. "Of course I'll stay with her." She moved in closer to her friend. "It'll be all right, honey," she said, gently peeling Naomi's grip from Lucas.

Before he turned, he kissed her forehead. "I'll find them," he promised. "You stay with Darla. Okay? I have a radio. Let me know if they come back."

"No!" Naomi clawed at his shirt. "I'll come with you. We can look together."

Lucas shot Darla a glare. She wouldn't make it. Her body shook so hard she couldn't even stand up straight. "You need to stay here," he said as gently as possible. "Just hold on, baby. I won't come back without them."

Chapter Twenty-four

Naomi darted after Lucas again but Darla pulled her back. "Let him go," her friend ordered, blocking her way. "You're in no condition to run up that trail."

It was true. Naomi knew it was true. She was already shivering with sweat, on the verge of throwing up.

"I can't believe this." A stark helplessness gouged her. She turned to her friend, her knees buckling. "Why did I let him take her up there?"

Darla took Naomi's cheeks in her hands, steadying her with a long, sure glare. "This isn't your fault. This isn't even Mark's fault. No one could've predicted this would happen."

"I could've," she sputtered, her heart floundering in the hollow feeling that stretched all the way through her. "I should've set more boundaries. I should've forbid him from taking her away from the house."

Her friend shook her head slowly, eyes focused and

intent. "Mark's a great guy. You know that. He would never put Gracie in danger on purpose."

Tears clogged her eyes. They wouldn't stop. The fire's thick haze hovered over her, tinted with that nightmarish smell. Everything was burning. Her world was burning.

"Come on. Let's get you into a chair." Darla half-dragged her to her car. She popped the trunk and pulled out a folded camping chair. Once she'd set it up she sat Naomi in it, then shoved a water bottle into her hand. "You look like you're about to pass out."

Naomi wanted to. God, how she wanted to. Close her eyes and wake up from this nightmare. Her eyes blanked. All she saw was that trail. Leading up the mountain into a fog of smoke.

Chaos hummed all around her—cars and people and ATVs. But it seemed to be happening in a movie—like she was watching someone else's tragedy unfold.

Closing her eyes, she fisted her hands and fought the hopelessness that spread through her like the smothering smoke. She had to fight it.

Blinking hard, she opened her eyes.

Dev ran over and put his head together with Darla's, murmuring in a hushed tone. The conversation was short and clipped—all business. When he hurried away, Darla knelt next to her. "Dev said they're mobilizing a team. They'll send the ATVs up after Lucas and try to get them spread out so they can cover more ground."

Her head nodded in what seemed to be slow motion. That small movement took so much effort. A painful hammering in her heart ordered her to get up and do something. Scream, tear up that trail after her daughter. Instead, she gripped Darla's hands and pulled herself out of the chair. She would not do this. She would not sit here helpless.

Darla squeezed her hands. "Your color's coming back."

"I'm better. Stronger." And she could help. She might not be able to run up the trail, but she could do something. "Come on," she said, tugging on Darla's arm. "Let's see how we can help."

She marched over to where Dev now stood with Hank Green, engaged in a heated discussion.

"I just heard from the fire chief," Hank informed them. "They suspect arson."

Arson. Outrage tangled with the fear that still thumped in Naomi's heart. "Someone set the fire on purpose?"

"Too early to say officially," Dev insisted, glaring at Hank like he wanted him to shut up before the rumors got going.

"But that's how it looks," Hank countered, scowling at the deputy. "And I'll bet I know exactly who's responsible."

"Enough." Dev's voice bordered on a shout. "We won't know anything until we get a handle on the fire," he said firmly. "No use pointing—"

"They're saying it started on the south side of the mountain," Hank interrupted. "Near the river. We all know who spends his time down there."

Naomi looked at Darla. The south side by the river. That was where Lucas had taken her fishing. But surely they didn't think he'd started the fire. "He was with me all morning!" She hadn't meant to yell, but desperation shattered her control. "There's no way he could've had anything to do with this."

"It's probably been smoldering for at least a day," Hank argued, as though he was enjoying her misery.

"Right now, this is all speculation." Judging from the

harsh edge in his tone, Dev was losing patience. "Besides, if he'd started the fire, why would Lucas be up there right now? Risking his life to search for Gracie and Mark?"

"Isn't it obvious?" the mayor sneered.

"What the hell is that supposed to mean?" Naomi backed up a step so she wouldn't haul off and hit him the way her daughter had hit the Dobbins kid.

"It's okay," Darla said, eyeing the mayor like he was parasite. "Hank's just blowing smoke again. Typical day in Topaz Falls."

Anger made the man's face glow. "It means he wanted to look like the hero. He set the fire so he could go and rescue your girl and make himself the hero." His lips curled in a self-righteous smirk. "He knew she'd be hiking up here this morning. Didn't he?"

Naomi refused to answer the question. "You don't even know him." Hank Green had always hated the Cortez family. He'd find every excuse to go after Lucas just to spite his father.

"I know what he is," Hank snapped. "The whole town knows what he is. You're the only one who's naïve enough to believe he's changed."

Naomi could've hit him then. She could've popped him right in the face if Dev hadn't stepped between them.

"Enough," he said again. The deputy put a hand on Hank's shoulder and directed him away. "We're not discussing this now. We have a hell of a lot to do, the most important thing being locating two missing persons and getting them off that trail."

He led the mayor away, but something told Naomi that wasn't the end of it.

* * *

The fire seemed to have spread to his lungs. Lucas hadn't broken his swift jog since he'd left the trailhead. It felt like years ago, but he'd only gone a few miles. Every five minutes he checked in with Dev, but even with the firefighters spreading out all over the mountain, no one had seen any sign of Gracie and Mark.

He stuck his fingers in his mouth and whistled again because that was all he could do. *Keep shoving one foot in front of the other. Keep whistling. Stop and listen.* He did that all the way up the side of the mountain. As he climbed higher the air grew murky, but the smoke rose above him, pouring in from the south.

He hadn't seen any flames yet, but he kept a close eye on that wind as he followed the trail. The forest was restless, quiet, but full of sounds that kept startling him to a stop. Cracking twigs, rustling leaves. Every time he heard something, he'd pause and suck in his breath, wishing his fucking heart would slow down so he could hear better.

Jogging up a steep section of the trail with sweat trickling down and burning his eyes, he yelled Gracie's name for what had to be the hundredth time. Each time her name scraped his throat, he prayed she'd answer.

The trail veered more to the south, winding around a sharp curve.

Lucas hesitated. Here the air was thicker, darker, almost like dusk was descending in the middle of the afternoon. A form appeared a ways off and at first he gasped a hopeful breath, but then a fireman's yellow gear came into focus.

The guy was running toward him. "You shouldn't be out here," he called.

Lucas didn't recognize him. He held up the radio, hoping he'd think Dev had given him free rein. Truthfully, the twenty minutes Dev had given him had ended a while ago. The deputy had called him back and he'd lied, saying he was on his way down.

But he couldn't go down there. Not without Gracie. He couldn't face Naomi. "I'm looking for the missing hikers," he said, battling a cough. "A little girl and a man in his late twenties."

"We're keeping an eye out." The firefighter frowned, eyeing the smoke that seemed to be creeping closer. "But the wind's shifting again. We have no idea what this thing's gonna do."

He didn't care what it would do. He couldn't go back to Naomi without Gracie. "I'm guessing they went off the trail." Mark would've taken Gracie in the opposite direction when he saw the smoke. "I'll head north," he said. "Hopefully I'll meet up with—"

A muted shrill cut him off. Once again, he held his breath. "Did you hear that?"

The firefighter removed his hat. "What?"

"A whistle." His blood pumped hard. "I heard a whistle." It had to be.

The guy looked at him like he'd lost it, but Lucas strained his ears and headed a few steps to the east. Something trilled again. So faint. He jerked his head to look at the fireman.

The man nodded. "It's definitely something."

Lucas stuck his fingers in his mouth and whistled. They both stilled. Seconds stretched into a torturous minute. Then the sound rang out again. A whistle and a bark.

"Bogart!" Lucas darted around a spruce and bolted to

the east, calling to the dog and whistling like he'd lost his mind.

The answer came faster this time. Louder. Dodging trees and rocks, he tore down the mountainside, then stumbled along a rocky slope, his feet slipping on the loose gravel. The fireman stayed close behind him, barking into a radio. But Lucas was afraid to call Dev. To get Naomi's hopes up. What if it wasn't Gracie?

The rocks got bigger, forming a series of jagged shelves that hung over the mountainside. Down below, Bogart sprinted into view.

"Gracie!" he yelled.

"Lucas!" She wasn't far behind the dog. "Lucas, Dad needs help!"

"We're coming," he told her, picking his way down the rocks.

Moments later he pulled her into his arms and she hugged him so tightly he couldn't breathe. "Gracie. Oh God, Gracie girl." Bogart jumped and whimpered like he wanted to be held, too.

"Dad slipped on the rocks when he was trying to help me," she sobbed. "He hurt his leg real bad."

"Can you show us where?" Lucas held her tighter, trying to stop her trembling.

Bogart tore away from them, staying near the edge of the boulders.

"That way," Gracie said, pointing after the dog. "Bogy knows."

The fireman ran ahead of them, following the dog, yelling into his radio. "We've located the missing hikers." He rattled off some coordinates, his voice growing fainter as he disappeared around a bend.

Lucas tried to breathe, his feet suddenly clumsy. He set Gracie down and knelt. “You’re okay, though?” he choked out, his eyes full. He couldn’t blame that on the smoke.

“I’m okay,” she murmured.

“What happened?” He stood and took her hand, continuing toward the sound of Bogy’s frantic barks. “How’d your dad fall?”

“When we got to the waterfall, we smelled all that yucky smoke. At first we thought it was a campfire, but then it got so dark.” Gracie slowed, her eyes reading the ground. She guided him past a small cave in a rock face. “Dad thought the smoke was coming toward us, so we ran off the trail and came down this way.” Her voice wavered. “I couldn’t do all the big rocks so he was helping me, but his foot slipped and he fell.”

“I’m sorry, honey,” Lucas murmured. “I’m so sorry that happened.” That she’d had to witness something so terrifying.

“I just want him to be okay.” She rubbed the tears from her cheeks as though she was trying to be strong.

“He’ll be okay,” Lucas assured her. “They’ve got all kinds of people ready to help him.”

They skirted the base of one more cliff before Lucas caught sight of Mark, propped up against a fallen tree, his legs stretched out in front of him.

Bogy licked his face while the fireman asked him questions.

“Boy, am I glad to see you guys,” Mark said as Lucas and Gracie approached. Sweat and obvious pain had turned his skin sallow.

“We’re glad to see you, too.” Lucas took a quick look at the leg. Judging from the blood, it was a compound fracture.

"Will he be okay?" Gracie asked fearfully, her eyes wide and teary.

Lucas lifted her into his arms again. It was finally hitting him that they'd found her. That she was safe. "He'll be fine. You were so smart to use your whistle." And thank God they'd had the dog with them.

"Thank you for finding us," she whispered.

"You saved him," Lucas told her. "You were so brave. We found him because of you. And now he'll get the help he needs."

The fireman stood. "It's a nasty break," he said grimly. "They're sending up a UTV."

"Hear that?" Lucas brushed a kiss on the top of her head. He held the girl tighter. Couldn't seem to put her down.

"I was so scared." Gracie laid her head on his shoulder.

He closed his eyes, savoring the feel of holding this precious little girl in his arms.

"You don't have to be scared anymore," he told her. "I'll always protect you."

Chapter Twenty-five

Gracie hadn't let go of him since he'd first seen her. All the way down the mountain she'd sat wedged against him in the UTV, holding onto his hand as though they were teetering on the edge of the cliff. Bogy lay on the other side of Gracie, his head in her lap.

When they broke through the trees and blitzed into the trailhead's parking lot, Gracie sat up straight, her eyes searching.

The thing skidded to a stop and Naomi called out, running over to meet them. Then the girl ripped away from him and threw herself into her mom's arms, sobbing as though she could finally let go. Bogy barked, happily circling them.

"Oh, baby. Oh, Gracie. I was so worried." They sunk to the ground, tangled in an embrace no one else could touch. Both crying. Both laughing. So much a part of each other.

Lucas gave them that moment and hung back by the UTV, making sure the paramedics went easy on Mark.

As they loaded him onto the gurney, Lucas shook his hand. "She's lucky to have you for a dad," he said. He could appreciate all the man had done to protect Gracie up there. He was a decent guy. They'd all come a long way since high school. Including Mark.

Pain still gripped his features, but Mark held the firm handshake. "She's lucky to have all of us."

They wheeled the gurney toward the ambulance. As they passed Naomi and Gracie, both of them stood.

Gracie perched on her tiptoes to give Mark a hug and Naomi reached out to squeeze his hand. "Thank you for taking such good care of her." She brushed away her tears.

"Actually, she's the one who took care of me," Mark said with a laugh. "I'd hate to think what would've happened if I'd been on my own out there."

"I'm just glad you're both okay." She put an arm around her daughter as though she'd never let her out of her sight again. Lucas could relate to that feeling.

"All right. We gotta get him to the hospital." One of the paramedics eased the gurney down the hill.

As they wheeled him away, Mark waved.

"See you at the hospital soon!" Gracie called. Then she and Naomi walked over to where Lucas stood, with Bogy right on their heels. Wordlessly, Naomi slumped against him and he wrapped his arms around them both.

"Thank you," she breathed against his neck. "Oh God, Lucas. Thank you." He kissed the skin right under her ear, fighting the tears he'd already held off too long. These two girls meant everything to him.

Naomi pulled back. "Can we go?" she whispered. "I'd like to take Gracie home. Get her cleaned up."

He hesitated. "I'm guessing they can use my help here.

But you can take my truck. I'll hitch a ride with someone else." Surely Levi and Lance would be up to help as soon as they heard...

"No." Naomi's voice broke. "I want you to come with us. We need to go." An urgency slipped into her tone. "Please, Lucas. Let's just go."

He wanted to go, take Gracie and Naomi away from here, but how could he leave when they obviously needed all the help they could get? "Let me talk to Dev." He'd spotted him standing by the table where they'd spread out the maps.

"No." Naomi tried to pull him away.

He studied her eyes. "What's wrong? What's going on?"

Before she could answer, Dev sought him out.

"Nice work," he said, clapping Lucas on the back. But a look of grim concern pulled at the corners of his mouth.

"Can't take all the credit." Lucas slipped his arm around Naomi. "Her mom's the one who stashed a whistle in her backpack. And Bogy here made sure we knew where to go." He gave the dog's head a good scrub. That's what had saved them both.

Neither Dev nor Naomi smiled. They shared a look. "We need to talk," Dev said. He glanced at Naomi. "Why don't you take Gracie over to get some water?"

Her mouth opened like she wanted to argue, but she must've thought better of it. Instead of speaking, she gave Lucas's hand a squeeze and led her daughter away.

"What's up?" he asked. He didn't like the man's troubled look. They should've been celebrating the fact that they'd located Gracie and Mark. Something was off.

Dev glanced around like he wanted to make sure no one would hear them. "Wanted to give you a heads-up." His voice was low. "Investigators already found evidence of arson on the south side of the mountain. Near the river."

The south side. His favorite fishing spot. "Someone did this on purpose?"

The deputy nodded, still keeping a wary eye on anyone who passed by. "They found a bunch of empty turpentine containers. And receipts they've already traced to a hardware store in Denver."

"Shit." Just like that, the adrenaline was back, pumping through him, clenching his muscles into stone. Someone had started the fire. It could've killed Gracie...

Dev pulled him to the outskirts of the parking lot. "Thing is, they were purchased around the same time you were down in Denver."

An icy realization slid down his spine. He was being set up. "I didn't do this." That was crazy. How could anyone think he'd be that stupid? "You really think I'd leave evidence out in the open like that?"

"I know you didn't do it," Dev assured him. "But someone wants it to look like you did."

And he knew exactly who that person was. Rage simmered beneath his skin, making his body freeze and burn at the same time. "He could've killed her." Lucas went to step away, to search for the man responsible.

"I know." His friend pulled him to a stop. "I'll do everything I can to clear you. But the chief is gonna go by the book on this. And so far the evidence is pointing to you."

Of course it was. God. He'd been so stupid to think that Marshal wouldn't keep looking for a way to get rid of him. "It was Dobbins. It had to be."

Based on Dev's sure nod, he was already thinking the same thing.

The shock of it still pounded through him. "This is attempted murder."

"We don't know if he realized Gracie would be up here today," Dev reminded him. "It could be shitty timing. But it's pretty obvious he has it out for you. We need something definitive to nail him." The deputy started to walk away. "I'll keep searching. But you need to steer clear. Understand? I'll keep you posted. But I think it's best if you take Naomi and Gracie home. Lay low for a few days."

"I will. Thanks." What other choice did he have?

Dev gave him one last nod before joining a group of volunteers gathered near the command post.

Lucas walked back to Naomi in a stunned fog. She already knew what Dev had told him. That was why she'd wanted to get him out of there so fast.

Before he could say anything, Gracie inserted herself between them, holding both of their hands. "We should go to the hospital," she said. "I don't want Dad to be there alone."

"We will," Naomi promised. "But first we need to go home and get you cleaned up." She kept stealing worried glances at him as though she could see the darkness in his eyes.

He didn't try to hide it from her. He knew Marshal was a loose cannon, but this was far worse than anything he could've imagined.

Together they walked to the truck, Bogy attached to his side as though he didn't want to be left behind, Naomi and Gracie talking about what they could bring to the hospital to help Mark feel better. Lucas wasn't listening. He couldn't. How much had Naomi and Gracie suffered in the last week because of him? Because of his past? It wasn't worth it. He couldn't do this to them. He'd promised Gracie he would protect her. But he couldn't.

Which only proved he should've left Topaz Falls a long time ago.

* * *

He was drifting away from her again. Naomi studied Lucas's stone-faced profile as they drove down the highway. He hadn't said a word, not that anyone could get in a word around Gracie's chatter. The trauma of the experience seemed to be wearing off and now her daughter kept reliving every detail of her harrowing morning as though fascinated by the adventure of it.

"And then I heard a whistle. I knew it was a whistle!" she prattled, petting the dog's head. "So Dad told me to follow the rocks and see if I could find anyone. But he said not to go too far. He wanted to be able to hear me still."

"You did so good," Naomi told her daughter, reaching back to squeeze her arm—to touch her again. She might just sneak into her bed after she was asleep later and hug her all night.

"I've never met such a brave ten-year-old." Luca's tone was too controlled. A storm brewed in him; Naomi could see it. Dev had filled her in on everything just before they'd brought Gracie back. Someone was trying to frame him for arson. They'd endangered Gracie in the process, and now Lucas looked like he wanted to kill someone.

She feared the anger she sensed building in him. Not because she thought he'd act on it, but because she knew Lucas well enough to know that he would protect her and Gracie at all costs. Even if it meant him giving up something he wanted.

Her heart was heavy with the remnants of fear, relief…

and devastation that someone could be so calculated and callous. She reached over to Lucas, massaging his neck, his shoulders, trying to tell him they would figure it out. They would overcome this, but she saw the doubt in his features.

He pulled into her driveway and cut the engine.

Gracie scooted out of the truck, likely intent on hurrying so they could get over to the hospital, but Lucas didn't budge. He sat and stared straight ahead.

"You take Bogy into the house," Naomi called to her daughter. "We'll be there in a minute."

Once her daughter had disappeared, Lucas turned to her.

"I can't do this. I can't do this to you. I can't do this to Gracie."

"*You're* not doing anything." Her voice rose against the injustice of this. They'd waited so long for this chance to simply love each other. They'd been through so much. "Dev will get him. He'll find something and he'll lock Dobbins up." Tears soaked through the words. She took his hands in hers, wondering how she'd lived without him all this time. Knowing she couldn't live without him anymore.

Lucas stared down at their hands. "Until he does, I have to leave. I have to go back to the McGowens'."

One by one the tears fell, streaking down her cheeks. He leaned in and kissed them away. "You and Gracie mean everything to me. Everything," he uttered, his own eyes glistening. "I can't let anything happen to you. I can't even risk it."

"I'm not afraid of him." Things would work out this time. They had to. They deserved it.

"I could end up in prison again. If Dev doesn't find anything. If all of the evidence points to me."

"But Dev knows you didn't do it." She let the desperation

in her voice speak what she couldn't say. If he left again, he would break her heart. He would break both of their hearts. She'd let him in and now he was part of their lives.

"Who knows if anyone'll listen to Dev? I can't risk it." He pulled her close and kissed her lips slowly, savoring, clinging to her. "I love you. I've always loved you. No matter what happens, that'll never change. You're the light that's seen me through all of the darkest times in my life."

"And I'll see you through this, too." She wrapped her arms around his neck, holding on as though she could keep him there with her forever.

Chapter Twenty-six

She had to keep busy. Naomi put away the last of the dinner dishes, carefully stacking the plates, reorganizing the cups three times. Heartache clung to every movement and made everything seem heavier. Lucas hadn't come in with them after he'd brought them back to the ranch. He'd said he had things he needed to take care of and she hadn't found the courage to ask him what. She suspected those things had to do with packing and preparing to go back to the McGowen ranch, but she refused to acknowledge it. Refused to believe he could walk away so easily.

Rinsing a rag in the sink, she went to work scrubbing the countertops.

All afternoon, she'd made sure she hadn't sat still. After getting Gracie cleaned up, the two of them had gone straight to the hospital to see Mark. His surgery had gone well, and they expected him to be released within a few days.

After they'd gotten home Gracie kept asking to see Lucas, but Naomi hadn't been able to get ahold of him.

So the two of them had a quiet dinner and then Gracie had fallen asleep in front of *The Little Mermaid*. As Naomi clumsily hauled her to bed, she remembered how Lucas had carried her, so careful and competent, as though he'd tucked in a little girl every night for years. There was nothing quite as sweet as seeing a strong man carry a little girl so tenderly.

Her hand bore down on the counter, working at a dried splotch of orange juice that had been there since the last time her emotions had driven her to clean. By the time she was done in here, every square inch of the kitchen would sparkle. It wasn't as if she'd get any sleep tonight, anyway.

She scrubbed and scoured and scraped until a knock on the front door finally gave her a reason to throw down the rag.

Anticipation beat all through her. It was amazing how even the thought of seeing Lucas standing at her door fixed her. Fixed everything.

She hurried down the hallway, carried by the craving to be in his arms, to feel the comfort of his body against hers. Bogart grunt-barked at her heels all the way to the door as though he was as hopeful as she was.

She opened it, ready to fall against him, but it wasn't Lucas. Levi stood under the porch light, shoulders hunched, hands stuffed deep into his pockets. Behind him stood Lance and Jessa, and Luis.

Oh God. "Is everything okay?" She took ahold of the door to steady herself. Had Lucas left without saying goodbye?

None of the men would look at her directly, so Jessa pushed her way in. "Everything *will* be okay. But there's something we need to tell you." She glanced over her shoulder. "*Right*, guys?" she prompted sternly.

"Right," all three of them responded in a mumbled chorus.

"Okay..." Naomi backed away from the door so they could come in.

"You'd best sit down for this." Jessa quickly guided her to the overstuffed chair near the fireplace.

Levi, Lance, and Luis all sat on the couch, stiff and uncomfortable, but Jessa sat on the arm of the chair, settling in next to Naomi with a reassuring arm around her shoulders.

"What is it?" She couldn't bear the silence. Something terrible must've happened.

"Ahem." Her friend cleared her throat loudly and widened her eyes at the men.

Levi scooted forward on the couch, hunching over so that his elbows rested on his knees.

For once the youngest Cortez brother looked serious. The charismatic light that always illuminated his eyes had dimmed. "There's something you need to know."

"So tell me already." It couldn't be any worse than what she was imagining in her head. "Did Dev arrest Lucas?"

"No," Jessa said quickly, shaking her head as though disgusted by Levi. "Lucas is up at our place."

She let out the breath she'd been holding since they'd come in.

"But he's not doing so good." Lance's gaze barely lifted to hers.

"Is that why you came? Should I try to talk to him?" God, she wanted to. She wanted someone to give her permission to go to him, to bring him out of that dark place he'd gone to when he'd talked to Dev. "I'll convince him to stay. We'll fight back. We'll make sure no believes he started the fire..."

"First we need to make sure everyone knows the truth about the fire ten years ago," Luis said gruffly.

"The truth." Naomi glared at the three men, trying to understand what they weren't saying.

"This is all my fault." Levi finally raised his head. "His life is falling apart again because of me."

"That's ridiculous. This is Marshal Dobbins's fault," she nearly shouted. God, why couldn't everyone see that? Why didn't Lucas understand that?

Levi looked at her directly. "Maybe so, but it's all because of what happened before. Dobbins can't let it go. He wants Lucas to suffer for it."

"Which is insane," she reminded them. "Lucas already paid the price. He's already atoned for everything." She'd forgiven him. Gracie had forgiven him. His family had forgiven him. That was all that mattered. They would stand by him, no matter what some lunatic had tried to do.

"He didn't start that fire at the rodeo grounds," Levi said quietly. "I did."

"What?" Even as the gasp shot out of her mouth, everything clicked into place. Everything. The suspicions she'd had back then. The shock, knowing Lucas never got into trouble. It'd never made sense until right now.

"I started the fire," Levi repeated as though he was afraid she hadn't understood.

She had. She just couldn't move. Couldn't speak.

Lance shared a look with his future wife. "When Levi told us what he'd done, Lucas and I locked him in his room and came up with a plan." He said it as though he'd rehearsed his part ahead of time. "We decided he should confess. He'd never been in trouble, and we thought he'd get off easy."

Naomi gripped the armrests, desperately trying to stop her world from spinning.

"I was having an affair with Maureen Dobbins," Luis explained. "And Levi found out. He was angry. They all were. I wasn't there for them. Not the way I should've been. So if anyone takes the blame in all this mess, it should be me."

"It doesn't matter now." Jessa looked around the room. "It's in the past. All that matters is figuring out how to help Lucas." She turned her attention to Naomi. "We'll figure this out."

"Figure it out?" She blinked at them, the fury and anguish filling her eyes with fiery tears. "I can't believe this." Bracing her hands against the armrests, she pulled herself out of the chair and moved away from them. From all of them. "He lost everything. *We* lost everything." His own brothers had stolen years of his life away from him.

Lance stood, too, but he wisely stayed on the other side of the room. "It was what Lucas wanted. He was adamant. You know him. He wanted to protect the rest of us."

"And you let him." She wanted to yell at them, to scream, but she could hardly manage a whisper. "My God, you let him sit in a jail cell for three years for a crime he didn't commit. You let him give up on a life he'd dreamed about..." On a life they'd dreamed about together. Did they even realize how much they'd taken away from Lucas? From her?

"I'm so sorry," Levi said, his voice as strangled by emotion as hers. "I never would've agreed to do it if I'd known what would happen. We thought he'd get probation, community service. I never imagined he'd be sent to prison."

"Well, he was." Naomi didn't bother to wipe away her tears. "All these years, you've let him take the blame." She directed the words to Luis. How could a father hurt his own son that way?

"He didn't know." Jessa rushed to her side. "Luis didn't know anything until last fall, when I asked Levi and Lucas to come home."

"How long have *you* known?" she asked her friend. There was plenty of anger to go around. All of these people she loved had been lying to her.

"Lance told me not long after we got engaged."

"Why didn't Lucas tell me?" Didn't he trust her enough to tell her the truth? He'd known her suspicions about the fire, anyway.

"He was still trying to protect us," Levi said. "And I get that you're pissed, that you probably hate me now. That's fine. But we need to figure out how to protect Lucas. He'll need all of us."

Naomi crept back to the chair, overwhelmed by warring emotions—anger and hurt and fear. Would she lose him again because of what they'd done?

Jessa crouched next to her. "What do you need, honey? Do you want us to go? To give you some space to process everything? We could talk tomorrow…"

"No." Naomi grabbed her hand, holding on tightly. They were right; if they were going to help Lucas they had to do it now. "Tomorrow's too late." Lucas might be gone, or Dev might have to arrest him. "We need to come up with a plan." Lucas had spent his entire life protecting the people he loved. That was one of the things she admired most about him. But now it was time for them to rescue him. "What did you have in mind?" she asked his brothers, hoping like hell they had some ideas. Because she had nothing.

"There's a town hall meeting. Tomorrow night," Levi said. "An update on the fire. I'll tell everyone in town the truth then."

"That's great, but it won't make him stay." Her eyes heated again. "He won't stay unless Dobbins is in custody." As long as that man was a threat to her and Gracie, Lucas would leave. He wouldn't risk their safety after what had happened earlier.

"I think you and I can take care of that." Jessa shot her a calculating smile. "All we have to do is target the one person who can bring him down."

* * *

Naomi sashayed into the Cut Above Beauty Salon behind Jessa, five minutes late for their appointment with Jen Dobbins. She'd never been to the lone salon in Topaz Falls, opting to make the trip to Denver once every eight weeks instead. The place wasn't exactly regarded as a high-end establishment, and normally she didn't entrust her unruly hair to just anyone. But this morning they had a special mission.

"You sure you want these people to do our hair for the wedding?" she whispered. The salon's interior didn't exactly give her extra confidence in their capabilities. The space was decorated with outdated hair posters featuring women who looked like they belonged on a late-'90s sitcom. The whole place smelled like the solution they used on perms, likely because their business catered to the little old ladies who came in twice a month.

"How hard could it be?" Jessa whispered back. "All they have to do is put in some curls and do a few twists. It's not rocket sci—"

"Good morning." A young receptionist slipped in through a door off to the side and greeted them enthusiastically. Naomi supposed that was probably because they didn't get many patrons under the age of sixty walking through their doors.

"Hi there." Jessa smiled just as brightly. "We're here for the bridal hair trial run."

"She's here for the hair," Naomi corrected before anyone got any ideas about touching her curls. "I'm just here to watch and offer opinions."

"Right. You must be Jessa and Naomi." The woman didn't even check the schedule. The salon didn't exactly have a full house that morning.

"I'll go tell Jen you're here."

After she'd disappeared, Naomi tried to wring the nerves out of her hands. "I hope this works."

"Of course it'll work." Jessa glanced around like an undercover detective. "We'll figure out how much she dislikes her ex, and then see if she has any proof that he went to that hardware store in Denver last week."

According to Levi, Dev had already talked to Marshal Dobbins regarding his whereabouts. Supposedly, he was in town all week, but of course no one could vouch for him being around 24/7.

"She might still love him," Naomi reminded her. "Which means she'll try to protect him."

Before her friend could answer, Jen hurried toward them. "Hi there!" She was a pretty girl. Plump and cheerful. Her long blond hair was streaked with pink. "Welcome to a Cut

Above!" She leaned in for hugs as though the three of them were old friends.

"Oh, wow. Hi." Naomi patted her back awkwardly, then pulled away. She knew *of* Jen. They'd both gone to Topaz Falls High, though Jen was a few years younger. Now her son went to Gracie's school so they ran into each other at some of the events. She'd already decided not to bring up the whole issue at school the other day, though it was tempting. Telling on Jen's son wasn't exactly relevant to their mission.

"Oh my God! I'm so excited to do your hair for the wedding!" Jen squealed. "Come on back. Let's get started!"

Jessa squealed, too. Naomi followed them while they chatted all the way to the stylist chairs in the back.

"Can I get you anything?" Jen gestured to a small kitchenette at the back of the shop. "Coffee? Tea? Bottled water?"

"No thanks," Naomi answered for both of them. Best to make this as quick as possible.

But Jessa sat down in the chair and settled in. "Actually, I'd love some coffee. Do you have any flavored creams? Hazelnut is my fave."

"Coming right up." Jen spun and booked it to the coffee pot.

"You're sure enjoying this," Naomi mumbled.

Excitement glittered in Jessa's eyes. "It's my first undercover investigation." She spun the chair around. "We're like Sherlock and Watson. Or Castle and Beckett!"

"Or Lucy and Ethel," Namoi said, considering she had a feeling this whole sham might end in a comedic disaster.

"Ohhhh." Jessa sat up straighter. "Can I be Lucy?"

"Lucy who?" Jen came back carrying a steaming mug.

"Lucy Ricardo," Naomi mumbled with a glare at her friend. "It's one of Jessa's favorite shows."

"Oh." Jen gave her skeptical look. "Is that how we're doing your hair for the wedding?"

Judging from the dramatic lift of her eyebrows, Jessa was tempted, so Naomi stepped in. "You were talking about having it half up and half down with some flowers, right?" She didn't want Jessa to make any hasty decisions she'd regret later.

"Oh. Right." Her friend's excited expression mellowed.

"Sure, we can do that." Jen fluffed the edges of Jessa's hair. She turned to the tower of plastic drawers that sat next to an oval mirror. "We'll need quite a few pins. And I can talk to the girls over at the flower shop about what we can use on your big day." She sighed dreamily. "I love weddings." As she turned around, her lips curled into a smirk. "If only everything that came after the wedding didn't suck."

Jessa widened her eyes in Naomi's direction with a covert message. That was exactly the opening they needed. "I was sorry to hear about you and Marshal," her friend said sympathetically.

"Yeah. It sucks." Jen started to comb out Jessa's hair. "I mean, it hasn't been great for years, but you always hope you can stick it out for the kids."

Sympathy rippled through Naomi. "Trust me. I get it. Being a single mom is no picnic." She knew that for a fact.

"Hell no, it's not. But it looks like that's where I'm headed." Her eyes brightened. "Hey! We single moms should stick together. Maybe we could hang out sometime."

"That's a great idea." Jessa sat perfectly still while the woman brushed her hair. "I mean, I'm not a single mom, but I do love a good girls' night."

Naomi shot Jessa a surreptitious glare. It felt so wrong to pretend to be friends with the poor woman when they were only fishing for information. Besides, they didn't have time for small talk. They couldn't strike up a friendship and go out and then ask what they needed to know. They didn't have time. A sense of urgency sputtered through her. "Jen...if you don't mind sharing...what happened with you and Marshal anyway?"

A panicked look thinned Jessa's lips, but the woman didn't seem to take offense. Jen simply sighed. "Honestly, he kind of lost it after his dad passed away." She set down the brush and fired up the curling iron that sat on her station. "I'm pretty sure he's been using again. Meth," she clarified. "So I finally told him to get out. I don't need another kid to take care of."

"I'm so sorry." She was. Sincerely. But she had to push; she had to find something that would help Lucas. "Do you two still talk?"

"Oh yeah. We have to." Jen took a section of Jessa's hair and wrapped it into the curling iron. "He picks up the kids for me a lot. Takes them out to dinner. Stuff like that."

Jessa narrowed her eyes at Naomi as though reminding her to be careful, but they were so close..."Do you happen to know if he was in Denver at all last week?" she blurted, earning another glare from her friend.

"He went a little over a week ago," Jen said warily. "On Wednesday. I wouldn't have known but he was supposed to pick up the kids from school that day. He called me to say something came up so I tracked his phone." She released Jessa's hair from the iron and a curl bounced down around her shoulder. "He's always lying so I wanted to see where he was." Setting down the curling iron, Jen eyed Naomi. "Why?"

Naomi approached her. They had him. They just needed

her to tell Dev. "Jen... you might want to talk to Dev. They found accelerant where the wildfire started yesterday. Turpentine. Traced from a store in Denver."

The woman gave her a blank stare as though she didn't understand.

"I think..." How could she say this delicately?

"Marshal might be trying to frame Lucas for starting the fire." Jessa didn't seem to care anymore about being delicate.

"What?" The woman gaped at them like they were crazy. "No. No way..."

"But you've noticed a change in him since last fall," Naomi prompted, ready to lead her out of there and drive her down to the station.

"Yeah..." She drew the word out as though considering everything. "He was more of a dick than normal. And he's been completely unreliable. But I can't imagine he'd do something that insane."

Before last week, Naomi never would've imagined it, either. "Anger makes people do crazy things." Not to mention drugs.

"Oh my God. Wasn't Gracie out there when the fire started?" Jen asked with a horrified expression.

"Yeah." That feeling of helplessness washed over Naomi again. But they weren't helpless. They could make him pay. "And Mark. Her dad. He broke his leg trying to get her out."

The woman's face paled. "You think... Marshal did that?"

Jessa pushed out of the chair and went to Jen's other side. "Like you said, he hasn't been himself. He's unstable. But if he started that fire, he needs to be held accountable."

Jen nodded slowly, her eyes wide, her mouth slack.

"Will you come with us to talk to Dev?" Naomi asked. Jen was their proof that Marshal had been in Denver at the same time Lucas was. Maybe it would be enough for him to get a warrant. "Just to hear what he has to say?"

The woman's expression shifted from shock to anger. "If it's true—if he really started that fire—I'm not gonna cover for his sorry ass."

That was what they'd been counting on.

Chapter Twenty-seven

There was no way around it. He was screwed. Lucas stared out his bedroom window. He could see Naomi's house right down the hill, but he couldn't be there. Couldn't be with her. Once again, the realities of his past barreled straight for him and hit him with the force of a freight train.

By now, everyone in town must've thought he'd started the fire to look like a hero. So he could run in and rescue Gracie, and be crowned as some kind of savior. Dobbins must've planned it all out. Everything. Even going to Denver the same time he'd been there to buy the Turpentine. *God.* He should've known. On his way out of town that day, he'd stopped by the gas station right next to Marshal's auto shop, and he'd made the mistake of telling the cashier he was on his way to Denver. He hadn't thought twice about it. Crazy how one friendly conversation had led him here.

He looked at the mess of clothes on the bed, at the half-packed suitcase. He couldn't go back to prison. Couldn't live in confinement again. Especially after having a taste of what it would be like to be with Naomi.

Going back now would kill him.

The door creaked open. Lance stuck his head in. "You ever gonna leave this room?"

"Won't have a choice when they come to arrest me." They'd haul him right back into his nightmare.

His brother stepped into the room but hung out near the door. "Dev'll find something. He knows you didn't do it."

"He might know, but no one else does." And if the evidence pointed to him, the town would be all too eager to hang him. "I never should've come back here. It was a mistake." It'd only caused trouble for Naomi and Gracie. And hell, it might cause trouble for Lance and Jessa, too. They were supposed to get married on Saturday. If this thing blew up and he got arrested, it'd ruin everything for them.

"That's bullshit," Lance said. "You belong here. With us. With Naomi. I don't care who Dobbins is and what kind of evidence he planted, you're not going back to prison."

"How can I stay here?" He'd seen the glares people were giving him at the trailhead after he'd brought Gracie down. They looked at him with anger, mistrust. "By now it's all over town that I set the fire so I could be a hero." He'd heard Lance and Jessa talking about it last night. It'd happened before in Colorado. A ranger who'd wanted some recognition set one of the biggest wildfires in the state's history. Everyone thought Lucas was just following in her footsteps.

His brother eyed the suitcase on the bed. "The truth has to come out eventually."

"Until it does, I think it's best if I go back down south."

If they even let him leave town. "Can you imagine what it would be like for Gracie to hear people saying I set the fire? It could've killed her." The kids at school were already giving her a hard time. Now it would be even worse. That was it; what got to him the most. He knew Naomi could deal with the gossip. But Gracie... she was ten.

"Gracie will know it's not true." Lance faced him. "She knows you would never do something like that."

"She may have known that before but then she found out I didn't tell her the truth about my past." Now she wouldn't trust him any more than Hank Green did.

Lucas went to the bed and shoved more clothes into the suitcase. "I've gotta pack." Then he'd force himself to go down to Naomi's house to say goodbye.

"Take it easy." His brother took another bundle of clothes out of his arms. "Wait until Naomi gets here."

That got him to stop. "She's coming here?"

Naomi stepped into the room just then, her eyes narrowing when she looked at the mess of clothes on the bed. "What're you doing?"

"I'll give you two a minute." Lance quickly ducked out of the room.

Naomi marched over to him. "What are you doing?" she asked again.

He couldn't look into her eyes. "I'm packing."

"For what?" Her eyes fired up as she stepped between him and the bed.

"I have to go." He couldn't explain why. Couldn't utter one damn word past the painful knot in his throat. Leaving her again would wreck him, but if it meant protecting Gracie—and Naomi—he'd do it. He'd suffer the rest of his life to make sure they never did.

Naomi moved closer to him. She was so captivating and delicate, but such a force to be reckoned with. She seemed to ignore the mess on the bed, the clothes, the suitcase. "Why didn't you tell me the truth about the fire ten years ago?"

He sank to the bed. Obviously she'd been chatting with his brothers. "Telling you the truth wouldn't have changed anything." They still would've lost all of those years. They still would've had to start all over.

She sat next to him. "I knew it wasn't you. I always knew."

Even just the feel of her thigh brushing against his was enough to flash the memories of holding her against him while they made love. "I wish I could go back and change things." Everything. Every decision he'd made that day that had brought them to this moment. The moment he had to say goodbye to her again.

He had to. Every time he thought of those seconds he'd spent searching for Gracie, he went back to that place where fear had sickened him. The outcome could've been so different…

"What happened wasn't your fault." Naomi turned to him, threading her fingers through his as though she could sense how much he needed her touch.

"I could've made sure it didn't happen," he murmured, running his fingers over her knuckles. Her skin was so soft…

"Bad things are going to happen sometimes. It's not up to you to stop them."

Maybe not, but he didn't need to provoke them, either.

"This isn't your fault," she told him for the umpteenth time. "You can't put that burden on yourself."

Too late. "I should've walked away from him at the bar

that night. I shouldn't have let it get to this point." He should've hauled Levi out of there before the fight started.

"You listen to me, Lucas Cortez." Naomi drew his face closer to hers. "I don't need you to save me from anything." Even though her voice had a harsh edge, her eyes were soft and open. "I only need you with me. Like you have been these last few weeks. Holding me. Letting me cry."

"It's not enough." He should be able to protect her from pain. Instead he'd brought it on her…

"You're enough," she whispered, emphasizing the words with a kiss. "Do you know that?"

"No." He didn't feel like enough. He'd never felt like enough.

She laid her hand on his cheek. Her touch was healing. "You're already good enough for me. Perfect. Nothing you will ever do could make me want you more than I want you right now." As if intent on proving it, she moved into his lap and brought her lips to his again. It held so much power; the way she kissed him, the way she touched him. She did want him. He could feel it in the fast pounding of her heart against his chest.

He held her tightly, kissing her slowly, letting her sweetness take him away from everything else. Maybe Naomi made him enough. Maybe it was them together. He started to lower her to the bed; he couldn't help it. When she was with him, he forgot about everything else.

"I need you to go somewhere with me," she murmured in the same soft tone she'd used right before they'd made love. "Please? It won't take long."

Her touch had so much power over him—already the troubles that plagued his life didn't seem so terrible. She was soft and warm, priceless…this lost treasure he'd searched for his whole life, but had never been able to hold onto.

"Okay." He sighed, focused on her lips. Their softness provoked that bottomless hunger, making his body plead for one more taste of her—to take her to the bed and make love to her, to lose himself inside of her...

"Okay," she repeated, sitting up. "Let's go."

He didn't ask where. He just let her lead him out the door.

* * *

When Naomi pulled up in front of the community center, Lucas didn't take off his seat belt. "What're we doing here?" Cars packed the parking lot, but only one or two people stood near the entrance, making their way inside.

"You'll see." She cut the engine and withdrew the keys. "We're already late. We have to hurry."

Hurry? "I'm not going in there." Especially if the whole town was there.

"You *need* to go in there." She drew closer and brushed a kiss over his lips. "You trust me, right?"

"Yes." He trusted her fully. Trusted that she'd only want what was best for him. "Don't know if I trust myself, though." If he saw Dobbins in there, he couldn't say what would happen.

Naomi must've seen the apprehension building in his eyes. "There's a community briefing about the fire," she explained. "And we're already late, which means we can sneak in the back. No one'll even see us."

He was tempted to send her in and tell her he'd wait in the car, but she likely wouldn't let him do that, so he got out and followed her through the entrance.

The community center was nothing like those fancy rec centers you'd see in a big city. It had once been the Episcopal Church, complete with a white steeple. They scooted quietly through the old wooden doors and into a small foyer. Beyond that, the space opened into a sanctuary with rows of staunch wooden pews that faced a small stage. Stained glass windows gave the room a holier-than-thou feel. As if this town needed any help in that department.

Lucas followed Naomi into the sanctuary, keeping his head down and trying to remain inconspicuous. Hank Green, king of sweater vests and bow ties, already stood at the podium speaking in his lofty monotone. Luckily the man didn't glance up from his notes as he and Naomi snuck in behind the back row and sat in a couple of vacant chairs.

"Right now we have level-one evacuation orders for all neighborhoods west of River Valley Road. The high school gym is being converted into a shelter for anyone who has nowhere to go," the man intoned. "But I also know the good citizens of Topaz Falls will come together and open their homes to offer the kind of hospitality this town is known for."

What about him? Lucas wondered. Green had one of the largest homes in town and had never had a family. The man could probably shelter fifteen people.

"We'll hand out maps after the meeting," Green went on. "Along with a list of what everyone can do to help. We'll need food and water donations for our fine firefighters who are on the front lines. Even with the state's resources, we'll all have to pull together to fight this thing."

A murmur of support bounded around the room. Lucas

kept quiet. He still didn't know what he was doing here. If anyone turned around and saw him, there was a good chance this meeting would turn into a public flogging.

Naomi smiled at him and snuck her hand into his as though telling him not to worry.

At the podium, Green gathered up his notes. "Now, before we close, are there any questions?"

An older woman Lucas didn't recognize waved her hand. "Is it true someone started the fire on purpose?"

This ought to be fun. He edged against the back wall and ducked his head.

"The fire chief has not officially released the cause yet," Green said stiffly. "But yes, we have reason to believe it is arson."

A commotion broke out as people began talking and looking around.

"Any other questions?" Green asked above the noise.

"Yeah. I have one."

Lucas's head snapped up. Why the hell was *Levi* sitting in the front row at a town hall meeting?

"In fact, mind if I take the mic for a minute?" His brother didn't wait for Green to answer. He simply walked up the aisle and nudged the man out of his way.

"This is highly inappropriate," Green huffed. "We're here to talk about the fire, not—"

"This is about the fire." Levi glared at the man until he shut his trap and stepped aside. "This about both fires. The one that started yesterday and the one at the rodeo grounds ten years ago."

"What's he doing?" Lucas started to stand, ready to pull his brother off the stage before he made a huge mistake, but Naomi kept ahold of his hand.

"Let him," she whispered. "It's time. He needs to do this. For you and for himself."

Restlessness needled him, but he forced himself to sit still, forced himself to watch Levi, the little brother he'd always protected, stand up in front of the whole town to make his confession. He slipped an arm around Naomi and braced himself for what was coming.

Levi bent down to the mic. "Lucas isn't responsible for the fire at the rodeo grounds. I am."

A rumble of murmurs grew into a roar.

The noise didn't seem to faze Levi. "I used lighter fluid and a match and then ran away when it got out of control."

"What on earth?" Green asked, but Levi didn't give him a chance to finish.

"Lucas took the blame. He went to prison for my mistake. And I don't want him to pay anymore. He's given up enough for me."

Lucas glanced at Naomi, at the tears that ran down her cheeks.

He slipped his arm around her. "I'm sorry." They'd lost so much time…

"Don't be. Not anymore." She leaned her head on his shoulder. "You're selfless, Lucas. It's one of the things I love the most about you." She peered up at him. "But you don't have to sacrifice your happiness anymore. Not for your family. Not for Gracie. And not for me."

At the front of the room, Levi cleared his throat and waited for the crowd's noise to die down. "You can all stop judging him now that you know the truth. You can stop trying to run him out of town."

Lance left his seat near the front and joined Levi behind the podium.

When was the last time *Lance* had attended a town meeting?

"And you can stop blaming him for the Topaz Falls fire, too," his older brother said into the mic. "He had nothing to do with it."

"You're all in on it." Lucas gazed down at Naomi. That's why she'd dragged him here.

"It's our turn to protect you." She nestled closer, and that feeling of having her by his side made everything right. All of those years they'd spent apart didn't matter now. All that mattered was their future together. Their future with the family they'd always wanted.

"You have no proof he didn't start the fire," Hank Green barked. "Then or now."

"Actually we do." Dev appeared near the back doors.

Somewhere in the middle of the crowd, there was a scuffling sound. Marshal Dobbins stood and started to make his way toward a side exit, but Dev quickly cut off his escape route. "Marshal Dobbins, you're under arrest for first-degree arson."

The man tried to bolt, but Dev tackled him and wrestled his arms behind his back.

Lucas blinked five times to make sure this was really happening, that Dev had Marshal in handcuffs and was leading him out of the sanctuary.

Loud chatter swarmed the room, swallowing the stunned silence.

Green whistled and took the podium again. "In light of the circumstances, I'd say the meeting is adjourned." Without acknowledging any of the Cortez brothers, the man hurried out after Dev.

Everyone stood and started to gather their things,

whispering in hushed tones, casting glances back at Lucas.

He sat right where he was, gaping at Naomi. "How the hell did that happen?" Given her beaming smile, she'd had something to do with all of this.

"Jessa and I had a talk with Jen Dobbins."

He couldn't stop himself from interrupting her with a kiss. He would kiss that beautiful smile every morning. Every night. As much as she'd let him for as long as she'd let him.

"Jen knew Marshal went to Denver last week," she said when he pulled back. "Dev was able to get one of the employees at the hardware store to identify him as the customer who'd purchased the turpentine."

"I can't believe this." He gathered her into his arms. "You fixed everything."

"*We* fixed everything," she corrected. "Levi and Lance and Jessa. And your dad. We all came up with the plan together."

"Thank you." He brought her fingers to his lips. "I'd almost given up."

"I wouldn't have let you." She moved in closer as though she was ready to kiss him again.

But a hearty throat clearing snagged his attention. "Hate to interrupt..."

That was a flat-out lie. Levi loved to interrupt.

Somehow Lucas managed to look away from Naomi. The room had emptied except for his family. At some point, they'd all snuck in—Jessa and Luis and Evie and Gracie stood with his brothers.

"Lucas!" Gracie launched herself at him. He caught her and pulled her into his lap. That same overwhelming relief that had flooded him after he'd found her out on the trail welled up again.

"I'm sorry." She smothered him with a hug. "I'm so sorry I got mad at you. I'll never get mad at you again. Not ever," she promised.

He gazed down into her precocious eyes. "You might," he told her. Especially if he had the privilege of being her stepfather. "You might get mad at me again someday." He leaned in. "But you know what? I can take it." As far as he could tell, parenting had some gut-wrenching moments, but the happy ones—the ones that lit you with joy from the inside like this one right now...those made the hard ones worth it.

"You're not a bad guy," Gracie told him earnestly. "You're the best guy in the whole wide world."

He laughed.

"It's true," Naomi said, scooting closer to him.

"It's true," Levi echoed.

"You deserve all of the happiness you were denied for too long, son." His father laid a hand on his shoulder.

Lucas covered it with his own. "It means everything to be back with my family. I can't believe you guys did all of this." It'd been a long time since he'd had anyone on his side. But maybe that was his fault, too. He could've come home sooner.

"Aw, it's no big deal." Levi always had to ruin the moment with a smart-ass comment. "Besides, it's not like they can prosecute me or anything. You already did the time. Compared to that, telling everyone the truth is nothing."

They both knew that wasn't true. Sometimes the backlash from regular people was worse than what the law could do to you. "Think it'll have any implications for your career?" His fans wouldn't like it when they found out what Levi had done as a teen.

"Nah." Levi seemed to brush it aside. "If anything, I'll get eaten alive on social media. But I've already got some ideas for how to repair the damage. Starting with launching a campaign to rebuild the grounds and bring the rodeo back to Topaz Falls."

"I'll do what I can to help," Lucas promised, still holding his girls against him. "Now that I'm sticking around for good."

"Awww." Jessa dabbed at her eyes. "We need to go out and celebrate! Darla said she'd close down for a private party. She's making a chocolate torte."

"Chocolate!" Gracie squealed, jumping out of Lucas's lap. "Let's go!"

"You can ride with us." Jessa herded Lance and Gracie toward the doors.

"And I'll give you two a lift," Levi offered to his father and Evie.

Luis nodded. "We'll see you two over there."

His family hadn't even cleared the doors before Lucas pulled the woman of his dreams into his arms again. "I hated thinking about leaving you." He would've, if he thought it could protect her from more pain, but it would've cost him his soul.

"I wouldn't have let you leave. Not this time," she said, touching her lips to his. "I would've hog-tied you and hid you in my bedroom."

"Is that plan out the window?" he wondered aloud. "Because it could be fun…"

He loved her laugh. Loved how it made him want to laugh

and hold her and let it soften all of the rough edges life had given him.

"Come on," Naomi said, linking her arm through his. "Let's get out of here. We might have a little time before we have to show up at Darla's..."

"No." They didn't have to be in a hurry. "We have more than a little time." He slid his hands onto her arms and brought her to face him. "We have all the time in the world." For once.

Even after he'd finished his prison sentence, he'd still been a prisoner. He couldn't have what he wanted, what he'd dreamed about. Naomi had changed that. She'd given him back a life—a real life with the potential for love and joy and intimacy.

For the first time in ten long years, he was free.

Chapter Twenty-eight

The unmistakable pitter-patter of rain on the roof drew Lucas to the window. He gazed out at the mountains, at the low-hanging clouds, at the dry ground finally being drenched. "About damn time," he said, rejoining his brothers in Lance's kitchen.

"Isn't rain on your wedding day a bad sign?" asked Levi.

Lucas flicked him in the ear. Something he'd missed doing. It'd been his favorite form of torture to inflict on his younger brother back in the day.

"Ow." Levi rubbed at his ear, revealing the same disgruntled expression he'd worn when he was six.

"Given how dry it's been—and the fact that there's a wildfire raging dangerously close to town—I'd say rain is a sign of good luck," Lucas told Lance. "Not that you'll need luck." Jessa was made of some strong stuff, and he had no doubt that their marriage would thrive.

"Jessa loves rain anyway." Lance sipped the good whiskey. "Says it makes everything more romantic."

"Well, she'd know." She was definitely an expert in that area.

"Speaking of romance..." Levi elbowed him. "You've been staying at Naomi's place this week, huh?"

"Sort of." He had dinner with them every night. Then, after Gracie went to bed, he and Naomi retreated to her bedroom, but he always left before Gracie woke up. Naomi wasn't quite ready to deal with her daughter's questions yet. But God, he couldn't wait until she was. Until they could have lazy mornings together...

"So what's your plan?" Lance awkwardly straightened his tie. Thankfully Jessa hadn't gone the tux route with the wedding. She likely knew they would've revolted.

"Plan for what?" he asked, playing dumb.

"Plan for the future," Levi said impatiently. "Plan with Naomi. Don't forget I stuck my neck out for you." And he'd made it known far and wide that he was already getting shit for it. The local Denver stations had run a story on the whole thing, and two days ago the national media had picked it up. They kept calling Lucas for exclusive interviews, but he turned them all down. He had more important things to focus on at the moment.

"You two getting hitched?" Lance came right out and asked.

He guessed it wouldn't hurt to share. "You two'd better keep this to yourselves. Got it?"

"Got it," they said in unison.

He reached into his pocket. Flicking open the lid on the ring box, he showed off his purchase. "Had to go to Denver to find it." He looked again at the wide platinum band, with its two carats of diamonds set into an intricately scrolled design.

"Whoa," Levi muttered.

"It's almost exactly like the one she saw when we were in high school." When he'd taken her on that date to Denver right before he was arrested.

"What're you waiting for?" Lance demanded. "After all this time, you should've had that ring on her finger the day after everything went down at the meeting."

"Don't want to steal your thunder." Lance and Jessa didn't need him to take the focus off them right before their wedding. "Figured I'd wait until you two were back from Maui. So we could all celebrate."

"Don't wait," Lance said. "Not on our account. Jessa's been hounding me, asking me every day if you've bought the ring yet. When I said I didn't know, she told me to go through your things."

"Sounds about right." Given what he knew about Jessa's penchant for happily ever afters.

"She'd love it if you proposed today." Lance set down his empty glass. "It'd make our day that much better." He grinned. "It'd get her off my back, too, so in a way you'd be helping me out."

"I'll think about it." It didn't have to be a production. He didn't have to take the focus off Lance and Jessa. He could pull Naomi away from the crowd, maybe during the reception…

"I could prepare a special karaoke number," Levi offered. "Do a little serenade to set the mood for ya."

"Thanks, but I don't need help setting the mood." He'd been setting the mood for over two weeks. And truth be told, the ring was starting to burn a hole in his pocket. Even after only three days.

Now that Lance had given him permission, he didn't want to wait anymore.

* * *

"How can you be so calm?" Naomi demanded, peeking out the shelter's window. "Half the town is out there hunkered under a tent and it's raining cats and dogs."

There'd be mud and mess and everything would get wet…

Smiling like a woman in love, Jessa handed her one of the fancy umbrellas she'd ordered just in case. "There could be a tornado out there and I still would feel like this is the best day of my life."

"It'll be the best day of mine if I get to third base with that guy sitting in the last row right there," Darla said, her gaze stuck to the window.

"What guy?" Jessa looked out over her shoulder.

"The one in the black suit. Blond hair?"

"That's my cousin," Jessa scolded. "And he's twenty."

"Damn." Darla's gaze roved away from him as though searching for another potential victim.

Naomi turned from the window and checked Jessa's hair and makeup again. "You look so beautiful," she murmured, shaking a wrinkle out of Jessa's train, trying not to think about what the mud would do to it. She'd stashed a Tide stick in her purse, but that wouldn't cut it.

"This'll be you soon, huh?" Jessa's eyes probed for information.

"Um…maybe…" she said quietly so her daughter wouldn't hear. Gracie was across the room with Jessa's mother, brushing Ilsa and decorating the pig's collar with small white flowers.

The thought of marrying Lucas was enough to send her heart spiraling. "But I've done the whole wedding thing."

Even though she'd been pregnant and only eighteen, her parents had insisted on a church wedding and had gone all out for the reception. "I don't want to do that again."

"Really?" Cassidy joined them.

"Really." There was so much stress around it all—the planning and the invitations and the food…

"I've always thought eloping would be romantic," Darla mused.

"I guess so." But she didn't care much about the day itself. Or whether they were in the mountains or on a beach. Naomi looked out the window again. Lance, Lucas, and Levi had taken their places in front of a beautiful white arbor that stood before the crowd. Lucas looked so handsome standing there, so proud and strong. "I just want to be married to him." She didn't want to have to jump through all of the hoops and make it some big production.

"I hear you," Jessa said. "At least my mom did most of the planning. If it would've been up to me, we would've done a hoedown."

They all laughed.

Outside, the music changed.

"Oh!" Darla started to scramble. "That's our cue."

As the band started to play "Lucky" by Jason Mraz and Colbie Caillat, Naomi rushed over to get Gracie ready. She looked so grown up in her white tulle dress. Jessa had had it made to match her own.

"Oh, this is so exciting," Cassidy gushed as they lined up. Gracie and Ilsa would lead the procession, followed by Naomi, then Cassidy, then Darla. Since her father had passed away, Jessa's mom would walk her down the aisle.

During the ceremony, all of the bridesmaids and groomsmen would stand off to the side as couples. Naomi could hardly wait to share this memory with Lucas. She hadn't seen him all day.

The song started to play through again, and just as they'd practiced, Gracie opened the door right on time. Naomi handed her Ilsa's leash, then they all put up their umbrellas in a chorus of rustles and creaks. Holding her head primly and straightening her shoulders, her daughter led them to the tent.

After ditching their umbrellas on the outskirts they walked down the aisle one by one, and when Naomi saw Lucas step out to take her hand she was thankful she'd opted for the heavy-duty waterproof mascara.

When they reached their assigned spot, he didn't let go of her hand. They both turned to face Lance but she could feel Lucas looking at her. Keeping her head still, she slid her gaze to meet his.

"It's not fair to the bride for you to look this beautiful," he murmured.

"You're looking pretty handsome yourself," she whispered without moving her lips. Handsome? He looked panty-melting hot right about now. She tried to keep a straight face as she watched Levi and Cassidy step formally to their spot.

After Cass, Darla took her time moseying down the aisle. Naomi was pretty sure she wasn't all that excited about being stuck with Tucker, the Cortezes' stable manager, though her friend did graciously let Tucker take her arm and lead her to their designated place.

After that, Naomi motioned to Gracie to sit down. Though the pig fought it, her daughter picked up Ilsa and sat next to Colton in the front row.

Whew. She relaxed.

"You gonna save me a dance later?" Lucas murmured.

"We have to pay attention to the wedding," she whispered, keeping him in suspense.

The musicians stopped singing, letting the instrumental swell as Jessa paraded toward them, her face beaming with joy. "Look at her." She blotted the corners of her eyes with a handkerchief.

"She looks pretty happy," Lucas agreed.

So did Lance. Naomi had known him for years. She'd lived on the ranch since Gracie was a baby, and she was sure she'd never seen him smile that way, with tears running down his face.

The two of them embraced, and it was such a beautiful picture with the soggy mountains in the background.

"My God, I love that dress on you," Lucas murmured, leaning in closer. "What're you wearing underneath it?"

"Pay attention," she scolded. "They're about to start the wedding."

"There's a wedding?" he teased.

She shushed him, holding back a laugh.

In front of them, Lance and Jessa turned to Luis. The old man looked so distinguished in his smart white button-up shirt and black vest. He'd even left off the cowboy hat to reveal his tufted silvery hair.

"We want to thank everyone for coming out today," he said, projecting his voice without the assistance of a mic. For being such a quiet, humble man, he was very well-spoken. "It means a lot to Lance and Jessa. A lot to our whole family. I have to admit I wondered if this day would ever come."

A murmur of laughter went around the tent.

"But I think I speak for all of us when I say it was worth the wait." Luis reached out and squeezed Jessa's hand. "You are a treasure, Jessa Love, and we're sure lucky to be welcoming you into our family."

The tears came faster, blinding Naomi. She tried to blink them away.

"When Lance and Jessa asked me to do the ceremony, I thought they'd lost their fool heads," Luis said to another round of laughter.

"But then I realized what a privilege it'd be to stand up here. I didn't always do everything right, but I'm damn proud of my boys. All of 'em." He looked over at Lucas. "And nothing makes me happier than seeing them build their lives on love."

Naomi squeezed Lucas's hand and smiled at his father.

He smiled back, that white mustache twitching. "If I've learned anything in my life, it's that, if you work at it, love will always find a way. That's my prayer for you, Lance and Jessa. That you'll always work at it. That you'll always put each other over the demands life will bring."

Naomi sniffled a bit, struggling to hold the emotion inside. Lucas pressed a kiss against her temple.

"Now, Jessa Mae Love, I'll ask you to repeat after me: Lance, I promise to choose you every day, to love you in word and deed, to do the hard work of making now into always."

Jessa repeated each word with a joyful wobble of emotion.

Luis waited for her to finish then continued. "I promise to laugh with you, cry with you, and grow with you. To be your support and your partner in all of life's adventures. Loving what I know of you and trusting what I don't yet know, I give you my hand. I give you my love. I give you myself."

Lance repeated those same words, pausing every so often to get ahold of himself, but why should he? Everyone else seemed to be crying. Naomi was pretty sure her heavy-duty waterproof mascara was running down her face.

Luis guided them through exchanging rings, and it was so wonderfully sweet how they held each other's hands reverently. The whole time, Lucas ran his thumb over Naomi's knuckles as though telling her he couldn't wait to put a ring on her finger, either.

"Well," Luis said proudly. "I guess that's about it. You two kids are officially hitched. Son, go ahead and kiss your new wife."

A cheer rose up, but Lance and Jessa didn't seem to hear it. They were staring into each other's eyes with a loving lost look Naomi completely understood. Lance pulled his wife into a passionate kiss as if it were just the two of them standing in front of a beautiful mountain backdrop.

While Lance and Jessa made their escape, the band started playing "As Time Goes By"...of course. *Casablanca* was one of Jessa's favorite movies.

As Naomi and Lucas paraded down the aisle behind Levi and Cass, he snuck a grab at her ass. When she stared up at him, he planted a quick kiss on her lips, and she let him.

The rest of the afternoon flew by in a blur of pictures and bites of delicious hors d'oeuvres and small talk with people in town. Everyone seemed to want to talk to Lucas, but no one seemed brave enough to bring up the fires. The men asked him about life on the McGowen ranch and the women tried to flirt, but every time one of them smiled at him, he'd touch Naomi, kiss her on the cheek, or slip his hand into hers or drape his arm over her shoulders.

When the sun started to set, the crowd thinned out and he snuck up behind her, lacing his arms around her waist and drawing her close. "Dance with me?" he asked sweetly.

She turned into him, clasping her hands at the back of his neck. "Thought you'd never ask."

He swayed her out to the dance floor where the band was still playing. A few other couples danced lazily to a slow country song, but she was too distracted with Lucas to care much who they were. A few feet away Gracie and Cassidy sat at a table watching YouTube videos and giggling hysterically.

"It was the perfect day," she sighed, leaning into him, inhaling the rain and the mountains. Her bare shoulders had started to chill, but Lucas's body warmed her right up.

"It's perfect now," he murmured against her hair. "I've been waiting all day to get this close to you." Dancing her into a quiet corner, he kissed her lips softly and made her wonder how quickly they could get out of there. Gracie had begged to spend the night with Cassidy, which meant she and Lucas would have her place to themselves for the first time.

"Think anyone would miss us if we snuck away?" she asked, resting her head against his chest. Outside the tent, the sun had broken through the clouds just in time to set. Rays of light poked through, spotlighting the peaks. It made everything seem so alive—new and fresh, still glistening with traces of the earlier rain.

"We can't go yet." Lucas stopped dancing and gazed down at her. His thumb grazed her jaw. "I love you, Naomi. And I love Gracie."

"We love you, too." Both of them. He had to know that. Gracie had been ecstatic having him around more these last few days. At the dinner table, she'd tell him every detail about camp, and at bedtime, she wanted him to tuck her in.

Lucas glanced around, then fished something out of his pocket. "I was going to wait for a while, but after today I don't want to wait anymore."

"Wait for what?" she asked, focused on the small box in his hands. It was a silly question. She knew. Her heart had started to beat wildly even before he'd dug it out of his pocket.

Lucas dropped to his knee. "I never thought I'd be lucky enough to get another chance with you," he said, steady and clear, even with tears in his eyes. "And I don't want to waste it. I don't want to waste one more second. I've loved you forever, Naomi, and I want to be with you the rest of my life." He opened the ring box and her breath caught. That ring. Memories flooded her of that night he'd taken her to a Moroccan restaurant in downtown Denver. Before dinner, they'd walked around beneath the big city lights, and she'd been awed by all of it. When they'd passed a jewelry store, her gaze had skipped over all of the typical rings, fixating instead on the most beautiful diamond-studded band.

"Marry me." Lucas gazed up at her with a shameless tenderness. "Let's build a life together. As soon as possible. You and me and Gracie."

"Yes. Oh my God, yes." She tugged on his hand until he stood and kissed her, then he slipped the ring onto her finger. It caught the sparkles from the globe lights hanging in the tent above them.

"Did you just get *engaged*?" Jessa shouted from across the tent. She hiked up her dress and ran over, dodging tables and chairs and the few people who were lingering. "Oh my

God!" She reached them, out of breath. "Did I just see you on your knee? Is that a ring?"

Her elated yelps attracted attention. Before Naomi knew what was happening, Cassidy and Darla and Jessa were all crowded around gawking at her finger.

"That's gotta be platinum," Darla said, eyeing the ring.

"It fits you perfectly," Cassidy added, patting Lucas's shoulder with approval.

Ignoring them, Naomi searched frantically for Gracie. Her daughter stood on the outskirts of the circle, her jaw hanging open and her eyes wide.

Lucas seemed to spot her at the same time. He elbowed his way past Naomi's friends and stooped to a knee in front of her daughter. Once again, he reached into his pocket and pulled out a box. "Gracie, will you be my stepdaughter? I promise to be the best daddy I can be." He opened the box and revealed a beautiful heart-shaped locket. "I want us to be a family. I'll always be there for you, no matter what."

Blinded by her own tears, Naomi stumbled over to them and sank to her knees next to Lucas.

Gracie reached out and touched the necklace as though she wanted to make sure it was real. "It's so pretty," she gasped. Her gaze shifted to Lucas's face. "You didn't have to get me something. I'd still want you to be my stepdaddy. That's what I've been hoping ever since Mom almost ran over you on the road."

Even though everyone had given them some space, they all laughed.

Lucas managed to get the necklace out of the box and clasped it carefully around Gracie's neck. She touched the pendant again. "Isn't it so beautiful?" she asked Cassidy.

While the women oohed and aahed over Gracie's bling, Lucas helped Naomi to her feet.

Levi and Lance must've finally caught on to what was happening from their post at the bar and took turns shaking their brother's hand.

"So when is it? When's the wedding?" Jessa demanded, as though she'd forgotten they were still at her wedding.

Naomi and Lucas looked at each other. "We haven't really had time to discuss the details," he said, taking her hands. "But soon."

"Sooner than soon," Naomi added.

"How 'bout now!" Gracie blurted. "Papa Luis knows how to do a wedding!"

"Now?" she echoed.

"Yeeessss!" Jessa hissed, the excitement clearly going to her head. "Everything's still set up for a ceremony! And all of the most important people are here!"

"Except for her *parents*." Lucas looked at Jessa like she'd lost her mind.

But...actually it *wasn't* that crazy. Naomi turned to him. "My parents would understand."

Now his incredulous expression targeted her. "You want to get married *now*?"

Yes. She did. The decision was so simple. She didn't want to go through months of planning and agonizing over the details. She wanted this man in her life now. Tonight. She wanted him to stay in bed with her into the next morning. And every morning after that. She knelt in front of her daughter. "I know this is fast, Gracie girl."

"Mommy..." Tears streaked her daughter's cheeks. "I love Lucas," she said, grabbing on to his hand. "And I know he loves us. This is the best. Day. Ever."

That got everyone crying. Lucas lifted Gracie up and caught them both in his strong embrace.

"What d'you think, Dad?" he asked. "You wanna perform one more ceremony today?"

"I'd be honored." The old man beamed. "'Course you'll have to go on down to the courthouse sometime soon to get a license and make it official."

"We can do that next week," Naomi said, brushing the logistics aside. "All I care about is the ceremony. The friends we have standing with us. And marrying the man I've always loved as soon as possible."

Excited chatter flitted among Gracie, Jessa, Cassidy, and Darla.

"Oh, this is so exciting!" Jessa sang. "Lance, go talk to the band. See if they can hang out a little longer!" She threw her arms around Naomi's shoulders. "I can't believe we'll share an anniversary! This is the best!"

The women all scattered, talking about musical selections and fighting over who got to be the maid of honor.

Lucas set Gracie on the ground, still looking stunned. "We're getting married," he marveled.

Gracie giggled. "We're getting married!"

Epilogue

Thanksgiving had always been Naomi's favorite holiday. Don't get her wrong; Christmas was great, too, but the gifts that came with Thanksgiving had more to do with family, friends, and love than with beautifully wrapped packages.

She bustled around the kitchen of the Hidden Gem Inn, stirring the cranberry sauce on the stove and checking the temperature of the turkey Lucas had brined and put in the oven even before she and Gracie had awakened. Tomorrow they would welcome their very first guests to the inn, but first, they were christening it with a large Thanksgiving dinner in their expansive dining room.

Everyone would be there—Lance and Jessa, Luis and Evie, Levi, Darla and Cassidy, Colton and his long-distance boyfriend, Owen. Even Mark and his family had agreed to come and spend the day with them. He'd been up to visit every other week since the summer, and last month he'd brought his wife and their son to meet Gracie.

Of course it looked nothing like the family Naomi had once imagined for her and her daughter, but she was grateful all the same. Logistics didn't matter so much when people loved each other well.

Once again, she made her way through the dining room, admiring the beautiful fall decorations Jessa had helped her place—ornate foliage with colorful leaves and miniature pumpkins. A wicker cornucopia overflowing with real fruit sat in the center of the table set elaborately for fifteen. And there was still room to spare. She checked the place settings again, smiling to herself for strategically placing Cassidy next to Levi. The woman claimed to harbor a serious irritation for him, but Naomi had also noticed that her cheeks seemed to get a little pinker whenever he was around.

"This place looks incredible." Lucas came up behind her, kissing her neck. "And you smell incredible."

She leaned against his chest. "I think it's your turkey that smells incredible." She smiled up at him, still amazed he was here. That they were here together. In their bed and breakfast. They'd moved in at the beginning of October and it had felt like home right away.

"Where's Gracie?" she asked. Earlier, while she'd kept an eye on their dinner, Lucas and Gracie had gone out to deliver Thanksgiving meals to families in need through the local food bank.

"She's outside playing with Bogy," he said, giving her shoulders a good massage. He was always doing that, doting on her.

"You might want to call her in here." Naomi turned to him. "Because we have something to discuss."

"Yeah?" He drew out the word into a hopeful question.

"Yeah," she confirmed, not offering him anything else.

He bounded out of the room with a grin and came back with Gracie slung over his shoulder like a giggling sack of potatoes. She squealed as he hauled her up higher in the air, then set her feet on the floor.

"That was fun!" Her cheeks were pink from the cold and the laughter, and her red hair was happily disheveled.

"Your mom has something to discuss with us." Lucas glared at Naomi as though he didn't want to wait one more second.

Neither did she. "You know how we'd talked about making the third bedroom an office?" she asked, unable to hold back a happy smile.

"Uh-huh..." His eyes got as wide as hers.

"And I said we had to save it for a brother or sister instead," Gracie reminded them.

"Well, Gracie girl...you were right. We're having a baby." She brushed a kiss first across Lucas's lips and then one on the top of her daughter's head. "A beautiful little baby."

"I knew it!" Gracie hopped up and down, clapping her hands and squealing. "We're having a baby! We're having a baby!"

"You're sure?" Lucas looked down at her, completely focused and intent, completely hers.

"I'm sure," she confirmed. "I took the test while you were gone." She'd been feeling off for weeks, so she'd bought a pregnancy test, figuring the odds were rather high given the fact that they'd been diligently making up for lost time. In case he needed proof, she held up the plastic stick and showed him the two lines.

Laughing, he threw his arms around her, kissing her forehead, her nose, her lips. As Gracie hopped by, he snagged her arm and pulled her into the hug with them, joining in her song. "We're having a baby! We're having a baby!"

The front door crashed open, bringing in a jovial flood of voices and chatter. Their family poured into the room, carting along their savory and sweet-smelling dishes.

Gracie's voice rose above them all. "We're having a baby!" she announced, breaking free to skip around the room and give everyone hugs. "We're having a baby!"

"A baby?" Jessa looked at Naomi as though wanting confirmation.

Naomi deferred to Lucas with a smile.

"That's right." He picked Gracie up into those strong arms of his. "Gracie's gonna be a big sister."

Gracie squealed again, hugging Lucas tight. "I've always wanted a baby! That's what I asked for in my letter to Santa and he's giving it to me early!"

A hearty round of congratulations broke out. Luis butted his way through everyone until he could hug Naomi. Then he took Gracie out of his son's arms. "I get to be a papa again."

"Let's break out the bubbly," Levi added, disappearing in search of glasses.

"You two sure don't waste time," Darla said with a smile.

Cassidy was running around hugging everyone. When she got to Levi, she froze. But he wouldn't let her off the hook.

"Come here," he said, casting her that charming grin that seemed to work on all the ladies.

Cassidy raised an eyebrow at him as he leaned in for a hug. Naomi had never seen the woman stand so stiff and straight.

"Congratulations, Naomi." At some point, Mark and his family had walked into the commotion.

"Thank you." She gave him a hug. After the incident on the trail, she'd given up on resenting him. Life was too short, and Gracie needed as many people as possible to love her. "I'm so glad you could be here," she said to Mark's wife Beth.

The woman leaned in to give her a hug. "The invitation means so much to us."

"Hey, do you want to see my room?" Gracie asked Ben, her half-brother.

"Sure." He looked up at her with all of the admiration of a little brother and she took his hand, leading him away.

Mark got busy introducing his wife to everyone else.

"When are you due?" Jessa asked, catching Naomi by the arm. "How far along are you? Are you feeling good?"

Naomi laughed. "I feel great. And I know nothing, yet. I just took the test this morning."

"You'll have to get in to see the doctor as soon as possible," her friend instructed. "I know the best OB—"

"Let's move this party to the dining room," Lucas called. "Don't want the turkey to get cold."

Everyone scattered, chatting and congratulating while they carted the many amazing dishes from the kitchen out to the table. After everyone had found their seats, Lucas clinked his glass. "I'd like to make a toast."

Amazingly, the room quieted.

"To the blessings of family and second chances," he said, raising his glass.

Everyone echoed the sentiment.

"And to a new baby," Jessa added.

Another round of cheers went around the table.

"A baby!" Gracie echoed, leading Ben to his seat next to hers. "I hope it's a boy. No, wait. I hope it's a girl." Her eyes grew big. "No! I hope it's twins! Then we can have one of each!"

"Whatever this baby is, we'll be grateful." Naomi rested a hand on the small swell of her belly. This little baby was the resurrection of dreams she thought had died a long time ago. And after losing them once, she understood how priceless they were. Having them back—having Lucas back—was a gift she would never take for granted.

Don't miss the exciting next installment of Sara Richardson's Rocky Mountain Riders series, featuring Levi and Cassidy!

Renegade Cowboy

Available Winter 2017

Please see the next page for a preview.

Chapter One

Welcome to Topaz Falls, Colorado
Elevation: 7,083 feet

Cassidy Greer blew past the green welcome sign. She knew full well that she had another two miles before she'd pass Dev's patrol car, which would likely be stashed off the south side of the highway while he waited for unsuspecting drivers he could slap with a $300 fine. The town had to make money somehow, but, seeing as how it was May, their modest ski hill wasn't open. During the spring and summer, traffic tickets were the town's main revenue source.

Right at mile marker 316, she tapped the brakes, bringing her old Subaru's speed down. She knew pretty much everything there was to know about this town. Living within the same eight square miles for her entire twenty-four years meant there were few surprises in her life.

She knew that, every Tuesday and Thursday, Betty Osterman and her group of blue-haired patriarchs did their morning jog-walks down Main Street, arms swishing, hips swinging while they gossiped about which names had shown up in the latest Police Calls column of the local paper.

She knew that, when she drove past the fire station on Sunday mornings, all those hot volunteers would be in the third bay with the garage door rolled up while they pumped iron, shirtless and sweating. A girl had to get action somehow. It was fair to say she hadn't gotten much over the past six years. Okay, she hadn't gotten any. She'd been too busy putting herself through nursing school, working as an EMT, and trying to keep her mother alive. So every Sunday morning, she, along with at least twelve other women ranging in age from sixteen to ninety-three, made sure to take the long way to the grocery store, passing by the fire station nice and slow to keep her lady parts activated. Because someday she might actually have a life.

A cautious wave of excitement rippled deep inside her chest. Someday soon…

Slowing the car, Cassidy took a quick right on Main Street. The town looked the same as it always did. Eclectic shops and small restaurants were all laid out on the cobblestone sidewalks. Nothing had changed, and yet today everything looked different. Topaz Falls had always been her home, but it might not be much longer.

She applied more pressure to the accelerator. She hadn't seen Dev's patrol car, and she was in a hurry. She'd just come from Denver. From an interview with one of the most prestigious pediatric nurse residency programs in the country, and it had gone well. Really well. They told her they'd let her know within a month, but the director had given her a smile as she'd shaken her hand. Kind of a silent *Don't worry.*

Don't. Worry.

Easy for her to say. All Cassidy had to do was catch a glimpse of her house down the street and pure, unadulterated worry crammed itself into her stomach so tight she couldn't find the space to take a breath. Now she knew why she hadn't seen Dev's patrol car out on the highway. He was at her little house on Amethyst Street, cruiser parked at an angle, lights flashing.

She floored it down the block and jerked the wheel, bouncing the car to a stop in the crumbling driveway. "What the hell happened?" she called as she threw open the driver's door.

Dev stood on the front stoop, his broad shoulders barely stuffed into the crisp navy blue uniform. She'd gone to school with Dev back in the day. He'd always been a man of few words, and true to form, he waited for her to hightail it up the steps to where he stood.

"Got a call from Turnasky," he said, eyeing the front door like he half expected a serial killer to emerge.

"What did he say this time?" Turnasky was a tyrant who lived in the house behind her. He was always complaining about the leaves from her aspen tree falling into his yard.

"It's an indecent exposure call," Dev clarified awkwardly. "Seems your mom's runnin' around the backyard without any clothes on."

That inspired a contemplative pause. Well, shit. This was a new one. "What do you mean she's running around without her clothes on?" Cassidy demanded, finally shoving past him.

He stayed right where he was on the stoop, poking his

head inside the door and squeezing his eyes shut like he wanted to make sure he wouldn't witness anything he couldn't unsee. "Hell, I don't know, Cass. Okay? All I know is Turnasky called me and said your mom was jogging around the backyard in her birthday suit and that the little kids next door were standing on the fence laughin'."

That last part put another kick into her step. She loved little Mellie and Theo. She'd hate to see them move away because of one of her mother's episodes.

Skirting the kitchen table, which was strewn with empty wine bottles, she bolted out the open back door. Sure enough, there was her mother, now crawling across the grass on her hands and knees, white ass in the air while she called to Loki, their cat, who was cowering behind the overgrown juniper bushes in the corner of the yard.

The kids were gone, thank the lord, but Turnasky was standing on a chair on the other side of the fence, getting quite an eyeful.

Cassidy gave him the look of death and hurried to her mom, snatching the cushion off the wicker loveseat on the way. "Mom?" She knelt down next to her, nearly knocked over by the same pain that flashed whenever she smelled the woman's lilac scent. It was the scent Cassidy remembered from her childhood. The scent that used to mean comfort and security and assurance.

"Cass-a-frass!" Her mom turned, white hair frizzed and unwashed, her eyes glazed with the telltale gloss of a drunk. "You're home!" she sang, completely oblivious to the fact that Dev now stood behind them on the deck, his hand covering his eyes.

"Is she okay?" he asked, eye protection still firmly in place.

"Of course I'm okay!" Lulu Greer sang. She abruptly stood, dusting off her thighs the way she might've done with pants, had she been wearing any.

Cassidy quickly shielded her mother's skinny front half with the cushion. "Mom..." She wasn't oblivious to the fact that this tone was the same one her mother used to use on her and Cash when they'd done something stupid. But that was before Cash died when he was twenty. Before her mother broke and Cassidy was forced to become the adult in the relationship. "What happened to your clothes?" she demanded. "Why are you out in the backyard naked?"

Her mother laughed. "It's our backyard, honey," she said, as though that made a difference. "It's not like I'm running down the middle of the street giving the neighbors a show."

"Actually you are giving the neighbors a show," Cassidy pointed out, nodding toward Turnasky. When they all looked at him, he quickly climbed down from the chair and dragged it away.

She turned back to her mother, a familiar sorrow leaking through the anger. Once again, she wondered how they'd gotten here. How had her healthy, devoted, superhero of a mom collapsed? "You can't do this. You can't just walk outside naked. The neighbors have little kids," she reminded her.

"Well, what was I supposed to do?" Her mother slung her hands onto her bony hips. "I was in the bath, and Loki climbed right out the window. I had to go after him! He knows he's not supposed to go outside!"

Cassidy's heart uttered a quick prayer of thanksgiving that her mother had gotten out of the bathtub. What would've happened if she'd passed out and drowned? That was all it took to diffuse the billow of exasperation. "Come on,"

Cassidy murmured, nudging her mom toward the back door. "Let's go inside."

Lulu stomped through the door like a pouting two-year-old and headed straight for the hallway that led to their bedrooms. "Sheesh. A woman can't even step out into her own backyard without a public inquiry anymore," she muttered.

"Put some clothes on, Mom," Cassidy called after her. "We have to be at the ribbon-cutting ceremony in thirty minutes." Which would be about as much fun as finding her mother wandering around the backyard naked. She had no desire to see Levi Cortez receive a standing ovation for his work rebuilding the rodeo grounds over the past year, but she'd lost a bet with her friend Darla.

Before she forgot, she dashed back outside and crawled through the prickly bush until she reached Loki. "Come on, you turd." She grabbed him by the scruff of the neck before bringing him in close for a snuggle. "Look what happens when I leave you in charge," she muttered as she hauled the cat back inside and set him on the floor. He promptly swung his ass in her direction and pranced to his favorite spot underneath the table.

Dev had already retreated into the living room and was hanging out by the front door, pretending to be completely engrossed in the old pictures she'd hung there—of her previous life, of her perfect family. If she didn't have the proof in the pictures, she'd question whether it had been real.

"I'm sorry about this, Dev," she said, walking him outside. "I was gone overnight. She doesn't do so well on her own when I'm away." Which would really throw a wrench in her plans to go to a nurse residency program. She'd thought about it all the way home. Maybe Mom could come with her and they could get an apartment close to the hospital. But the truth was that she'd be working full-time—twelve hours a day at least three days a week. She wouldn't be able to keep an eye on her mother. And who knew what kind of trouble Lulu would get into in a big city like Denver.

Sighing, Dev gave her that empathetic look she'd come to hate. The one that blended pity with embarrassment. "Yeah, I get it. No big deal. Just make sure it doesn't happen again. Got it? You don't want your neighbors to press charges."

"Nope. Definitely don't want that." She didn't have the money to bail out her mother or pay any fines. While Cassidy worked long hours as an EMT and Lulu received a modest retirement check from her years as a mail carrier, there wasn't exactly anything extra.

Dev hesitated before he got into his cruiser. "Hey, Cass...have you thought about getting her some help? Maybe you could take her to an AA meeting or something."

"Yeah, I'll look into it," she said, brushing him off. She'd tried a few times in the last couple of years, but her mother wasn't interested in AA. In all honesty, alcohol wasn't Lulu's biggest problem. It was depression. The heavy weight that seemed to cling to her, that told her to stay in bed. That's why she drank. She was trying to lighten her load.

"Let me know if I can help out. Okay?" Dev slid into the driver's seat. "I can give you some brochures. There're a lot of resources out there."

"Sounds great," she said, straining the muscles in her cheeks to keep her smile intact. "Thanks, Dev."

After a sympathetic nod, he tore out of there, and she turned to face her little dilapidated house. She'd purchased the small two-bedroom for her and Mom after her dad decided he couldn't handle the grief and left for Texas. While it might've been the wrong color blue and the epitome of a bad 1970s remodel, Cassidy loved the house because it was hers.

She trudged back up the walkway. Facing the house was the easy part. Facing what was inside would hurt more, but she didn't have a choice. This had to stop. Her being the parent. Her bailing her mom out of trouble. Her begging Lulu to get up, to get dressed, to eat something.

Somewhere inside that shell of a woman, Lulu Greer was still there. She was still funny and compassionate and friendly and honest. She was still Cassidy's mother.

Rolling up the sleeves of her sweatshirt, she opened the door armed with a purpose and a deadline. If she got into that nurse residency program, she had just over one month to turn her mother into a functioning adult again so Cassidy could move on and have her own life.

She'd better start now.

* * *

Levi Cortez had spent his fair share of time in front of the cameras.

As a bull rider, he'd competed in front of the cameras, he'd done interviews in front of the cameras, he'd posed with fans in front of the cameras. Hell, his main sponsor, Renegade Jeans Co., had even taken countless pictures of his ass filling out designer denim. So he was no stranger to cameras. No stranger to attention from large crowds. Even in an arena filled with thousands of spectators, he'd never once been nervous.

Until now.

As he made his way to the cheap, portable podium the town council had set up in front of their new rodeo facility, the hundred or so people gathered around whispered and elbowed each other. Some wore scowls, some narrowed their eyes with suspicion, as though they were waiting for him to make a mistake. *Another* mistake.

Admittedly, he'd made plenty of them in his life. The worst one being letting his brother take the fall and go to prison for three years because of something Levi had done. When the truth had come out last year, everyone discovered he was the one responsible for burning down the rodeo grounds when he was a delinquent teen, and these same people standing around had done their best to run him off.

Hank Green, the uncontested mayor of the town, had even started a Facebook page calling for Levi's voluntary banishment. But he couldn't do it. He couldn't leave. For once in his life, he'd stuck around, determined to make things right.

Levi placed one hand on either side of the podium and faced the crowd directly. Their faces blurred together. A dribble of sweat itched on his back. Speaking in front of cameras was a hell of a lot easier than speaking in front of a whole crowd of people you'd disappointed. Cameras didn't tend to see through a façade the way people did.

But this was it. This was him. A screw-up who'd hurt the town, disgraced his family, and had spent the last year doing penance to save his career and reputation.

He inhaled a deep, even breath. *Don't let them smell fear...*

"I wanted to thank you all for coming out today," he said, well aware that some of them had likely been bribed by his brother Lance and sister-in-law Jessa. Those two stood in the very front row, Jessa snapping pictures on her phone like a proud mom.

She waved at him, and he gave her a grateful smile.

"Over the last year, I've worked hard to make up for the hardships my actions caused..." That was an understatement. He'd spent every hour he wasn't competing fundraising and draining his own investments in order to raise enough to rebuild an arena and stables, a place where the town could host rodeos again. "Which is why we're here." He glanced over his shoulder at the new facility. It was ten times nicer than the old one—complete with a covered metal roof. The old arena had consisted of stands, a small call box, and lackluster stables. But during the rebuilding phase, he'd gone big. "My goal in leading this effort was to give our town a place to gather, a place to compete, and a place that will make Topaz Falls one of the most popular stops on the circuit again."

A murmur buzzed around the crowd. Someone actually applauded.

Levi eased out a breath, motivated by the minimal show of support.

"There's still more work to do. But I'm thrilled to be here today to dedicate phase one of the project. And I promise that I will keep working until we expand the stables and add the educational spaces we've promised."

This time Jessa started to clap. She elbowed Lance, and he joined her, rolling his eyes. The rest of his family joined in on the applause—his father, Luis, and Evie... Levi still wasn't sure exactly what to label her. Girlfriend, probably, though neither one of them would admit it. And then there was his brother Lucas and sister-in-law Naomi, who stood off to the side. She was about a month from giving birth and was fanning herself with the flyer they'd passed out earlier.

He scanned the crowd again. More people had started to clap. That was a good sign, right? The tension that had pulled at his neck dissolved. "I'm proud to officially welcome you all to the Cash Greer Memorial Arena." A tremor ran through his voice, but he didn't care. Cash had been his best friend and everyone knew it.

As they'd rehearsed, Hank Green walked forward and handed him the giant scissors. Levi cut the large red ribbon that Jessa had made, then gritted his teeth real tight and shook Hank's hand. They both walked back to the podium and Levi stood off to the side while Hank launched into one of his famous monologues. The man loved to hear himself talk.

"I would like to thank Mr. Cortez for his contributions to ensuring our town's bright future..."

Levi tuned him out and scanned the crowd again. No one seemed to be listening. Most people were either staring at their phones or chatting. His gaze moved to the back row and a punch of air hit him in the lungs.

Cassidy Greer stood next to her friend Darla. Shock rolled through him, rooting his boots to the ground. She'd come. And she looked good—like she was dressed to go out. The sleeveless sundress she wore showed off her tanned shoulders. Her mid-length blond hair had a wave through it, shining in the evening sun.

Daaammmnnn. His body heated. He shouldn't be looking. He knew that. She was Cash's little sister, and she'd always been off limits. That was how she seemed to want things, anyway. Ever since he'd come back to Topaz Falls, she'd blown him off. If she wasn't glaring at him, she was ignoring him. And he got it. He knew she blamed him for what had happened to his brother. She seemed to blame all bull riders.

But she'd come…

"We'd like to invite everyone far and wide to our first rodeo event in twelve years," Hank said dramatically into the blipping microphone. "Mr. Cortez has put together a benefit rodeo featuring some of his famous friends to raise money for the completion of the facility. You should have received a schedule of events. We hope to see you all tomorrow."

Another round of applause rose, louder this time, actually bordering on enthusiastic. A newspaper reporter stepped forward and snapped a quick picture, but Levi wasn't looking. He held his gaze on Cassidy as the crowd started to scatter.

She'd already made it to the edge of the dirt parking lot when he finally caught up with her.

"You came," he said behind her.

She stopped but didn't turn around. "I didn't have a choice. Darla made me." Her tone could've formed icicles in his eyebrows.

He moved in front of her so she'd have to look at him. Hadn't she punished him long enough? Everyone else in town had forgiven him for his past sins. Hell, they'd actually cheered him on up there. Everyone except for Cassidy Greer.

"I'm glad you're here," he said, wondering how things could be so awkward with this woman he'd once known like a sister.

"I can't stay." She looked past him. "My mother's waiting in the car."

Lulu had come? God, he hadn't seen much of her since he'd been back, either. "You should go get her. I'm sure she'd love to see the sign with Cash's name on it."

The woman's striking blue eyes dulled. "She's not feeling well." Cassidy moved to step past him, but he reached out and snagged her shoulder. He couldn't let her walk away again. Not this time.

"I'm sorry," he murmured, emotion mucking up his throat. "I'm sorry I couldn't stop it from happening. I'm sorry I couldn't save him."

Her full lips parted in surprise as she stared up at him. "Seriously?" Her sigh condemned his ignorance. "I don't blame you for Cash's death, Levi."

"Well, you obviously blame me for something," he shot back before she walked away. This was the closest thing they'd had to a real conversation in years. "You've been giving me shit ever since I came back, so I just assumed..."

"Cash's death was an accident," she said, her voice gentling. "It wasn't anyone's fault."

"That doesn't mean I don't wish I could go back." It had just been him and Cash out the corral that day. Training, trying to one-up each other like always. They'd done it so many times. But his friend had lost his grip and slid off the back of the bull, getting trampled before Levi could save him.

"None of us can go back," Cassidy said, her eyes lowering to the ground. "We all had to move on. It wasn't as easy for some of us as it was for others." Her gaze targeted his. "Some of us are still trying to move on."

The words jabbed him. Yeah. He'd moved on. He hadn't been able to face everything in Topaz Falls after Cash's death, so he'd left as soon as he could. Was that why she couldn't stand him?

"I have to go," she said, before he could find the courage to ask. "I need to get Mom home." Without a goodbye, she hurried across the parking lot and got into her car.

"Wow, you sure know what to say to a woman." Lance walked over. His eldest brother never missed an opportunity to give him a hard time. "I think she was actually jogging to get away from you."

"Not in the mood right now." He turned to walk away, but Lance followed on his heels.

"Why does it bother you so much? So she doesn't like you. Who cares?"

He paused. Why indeed. "Cass is..." Special. There. He said it. Okay, he thought it. She was special to him. They'd grown up together. He'd been a part of her family. And there was a time she'd liked him a whole lot.

His brother's eyes narrowed. "Cass is what?" he asked suspiciously.

He and his brothers had come a long way in the last year and a half, but Lance didn't need to know what he thought of Cass. If Levi told him how he really felt, he'd never hear the end of it. "She's a friend. She *was* a friend," he clarified. Once. They'd been close. They shared a history and a deep grief. Instead of bringing them together, that's what stood between them.

But maybe it didn't have to.

Acknowledgments

This is my favorite part of every book I write! When I finish a project, nothing means more to me than taking the time to recognize all of the people who continue to help, encourage, and inspire me on this journey.

First, to my readers, I love how stories bring people together and give us a chance to share a special connection. Thank you for faithfully reading and for reaching out to share your own stories and thoughts and insights. I treasure each word.

The team at Forever continues to amaze me. It's incredible to work with such a diligent, talented, and creative group of people. Special thanks to Megha Parekh for knowing how to fix all the things, and for the smiley faces on my revisions.

Thank you to Suzie Townsend and Sara Stricker at New Leaf Literary for making sure I get to write more books.

To Julie Pech, owner of the real Chocolate Therapist in Downtown Littleton—thank you for allowing me to borrow your brand for this series! And thank you even more for making the best chocolate I've ever tasted. Seriously. You all need to try the Down by the Sea Salt bar. That's what gets me through my deadlines.

A writer could not survive without her writerly friends. Thank you, Elaine Clampitt and Kimberly Buckner for the hours at Starbucks, the brainstorming during Avalanche games, and the professional retreats by the pool in Mexico. I would not have finished this book without you!

To my big sis, Erin Romero, thank you for loving my books so much that you share them with all of your friends. And even some strangers. Thanks for being one of my biggest cheerleaders.

I will never run out of words of gratitude for my forbearing husband. Being married to a writer is no easy task, and he has truly become my hero. Will, you might be the most patient man alive. I love you. Last but never least, to my two cherished sons, AJ and Kaleb—thank you for making my life such a joyful adventure.

About the Author

Sara Richardson grew up chasing adventure in Colorado's rugged mountains. She's climbed to the top of a 14,000-foot peak at midnight, swum through Class IV rapids, completed her wilderness first-aid certification, and spent seven days at a time tromping through the wilderness with a thirty-pound backpack strapped to her shoulders.

Eventually Sara did the responsible thing and got an education in writing and journalism. After a brief stint in the corporate writing world, she stopped ignoring the voices in her head and started writing fiction. Now she uses her experience as a mountain adventure guide to write stories that incorporate adventure with romance. Still indulging her adventurous spirit, Sara lives and plays in Colorado, with her saint of a husband and two young sons.

Learn more at:

SaraRichardson.net
Twitter, @SaraR_Books
Facebook.com/SaraRichardsonBooks

Fall in Love with Forever Romance

PRIMROSE LANE
By Debbie Mason

"[The Harmony Harbor series is] heartfelt and delightful!"
—RaeAnne Thayne, *New York Times* bestselling author

Finn Gallagher returns for a visit to Harmony Harbor only to find that the town's matchmakers have other plans. Because it's high time that wedding planner Olivia Davenport gets to plan her own nuptials. And finding true love is the best reason of all for Finn to move home for good.

Fall in Love with Forever Romance

COMEBACK COWBOY
By Sara Richardson

In the *New York Times* bestselling tradition of Jennifer Ryan and Maisey Yates comes the second book in Sara Richardson's Rocky Mountain Riders series. When Naomi's high school sweetheart comes riding back to town, this self-sufficient single mom feels something she hasn't felt in years: a red-hot unbridled need for the handsome cowboy who left her behind. As much as Naomi's tried, a woman never forgets her first cowboy…

Fall in Love with Forever Romance

ON THE PLUS SIDE
By Alison Bliss

Thanks to her bangin' curves, Valerie Carmichael has always turned heads—with the exception of seriously sexy Logan Mathis. But Valerie is determined to get Logan's attention, even if it means telling a teeny little lie to get a job at his bar...Logan can't remember a time when Valerie didn't fuel all his hottest fantasies. Now the she-devil is working behind his bar and tempting him every damn night. But no one warned them that sometimes the smallest secrets have the biggest consequences...

Fall in Love with Forever Romance

THE HIGHLAND COMMANDER
By Amy Jarecki

As the illegitimate daughter of a Scottish earl, Lady Magdalen Keith is not usually one to partake in lavish masquerade balls. Yet one officer sweeps her off her feet with dashing good looks that cannot be disguised by a mere mask…Navy lieutenant Aiden Murray has spent too many months at sea to be immune to this lovely beauty. But when he discovers Maddie's true identity—and learns that her father is accused of treason—will the brawny Scot risk his life to follow his heart?